Eliz

storyt... ...g ..., w... the ... ...ly ...
her doorstep, never lacks a glorious setting for her
books. Elizabeth tried horticulture, higher education
as a mature student, briefly taught English and worked
in an office, before finally turning her daydreams
about dashing, piratical heroes and their stubborn
and independent heroines into her dream job; writing
Regency romances for Mills & Boon.

Regency Rogues

Regency Rogues:

A Winter's Night

ELIZABETH BEACON

MILLS & BOON

First Published in Great Britain 2019
By Mills & Boon, an imprint of HarperCollins*Publishers*
1 London Bridge Street, London, SE1 9GF

REGENCY ROGUES: A Winter's Night © 2019 Harlequin Books S.A.

The Winterley Scandal © 2016 Elizabeth Beacon
The Governess Heiress © 2017 Elizabeth Beacon

ISBN: 978-0-263-27685-5

1119

MIX
Paper from
responsible sources
FSC™ C007454

This book is produced from independently certified FSC™ paper to ensure responsible forest management.

For more information visit: www.harpercollins.co.uk/green
Printed and bound in Spain
by CPI, Barcelona

THE WINTERLEY SCANDAL

Chapter One

It's so hot tonight I am only wearing my new rubies as I write. The stones are glorious, but the settings—oh, my diary—so old fashioned I could scream. Still, only the diamonds to coax out of Lord Chris now—and how his brother the Duke of Linaire will gobble with rage when he sees me wear them.

No, I shall wear every last one of Lady Chris's jewels, ancient settings and all, the day I get hold of the lot. The Duke of Linaire wants them for his fat mistress, whatever he says about them belonging to his nephew. He doesn't even like the boy—and how dare he threaten to have me whipped at the cart tail because his little brother loves me to distraction?

Chris's plain wife is dead and the jewels her vulgar father showered on her never looked half so well on her anyway. The truth is the Duke hates Chris for being young and handsome and having

*me. After marrying that plain heiress the old Duke
insisted one of his sons wed when Lord Horace
ran off to the Colonies with that odd female who
paints, rather than shackle himself to a nabob's
daughter.*

*Chris deserves some fun. He endured that low-
born creature in his bed for so long it must be
bliss to share it with me—and his son can't wear
the jewels, can he? So what use are diamonds of
the first water to the horrid brat?*

Colm Hancourt carefully put down the expensive notebook lest he throw it across the room and let out the
breath he hadn't known he was holding in an uneven
gasp. As the horrid brat in question, he could argue for
a hundred better uses for a fortune in gold and jewels
than decorating a vain and adulterous *demi-rep* with
them all. The fortune she had been busy spending had
been his as well—or it would have been if his father
hadn't stolen it before Colm was old enough to argue.
Whatever Lord Christopher Hancourt had done with his
son's fortune, inherited from Colm's fabulously wealthy
maternal grandfather Sir Joseph Lambury, those jewels
should be in the bank, waiting for Colm to take a wife.
So here was proof, if he needed it, they were long gone.
Colm's maternal grandfather might have left his entire
fortune to his only grandson, but that hadn't stopped
Lord Chris from spending it all before Colm was old
enough to go to school.

He bit back a curse as the shock of that betrayal hit
anew. All the wishing and cursing in the world wouldn't

make his lost fortune reappear and he should know; he'd tried every one when he was younger and seething with fury about the hand life and his father had dealt him. Rage and hurt fought to rule him even now, after eight years of soldiering and learning self-control at the charity school his eldest uncle sent him to before that. So how could he *not* curse his father for putting this heartless woman ahead of his children? That was the real question he had to answer if he was ever going to be content with what little he had left.

One thing he did know was that he should never have agreed to come here to Derneley House and meet the past head on like this. Pamela had grown up here, under the so-called care of her sister and brother-in-law, and reminders of the wretched female were everywhere. Portraits of the infamous Pamela seemed to jeer at him from far too many walls and it almost felt as if he might catch her and his besotted father up to something disgraceful if he turned round fast enough at times, although they had both been dead these fifteen years and more.

Still, he did owe the only one of his father's brothers prepared to own up to him quite a lot. The current Duke of Linaire was so sheepish about asking him to come here that he couldn't even claim he was bullied into it. No, he played down his revulsion at the idea of living in this house for however short a time he would be needed and had come here of his own free will, so he must endure this stupid suspicion that the woman who ruined his life was busy laughing at him from her front-row seat in hell.

He'd had to slot back into his old familiar disguise to live here for as long as this took as well. The Duke of Linaire's librarian had been dismissed for selling one of the finest volumes in the Linaire Library to a rival collector and expecting the new Duke not to notice. As Uncle Horace would never find a man he could trust to do this task in such a hurry, here he was, Uncle Horace's long-lost nephew, doing his best to do a good job with the neglected Derneley Library where he'd spent the last eight years with only one book at a time to his name, to be read and passed round other readers who liked to lose themselves in a book when life was almost unendurable on campaign. So he couldn't even be himself now that he was back in London after all these years. Lord Chris's son would never be welcome under this roof while Lady Derneley lived under it as well. She still raged about what she called the murder of her little sister to anyone who would listen and Lord Chris Hancourt *had* driven so recklessly along an Alpine road at twilight that the coach missed a bend and he and Pamela hurtled to their deaths. So here he was, Colin Carter again—just as he'd been in the army. He wanted to push aside the thought that he might have died under that name at Waterloo, if not for his sister Nell and the new Duke, but somehow it haunted him.

Nell had coaxed, or bullied, Uncle Horace into taking her to Brussels when everyone else was fleeing it as battle roared only a few miles away. Revulsion at what his little sister must have seen ate away at Colm every time he thought of Nell viewing the hell of slaughter and corruption the day after Waterloo. She had scoured the battlefield until she found him, dazed and half-conscious from loss of blood, and somehow got him back to Brussels to be nursed at the new Duke of Linaire's expense. When he was pronounced likely to live, Nell raced back to England and her position as governess to four orphaned girls. Colm's hands tightened into fists; his sister had to rescue him rather than the other way about and he so wanted to protect *her*; give her back the life she was born to. In his daydreams she was fulfilled and happy with a man who would love and cosset her as she deserved for the rest of her life. A reminiscent grin spoilt his frown as he reminded himself this *was* Nell he was thinking about. She wouldn't thank him for such a husband, even if it meant escaping her life as a governess. He might as well forget the fantasy of giving Nell a Season so the world could see what a wonderful woman she was. She would chafe at the controls society put on marriageable young ladies and ask for her old job back.

So where was he? Ah, yes, Uncle Horace—the second eldest of his father's three older brothers and the only one Colm liked and might even learn to love one day. Uncle Maurice, the next Hancourt in line after Horace, hated Colm for being his father's son and he'd hated Lord Chris even more for succeeding with Pamela when he failed. Maurice ought to be grateful to have escaped her clutches, but Colm knew he would never forgive that slight to his reputation as a devil with the ladies. Colm frowned and decided he could well do without his Uncle Maruice's approval, but Pamela probably chose the younger brother because he'd wed an heiress. Whispers of the fabulous Lambury Jewels locked away in a bank vault would have seemed too delicious to resist as well.

Drat, he was thinking about the wretched female again and how she had seduced and nagged and wheedled that part of his inheritance out of Lord Chris. So where had he been before Pamela interrupted his thoughts? Ah, yes, Uncle Horace—he was a much more pleasant member of the family to think about. As soon as Colm was declared likely to live, the doctors insisted Colm convalesce before he settled into his new life, and neither the Duke nor the Duchess of Linaire would listen when he insisted he was fit to work. They even packed him off to the seaside to recover, so how could he turn his back on the only other members of his family willing to own up to him?

Uncle Horace had only come back to England when he'd inherited the dukedom last year. He probably didn't realise how huge the scandal had been when his youngest brother had run off with Pamela Verdoyne and then died with her on their way to a party she'd insisted on attending whatever the weather. Uncle Horace had been cut off for refusing to marry the heiress Colm's father had wed instead by then. Sensible Uncle Horace, Colm thought wryly, and almost wished his father had run off with a woman he could love instead of meekly marrying that unlucky girl as well.

No—he was brought up short by the thought of the woman his father had loved so deeply and unwisely after Colm's mother died—he decided Sophia Lambury was a far better parent to own up to than the current

Viscount Farenze's first wife. His mother might have been the pawn her father sold for a title and a convenient wife Lord Chris didn't love, but at least she wasn't a lovely, heartless harpy.

He shot the portrait of Pamela Verdoyne-Winterley hanging over the fireplace a hostile glare. She had been ripe and lush and beautiful, he conceded, but the mocking sensuality in her sleepy blue eyes said how aware she was of her power over fools like Lord Christopher Hancourt and how she revelled in enslaving lovers until they satisfied her every whim, whatever it cost them and theirs.

He compared her image to his shadowy memories of his mother and, yes, he definitely preferred having gentle, plain Sophia as his dam. So how *would* it feel to have Pamela's blood running in his veins? Appalling, he decided, feeling sorry for the girl with that burden on her young shoulders. He didn't know her, but for some reason he'd waited in the shadows to catch a glimpse of Lady Derneley's niece tonight with the other servants. Miss Winterley had looked self-contained and almost too conscious of her mother's sins, or was he being fanciful? Dark-haired and not quite beautiful, she looked very different from her notorious mother. He had to try not to snarl at the near-naked portrait of Pamela whenever he was in this room, but now he examined it for signs that her daughter had inherited her bold sensuality. Miss Winterley had her nose and slender build perhaps, but her eyes, the shape of her face and her height were all very different. Pamela's daughter looked as if she, too, could be haunted by her mother's sins a decade and a half after they had ended so abruptly on that Alpine pass.

So at least he didn't have to fear a feral beast might lie under his own skin as Miss Winterley looked as if she did in her worst nightmares. Lord Chris was a fool who had loved a noble doxy beyond reason, though, and Colm hoped and prayed he would never love madly and without limits like his father. So they were equal in some ways. He sat back to brood on fate and their very different destinies and concluded that was all they had in common.

Miss Winterley was doted on by her family; Colm barely acknowledged by his. Now Uncle Horace was Duke of Linaire he had a roof over his head and a job, but Uncle Maurice was next in line; he would turn Colm out the day he succeeded to the title. Colm liked his new relative very well, but if anything happened to the current Duke he would have to support himself on one good leg and nothing much a year. So if Uncle Horace wanted him to list and pack the entire library to make sure Derneley wasn't selling off the best volumes to dealers behind his back, Colm would stay here and do it and Mr Carter could live on for another week or two.

Miss Winterley's presence in this house tonight, when he was sure she didn't want to be here, was still something of a mystery. He wondered how Lady Derneley managed it, when the distrust between Pamela's sister and the Winterleys, once Pamela openly gave up on her marriage, never seemed to have been bridged by either family. Luckily the maids hired for the evening whispered and why shouldn't another servant listen to gossip? Colm thought with a wry smile at his own expense. Apparently Lady Derneley had put it about that this party was to be held in her niece's honour, as a peace offering in a war where she would hear not a word said against her late sister, and the Winterleys had, not surprisingly, not a good word to say in her favour so they said nothing at all. The Winterleys had to attend or let the world know they were openly at odds with Miss Winterley's relatives. Since it was Viscount Farenze's mission in life to keep scandal at bay whenever he could, he would be furious to be forced into a corner, but his wife and daughter would even endure an evening at Derneley House to keep the peace.

That was the how of it all, so what about the why? Lady Derneley was a widgeon and all the brass and cunning in the family must have gone to her little sister, but was there a deeper reason behind her husband's scheme to get his wife's niece here tonight? Colm shuddered at the idea, but Miss Winterley had a strong protector in Viscount Farenze and he had powerful friends. Derneley wouldn't risk all that power and influence turning against him, would he? Unless he was going to flee to the Continent to avoid his debts and thought the Winterley interest didn't reach that far. No, it was too much of a risk, so Colm had imagined a furtive air about the man nobody else saw as he greeted his 'long-lost niece' as if he might cry like a stage villain over her at any moment.

Anyway, what better way was there for the Derneleys to fool their creditors a family reconciliation had taken place? The Winterleys were rich and powerful and it might work, and there were no bailiffs in the hall or toughs in the kitchens tonight. He shivered at the idea of anyone being imprisoned for debt and resolved not to long for the wife and family he might have had if things were different. Derneley's ruin was all his own work, though; Colm had nothing in common with that noble idiot. Even he knew selling the Derneley Library to the new Duke of Linaire wouldn't keep Derneley solvent long, but the man didn't seem worried. Colm wondered how the guests would feel if the bailiffs turned up for dinner, dancing and a nice little gossip with the nobs. Delighted, he suspected; they had come here to be entertained after all.

Colm eyed the beautifully bound book Pamela confided in and refused to be sorry it was probably the closest she ever got to a friend. She had hidden her diaries behind a row of sermons and he wondered that they hadn't burnt holes in the worthy volumes. The library was being taken apart and shipped to Linaire House book by book, so they would have been discovered sooner or later and Colm was suddenly very glad he was the one taking it apart, not some poor clerk happy to sell such deliciously scandalous diaries to the highest bidder. Some of the lower branches of the publishing world would love to get their hands on such 'work'. But what on earth was he going to do with them? Burning seemed a fine idea with that prospect in his head, but he wanted to find out more about his father. Lord Chris died when Colm was eight, but he'd left his children before then.

Stuffing the expensively bound books into a portmanteau and limping off into the night was a tempting idea, but his work wasn't finished and the tale that would do the rounds if he was caught creeping out of the house with Pamela's diaries would enliven the radical press for years to come. Someone might recognise his name and if Captain Carter of the Rifles was smoked out as Lord Chris's son how the *ton* would sneer at a duke's grandson forced to serve in a regiment famous for dash and daring, but officered largely by tradesmen's sons and great gruff soldiers promoted on merit.

'Oh, no, my dear, the fellow's totally unsuited to polite company even without those unsightly infirmities. Not a penny to bless himself with and even a cit's daughter wouldn't risk marrying Lord Chris's son since he's likely to spend her fortune on a doxy like his father.'

It was uncomfortable enough to imagine, what if he had to listen to real asides and furtive titters when he was openly his uncle's nephew? He'd end up calling some fool out and he didn't want to flee justice, or shoot some idiot in a duel. Nell would be furious and the thought of his lion-hearted sister made him smile. If she were here, she would bid him get on with his life and forget the past. Well, he couldn't quite manage that yet, but he would put most of Pamela's diaries back and hope nobody chanced on them before he could think what to do with them. Then, if he could only forget his sister had to work for her bread because of the selfish adulteress who had bled their father dry, he might be able to enjoy the novelty of not being shot at on a regular basis and be himself for the first time in eight years.

Colm cursed the day Lord Chris set eyes on Pamela

as he limped towards the steep little stair to the upper shelves of the library to replace the rest of her diaries and the Derneleys' guests enjoyed the remnants of their host's once-fabled wealth only a few rooms away.

Eve Winterley still couldn't work out how her step-mama talked her into attending this wretched party. She wished clever Lady Chloe Winterley, Viscountess Farenze, hadn't right now. First there was Aunt Derne-ley's delusion they doted on each other to endure, then Lord Derneley trod so clumsily on her skirt in passing as she curtsied to her dance partner that she had to hastily leave the room. If not for that the appalling old man who waylaid her on her way to find a maid to help mend it she could have left this horrible house by now… Ugh, no, she didn't want to think about him yet, but how she wished she had invented a headache to keep her at home tonight.

She didn't care if the gossips gloated over the split between the Derneleys and the Winterleys. Her mother had willed her to die in the attic of this place once upon a time, so little wonder she couldn't wait to go home even before… No, she wasn't going to think about that awful old wineskin until she was safe. She wasn't sure she could endure the thought of him and what he might have done even then. Papa always said the best thing her mother did was reject her and usually Eve agreed, but tonight a small part of her wanted to throw something fragile because Pamela did her best to starve Eve to death in the attics here instead of being any sort of mother to her newborn babe.

Pamela didn't matter. Dear Bran was brought here to nurse Eve and then Papa rescued them both. Eve grew up knowing she was loved as surely as the sea beat on the rocks below her father's northern stronghold. Then Papa married Lady Chloe Thessaly when Eve was sixteen and what a relief to love and be loved by such a remarkable woman, she reminded herself, and supposed she would have to forgive Chloe her part in this wretched evening after all.

A nasty little voice at the back of her head whispered she couldn't escape the past in this down-at-heel mansion the Derneleys were clinging on to somehow. *What if the gossips and naysayers are right when they whisper, 'Like mother, like daughter,' behind my back?* her inner critic goaded. *What if one day I meet a man who wakes up the greedy whore in me and she makes me need ever more wild and wicked things from him and the rest of his sex as Pamela did?*

No, never, she denied it as her headache beat in her ears and she scuttled down the next half-lit corridor in the hope of sanctuary. She was a Winterley—everyone said how closely she followed her father in colouring, build and character. Even after three years out in society not a whiff of real scandal tainted her name, despite all the rakes and fortune hunters who tried to blast it so she would have to marry them or accept a lover. Still those whispers circulated without proof to back them up and malicious eyes watched for signs she was like Pamela. Anyone who mattered knew her and not the creature gossip said she was, but ageing rakes like Sir Steven Scrumble still thought they could force her into an unlit room and make her agree to marry him because she must be like her mother, or so he'd mumbled as he did his best to make sure she was the next Lady Scrumble. She shuddered at the memory of his wet mouth and invading hands and wiped a hand across her lips to try to rub out the feel and taste of him. Hadn't she just promised herself not to revisit that horror?

If she collapsed into a weeping heap everyone would know she had something to cry about and she hadn't got her flounce mended either, so she had to hold it out of the way not to trip over it and now she was lost. The wicked old fortune hunter fell into an agonised heap when she'd kneed him sharply in the privates, though, so she doubted he'd be on her tail. Uncle James was a most satisfactory mentor for a young lady who didn't want to be landed with a husband she hated. If that tactic failed, there were more to fall back on so thank heavens she belonged to a powerful clan; if she was poor and alone her mother's wild life and blasted reputation would have ruined her years ago.

Her first real suitor came so close to doing it she shuddered at the thought of her youthful stupidity. How had she ever thought herself so in love with a fool? Papa and Chloe had warned her he wasn't the man she thought. It wasn't until she told him she wouldn't elope that the gloss and excitement of having her first grown-up lover melted. He wanted her *because* she was her mother's daughter, not despite it. Memory of the hot, greedy need in his eyes as he tore her gown and got ready to rape her made her feel sick even now. That was when Uncle James intervened and, as that boy hadn't shown his true colours since, maybe his punishment worked.

Fighting the memory of that night and all the times since when even a quiet and outwardly respectable man would look at her with the memory of her mother in his hot eyes, she looked for somewhere to ply the needle and hank of thread snatched from the deserted ladies' withdrawing room. Opening a promising door warily, she checked for fat and lazy fortune hunters, then slipped inside. There was an air of peace in the old-fashioned book room; a very small fire and one branch of candles cast mellow shadows. Her uncle by marriage would never come in here for a quick read; he was probably allergic to printers' ink. She moved the candle and sat on a stiff and old-fashioned sofa by the fire to whip quick, impatient stitches into her torn flounce, glad to be alone for a few precious moments. Shifting the material round so she could reach the tear, she made herself sew more neatly, so it would look as if a maid mended it for her and that was where she had been all along.

There, that was the tear darned. Once she had the strip of fine French braid tacked neatly in place she would be respectable again. It was still trailing like a tail behind her when a suspicion this wasn't such a wonderful place to hide crept up on her. One of Uncle James's rules was assess all escape routes when you entered a strange room. She froze in her seat, needle in mid-air and every sense alert now it was too late. Another faint movement made her look round and see there was a gallery to this faded room she should have noted of earlier.

Someone was coming down a hidden stair so slowly and quietly a superstitious shiver ran down her back.

Too late to avoid whoever it was now, she wasn't about to run back to the ballroom with her braid trailing behind her, so she grasped the needle like a weapon and hoped it might work. Lord Derneley's cronies were too soft and idle to fit into the narrow confines of the ladder-like stair she could see now her eyes were used to the dim light, so this was a less substantial person. Halting steps met the marble floor at last and she squinted against the candlelight and deep shadows it cast to see whom she must defend herself against this time.

Chapter Two

'What the devil are you doing here?' a gruff male voice rumbled as Eve froze, staring at the stiffly held figure and telling herself he wasn't made of shadows.

He took a step forward and stared nearly as rudely back. He looked both old and young at the same time and she wondered how such a shabby gentleman could seem so arrogant it was as if he owned the room and not Lord Derneley's creditors. His overlong hair was neither brown nor gold but a mixture of both and his nose had been broken once upon a time. There was an air of contained power about him that didn't fit his modest shirt points and a very ordinary dark coat and breeches. He shouldn't be in the least attractive to a lady like her and yet he was. Now he turned his head as if to listen for more intruders into his domain and the candlelight struck his face full on. She could see a still raw scar high on his forehead that made her gasp, then wondered how much damage his tawny pelt hid and if that explained why he let it grow. Something wary and proud in his unusual eyes stopped her answering his question with a casual put down from lady to upper servant. Even from several feet away and by weak candlelight those eyes looked dark and light at the same time. He came a little closer to peer down at her as if she was an exhibit in a museum and she gazed up and saw his irises were brown, but his pupils were rayed with flares of light gold that made them look paler.

Here was a man who kept his hopes and dreams hidden, but when their gazes met something sparked between them that she didn't understand. It felt as if he was important to her somehow, but he couldn't be so, could he? Looked at coolly he was a young clerk in shabby day clothes and had nothing in common with the Honourable Miss Winterley. Still she felt an eager leap of the heart she had heard about but never experienced before; the dawn of something huge she never believed in until now. It threatened to turn her world upside down as they gazed at each other as if under a spell. Which was just plain nonsense, wasn't it? There might be enough mysteries in this stranger's striking eyes to intrigue a flock of unwary young ladies, but she was Eve Winterley and he was an upper servant by dress, if not his arrogant manner as he silently dared her to set him down as nobody.

'You took the words out of my mouth,' she informed him huskily, doing her best to act the composed society lady in the face of his impudence.

'Her ladyship's ball is that way, Miss Winterley,' he said and Eve felt that tingle of warmth she'd been trying to fight turn to ice. The coldness in his voice made her shiver and something like disapproval iced his gaze as he dwelt on her exposed ankles and calf, then he looked away as if she offended him.

'You have the advantage of me, sir,' she said stiffly.

'Carter, ma'am,' he said unenthusiastically.

'And now I know?'

'The Duke of Linaire engaged me to sort the Derneley Library and have it packed up and sent to Linaire House or the bookbinders.'

'Well, it's a fine collection and Lord Derneley is desperate,' she said, then wondered what demon had got hold of her tongue tonight.

'His father was a notable scholar,' the man said as if every word must be paid for and he was unwilling to waste them on the likes of her.

'Maybe his son is a changeling then,' she said, her temper prickling. She refused to tell polite lies after the evening she'd endured so far and this man's hostility seemed to be coming towards her in waves now he'd taken a good long look at Miss Evelina Winterley and decided he didn't like her one little bit.

'Lord Derneley is my host,' he reproved her, as if she had no idea it was rude to make comments about one when you were under his roof.

'And therefore above criticism? I shall employ you to sit in my father's library and whisper my grace, talent and general omnipotence in my ear when I feel less than pleased with myself and the world.'

'I shall be very ill occupied then,' he said unwarily—so that was what he thought of her, was it? 'I beg your pardon, I'm sure dozens of fashionable gentlemen queue up to praise your elegance, beauty and cleverness, Miss Winterley,' he added patronisingly, as if that should make her feel better.

'Since we seem to be jumping to conclusions about each other so freely tonight, you must be a cynic and a Jacobin, Carter. Why else would you take against a lady you don't know, unless you hold a grudge against my family, of course?' she demanded, suddenly very tired of being Pamela Winterley's daughter. Tonight was bad enough without a stranger sniping at her as if she must deserve it.

Colm tried to rein in his temper, but the sight of her looking as if she had only just left the arms of her lover made him deaf to the voice of reason. *Apologise, then bow politely and leave her to her sewing, you blundering idiot*, it whispered, but this was a very different Eve Winterley from the one he saw enter Derneley's hall tonight. Then she was pale and composed; a dark-haired version of the Ice Queen, so cool and distant she could have been made of bronze and cold painted. Now she was ruffled and flushed and he still wanted to touch her, not to find out if she was real this time, but to carry on the work of the lucky devil she must have been kissing in the long-disused conservatory at the end of this corridor.

He sounded like a jealous lover and how could that be when he didn't even know her? He still wanted to be the one who tousled all that cool perfection, though. If he had sent her racing along dusty passage ways to find the least-used part of this rambling old place and set herself to rights after their amorous encounter, now that would be *much* more acceptable. Even the thought of being the one whose kisses set her delightful breasts rising and falling with every fast and shallow breath made him hard. Exploring even the edges of passion with her warm and willing in his arms wasn't to be thought of. *No, it really, really wasn't*, he argued with his inner savage.

Colm felt the gnawing of bitter envy as he let himself sneer ever so slightly at the difference between her public face and private morals. Miss Winterley was set fair to follow her disgraceful dam after all. He recalled Pamela's shocking declaration that she was writing her diary wearing nothing but rubies and that did nothing to help his wild fantasies about seeing her daughter in a similar state of nature.

'How can I feel anything about your family when I don't know them?' he asked as coolly as he could while he tried to shackle his inner sensualist.

'I don't know; how can you?'

'Obviously I cannot.'

'Yet you have your shallow prejudices about me and mine and seem to think it quite acceptable to show them off. For a mere librarian you are very daring, Mr Carter,' she said with a pointed stare at the scar on his forehead he usually felt so defensive about.

'Librarians do not spring fully formed from the head of Zeus like the goddess Athene, Miss Winterley.'

'Waterloo?' she demanded rudely and he supposed he'd asked for it by leaping to conclusions about her as well.

He nodded, still unable to talk about that terrible day. Not even Nell knew the terror he had felt, the dreadful urge to turn his back on his men and this hell of powder and shot and pounding artillery all around him and walk off into the woods to find peace. Now that his emotions seemed too close to the surface he was afraid he might let her see things he didn't want any other human being to know about. She was his enemy; Winterleys and Hancourts had hated one another since his father ran off with her mother. It was probably his duty to think the worst of her, but as his lust and temper cooled he took a second look and wondered if he misjudged her.

'I can see how a library might offer peace and quiet after that,' she added as if she understood a bit too much. 'Will this be enough for you after a life of action?'

'I don't know, Miss Winterley. No doubt I shall find out when these books are safely housed in my employer's various houses.'

'And rescued from the neglect of nearly half a century,' she agreed rather absently, as if her real thoughts were elsewhere.

'Indeed,' he said, sounding stuffy even to his own ears. 'I wonder they are not in worse condition.'

'Fascinating as you find this topic, Mr Carter, I need to get back to the ballroom before people notice I have been away too long. Kindly turn your back, or go away, so I can finish sewing this braid back in place and go.'

'I still have work to do tonight,' he said, wishing he had pushed the open volume of Pamela's diary he had kept out to read under something else, so there was no risk she might spot it if she wandered closer to the library table to see what he had been doing. 'Here, let me move the candle so you can see better and be gone all the sooner,' he offered ungraciously and moved it before she could argue. Then he meekly turned his back as ordered and hoped that was distraction enough from her mother's appalling scribbles.

'You are almost as eager to see the back of me as I am to go,' she said, her voice muffled because she was paying close attention to her gown.

Colm was tempted to use the old mirror nearby to sneak another look at her fine legs and ankles as he fantasised about the thread pulling up her hem as she worked on the most awkward part of the braid once again. The unresolved question of who did that damage plagued him and he could still hear her move, feel her presence in this shadowed and oddly intimate room and long to be someone else.

'You can't marry a librarian if we are caught here in such a compromising position,' he explained gruffly.

'Even if you are a hero?'

Wouldn't it be fine if they truly felt easy enough to laugh together? They never would if she knew who he really was. After tonight they could go back to different worlds. Except he thought Uncle Horace and his Duchess had plans that might make those worlds collide. Heaven forbid, he thought. He hated the idea of who he really was frosting Miss Winterley's eyes when they met as polite strangers.

'I am nobody's hero, Miss Winterley,' he said dourly. 'They usually end up dead and not maimed like me.'

'If that scar was on the back of the head I suppose I might believe you got it running away,' she said as the faint sound of her needle penetrating the heavy satin of her gown reached his over-sensitised hearing and he held his breath against the quiet catch of her breathing and what it was doing to his dratted body.

'Maybe I walked backwards from the guns?' he said wryly and she chuckled. The warm sound of it brought back all the temptations he had been fighting since she walked into the room and he saw her all flustered and compelling from his perch at the top of the spiral stairs, before she even knew he existed.

'And maybe a bullet bounced off somewhere else and hit you in the leg, but somehow I doubt it.'

'I could have been devilishly unlucky.'

'You could.'

'Are you done yet?' he asked sharply, because it felt dangerous to argue, then almost laugh with her.

'Eager to be rid of me?'

'Eager to keep my job, Miss Winterley. That will not happen if we are found alone here with the door shut.'

'Yet the new Duke seems such a reasonable sort of man,' she said as if he could be explained away with a careless smile and a shrug that said of course we were not up to anything untoward, how could a viscount's daughter and a librarian be anything but strangers?

'Your papa doesn't look so where you are concerned.'

'True, but he's not here and now I'm set to rights he won't need to be.'

'Kindly hurry away then and make sure of that, if you please. Can I turn round, by the way?'

'Yes, I am quite neat and unmarred again,' she said and he frowned as he turned and met her challenging gaze. 'I cannot say it has been a pleasure meeting you, Mr Carter.'

'Good evening, Miss Winterley,' he said curtly and wished she would go away and leave him in peace.

'Good evening, Mr Car...' she began, then faltered as the sound of hurrying feet sounded outside. 'Where can I hide?' she demanded urgently.

He darted a look at the alcove set aside for a clerk to catalogue new finds in the days when Lord Derneley's father collected rare volumes from anywhere he could. Even that dark corner couldn't conceal a young woman in pale and rustling silk. She gave him an impatient look and darted towards the narrow wooden stair he had climbed down so carefully only minutes ago. She scrambled to get out of sight and was lost to his view, if not to his senses, just in time not to be seen when the door opened and Lord Derneley sauntered in.

'Thought you could have helped Lady Derneley with the wallflowers, Carter,' he said distractedly, looking round as if this half-empty room was a surprise to him.

The thought of Miss Winterley standing so near and still made Colm tense as a drum. He breathed more shallowly for fear she might make a noise and be found and what on earth would they do then? An offer of marriage from him would hardly quiet the scandal. Yet there was something furtive in Derneley's pale eyes that said he knew she had flown somewhere to set her appearance to rights and he intended to find her. That suspicion he had earlier that the man was up to something devious as far as his wife's niece was concerned returned in spades. He felt a fierce need to protect her from whatever moneymaking scheme the rogue had thought up at Miss Winterley's expense.

'It seemed best that I not embarrass the young ladies, your lordship,' he said and when the man looked baffled Colm pointed at his damaged leg.

'Oh, aye, quite right. Forgot you're a dot-and-carry one and can't dance. Make the poor little things a laughing stock if you tried, I suppose.' The man's glassy gaze lingered on the scar high on Colm's forehead, then flicked away as if he was being delicate about mentioning yet another reason he could not show his face in public.

'Quite,' Colm managed flatly, willing the girl hidden so precariously nearby not to move even a finger while this noble rat was in the room to hear her and force her to do whatever he had in mind.

'I'll tell her ladyship that's why you're hiding yourself away then, shall I?'

'Thank you, my lord,' Colm made himself say as humbly as a clerk should when invited to join the nobility at play, even if it was only to dance with wallflowers.

'Ah, there you are, Derneley,' Viscount Farenze said from the doorway.

Colm knew who he was because he was standing by his daughter's side earlier, looking formidable and aloof and ready to challenge any man who put a finger on his eldest child against her will. Colm marvelled at Lord Derneley's stupidity for thinking he would get away with whatever he was up to without being flayed alive.

His fury sharpened as he wondered if Derneley had been forcing his attentions on a girl he shouldn't even think of touching, but no, he looked too sleek and fashionable to have done anything so repellent. No doubt it would take hours to redress, so that was one horror he could discount. Which left his first thought when he saw Miss Winterley so disarrayed and seductive looking; she had a lover and Derneley knew. And wasn't that a guilty secret she and her father would pay handsomely to keep that way?

Lord Farenze eyed Colm coolly before he took a quick scan of the room from the doorway, then stepped inside. Colm thought of Miss Winterley a few heartbeats away from disaster again and he didn't want her to be found out, lover or no. A sneeze or a snatched breath could give her away and then where would they be?

'Came to find Carter here,' the master of the house said uneasily under his one-time brother-in-law's stern gaze. He even managed to make it sound logical for the host to seek the humblest gentleman here in the midst of his own evening party.

Colm called on all his experience of hiding his feelings not to glare at the man. If it wasn't Miss Winterley who was a hair's breadth from disaster, he might be stifling laughter instead of a savage growl as the man let his gaze shift past half-empty book stacks and sharpen on the deepest shadows as if he was looking for her. There was something damned odd going on; he hadn't been imagining things earlier. Colm couldn't help wondering what Miss Winterley was thinking, standing in semi-darkness and wondering what Derneley was up to as well.

'I'm weary of cards and gossip and my wife is deep in conversation with Lady Mantaigne, Derneley. I might as well keep Linaire's librarian company for you, as you have a great many other matters to attend to tonight. You know how I dote on books and a good host can't absent himself from his own party for long, can he?' Lord Farenze said so genially Colm shivered. The man's good humour had so much steel in it he was surprised Lord Derneley wasn't shaking in his boots.

'Always knew you were an odd fellow, Farenze, but I suppose you're right. Best get back to m'wife's party before anyone notices,' Derneley agreed airily.

'I'll join you as soon as I've picked this learned young man's brains,' Lord Farenze replied and Colm eyed him uneasily as Lord Derneley finally ran out of reasons to stay in his own library and left with one last frustrated look round the room, as if he might spot Miss Winterley climbing a half-dismantled book stack, presumably desperate for a good read.

Chapter Three

'Hold still,' Lord Farenze murmured, as if he could see through all that finely carved wood and a wall to his daughter's hiding place. Colm held his breath as Lord Derneley's steps faded rather slowly down the marble-floored corridor and Lord Farenze finally shut the door on him. 'It's safe to come out now, Eve,' he said softly.

'How did you know I was here, Papa?' she said and did so as if nothing much had happened.

Colm took a second look to be sure she wasn't on the brink of hysteria. No, Miss Winterley's blue-green eyes even had the hint of a smile in them now. If not for the way her fingers fisted into her palm on the side her father couldn't see, he might think her calm as a millpond.

'The same way I did at hide and seek when you were a child; you are in the place that makes the most sense,' her father said.

'Oh, I see,' she said and Colm wondered why she still looked so white and strained now her father was here to make all right if another lord came in and caught them having a bookish discussion instead of dancing.

'I wish you both goodnight, my lord, Miss Winterley,' he said stiffly, feeling he was the invisible upper servant everyone thought and it hurt his pride somehow now he'd finally met Miss Winterley face to face.

'First promise not to tell anyone I was alone here with you tonight.'

'I am not a braggart, Miss Winterley,' he argued before he could think straight. Colm saw Lord Farenze's eyes harden and found it difficult to meet the steely distrust in the man's level gaze, but he did.

'If any scandal is whispered about my daughter, the person who spread it is likely to regret he was ever born,' the Viscount threatened so quietly it was far more potent than if he'd shouted and shaken his fists.

'Don't, Papa,' Miss Winterley said with a weary wave of her hand that touched Colm far more than feminine hysterics ever could. 'I think we can trust him.'

'I don't trust any man with your safety and peace of mind tonight.'

'Please give him your word as a gentleman not to reveal I was here alone with you, Mr Carter, or we'll be here all night,' she said with a pleading look Colm couldn't resist, however little he'd wanted to be part of this scene.

'I promise not to whisper scandal about Miss Winterley, my lord.'

'You seem to be a man of words, Carter.' The man gestured at the chaos of packed books and the stacks waiting to say Colm might not be beyond writing scandal even if he didn't speak of it.

'I wouldn't write anything that damaged a young lady's reputation either.'

'I am suitably grateful,' Miss Winterley interrupted their silent battle with rather magnificent irony.

'And I have nobody much to write it to if I did,' he told her as if that ought to make this better. He doubted it did from the chilly look she gave him. 'I don't know what you're talking about anyway.'

Lord Farenze looked hard at him. 'Derneley is up to something and the servants will gossip, so you had better add a promise to tell me what they have to say about us to that gallant oath, Carter. Then I might trust you to leave my daughter's reputation alone and let you leave this room in one piece.'

'Very well, my lord. I vow to report faithfully what the servants are saying or not saying over breakfast. I hope that will be all?'

'Not quite, I am also unreasonable enough to expect you to come to Farenze House tomorrow and tell me about it in person. Do not put anything in writing.'

'I have work to do, my lord, but I dare say his Grace will spare me from it for an hour or so to take some air, if I ask him nicely,' Colm said not quite humbly enough to be truly Mr Carter, who only wanted his bed and an end to this ridiculous situation.

'Oh, come on, Papa. Leave the poor man be. Don't forget someone I wish I had never set eyes on could be back in the ballroom by now and busily spreading rumours,' Miss Winterley said with a pained look in the direction of the ballroom that said her ruin might be going on even as they dallied.

'Even Derneley isn't that stupid and I bloodied the nose of that someone else you are talking about. I doubt he'll say anything for a while, let alone admit he was bested by a slip of a girl he thought to force himself on, then knocked out by her very irate father,' Lord Farenze added matter of factly.

Colm went very still as he realised why Miss Winterley had really come in here to repair her gown. What a fool he was not to see the difference between a young woman dishevelled by her amorous beau and one attacked by a raddled old rake. His own convalescence in Brighton had given him the inside track on all the society gossip his breathless landlady gathered from friends who let out rooms or their houses for the Season. So he sorted through the guests he'd seen arrive tonight and came up with the ideal candidate. Sir Steven Scrumble was on the lookout for a wife with enough blue blood and powerful connections to drag him back to the heart of polite society. The man would pay generously for such a bride and Derneley must have sold him a perfect chance to rape Miss Winterley and force an April-and-December marriage on her. The very idea made his flesh crawl, so goodness knew what it did to hers. Scrumble was very rich, so selling a convenient accident to her gown and a neatly empty sewing room wouldn't trouble Derneley's conscience. He clearly didn't have one. Then, with his ill-gotten gains and the money he got from the Duke for his father's books, Derneley might have made it across the Channel and disappeared. Colm thought Derneley's creditors would soon learn Lord Farenze wouldn't lift a finger to

save his one-time brother-in-law and they would fore-
close. Serve the vicious sot right, Colm decided as the
Viscount frowned as if he wished him a thousand miles
away, then did his best to reassure his daughter.

'I made it clear you won't be marrying him if the
whole world is baying for you to do so; I'll kill him
first,' he told her.

'I'm not dashing round the world evading justice
even for you, Papa, and Chloe has had quite enough of
living in shadows. What if he tells everyone anyway?'

'And admit he was bested by a defenceless young
lady? The man's not that much of a fool.' Lord Farenze
went on with a sideways look at Colm that told him
not to be one either, 'Even in his cups he'll remember
what I threatened to do to him if he didn't keep a still
tongue in his head.'

Colm wanted to find the cur and add his fourpen-
nyworth to the mix. He could hardly threaten to have
the bastard drummed out of the clerks' guild though,
could he? Their inequality of power and rank would
forbid the man fighting if Colm challenged him to meet
at dawn, swords or pistols at the ready. Reminded how
little he and Miss Winterley had in common, he used
a trick he'd learnt in his youth and retreated into his
thoughts until he was calm again. He went back to the
table, realised Miss Winterley had put the candle back
in the ideal place to highlight what he'd been reading
before he got distracted and tried to slide Pamela's jour-
nal under a sheaf of ancient letters.

'Wait,' Lord Farenze said sharply, catching that furtive movement as if he was the one who'd spent eight

years sharpening his senses in the Rifles and not Colm. 'What have you got there?' he asked and came closer for a better look. 'I've seen a notebook like that before and that looks like my late wife's scrawl. Let me see.'

'My employer paid a fair price for any item in this room he chose to take away, my lord,' Colm protested half-heartedly.

'And it pains me to see such a fine collection neglected, but if that's truly a volume of my late wife's scribbles then it isn't Derneley's to sell. As her husband I lay claim to it.'

'Papa—' Miss Winterley touched her father's arm '—surely all her scandals are already out in the open by now? We really must go.'

'I'll not have them reawakened in the yellow press and we shall say you wanted to look at the portrait of your mother you knew Derneley had hidden away somewhere in this house. We can explain our absence to your stepmother when we return to the ballroom and the gossips will nod and whisper she has a great deal to bear, but I'm not leaving this room until you explain what you have there, Carter, and if there's aught else I should know about in this musty old collection.'

'I really couldn't say, my lord. I only found the first Lady Farenze's diaries hidden behind a shelf of sermons this afternoon.'

'You have to admire her cheek, don't you?' he said to his daughter and Colm saw the man behind the stern mask before he sent Colm another challenging stare. 'How much have you read?' he asked menacingly, as if it was an intrusion he found hard to forgive.

'Only this last one,' he said, refusing to stand here like a schoolboy sent for punishment and say nothing in his own defence. 'I certainly won't tell her secrets to anyone else,' he promised easily enough.

He had more reasons not to want them known than the Farenze family, and reading Pamela's words really hadn't got him any closer to his father. A woman that self-obsessed was hardly likely to waste pages describing her lover, was she? He would do better to put her and her entire family behind him forever the day he left this place and handing them over might help him do it. The sneaky thought that Pamela's daughter was more difficult to forget nagged at him, but he did his best to ignore it.

'Will you hand over anything else you happen upon before your work here is done?' Miss Winterley asked as if she had caught her father's distrust of him.

'Anything that concerns you, yes,' he said with a weary sigh.

'Good, now we must leave the lad in peace, Eve,' his lordship urged his daughter when she would have argued. 'He can rehash this argument with me in the morning, but you're right, it's high time we returned to the ballroom.'

'We can hardly carry a stack of my late mother's diaries with us. Will you bring them to Farenze House for us, Mr Carter? I would be most grateful.'

Since she didn't wheedle or make any attempt to charm him into doing her bidding, Colm saw no reason to object and delay their departure. 'I suppose it's easy enough for me to carry books in and out of here, so, yes, I'll bring them when I call on your father tomorrow. Now please, will you both go? I don't want to be caught up in the affairs of the great and the good any more than you want me to be.'

'Thank you,' she said and they were back to humble clerk and lady again.

'Goodbye, miss, my lord,' he said with a bow that would do a butler credit.

'Goodbye, Carter,' she replied with a dignified nod and took her father's offered arm to be escorted back to civilisation.

He watched them go and wondered. How would it feel to stroll back into that ballroom with them, sauntering confidently at their side as an equal in birth and fortune? For a moment he thought wistfully of all he once had and didn't regret it as much as he thought. The polite world looked bright and glittering and sophisticated from the outside, but he didn't think it gave the Miss Winterleys of this world much joy. He had grown accustomed to a life where worth and courage counted for more than birth and fortune. When you were all hungry and cold and miserable, on the retreat through harsh country already ravished by French troops, birth and privilege didn't count for much.

As for knowing young ladies like Miss Winterley outside the charmed circle of the *ton*, that was clearly impossible. He put the very idea behind him, limped back up those stairs one last time and packed the eight volumes he had found into a handy little box, stowed it under his arm and was glad neither Winterley was waiting below to see him descend on his clerkly behind as he needed one hand and his good leg to get him down again without disaster. Confound his weak leg and the suspicions Lord Farenze had put into his head about his fellow servants. They were probably too busy to search for such scandalous gems in the library their master had sold off tonight, but Colm turned the key in the lock and pocketed it when he left the library all the same.

'So are you going to let me read my mother's journals, Papa?' Eve asked her father as soon as they were safely out of earshot.

'Certainly not.'

'You do know you can't protect me from her sins for ever, don't you?'

'Yes, but please don't expect me not to try. Even when we're both old and grey, I shall still be your father and convinced it's my role to keep my daughter safe.'

'Nobody could guard me as carefully as you have done, Papa, but I am an adult now in the eyes of the law.'

'I know that too well,' he admitted with a frown that spoke volumes of his concern for her peace and future happiness.

Eve had to live with her mother's many scandals hanging over her, but the world must deal with her as she was, not as they expected from her mother's wild ride through life. 'I do love you, Papa, and Chloe and Verity and the boys, but I need to live my own life.'

'Your stepmother has told me time and again not to follow you about like a mastiff and glare at any young idiot who notices you are a woman. Don't ever fool yourself, I like watching you hurt yourself on briars that aren't of your setting though, my Eve.'

'If I am to live any sort of life I must find my own way through them, though.'

'I suppose so, but not right now. It's high time we got back to indifferent wine and weak lemonade and rescued your stepmother since not even she and Polly Mantaigne could keep the curious at bay for the amount of time we have been gone. The poor girl will have talked herself into a headache again by now.'

'You are a fine and remembering sort of husband; I do love you, Papa.'

'Don't try to wheedle your way round me with soft words, minx; I'm still not letting you read Pamela's selfish outpourings.'

'Spoilsport,' Eve pronounced him and took a look at herself in one of the long mirrors placed at strategic points even along this dimly lit and seldom-visited corridor. She looked remarkably unscathed. 'Aunt Derneley is the vainest woman I have ever encountered,' she said after she twitched a frill back into place and brushed a piece of lint from her skirt.

'Only because you didn't know your mother,' Lord Farenze said as he removed a cobweb from his daughter's dark hair. They re-entered the ballroom to run up against a clever scold from Chloe for avoiding their social obligations and a frown of concern for the headache Eve didn't know she had until now.

Chapter Four

'What's he like then, Eve?' Miss Verity Revereux demanded the next morning as she bounced on to Eve's bed before staring wistfully at herself in the mirror across the room and wondering out loud if she was developing a spot.

'What was who like? And it seems unlikely since you were blessed by far too many good fairies at your birth and never had a single blemish I know of,' Eve said.

Then she remembered what a grim situation her honorary sister was born into. Her mother died as she gulped in her first lungful of air and poor Chloe was left with a newborn to care for at the tender age of seventeen as her twin sister died in childbirth. Eve groped about for a rapid change of subject and hit on the least welcome one to hand. 'Whomever can you mean anyway?'

'The man you met last night from the dreamy look on your face.'

Eve frowned and did her best to avoid the apparently guileless blue eyes Verity had inherited from her father. Neither Captain Revereux nor his beloved daughter were the innocents they appeared, so Eve hardened her heart against the plea in her best friend's eyes and turned to her lady's maid instead.

'You were right, Bran, this colour looks better on me this morning,' she said with her head on one side as she studied the choice of morning gowns on offer. 'I'm not sure which sash to wear,' she added, hoping to divert Verity with fripperies. She ought to know better, she supposed. Verity might look like an angel sent to humble lesser beings with her golden beauty, but looks could be deceptive. When her father was at sea they were all inclined to spoil her and Eve wished the gallant captain would hurry home and check his beloved child's wilder starts before they got her into real trouble.

'I can stay here all day if I have to, Eve dear,' Verity told her. 'Miss Stainforth has agreed to go and see a dentist at last, so I have all the time in the world to plague you until she is feeling better.' Verity lounged back on the bed to prove it. 'I loved it at school, but I'm so glad Papa insisted on hiring Miss Stainforth to teach me instead. Now I can be with you and Aunt Chloe and Uncle Luke all the time when he has to be out of the country and you can't lie to me at a distance. I can't see why you treat me like some artless child who must be kept in ignorance of the important things in life, Cousin dear. I preferred you before you made your curtsy to society and became so *terribly* worldly wise.'

'No doubt your governess left you plenty to do, Miss Verity, and you ought to be doing it right now,' Bran said sternly.

'She was in so much pain she forgot and why should I have my head stuffed with more facts and figures that I shall be expected to forget the moment I set foot in my first ballroom?'

'Our sex makes up half the world, Verity, and if we were all wilfully ignorant it would fall apart. You should be worrying about the poor lady's pain and suffering, not gloating over your freedom like some horrid schoolboy let off his lessons,' Eve tried to scold. Verity looked unimpressed and went on sorting Eve's sashes.

'Lady Chloe will find you something useful to do since your poor governess was in too much pain to bother, young lady,' Bran added with a look at Eve that said her disturbed night was showing on her face.

'No, don't bother her at this hour of the morning,' Eve intervened. Chloe was in the early stages of pregnancy yet again and if this one went like the last two, her stepmother would not be ready to deal with her wayward niece for another hour or two yet. 'You can take a stroll with me to Green Park among the nursemaids and governesses. I need some fresh air and you will be working too hard this afternoon and poor Miss Stainforth won't be well enough to accompany you out anyway.'

'Sourpuss, but I'm not put off that easily. You didn't answer my question, Eve Winterley. Are you quite sure you didn't meet the man of your dreams last night?' Verity asked, being of an age when fairy tales weren't quite impossible and beckoning womanhood whispered how wonderful if they happened to her.

'I never had those sorts of dreams, but, no, I did not,'

Eve said firmly, pushing a mental picture of the gruff, wounded and annoyingly unforgettable Mr Carter out of her mind. 'If Betty comes with us to the park, will you stay and make some of your peppermint tea for Lady Chloe, Bran?' she asked once Verity was fully occupied with finding her pelisse and muff, then dragging her favourite maid away from her duties as well as the second footman. Verity loved a romance and as Eve refused to live one for her, she must have decided to promote that one instead.

'Of course I will. You have a good heart under those stubborn ways, haven't you, my chick?'

Eve eyed her own reflection in the mirror and saw an almost perfect lady of fashion staring back at her. She almost expected a magical image of Mr Carter to peer into the glass behind her and smile mockingly, so she turned away with a sigh. Hadn't she had just told Verity she didn't have daydreams and here was the least comfortable hero she had ever encountered intruding into them?

'I'm too old to be anyone's chick now,' she replied to Bran's question lightly enough before she left the room.

'You'll never be too old for that, my love,' Bran whispered as she watched the almost sisters join up on the wide landing, then go downstairs for their walk. 'And perhaps I've good reason to worry about the dark circles under your eyes and stubborn set to your chin this morning.'

'Ah, now don't remind me, I'm determined to recall your name for myself, sir. There now, I knew it would come to me if I thought about it hard enough. You're Mr Carter, are you not? I dare say you have been calling on my father?' Miss Winterley's pleasing contralto voice asked Colm as if they had met at some fashionable soirée.

Damnation, Colm thought darkly; he thought he was safe out here, trying to get some air into his lungs before making his way back to Derneley House. Lord Farenze's daughter wasn't as indolent as most of her kind and fate wasn't on his side this morning either.

'Good morning, Miss Winterley,' he managed dourly.

'It is, isn't it?' she replied brightly, as if his failure to sneak past her unnoticed made it a lot better for some reason.

'We should not linger together in public or private, ma'am,' he told her in an undertone he hoped he'd pitched too low to carry to the ears of a nearby knot of overgrown schoolgirls giggling over something best known to themselves.

'We should not linger anywhere, then? You are very unsociable, Mr Carter, and the title *ma'am* is reserved for ladies with considerably more years in their dish than I have.'

'Forgive my ignorance, Miss Winterley. It's as well I have no inclination for high society and it has none for me,' he said with an odd pang at his exile from the polite world that felt nothing like the burning resentment he had once struggled with.

A Mr Carter had to shape his life around his work, so Colm tried hard not to meet Miss Winterley's challenging gaze with one of his own and wondered how it would feel to have the wealth and status his father took for granted back right now. Perhaps then he could meet her gaze for gaze and it wouldn't matter that his father once ran off with her mother. With all that noble blood and nabob wealth at his back Colm Hancourt might have challenged Miss Winterley back and...

No, there was no and...for them and there never would be. Even when he was under his uncle's roof and being himself again he wouldn't have much more than a rifle and a tiny annuity. Mr Hancourt worked for his uncle and most of his salary would go on being the Duke of Linaire's nephew. He must have better clothes and a sturdy horse and anything else could go into a small dowry for his sister. He and Miss Winterley would still not meet as equals and she would probably hate him for who he was when she found out. So he hoped she would tire of such a stiff-necked block and dismiss him before he said something disastrous.

'You go off into a world of your own at the drop of a hat, don't you, Mr Carter? That could get you into all sorts of trouble at Derneley House,' she warned lightly.

'I beg your pardon, Miss Winterley,' he said. 'I'll go about my business and leave you to enjoy the sunshine.'

'Please don't go,' she protested impulsively. 'My cousin has met some old school friends and is catching up on all she's missed since they last met.'

The three of them were standing a few yards away, so absorbed in excited conversation they might as well be the only people in the park. 'I thought your cousins were still in the nursery,' Colm said, revealing he knew more about her family than he wanted to admit.

'Uncle James's various chicks are, but Verity is my stepmama's niece. I'm surprised you haven't heard the story yet; it caused a sensation five years ago when my father married Lady Chloe Thessaly and the truth had to come out.'

'I have spent the last eight years in the army. The sayings and doings of the great and the good passed us by for most of that time.'

'I suppose you had more important things to think about than gossip and scandal, but you must have been little more than a boy when you took up your commission to have been in the army for so long, Mr Carter.'

'A compliment, Miss Winterley?'

'An observation,' she said with a slight flush on her high cheekbones that told him she thought it might have been as well.

'I was sixteen,' he said, his eldest uncle's brusque dismissal of his hopes and dreams of being a writer and scholar one day like his determinedly absent Uncle Horace sharp in his voice. He heard the gruff sound of it, shrugged rather helplessly and met her gaze with a rueful smile. 'I thought myself the devil of a fellow in my smart green uniform,' he admitted and suddenly wished he'd known her back then.

He'd felt so alone under his boyish swagger the day he entered Shorncliffe Camp and began the transformation from scared boy to scarred Rifleman. Mr Carter came into being in a regiment where officers won their rank largely by merit and gallantry in battle. Colm wanted a plain name to go with his dashing uniform mainly because he wanted to fit in and the Hancourts wanted nothing to do with him and Nell. Eight years on he must be Carter for a little longer, but at least nobody was trying to kill him.

'Were you a Rifleman, then?' she asked and he supposed he must have looked bewildered. 'Since you wore a green uniform it seems a strong possibility,' she added logically.

'Aye,' he said, 'some folk call us the Grasshoppers because of it.'

'To survive eight years as a Rifleman you must be brave as well as fortunate, whatever they called you,' Eve managed to reply lightly enough.

Instinct warned her not to let him know how she pitied a boy who began his dangerous career so young. What if he was born rich and well connected instead? Would she have met a rather dazzling young gentleman in an expensive drawing room when she came out and fallen for his easy charm? Or would she have thought him as shallow and unformed as the other young men who paid court to her with an air of fashionable boredom she didn't find in the least bit flattering? She could have found the way his thick honey-brown hair curled despite his efforts to tame it fascinating. His gold-flecked eyes might have danced with merriment and lured a discerning young lady into falling in love and his scarred forehead would be unmarred. As for that lame leg—that would be as long and strong and lithe as the rest of him. That charmed and charming man would laugh and smile with her, then grow serious long enough to look deep into her eyes with his soul alive and clear in his own. And then he would kiss her.

Her breath caught in heady anticipation in the much less magical here and now and she almost gave her thoughts away by moving a little closer to him and behaving like a besotted ninny. A dreamer deep inside her whispered it would be almost unbearably glorious, whichever version of him did the kissing, but that might be Pamela's daughter speaking and Eve didn't want to listen to her. Carter certainly didn't adore her and he was the Duke of Linaire's clerk and librarian, for goodness' sake.

'I was just lucky, I suppose,' he said with a self-deprecating shrug as if nothing else could account for it.

Eve shivered at the thought of a stray bullet or sabre slash that might have ended his life and refused to think of the number he must have survived right now. 'I doubt any officer could survive long on luck in a regiment like yours,' she challenged.

'You would be surprised and at least I had enough of it to know when it ran out. This summer I was at the end of it and sold out as soon as I recovered enough to sign my name after Waterloo.'

'You seem determined to make light of your experiences.'

'A limping man stands little chance of surviving a forced march or fighting retreat, but let's not speak of such horrors on a day like today. Didn't you promise me a fine story about your cousin by marriage and your stepmama just now?'

'Did I?' Drat the man, having a conversation with him was like trying to hold a slippery trout wet from the river. Last night he seemed almost too dashing to be an upper servant, today he carried his shallow dark hat as if itching to have it back on his head and go before someone caught him speaking to a lady. 'It's no secret now, so you might as well hear it from me. Lady Chloe and Verity's mama were twins, Mr Carter. At much the same age as you joined the army, Lady Daphne Thessaly wed a young naval lieutenant to avoid an arranged marriage. Her father was furious at being robbed of what he saw as his right to sell his daughter to a rich old man so he had her husband pressed, then left his twin daughters to birth her baby in such dire conditions it's a miracle Verity and her aunt survived, but Lady Daphne died in childbed. Lady Chloe spent the next decade acting as Verity's mother and became a housekeeper, then my father spent most of it trying not to be in love with her.'

'And when he couldn't resist any longer they told each other their secrets and seized the day?'

'I don't recall it being that simple, but the end result is they are very happily wed and Verity lives with us when her father is at sea,' she said and wondered why she hadn't let him go in the first place. It was that bland mask of the onlooker on life that did it, she supposed. For some reason she itched to rip it off and show the world a real man stood here, despite the repressive black garb and his fiercely guarded aloofness. Now she waited for his stiff farewell and told herself to let him go this time.

'Would my sister had had an aunt like your stepmother to love and protect her when I was sent off to school by our uncle,' he said instead and why was she this glad he hadn't mumbled a hasty farewell and limped away?

'What happened to her?' she said with all the horror stories of girls sent out as apprentices by their cruel relatives in her mind as she saw him frown.

'Oh, nothing very awful, she was put in the care of a governess until she was old enough to go to school and our family could forget us. My wicked uncle still found her useful as a stick to beat me with; if I ran away from school or tried to argue with the career he had in mind, my sister would be apprenticed to a milliner. I'm sure you know what happens to most girls bound to that trade, Miss Winterley. Even at eight years old I knew I must be a pattern card to save her from such a fate.'

'How cruel,' she exclaimed and felt furious with his appalling relative when he shrugged.

'It's the way of the world, my father annoyed two of his brothers so much they would have loved to have nothing to do with his children, but the scandal would have deafened them if they let us go into the poorhouse.'

'What did your mother's relatives have to say for themselves?'

'She was an only child and her parents died before her. If she had any relatives I don't know of it,' he said as if he wished he'd never told her so much in the first place.

'I am astonished her friends and neighbours let your uncle treat you both so, then,' she said although Mr Carter didn't want her to feel anything for him or his.

'They would shake their heads and mutter it was terrible we were left destitute, then whisper about bad blood and decide we were best forgotten,' he told her with some passion in his voice at last. 'Poverty stalked my sister's childhood and she is always a hair's breadth away from it even now, Miss Winterley. One wicked thought in an employer's head; a wrong word or unwitting action can get a governess dismissed without references. I can't endure the thought of such a life grinding her down as the years go on, so it is up to me to find a way out of such an existence for her, before it drives the youth and laughter out of her completely.'

Eve only had to see the purpose burning in his fiery gaze to know she was right about the hidden depths he tried to keep to himself. He wasn't the flat character he tried to be; he couldn't be if he pretended he was until doomsday.

'Your uncles are as guilty as your father of not making sure she is provided for. You will need very broad shoulders if you intend to take the sins of your entire family on them, Mr Carter.'

'You are very direct this morning, Miss Winterley.'

She shrugged. 'For direct I shall read rude, but I have no patience with pretend ignorance, sir, and if you had moved in polite society for the last three years you would not have any either. Your sister might count herself lucky not to be watched like a prize heifer by every idiot on the marriage mart if she knew how it felt.'

'Are they all idiots, then?'

'Not all, but no sensible man will hold an interesting conversation with a marriageable young lady for long unless he is in serious need of a wife.'

'So there is some merit in being ineligible after all,

then?' he joked and Eve felt a tug of temptation to make him do it again.

He was so unaware of how handsome he was when he forgot to guard his tongue that he could steal an unwary female's heart before she knew she was in danger. Lucky she wasn't unwary then, wasn't it?

'Why come to London for the Little Season then, since you dislike it so much?' he asked as if truly interested.

'The House is sitting and Papa hates coming on his own. My parents worry about me if I don't come with them and there's Verity's future to think of as well. If I refuse to take my part in this pantomime the *ton* plays out twice a year she will be an oddity by association. That would be so unfair when we're not related except through Papa and Chloe's marriage and a common link with my little half-brothers.'

'So you only dress and dance and behave like a fashionable young lady who is enjoying herself for the benefit of others?' he said with a sceptical glance at her fashionable pelisse and high-crowned bonnet that said he thought her vain and not very self-aware.

Chapter Five

Miss Winterley looked as if she might agree she was that saintly for a moment just to spite him, then mischief danced in her eyes and an irresistible smile tugged at her temptingly curved mouth. Colm had to struggle with a terrible urge to kiss her breathless, silenced and deliciously responsive—in the middle of Green Park for goodness' sake. What business had such a controlled and confident lady turning into an enchanting mix of funny, wise and daring when she smiled?

'I love my finery and attending the opera and theatres and real concerts that are not put on by supposedly musical ladies to show off their airs as much as their talents. I should not see my family and friends anywhere near as often as I do if we could not meet up in town either. My Uncle James has grown so fond of country life I sometimes wonder how Aunt Rowena manages to drag him here as often as she does though, but I can put up with the Lady Derneleys and Mr Carters of this world in order to keep in contact with the friends and relatives who truly matter to me.'

Thanks to his Brighton landlady even Colm knew of James Winterley's transformation from idle London rake to country squire and father of a ready-made family. Then there was the Winterleys' close connection to the Marquis of Mantaigne and his mixed bag of a family by marriage—oh, and Sir Gideon Laughraine and his lady. Here was the truth of things: Miss Winterley was at the heart of a group of impressive and powerful aristocrats and he was only even a secretary thanks to his Uncle Horace's bad conscience.

'Then I hope you enjoy your latest visit, Miss Winterley,' he said with a stiff bow and half raised his humble and unfashionable hat.

'Thank you, Mr Carter,' she replied with an ironic lift of her fine dark brows and a regal nod. 'How very kind of you to wish me well.'

'Good day, Miss Winterley,' he said repressively and got ready to limp back to his books and papers and packing crates.

'And a very good day to you too, sir,' he heard her reply lightly by way of dismissal from a lady to the upper servant he really was nowadays.

The thought of how much clear water lay between him and Miss Winterley mocked him all the way back to Derneley House and made him limp more heavily than usual for some strange reason. 'Even a lunatic wouldn't be fool enough to yearn for that particular moon, Colm Hancourt,' he murmured under his breath as he went.

He was fairly sure he was still sane, but that was about all he had to offer any woman deluded enough to want him. He was scarred and limping and about as penniless as a man could be without actually living in the gutter. Before he met Miss Winterley he had still been able to convince himself he only wanted his lost fortune back for Nell's sake. Now he had a sneaking suspicion he'd lied. Was there any hope Miss Winterley might ever look on him as a possible lover if he wasn't who he was? Of course not. The idea was ridiculous and he must put it from his mind right now.

So that left him with his sister Nell still to save from a life of genteel poverty or a rich man's bed and no wedding ring. The very thought of either fate for his bright, brave sister horrified him enough to make him put aside air dreams and concentrate on her future instead. There was one elusive possibility he'd been turning over in his mind since he read the last entry in Pamela's diary last night. He shrugged off the idea it had been wrong to read them before he passed them over to their rightful owner as ordered. He had as much right to know the wretched female's thoughts during the time she was with his father as anyone still alive. The woman was annoyingly evasive about the Lambury Jewels after that crow about the rubies, at least until the end of her diary when she must have left for that last wild adventure with her lover. Before she went she railed at her lover's refusal to hand over the last of his wife's jewellery: the magnificent diamond set Joseph Lambury had made up for his daughter after Colm was born. So when his father left England with his *inamorata* they should have been in the bank vault his uncle had sworn was bare as a pauper's pocket when Colm plucked up the courage to ask before he left for the army.

A slender thread of hope dangled in front of Colm's eyes as he speculated how much the diamond set might be worth. He vaguely recalled seeing his mother wear them when she was dressed up for a ball grand enough to warrant such splendour. There had been a tiara and a magnificent tumble of diamonds round her neck that sparkled fascinatingly in the candlelight when she came to bid him goodnight. Heavy bracelets weighed down her slender wrists and they laughed together as he playfully moved her hands so they would make rainbows from her rings even with the nursery night lights. A coachman shouted at a carter and their loud exchange of insults jolted Colm out of the past and into a very different world. For a moment he had been back there with her, sharing a careless moment of loving intimacy with his mother and remembering so much about her he thought he'd forgotten.

He felt almost sorry he had that memory to cherish when Nell was too young to remember much more about their mother than a vague impression of pale hair and warm arms. They had talked about their parents one night this summer in Brussels, when the pain of his wounds kept him awake and she insisted on waking with him. It taught him a lot, that time when even he wasn't quite sure if he was going to live or die. The most important thing he had found out was he and his sister still shared a strong bond, despite all the efforts two of their uncles and aunts made to keep them apart. All those years of pretending the Hancourt-Winterley scandal died with their brother and not even the last

Duke and their Uncle Maurice could make Colm and Nell strangers to one another.

Which brought him back to the diamonds; the last Duke of Linaire must have had them broken up and sold, he supposed. Colm thought about the hard-eyed man who informed him his father was dead as if he ought to be glad. That man was capable of it, but could he have got away with it? That was less certain and whispers of what he'd done would have haunted the cold-hearted devil to his grave. Nothing Colm had heard since he came back to England said any of those whispers existed. The diamonds might still be hiding somewhere, waiting to be found and claimed by him. A beat of wild hope thundered in his heart as he thought what that would mean for Nell's future happiness. A real dowry, a secure home and perhaps living under the same roof as her brother for a while before she wed a man who deserved her, if such a paragon existed. Colm almost smiled, then changed his mind as he realised how unlikely his latest daydream sounded. If he could find diamonds nobody had seen for fifteen years; if he could prove they were his; if he could sell them for the fortune needed to buy a modest home and a farm to support it; if Nell would leave her noble orphans and join him there…

So many ifs made a fantasy, but if there was some trace of his mother's diamonds, Uncle Horace might help him find them. Colm knew his uncle and aunt felt they had let his little brother's children down by staying away when their father died. Now they were back in England the duchy wasn't the rich inheritance it was before the last Duke and Colm's grandfather spent money like water. The current Duke couldn't afford to dower his niece and establish his nephew as the gentleman his birth argued, because Uncle Maurice would be watching his future inheritance like a hawk. The new Duchess was unlikely to produce a child after a quarter of a century of marriage, so Lord Maurice would insist on an allowance as his brother's heir before Lord Chris's children got a penny of Hancourt money beyond the twenty pounds a year already settled on them by the last Duke. Those diamonds might be a false hope, Colm mused as he made his way down the back steps of Derneley house, but sometimes it was better to have one of those than none at all.

The work of getting the Derneley Collection listed and packed up ready for its new home, so he could get out of this house, felt more urgent today. As Colm went about it he couldn't stop thinking of his latest meeting with Miss Winterley. He didn't number many fine ladies among his acquaintance, but something told him she was an unusual one. This morning she seemed as relaxed as if he was a fashionable gentleman in Hyde Park at the fashionable hour, instead of an almost servant in Green Park at some unlikely hour of the morning for a lady who had been at a party late into the night. He let his hands slow for a moment as he thought of her in the clear light of a fine autumn morning. Her skin was flawless, he recalled, and she was still young enough for a late night and early morning not to be written under her eyes. Her bonnet was modest by the standards of the current fashion for vast pokes that hid the wearer from view if there was any danger of shadows. So now he knew that her eyes truly were a rare shade of blue-green and could haunt a man to his grave if he wasn't careful. Add a slender but womanly figure and the smile that made her unique and he had best think about diamonds again and forget Miss Winterley as best he could.

Anything more than a stiff acquaintance between that lady and Mr Carter was clearly impossible, so he thought about that passage he had copied out last night in his room and with the door safely shut behind him. He took out the paper he kept in his jacket pocket lest some servant find it and scanned Pamela's words for anything that passed him by last night. He was bone weary at the time and his head so full of Eve Winterley and her icy father he couldn't think straight. There might be a stray word he'd missed the sense of as he wrote it down. The last page of her diary seemed to sum the woman up perfectly.

> *Knowing the full power of my own beauty at last and feeling men lust for me so deeply they can't fight it is wonderful, but jewels never fade. I don't intend to be deprived of a single stone, and they will never make me feel less than beautiful, however old I get.*

So had written the woman who would never get much older than she had been when she'd made that last entry in the diary.

Colm's mouth twisted in distaste as he re-read her self-centred ramblings, but he felt a spark of regret for a vivid life cut short all the same. He was sorry Lord Farenze would have to read his late wife's words and wonder what made her as she was. Colm had no idea how it felt to walk in the Viscount's expensive shoes, but he didn't envy him the memory of a wife no one man could satisfy. Her words told him enough about Pamela to know she would have left Colm's father for another lover, however deeply Lord Chris adored her. Colm was almost glad Lord Chris hadn't lived to watch the woman who cost him so dearly walk away without a backward look.

Emotions he didn't want to imagine underlay the dark fascination of a duke's youngest son and the runaway wife of a very young peer. If he let himself dwell on such wild passions he might feel an echo of them for some unsuspecting female. A picture of Miss Winterley looking horrified as he poured out his insatiable desire for her made him flinch, then smile at the next image of her speechless with shocked surprise that he could feel anything at all, let alone that. She was so unlike her dam, Colm felt guilty for misjudging her last night and uneasy about the thunder of passionate need in his own veins as he watched her ghost into his temporary lair breathless and far too desirable for her own good before they had even spoken to each other.

Eve had given her father time to read all Pamela's letters and diaries before confronting him the day after she met Mr Carter in Green Park. It must make painful reading for him and she doubted her mother's self-centred outpourings shone much light on what had made her long for a succession of ever wilder lovers.

'You really won't let me read a word of my mother's papers, will you?' Eve challenged as she followed him into his study after breakfast.

'I wish I could burn the lot right now, so there would be no risk of you or anyone else ever reading a word of her selfish drivel,' her father said with a preoccupied frown at the locked drawer of his desk where she guessed the diaries were sitting like a row of fat little grenades that could be so destructive in the wrong hands she shuddered at the thought of it.

'Then why don't you?' she asked with a nod at the fire burning steadily in the grate on this fine but chilly morning.

'Because it isn't right to deprive that boy of a chance,' he murmured as if he was fighting the urge to do it anyway.

'What boy? Oh, you mean Lord Christopher Hancourt's son, I suppose. I thought he was dead; nobody has heard of him for years and his family never talk about him or the little girl I remember someone mentioning once.'

'Their father spent the lad's rightful inheritance on your mother and I can't believe that fool was besotted enough to simply hand over all those jewels to her. She knew the Lambury Jewels weren't even his to give, but she seduced and sulked as only she knew how until she got them out of him. There isn't a single word of remorse about the boy and his sister in the books and papers Carter handed over.'

'It would be beneath him to hold back a single letter of hers once he made you that promise,' Eve argued against Mr Carter holding something over them. Her father's acute gaze focused on her as if he was trying to read her thoughts and feelings about a man she didn't even like. Of course she didn't feel anything for the stiff-necked idiot, how could she? She still felt the need to affirm his honesty for some reason. 'He wouldn't keep anything that didn't belong to him,' she added.

'That's what I'm afraid of,' her father murmured so low she wondered if she was mistaken. 'Nothing Pamela did should shame you, love,' he said out loud and with such sadness and concern in his eyes Eve felt guilty about reminding him of those dark days in both their lives, not that she could remember them.

'Nor you, Papa,' she said. 'She did enough damage when she was alive. Please don't agonise over her sins now she's dead. The memory of them kept you and darling Chloe apart for years, so don't fret about things she never felt a second's worth of unease about now.'

'Yet if I burn these books I might deprive that boy of the better life and we Winterleys have done enough damage in that quarter already. If there's any chance those jewels she writes about so gleefully can be found and I destroy a clue to where they are, then I shall be the one in need of a few scruples and not Pamela.'

'We must find the man Lord Chris's son must be by now and help him as best we can then. If that's what it takes to make you forget all the evil Lord Chris and Pamela did between them, we have no choice.'

'Any gossip now sleeping safely might wake up

and bite you if he or his sister come forward, love,' he warned with a brooding look Eve couldn't quite read.

'Don't you think I'm strong enough to ignore such poisonous gossip by now?'

'Sometimes I wonder if you're not too strong, Eve. If I had only worked my way past Pamela and caught your stepmother ten years before I did, you and Verity would have had easier childhoods. I was a fool not to seize the day and your stepmother a lot sooner than I did.'

'Well, there's no denying Chloe is perfect for you in every way my mother never was, but Verity and I did very well with one of you each for the ten years you two spent apart. We do even better now you're together and happy, instead of apart and secretly miserable, but there's no need to mourn what we didn't have because you were stubborn as a rock, Papa. We were both very much loved and cared for even before you and Chloe let yourselves be happy together.'

'I'm glad you know we love you, but are you sure you're prepared for the old gossip to be stirred up if I find Hancourt and help him search for any remnants of his inheritance that might be lying around unattended?'

Eve had had to prove over and over again how unlike her mother she was when she made her debut in society. The idea of facing that ordeal again was daunting and made her pause for a moment. No, peace wasn't worth having if it came from playing the coward, she decided. She would have to be more cautious than ever about dark corridors and deserted ladies' withdrawing rooms, but the sneaky thought that meeting an intriguing and gruff young gentleman at the end of her last adventure made it almost worthwhile was nonsensical, wasn't it?

'Even the whisper of a lost fortune could do that anyway, but I don't see how we can stand in his way, if he's still alive, of course.'

'And I suspect he is,' her father muttered with that odd look on his face again and Eve was tempted to stamp her feet and demand he tell her everything he was keeping back. She was a young lady now and not a harum-scarum miss, so she could not and she knew that look of old. He wouldn't even tell Chloe what was in his thoughts until he was ready and a show of temper certainly wouldn't help.

'Your Mr Carter might be in the Duke of Linaire's confidence, Eve. You could always ask him to find out what happened to Lord Christopher's children next time you meet him in Green Park.'

'How did you know about that?'

'Luckily Verity doesn't know it was meant to be a secret.'

'But it wasn't. I met the man there by pure chance. I suppose he was taking the air on his way back from delivering my mother's papers to you.'

'And yet you spoke with him at length in the sight of all those nursemaids and governesses. Don't deny it, Eve; I had the tale from more than one source.'

'I didn't think you listened to gossip, Papa.'

'I do when it concerns my daughter. Have a care, my Eve. Carter might be a wounded hero of however many battles of Wellington's he is old enough to have fought in, but he clearly hasn't a feather to fly with. He wouldn't be sorting dusty old books for Linaire at Derneley House if he had.'

'I never took you for a snob, Papa, and I only met the man two days ago. I am hardly likely to fall in love with such a rude and stiff-necked idiot anyway, even if I had known him since we were in our nurseries.'

'It doesn't take long to do that,' he warned her ruefully. 'Love can come without an invitation and when we're least expecting it. Be careful it doesn't creep up on you in the worst possible circumstances and bludgeon you over the head like it did your unwary papa.'

'It won't. I don't intend to succumb to passion. If I wed at all it will be to a gentleman I have learnt to know and respect after months, if not years, of friendship.'

'What of mutual attraction and downright lust? I know you're my daughter and I should be glad you are going to be so sensible about picking a husband, but I don't want you to miss out the crucial parts of a happy marriage.'

'Not many fathers encourage their daughters to become besotted with a gentleman they have not even met.'

'How do you know that if you only intend to wed a not-very-exciting friend? And I only want you to form a passion for the man if he is right for you.'

'Logic will tell me that, I have no need for the sort of insane urges that ruled my mother's life.'

'No, but you should think a little more about your own before you marry a block, love.'

'If I was really looking for one of those, Mr Carter would fill the bill very nicely.'

'Believe that and you'll believe anything,' her father said darkly and Eve wished she'd picked a better example than the Duke of Linaire's whatever he was: secretary, librarian, man of business? Possibly only the Duke and Mr Carter knew the answer to that question.

She remembered how it felt to have Mr Carter's gold-brown eyes focus intently on her when he forgot his false humility. No, he wasn't a wooden soldier at all. Papa was quite right; there was a sharply intelligent and sensitive man under that quiet exterior and she would do well to remember it if they ever met again, which seemed very unlikely as he was the Duke of Linaire's clerk and not part of the *ton*.

'My one-day marriage and Mr Carter aside, what do you mean to do about the Hancourts, Papa?'

'When I track them down, I shall make sure they know all I do. I don't know if that will help much, since I don't properly understand it myself.'

'What does she say, then, Papa? You can't hint at something that might be a clue, then refuse to tell me any more lest you offend my delicate sensibilities.'

Eventually he handed her a list he had copied out, and censored, from entries in Pamela's diaries where she gloated over the fabulous jewels she had coaxed out of her lover one by one. Eve could hardly believe any woman could lust after cold gemstones so ruthlessly and it left her with an unpleasant taste in her mouth, despite all her assurances to her father that Pamela had done her worst as far as her daughter was concerned.

Chapter Six

As she tried to go about her day as normal Eve was annoyed with herself for constantly drifting off into a reverie. She hoped her father wasn't right to be uneasy about Mr Carter. No, of course he wasn't. She was immune to love and passion; if she wasn't she would have let it carry her away long ago. An unwanted image of Mr Carter waiting to lead his men into battle flitted into Eve's mind all the same. He would exude confidence even if he was terrified and look unforgivably handsome in his Rifleman green uniform while he was about it. A silken voice whispered in her ear that was how a real man should look and never mind the marks of battle the great idiot thought wiped out any manly beauty he had—Mr Carter was more a man than the weak-willed and self-indulgent aristocrats he was supposedly inferior to.

Take Lord Christopher Hancourt, since he was in her thoughts as well today. That weak and overindulged man had never faced a moment of real hardship or danger until the very last seconds of his life, but Carter had defied both for nearly every day of the last eight years. How irritating if her father was right and he really had intrigued her too much for comfort. The one man she could never marry was the only one to make her think twice during this tedious time she had to spend away from her real life at Darkmere or Farenze Lodge near Bath.

Anyway, she had learnt long ago not to trust a man's passion for a willing woman the hard way, hadn't she? Her first real suitor seemed so earnest and naïve and in love she somehow fooled herself she loved him back. She doubted that spotty youth sat comfortably for a month after Papa and Uncle James thrashed him like a sniffling schoolboy, but she learnt a hard lesson that night. Her mother's wicked reputation would descend on her if she wasn't very careful indeed and she had been ever since. Too careful, perhaps, given how she was having to struggle to get not very humble and decidedly awkward Mr Carter out of her mind now.

It was probably the silly, rebellious part of it that once believed a boy's lust was love whispering that Mr Carter was uniquely formed to understand her. He could see past the gloss Winterley money and prestige added to her unremarkable looks. He seemed to know about the true heart she'd learnt to keep so safe, even she had almost forgotten she had one. He might do any and all of that, but it wouldn't do either of them any good. They were as divided from each other as the Ganges was from the Thames, or the icy poles at opposite ends of the earth. Made of the same substance, but thousands of miles apart in every way that really mattered.

Colm thought he would hear no more of the Winterley family, but it was only a few days after their last encounter that Miss Winterley confounded him all over again. He turned over the brief note an urchin had delivered to Derneley House before he ran off. No, the hastily scrawled words really were as brief and uninformative as he'd thought they were the first time.

> *Please come as fast as you can. I am waiting with a hackney at the corner of the mews. Do not tell anyone you are meeting me and try not to be seen.*
> *E.W.*

One of the more innocent letters Colm's father had sent to her mother years ago had fallen out of the sealed note to prove this wasn't a hoax. It was ten o'clock on a dark autumn night, for heaven's sake; even meeting him at this hour of the night would mean certain ruin if they were discovered. He shrugged into his dull coat and reached for his shabby hat, even as he told himself he was a fool to think of going anywhere with her. He still slipped into the garden through a side door and locked it after himself in the hope nobody would even notice he had gone.

'Hurry,' her low and deliberately gruff voice ordered as soon as he crept out of the garden gate. He saw a hackney doing its best to pretend it wasn't there and finally had to believe this was really happening.

'What the devil…?' he began only to have her reach out and tug him into the carriage as if there wasn't a moment to spare.

'Take us to the place we agreed inside ten minutes and I'll pay you twice the price,' she ordered the hackney driver as coolly as if she kidnapped limping clerks every night of the week.

The coach shot forward so fast Colm was surprised they didn't tumble out. There wasn't even time to gasp out another question before they were clattering over cobbled streets as if their lives depended on it and she wouldn't be able to hear him. Exclusive parts of Mayfair flashed past until they reached Oxford Street, crossed it at a reckless pace, then finally slowed as they neared Cavendish Square and stopped just short of it.

'Shush!' she whispered as Colm climbed down and stood on the cobbles, feeling like a mooncalf as he tried to make sense of the world and she handed two guineas to the jarvey, then grabbed Colm's arm as if she owned him.

As soon as the shabby little carriage was out of sight he stood stock still, so she had to let him go, fall over, or cling to him like a limpet. Luckily she did the latter, but gave an irritated click of her tongue, as if all this was his fault and he decided he'd had enough.

'Explain,' he demanded abruptly.

'Aren't you supposed to be a man of action and not words?' she muttered, as if she was having severe doubts about bringing him along after all.

'Not any more,' he replied gruffly.

'Imagine you still are and simply use the brains officers in your regiment are supposed to possess, although I see little sign of them right now.'

'Never mind trading insults with me; I'm not going a step further unless you give me a very good reason to do so.'

'My cousin has been reckless and silly and I must get her away from here before it's too late to remedy. You are here to help me do so—now *will* you hurry?'

'Your parents are responsible for her, they ought to know what she's been up to and make sure she never does it again.'

'Believe me, she won't. Now move, you great ox, before it's too late.'

Cavendish Square, now why did that ring a bell? Colm let himself be prodded into motion while he reviewed a half-heard conversation between Derneley and his lady about their evening.

'Lady Warlington's masquerade,' he murmured as it all fell into place.

'That will turn into a drunken romp long before midnight. Lady Warlington's brothers will see to it if nobody else does,' Derneley had joked. His wife agreed and put it with the slender pile of invitations they still received now they were so widely known to be drowning in River Tick.

'Exactly,' Miss Winterley said now, as if that explained everything.

'Why would Miss Revereux be anywhere near such an event, especially seeing that she isn't even out?'

'Because an empty-headed youth begged her to meet

him there and it probably seems like a huge adventure to her,' she muttered.

'Who is this idiot?'

'Verity is only fifteen and Lady Warlington's youngest brother is startlingly handsome, so I suppose it's understandable she sighs over the silly boy and imagines herself in love with him. He should never have dared her to meet him tonight, though. If she's at this wretched party dressed as I suspect she must be from the items missing from the dressing up box, she won't have a shred of reputation left to lose if we don't find her before anyone else does, for he won't care about ruining such a young girl's prospects. I suspect he would find it horribly amusing.'

Fuming at the very idea some lout might casually wreck such a young girl's future before she was old enough to be out of the schoolroom, Colm let Miss Winterley bundle him towards the back of Lord Warlington's town house and they waited for a chance to slip inside without being noticed. At last a door opened to let in cold night air and Colm finally saw the way Miss Winterley was dressed and he knew why she needed him with her and nobody else. Who but Mr Carter could Miss Winterley rely on to pass through the servants' hall at this time of night with little more than a raised eyebrow if they were caught?

She made a fine serving wench, he admitted numbly, as the fact he had been on hand at the right time and dressed more shabbily than any other male of her acquaintance stung more sharply than it should. Any doubts he had about her clever cover failing them when they got to the public rooms faded when she scooped up a discarded mask as if she was diligently tidying the chaos, then unearthed a domino from behind a classical statue. Thrusting both at him as if he ought to know what to do next without being told, she went to forage for her own disguise whilst he gathered his wits enough to meekly put them on. *Who am I supposed to be this time?* he silently asked his reflection in a nearby mirror. *A somebody pretending to be a nobody,* the false image mocked back at him. He looked almost like the man he could have been—a rich idler who thought it amusing to ape a clerk when he had never done a decent day's work in his life.

A loud bellow sounded along the corridor he had seen Miss Winterley disappear into just now and it was echoed by another drunken sot who sounded far too castaway to move very fast. He should have remembered what happened to the confounded female when she wandered about once-grand houses on her own. Cursing himself for being so glum about Miss Winterley's uses for him tonight, he had let her go by herself. Colm was halfway along it, and bad leg be damned, when she came dashing towards him as if the hounds of hell were on her tail.

'Hide me,' she gasped as heavy treads sounded behind her.

There wasn't a niche big enough to hold a classical statue or a handy cupboard, so he tugged her into his arms and put his body between her and whoever was trying to chase her down this time. He pushed her against the nearest marble column as if they had been aiming for the right place to dally with each other ever since they stumbled out of the ballroom frantic for one another only moments ago.

'Not like tha—' she was saying even as he kissed her passionately.

She struggled fiercely for a moment, then gave in with a huge sigh, went gloriously responsive and kissed him back as if she had been starving for this since the night they met as well. For a moment he let himself dream she wanted him as urgently as he did her. Her mouth first softened, then seemed to ask for impossible answers under his. *Are you my special he?* she might as well be asking as she explored his mouth with an edge of wonder under the inexperience. *Could you be the lover I have dreamt of since I was woman enough to ache for him?*

Yes, yes, to all of it. To every question you could ever ask of that man, yes, the true Colm under all his careful defences whispered back. He forgot where they were and what the world would say if it knew who he was and simply kissed her and let his senses drown in blissful unreason.

'Tally-ho,' the less drunken of the two voices bellowed almost in his ear.

Colm cursed reality and tried to think straight when all he really wanted to do was go on kissing Eve Winterley and feeling something beyond his wildest dreams for this dear enemy of his. He raised his head as if bitterly offended and impatient of any interruption of that soul-stealing kiss and it wasn't any effort at all to glare at the swaying idiot as if he hated him.

'I saw the pretty little vixen first,' the buffoon had the audacity to say, as if Colm would apologise and politely step aside then leave him to do his worst. 'Don't think we've met, I'm Louburn, y'know?'

'I don't think we have either, but my wife avoids drunken fools whenever she can and I am not about to introduce you to her,' he said and felt Eve shaking with nerves in his arms as he cursed the nearest buffoon virulently under his breath.

'You claim you're my sister's guests, yet you're married to a servant girl? That don't sound right to me,' the second drunk managed, and now Eve had two of Lady Warlington's notorious brothers on her tail. A flutter of panic joined the butterflies Mr Carter had set spinning about inside her with that heart-stopping kiss. If she was desperately unlucky one of these fools would be sober enough to realise who she really was and that she wasn't married to anyone, especially not to Mr Carter, usually to be found in the latest Duke of Linaire's library.

'Even cast away you should be able to recall you're doing your best to spoil your sister's masquerade and not in some dockside tavern, Louburn,' Carter told the elder Louburn brother so brusquely she wondered why she'd ever have thought him too withdrawn and mild-mannered to be an effective officer.

'We ain't met before, have we?' the slightly less drunken brother asked blearily.

'Let's just say your reputation goes before you and leave it at that, shall we?' her brave cavalier said icily and Eve wondered how the menace under that weary comment could pass these idiots by when it made her tremble and it wasn't even directed at her.

'Wife or not, she ain't wearing a mask, is she?' the more eager Mr Louburn asked, as if his stinking reputation was something to be proud of and he wanted a woman right now, so one ought to be instantly available—willing or not. The more she thought about Verity wandering unprotected about such a house on such a night the more anxious Eve was to find her and get them all out of here before tonight went even more disastrously wrong.

'No, and that's because we were looking for privacy and you interrupted us. Why would my lady need a mask when I know every inch of her and can recognise her even in the dark? Not that I need explain myself to a sot like you.'

Even Eve believed in the outraged aristocrat Mr Carter was pretending to be at the moment. He had put aside the would-be humble and workaday Mr Carter and spoken with such authority it almost seemed rude *not* to believe every word he said. She shivered at the thought that here was the true man under his mild disguise and decided it was a good idea to go along with him and pretend she was his modest wife, caught in not very modest circumstances. She buried her head against his shoulder for good measure and to stop the wretches from taking a second look at her and realising where they'd seen her before.

'Come on, Bart, there's far better sport to be had elsewhere without having to mill him down to get to it and I'm thirsty,' the less amorous brother said with fading interest in anything but his next drink.

'Two of us, don't you see? We can easily take him on between us, Rolly. Nobody'll be any the wiser if we throw him outside, then I can tup his wife in peace and they won't tell anyone, will they? Scandal as much on them as us, see?' he said, tapping his finger where he thought his nose ought to be.

Eve felt the tightly wound tension in Colm's surprisingly powerful body at that despicable threat to treat them both as if they'd been put on this earth to meet a lusty drunkard's convenience. The pent-up violence crackled in the air all around them now. Suddenly this farce had threatened to turn very dark and she didn't want Mr Carter to get hurt, any more than she wanted to be violated herself.

'And there are only two of you?' Carter drawled with such terrible confidence she wanted to cry out a warning that they were notorious brawlers and he must find a safer way to stop this threat to their safety and sanity. 'Hide your face,' he whispered to her as he pushed her behind him, then turned on his latest adversaries with such calmness her hands did as they were told before her mind could argue. She peeped at what happened next through shaking fingers and for a moment was quite sure her eyes were deceiving her.

It was over too fast for her to have time to pile into the mêlée and never mind Carter's high-handed efforts to keep her out of it. She would have kicked and bitten and clawed against the casual brutality of these two so-called gentlemen, except they were dealt with so swiftly and efficiently she had no time to form her hands into claws and spring into action. A sporting man might call it as pretty a display as he ever saw outside a boxing ring, she decided in dazed shock. Perfectly flush hits to the jaw one after the other and there was nothing left for either of them to do but stare down at a heap of unconscious Louburn brothers, until Carter shook out his protesting hands in brief agony and gave her a harassed glare. While she was still struggling to come to terms with his might and such an unexpected skill he dragged first one Louburn, then the other back into the ruin they had made of a once-elegant room and locked the door on them, then pocketed the key with an exasperated sigh.

'Well, I told you not to look,' he said gruffly as he straightened his domino and handed her one he must have found in that rogues' den the Louburns had made of their brother-in-law's home, along with a far prettier mask than the one that hid most of Carter's thoughts from her right now and made his eyes look even more intriguing when he stared down at her as if he wanted to read all the confused thoughts and feelings scurrying about in her reeling head. Not that she could afford to be intrigued by the man, she reminded herself hastily, as she numbly put on her new disguise and wondered what disaster they should expect next.

'I wasn't… Well, no, that's not quite right, I'm not…'

You were not what, Eve? her inner critic mocked. *Not shocked, not awed and feeling a little bit breathless at the power and deadly purpose of the true man under Mr Carter's pretend humility? Not secretly long-*

ing for him to repeat that kiss with interest added on to
say thank you for saving you from the worst of his kind
and that you did rather like it the first time?

'Never mind what you are or are not right now. How
the deuce are we going to find your little sister or cousin
or whatever it is you two call one another in this bear
garden?'

'Oh, yes, Verity,' she murmured, still so off balance
from that kiss and his heroics afterwards she had almost forgotten why they were here in the first place.
'She has no idea aping Caro Lamb in breeches could
get her into far more trouble than if she came dressed
as an opera dancer,' she blurted out Verity's disgraceful disguise and heard him groan even above the din
of excited chatter and laughter and the orchestra desperately trying to be heard above it all in the ballroom
at the end of this side corridor.

'Oh, good, now we only need to find the next riot and
suppress it, then lock up the rest of the Louburn family
and get out of here without being recognised, then we
should all be able to go home and sleep serenely as if we
never left our beds in the first place,' he said with such
irony and an angry glare that seen through the filter of
his dark mask looked almost fearsome, except he was
also looking rather deliciously mysterious, flighty Eve
pointed out helpfully. 'The girl is obviously not fit to be
let out without a keeper,' he growled and she sighed to
oblige that silly version of herself and wondered if he
might be persuaded to visit a more sedate masquerade
with her if she asked him very nicely.

Ridiculous idea, her sterner inner self pointed out,

and she tried hard to concentrate on what he'd said instead of feeling prickles of something that must be forbidden slide down her spine at the sound of his voice so gruff and dark and the stern glint of his eyes through that mask. She shivered, although for some reason she was incredibly warm, and even that didn't seem to put all these wicked ideas out of her mind and certainly did nothing for her rebellious body.

'She is only fifteen,' she said as if that ought to explain everything and she struggled with the fact her grip on this misadventure seemed to have slipped and she was following him like a meek little acolyte behind a high priest, or a besotted girl after the man she thought was the love her life.

If not for Verity, she would be quite content to drift among the elegant chaos of this rather wild party and feel deliciously daring yet utterly safe in the company of a tall, dark and compelling man of mystery. Mr Carter always wore a disguise, she decided; she doubted he ever let the world see the real man, even if he could afford clothes the dandies of the *ton* wouldn't shudder to be seen standing next to. Yes, if not for Verity she would be quite happy to stay until too close to midnight and run the tempting risk of being caught in the least desirable company the Honourable Miss Winterley could find herself in if she tried.

She hardly recognised the cool and controlled Eve Winterley she had made herself become when she realised how eagerly the *ton* was waiting for her to turn into her mother. The female clutching Carter's strong hand as if he was her rock and only chance of safety in a sea full of storms was a stranger. So much for not relying on a man to make her feel strong; for never looking for all the things her mother spent her life longing for. Eve still didn't want a man's unconditional surrender, or constant proof he worshipped her like some pagan goddess. The very idea made her shudder with revulsion, but a mutual surrender to something more than the coolly logical marriage she had thought she wanted seemed so very desirable right now it felt sinful. At least she understood that raw state of wanting a little better after his heady kiss and the shock of seeing Carter the fighting man emerge from the shadows. Another mask, she decided as the music and wild laughter got even louder. How many disguises could one man wear and not lose his true self?

Chapter Seven

'Eve…' The desperate whisper came before someone
noticed she and Carter were standing on the fringes of
this wild party and came to find out who was hiding
under their ingenious disguises.

If they weren't careful they'd be seen by too many
curious eyes under the glow of what looked like a thousand candles in the noisy ballroom ahead of them and
someone might recognise her. Eve could just see the
curtains of an alcove off the corridor they were almost
at the end of and thanked heavens they had not had to
brave the full glare of the crowd ahead to search for
her almost cousin.

'Verity?' she whispered sharply. 'What the deuce
are you doing here?' she asked, hoping the boy who
carelessly drew a fifteen-year-old girl into this rowdy
chaos didn't come to find out if she had turned up for
an assignation she was far too young to understand.

'I was looking for a way out,' Verity said, looking
very pale and deeply shocked by what she had seen so
far, as well as a bit woebegone.

Perhaps this latest escapade had overwhelmed even her high spirits and it would make her think twice about trying to run before she was ready to walk in so-called polite society. Eve couldn't think it very polite, or even glamorous after this circus herself, so maybe letting Verity see the dark side of it all wasn't such a bad idea, if they could only get her out of here relatively unscathed and with her reputation intact, despite Rufus Louburn's worst efforts.

'At least you have done one sensible thing tonight, then,' Eve whispered sharply, not inclined to be disarmed after what she and Mr Carter had already been through on this little madam's behalf.

'Leave her be for now, you can scold her once we have all got safely away,' Carter cautioned softly. 'And let's hope we don't have to go back the way we came. Those two drunken idiots could be awake and howling for revenge on us by now,' he murmured in her ear. She stifled a giggle as he managed to make a joke of what could have been a vicious struggle for more than she wanted to think about right now.

'Ah, I thought so. I knew there had to be more than one back stairway down to the vast basement there must be under the house,' he whispered as a jib door Eve hadn't even thought to look out for opened under his probing fingers and showed her once again that he was a lot more composed than she was after that earth-shaking kiss. It had seemed about to make her world anew for a wild moment and perhaps it was only one on a long list of such sweet encounters for him. Didn't soldiers have a sweetheart in every town they passed through? The contrast between dashing Mr Carter of the 95th Rifles and the shabby clerk she'd met that night at Derneley House made her wonder if there might be other versions of this complex man for her to discover, if she dared to look.

At least the narrow stair he'd found was lit by the occasional ensconced candle, she saw with a shudder. The bareness and gloom behind the narrow door made her feel as if the walls might press in on her, but this was what maids endured every day of their lives so their employers could enjoy the privacy and luxury of nigh invisible service. If she and Verity had been born to poverty they might be the ones labouring every hour God sent at this very moment; enduring the insecurity and danger that went with being young and female in such a household. Instead they were stumbling down the bare wooden stairs in Mr Carter's wake and Eve couldn't let her fear show with Verity between them and her fragile young shoulders shaking so hard she was clearly on the verge of hysteria.

'Oh, Eve, thank God you came.' Verity launched herself at Eve once they reached the bottom of the cramped stairway and it opened into a grim little stairwell with gloomy corridors stretching four different ways. A storm of frightened tears threatened until Carter bowed as if Verity was a lot more grown up than she appeared right now and bade her a smooth, 'Good evening, Miss Revereux.'

'You're Eve's Mr Carter, aren't you? I remember you from the park.'

'Maybe I am then, but we really must get out of here

before midnight when everyone is obliged to take their masks off, you know? If we meet any servants on our way, we shall have to pretend to be a very scandalous trio indeed. You and your cousin are going to be my pretty ladybirds for the night. Do you think you can act such a wild part? I know it's a lot to ask after all you witnessed tonight, but I really don't want to be dragged back into that ballroom and made to unmask, do you?'

'No,' Verity said with such a fervent shake of her head Eve wondered once again exactly what she *had* seen tonight.

'Very well, you only need endure this pretence for a few more minutes and then we'll have you out of here and back at Farenze House as if you were fast asleep all the time,' he said with a grin Eve caught herself being fiercely jealous of.

She wondered at herself again when he draped an arm round each of their shoulders and hugged her so close every inch of her skin felt man-warmed and prickly and responsive to him and him alone. Heaven forbid Verity felt even a hint of the sizzling excitement that was running through her like wildfire. At least that notion sobered her sharply enough to seem cool when he looked down at her with one raised eyebrow, as if to say, *Needs must when the devil drives, so don't blame me.*

'Is my scar visible?' he asked prosaically and she gave an almost wifely sigh and raised both her own brows at his unexpected vanity. 'I don't want us to stand out in any way but the obvious,' he whispered as if he had read her mind and couldn't believe she thought him so shallow.

'Set me free,' she demanded and reached up to ruffle his unruly hair until it curled as far as Mr Carter had left her length enough to work with. As she pushed and pulled it to hide the mark of his ordeal at Waterloo her hand shook as the reality of how close he'd come to death hit home and made her eyes water at the thought of never being able to know him at all. Reminding herself she couldn't afford to fall in love with this mystery of a man, she stood back and eyed her handiwork critically. His hair had felt as intriguing as she thought it might the first night they met. Soft and at the same time full of life and she still wasn't quite sure if it was more gold or brown in the dim light, any more than his eyes could decide between the same colours as they watched her with a question in them that had nothing to do with how unmemorable she had managed to make him.

'That's better,' Verity said in a whisper that barely wobbled at all, so at least she was beginning to recover some of her usual spirit.

'And don't push it out of your eyes when you're not thinking and ruin my handiwork, will you?' Eve chided him. And how had she let herself notice that he did exactly that when he was distracted? They had not met enough times for her to need two hands to count them on and she was picking up on his habits as if he was her lifetime study. This silliness really would have to stop. 'And you had best lean some of your weight on me and do your best not to limp as well,' she added briskly.

'I suppose I must,' he said ruefully. 'Now if you will both loosen your laces and ruffle your own hair and try to look a lot more undone than you are right now, ladies,

I think we will be able to get on with this private masquerade of ours *and* have you both safely back home before the clocks strike midnight.'

Two hours could drag by on broken wheels or be so full of incidents it was almost impossible to believe so little time had passed since she set out, Eve mused. Verity even seemed to be enjoying the joke now. She unbuttoned her velvet jacket and undid the laces of her shirt so it would gape open to prove she really wasn't the uninformed youth her breeches argued. If this charade reignited her step-cousin's adventurous nature, Eve supposed she had to be glad, even if she didn't want Verity thinking such folly should ever be repeated. She would just have to find a way to calm her down when they got home, lest Verity wake half the household with overwrought high spirits. Eve felt cool air on the exposed upper slopes of her own bosom as she did as Carter asked as well. Very adult emotions shivered through her when his gaze followed the soft stuff of her borrowed gown as it fell open, then he lingered hungrily on the last remaining slice of ribbon that left her shift straining on the edge of decency between her breasts, as if he badly wanted to undo it and explore even more of her than he already had.

'That will have to do,' she told him severely, because she badly wanted him to as well and that was wrong in so many ways she could hardly count them.

'At least that much temptation should distract any healthy males we happen to meet on our travels,' he said as if that was all that mattered, and he was right, wasn't he?

Luckily most of the servants were still upstairs waiting on the company and the kitchen maids too busy in
the scullery to see aught but steam and a mountain of
dirty dishes and pots and pans. Which only left a chef
sitting at the smaller table in the kitchen and trying not
to fall asleep in the remnants of one of his own creations
and a pastry cook to be shocked by the quality sneaking
out through their domain with a few flustered giggles
from the so-called ladies and a bad-dog smirk from a
happy-looking gentleman who was stealing away from
this wild party with a woman under each arm.

'Lucky dog,' the chef said with a regretful sigh and
a jaded look at the bridling cook, as if to say some men
had all the luck tonight and he wasn't one of them.

'Devils the lot of them and just look at that brazen
hussy flaunting her legs and everything else she has
like some doxy in the Haymarket,' the cook said in
disgust. 'All of them no better than they should be and
yet they calls themselves quality, disgusting is what I
say they are.'

Verity giggled delightedly and Eve gave Carter an
angry nudge to let him know he would have to put
more of his weight on her shoulders if he was to pass
as a run-of-the-mill rake and not a limping one. 'La,
but he's even more drunk than I thought he was,' she
hissed at Verity in a stage whisper, hoping any sign of
a stagger in his step would seem to be from too much
alcohol and not war.

'Let's hurry up then, before he finds another bottle
and climbs into it for the night,' her devious little relative by marriage replied in the affected tones of a lady

intent on being very unladylike indeed and daring the world to stop her.

Eve managed a false titter and even wiggled her hips so provocatively the chef ought to remember her walk and not Carter's, if anyone asked him to describe such a disgraceful trio, should the Louburn brothers escape and start baying for Carter's blood.

'You win,' he murmured so softly only she could hear him and he finally let some of his weight fall on her shoulder until they were safely across the vast kitchen and out of the open door, into the dark coldness of the night and up stone steps into the street that served the back of these tall town houses.

'Hush,' he ordered them both when Verity would have said something gleeful about their lucky escape and danced about in triumph, 'you're not safe home yet. Take off that mask now and button yourself up again before you catch your death, there's a good girl.'

Eve could sense Verity's mouth firming sulkily at being called a good girl after such a grown-up adventure, but if anyone deserved to be treated like a naughty schoolgirl tonight it was she. 'Or shall we call you a crass idiot for what you did tonight if you prefer not to be called so?' she whispered severely in Verity's ear.

'I'm so sorry, Eve, really I am,' the contrary, exasperating and disarming girl said humbly.

'There will be plenty of time for all that later,' Carter told them both impatiently.

Eve felt his fingers searching for the strings of her mask because she hadn't hurried to do as she was bid fast enough. *This has to stop*, she told herself, as her breath caught at the heady sensation of his fingers winnowing through her disordered curls. A foolish little shiver slid down her neck when he brushed against her vulnerable-feeling nape and the whole of her body wanted to respond to him as if he was her lover now. A longing she had never wanted to feel until she met him shook her right down to her toes. She told herself it was a sigh of relief that she let out when he found the strings of her mask, undid it and put the silly, frivolous thing in his pocket before she could grab it as a keepsake of a night she ought to want to start forgetting even before it was properly over.

'That's better, this time we are going to be a respectable, middling sort of couple with a very sulky young gentleman in our charge. As long as you keep that cap on and don't speak above a whisper we may get away with it in the dark, Miss Verity,' he said softly as he pushed the odd stray wisp of golden hair under the velvet jockey cap Verity had at least had enough sense to wear when she set out on this shocking scrape tonight.

Carter offered Eve his arm as if they were about to take a stroll in the park and what could she do but take it like the obedient wife she was supposed to be right now? Control of their latest misadventure had slipped inexorably from her fingers the moment they got into Warlington House and she supposed he had got them this far without disaster, so she might as well go along with officer Carter for a little longer. They crept round the most shadowy edge of the square and were soon out of it and back in the wider world again. Eve allowed herself a moment to imagine how it would feel to be creeping through the darkness without him and terror whispered in her ear. Luckily he was here, though, and she could wait to review imagined terrors when they were safely at home and in their beds. Right now it was still quite early by *ton* standards, so now and again a fashionable town carriage would rattle past on the way to a different party or to clubs and less public assignations. It wasn't as busy as it would be in the spring, but Mayfair was still lively on a chilly October night.

Eve was glad she could walk in Carter's shadow as they passed tall town houses where entertainments were being held tonight, or a smart coach swept past on the way to somewhere else. How could she feel so safe and oddly interested in how the night felt when she wasn't part of that busy round of doing nothing much in grand style? Because Carter was here, she let herself know. His muscular arm was warm under her fingers and his body so close it felt as though he was her security and such a sure strength—why would she let him go at the end of this reckless adventure? *You know why*, common sense and her mother's blasted reputation whispered in her ear and how ardently she wished they would go away right now.

'Is there some way you can get back inside without being found out?' Carter murmured when they finally reached Farenze House and all seemed serene, so at least neither she nor Verity had been missed.

'Yes,' Eve whispered. 'Goodnight and thank you, Mr Carter.'

'Hasn't he got a given name?' Verity asked a bit too loudly.

'Hush, Verity, and don't be nosy. Remember what you did tonight before you say another word to those of us who were forced to lie and risk far too much to rescue you from your stupidity.'

'I was going to say then we are deeply in your debt, whoever you are, sir,' Verity managed with almost grown-up dignity.

'Please don't mention it and I mean that in every sense, by the way. It will be best if we pretend we can't really remember one another if we ever happen to meet again, Miss Revereux. Now I must bid you both good-night and try to smuggle myself back into Derneley House unseen, before Mr Carter scandalises the whole neighbourhood by being caught out here with two young ladies so late at night.'

A brief touch of Eve's hand as if he was bidding goodnight to a nodding acquaintance and Mr Carter strode off into the darkness as if they had imagined him. He might be gone from their sight, but Eve knew somehow that he stopped to watch them creep inside the house and make sure they were finally safe. He was simply that sort of man, she admitted to herself as she rushed Verity up the stairs so she could light a candle and show it at the window just long enough for him to know they were safe home and had not been caught.

'Go to bed, Verity, you will answer to me in the morning and you're lucky I didn't call Papa and Chloe back from their dinner with the Laughraines. I only decided not to do so because I won't have Chloe upset by your idiocy at the moment and risk harming the baby.'

'I thought you weren't going to ring a peal over my head until tomorrow,' Verity said sulkily.

'Then you'd best hurry to get into bed before I change my mind, and before you do kindly hide that disgraceful disguise you stole before Bran finds it and raises the roof,' Eve ordered wearily, sinking down on to her own feather bed and wondering if she had it in her to undress, let alone brush her curls into good order, then hide the best gown she must somehow get back to the head housemaid's room in good order tomorrow, before the girl realised her box had been tampered with and it was gone.

'He is very handsome,' Verity said with a sneaky look, as she pulled off her cap and let her golden mane tumble down over her shoulders. Then she even had the cheek to sit and brush it with Eve's hairbrush as if this was a night much like any other. 'Lend me a nightdress and I will go,' she responded to Eve's unspoken demand to be left in peace.

'Why should I?' Eve demanded grumpily. It seemed unfair that Verity had come out of tonight's brouhaha looking like a part-time angel and Eve's whole life felt as if it had been turned upside down and she couldn't seem to get it right again.

'Because I don't want to be caught wandering the corridors at night in these very comfortable breeches and a gentleman's shirt. I won't go away and let you dream of Mr Carter until you let me change into something less improper.'

'You should have thought of that before you stole those breeches from the attic and remember you're the one with cause to feel ashamed of herself tonight and not me, Verity Revereux.'

'True, but I didn't drag the most intriguing stranger I ever met into the midst of a potential scandal, then watch him deal with it as if I couldn't take my eyes off him either.'

'At least I didn't risk my reputation for the sake of an idiot.'

'Rufus is very silly, isn't he?' Verity said with a heavy sigh that admitted she was shocked and disappointed by her evening.

'Yes, and his looks are only on the outside, Verity, inside he is no better than his brothers.'

'He didn't even bother to wait for me. I went to so much trouble to get into that horrid house undetected, but he was dancing with a woman old enough to be his mother when I got there. Then he kissed her and they disappeared for ages and ages,' Verity said tragically, then shrugged and went back to plundering Eve's drawers until she found a nightdress warm enough to roam draughty corridors and not catch cold. 'I realised Rufus is fickle as the wind and dim as a rushlight tonight,' she added mournfully. 'And he isn't even very nice either; I really can't imagine what I ever saw in him now.'

'Good, so now you know that very handsome males are often a little stupid and spoilt with it—I suppose they have no need to try very hard.'

'Your Mr Carter isn't an idiot.'

'Nor is he my Mr Carter; only imagine the fuss if he was,' Eve managed to joke weakly.

'I suppose there would be a whisper or two, since he

obviously hasn't got much money, but the tabbies would soon find something else to talk about if you two were boringly happy with each other and your father approved,' Verity said as she striped off her breeches and hastily pulled Eve's nightdress over her head.

'Do you really think so?' Eve said. The idea of being Carter's lady tugged at her heart and reminded her how wondrous it felt to be kissed by a man who really knew what he was doing. No, it was every bit as impossible now as it was the night she first met him and every night since. 'Papa would never allow it.'

'Maybe I was a fool tonight, but my parents' story tells me that it's folly to turn away from true love whenever it comes along. I had to find out if Rufus was only perfect on the outside, Eve. You know better than anyone that you can't judge a person by the family they were born into, although in his case I suppose I should have done.'

'It's as well you don't love him then, isn't it? Now go away, Verity. You're the last person who should preach to me about love after what you got up to tonight. Thank your guardian angel that we found you before the whole world knew you were abroad in breeches and then go to bed.'

'You went straight to Mr Carter as soon as you found out I was gone though, didn't you?' Verity said and left Eve sitting staring at a closed door and wondering if such chaste solitude was what she truly wanted.

Of course it was, she informed her inner doubter bracingly. She had not met the right man yet and sooner or later *he* would turn up to make perfect sense of her life. All she had to do was wait and refuse to be side-tracked by contradictory, gruff and unsuitable heroes like Mr Carter and her life would be as close to perfect as anyone's could be in this faulty world.

Chapter Eight

It took Colm another week to pack up the Derneley Library. With a sigh of relief he bade farewell to the few staff still working at Derneley House and limped out into a foggy autumn morning. It was time to bid farewell to Mr Carter and he must learn to be a Hancourt again. Someone had to stop the Hancourt estates slipping into chaos and it might as well be him. It would give him something to do, but as Uncle Horace and Aunt Barbara were childless he'd best not get too comfortable. Lord Maurice Hancourt would dismiss his nephew the day he inherited the dukedom, so somehow Colm would have to save enough from his salary to be able to offer his sister a home if she needed one, so he hoped the current Duke would live a long and happy life.

Nell wouldn't give up her post simply because he wanted her to, so perhaps he could suggest Uncle Horace needed her to stop his houses becoming dusty old book warehouses, because Aunt Barbara wasn't going to worry about housekeeping when she had so much nature left to paint. Nell couldn't claim she wasn't needed then, but he could almost hear her argue she was needed where she was now, thank you very much. He smiled ruefully at the notion his sister was quite happy in her current post as governess to four orphaned girls and virtual mistress of Berry Brampton House. If the Earl of Barberry ever set foot in the place, a single lady with any regard for her reputation would have to leave it though; so Colm had best start saving, even if Barberry had sworn never to visit the estate his family begrudged him so deeply.

Ten minutes later Colm limped up the steps of Linaire House, still mulling over his schemes to get his sister away from her current employment. The butler looked outraged when he limped up the front steps and coldly informed him servants used the rear entrance.

'I am expected. Mr Hancourt,' he informed the man with the cold authority he'd used on soldiers who thought him too young to be obeyed, but this man was made of sterner stuff.

'So you say,' the butler said with a regal sniff and a contemptuous look at Colm's shabby garb and the battered portmanteau he was carrying himself.

'My uncle is eager to have me supervise the unpacking and arranging of the Derneley Library. I wouldn't like to be the one who delayed that project,' he said and made as if to leave, even if he had no idea where he would go.

'His Grace did say he was expecting a member of

the family,' the man said dubiously, but at least Colm was allowed inside so his tall story could be examined.

Hearing voices, the Duke of Linaire emerged from his study. A smile lit his rather homely face and he hurried forward to make Colm feel more welcome here than he ever was as a child. 'Colm, my boy, how glad I am to see you at last. D'you know the bookbinder says he can't find that exact shade of Moroccan leather to replace the damaged covers?' the Duke of Linaire asked as if his nephew was so much a part of his life he didn't need to explain him to his staff.

'Let the boy settle in before you put him to work again, Horry.' Aunt Barbara emerged from the study behind him and greeted Colm with a kiss and a quick hug that made him blink and return it with a feeling he wasn't as alone as he'd thought. 'Not that I'm not delighted to see you as well, dear. Your uncle has been longing for a sympathetic ear to pour his tale of woe into all morning and I would dearly like to get some of this mist and murk in my sketchbook before the sun breaks through. So you are doubly welcome.'

Colm cast a look at the dreary townscape outside and raised an eyebrow at the unconventional Duchess to say there was little chance of that happening quickly.

'It seems unlikely now, but I don't have much interest in old books at the best of times and I'd forgotten how unreal London looks in the fog,' she admitted with a longing glance out of the window. Colm wondered once again how two people with such different interests could be so devoted to one another. 'That's enough of our woes, have you breakfasted, my boy?' she added, although it was nearly noon.

'Some time ago, Auntie dear,' he told her with a grin and she just smiled placidly and told him not to be disrespectful to his poor old aunt. Since his late Uncle Augustus once had him beaten for just speaking in his presence, this was a vast improvement on his last stay at Linaire House already.

'Then go on up and settle yourself in before your uncle puts you to work. He forgets how ill you were this summer and will answer to me and your sister Nell if he wears you out with his wrong shades of leather and the best way to arrange his musty old books. Then there's whatever real business you must sort out for us.'

'This is real business,' Uncle Horace protested, but shot Colm a concerned look and told him unpacking the undamaged books could wait until tomorrow.

Not quite sure he wanted a day of leisure when his thoughts were still so full of Winterleys, Colm went upstairs to unpack his bag before his uncle's valet could do it for him, then went downstairs again to find his uncle and see if he had forgotten he had given him the day off yet.

'Glad you're here at last, m'boy,' the Duke of Linaire muttered vaguely.

'It's good to be back. Is all well with the books I sent on?'

'Yes, yes, you did a good job. High time someone rescued that fine collection from Derneley, but I should never have sent you there. Barbara says I should be ashamed of myself for making you keep that disguise you've worn for so long.'

'Lord Derneley didn't look directly at me once he realised I was wounded at Waterloo and have the scars to prove it. I doubt he'd recognise Carter as your nephew if we happen to meet by chance.'

'Hah! Man's a buffoon; doesn't deserve what you and the other brave lads did to keep him safe in his bed. Not that it will be his bed for much longer if the rumours are true.'

Colm doubted it was officially his right now, but he didn't want to think about that selfish peer or his empty-headed lady any more. 'He certainly doesn't know how to treat fine books. Some are nearly beyond repair.'

His Grace shook his greying head and looked pained. 'I read your lists as they came in and warned the book-binders what to expect. Disgraceful, that's what it is and I had a good mind to drop my price to compensate for all the work that will have to be done in order to get them back to scratch.'

'I suspect your money is already spent.'

'Aye, and I shook hands on the deal; Barbara says she's coming with me if I negotiate for more than a child's primer from now on, but my word is my bond and I can't go back on it, can I?'

'No, even if your money goes the same way as the rest,' Colm replied and his uncle's one extravagance *was* dwarfed by Derneley's complete set.

'At least those fine volumes are safe now and I can't wait to see them set out in good order in their new home.

Barbara says I must wait for the plasterers and carpenters to finish before I ship any back to Linaire, though.'

When someone managed to distract the Duchess from her paints for the odd hour she was one of the most rational women Colm had come across. He didn't blame her for refusing to give up the joy and purpose of her life to run the vast houses her husband had inherited last year. If he had a wife himself, he wouldn't want her to give up her interests to devote herself to him either. Not that he could afford one, but his aunt and uncle's marriage was bigger than the usual society match and no wonder they sacrificed so much to make it happen. How wrong to visualise the wife he couldn't have as dark haired and possessed of a pair of fine green-blue eyes and the warmly irresistible smile Miss Winterley saved for best. She wouldn't have him if he had stayed the rich grandson of a duke instead of a barely solvent ex-army officer and it was high time he forgot her.

'Nearly forgot to give you this, Colm.' His uncle interrupted his thoughts, offering him a tightly sealed letter. 'Farenze's man brought it here with your real name on. Thought you wouldn't want it sent on to Derneley House.'

'No indeed, thank you,' he replied as he eyed the crisply folded letter with his lordship's seal stamped emphatically in the wax and wondered how he'd given himself away. Did he look like his father? Colm wondered, a little bit horrified by the idea and it was too long since he last saw him to know. The Derneleys hadn't seen through Mr Carter's plain old clothes to Lord Chris's son underneath so perhaps he didn't, but they would never truly look at a servant. A shrewd man like the Viscount might have seen Hancourt traits in him, but the idea felt disturbing.

'Do you mind if I read this right away, your Grace?'

'No more of that, lad. Be obliged if you'd call me Uncle Horace. When someone *your Graces* me, I still think they're talking to my father or Gus. Makes me shudder if you want the truth.'

'Me, too,' Colm admitted.

'Both tyrants, but they're dead now,' said the Sixth Duke with a furtive look round as if to make sure. 'Had the devil of a job persuading Barbara to marry me because of them and she's been the making of me. You should find yourself a fine girl with a mind of her own to make you happy after all you went through in Spain and Belgium.'

'I doubt if I could persuade her to see past my father's scandal and my empty pockets.'

'Nonsense, a lady of character will see what a fine fellow you are and never mind the rest.'

The only lady of character he wanted to know that dearly was uniquely designed not to be able to see past who he was, so Colm shook his head, then turned Lord Farenze's letter over as if that might tell him what the man had to say to Lord Chris's son without him having to open it. *Stay away from my daughter you lying rogue?* His heart sank at the idea she knew who he really was and still played the game of pretending he was Carter. Had she and Miss Revereux laughed together about his credulity after their misadventure? *Stop tor-*

turing yourself and read the confounded thing, his inner officer ordered impatiently.

'Go and read it before you wear it out, lad. Oh, and your Aunt Barbara has sent for a tailor; he's to wait on you today so he'll probably be here soon. Don't argue, my boy, Barb says she can't endure dining with a nephew dressed like a curate much more than a week. The man's to send his bill to me, so don't argue about that either. Consider it a uniform if you won't accept it as a gift to my nephew.'

'I had to pay for my uniform,' Colm objected half-heartedly.

'Then take a few decent clothes in the spirit we offer them,' his uncle said wearily. 'Dashed if I ever came across anyone as poker-backed as you are.

'Thank you then, it will be a relief not to worry about paying my tailor,' Colm said and wished it was really a joke as he wandered upstairs, past his bedchamber and the chance of meeting that tailor before he'd had chance to put Mr Hancourt back together, then up more stairs to the bare rooms where the last Duke grudgingly housed him and Nell until they were old enough for school.

It looked the same as ever; no need to make it bright and comfortable for children his uncle and aunt didn't have. Colm wondered fleetingly if he might be Duke of Linaire himself one day if Uncle Maurice's wife kept producing daughters. It wasn't a prospect he relished, even if he and Nell would have half a dozen old-fashioned homes to choose from. He liked the Duke and the Duchess and would rather have the modest house and a wife to make it a home he had dreamed of when trying to sleep on a bare mountainside or as he and his men were waiting for battle.

Colm went to the governess's desk and extracted a penknife to slip under Lord Farenze's seal. He should have known the man was too shrewd to take anyone at face value, but what did the Viscount want? He'd best read the letter instead of staring at it as if it might bite. Addressed in a bold, impatient hand, it was a masterpiece of distant politeness. They had matters to discuss arising from certain documents delivered to Lord Farenze. Since his lordship now knew who Colm was, they probably did as well. Tempted to wait until he had new clothes and looked a little more gentlemanly, Colm limped up to his room and wrote out an offer to call on his lordship tomorrow morning instead.

Chapter Nine

'Mr Carter, my lord,' the Viscount's stately butler announced Colm solemnly the next day.

'Come in, Carter, and bring burgundy, please, Oakham,' Lord Farenze said as if it was quite normal to offer his good wine to a humble clerk.

'Good morning, my lord,' Colm said quietly.

'Don't stand in the corner like a nervous sheepdog, man, take a seat,' his host ordered him impatiently.

'Thank you, my lord,' Colm said and did as he was bid.

'Should I feel rebuked by your faux humility?'

'Of course not, my lord. What right has Mr Carter to correct the manners of his elders and betters?'

'Oh, *touché*; you learnt more than you want to admit in your old employment.'

'Old employment, my lord? What work could a humble clerk do to teach him to be bold?'

'Recently healed scars and a halt in a man's step are all too common since Waterloo, so pretending the whole business was nothing to do with you attracts attention rather than deflecting it, Hancourt and you will have to resume your true identity under your uncle's roof, won't you?'

'Did my uncle give me away somehow?'

'No, your father did. You are the spit of him at the same age,' the Viscount said dourly, as if he was trying not to hold it against him.

'Barring the scars, I suppose?' Colm said, wondering how he felt about being so like his father and what conclusions this man had made about him on the strength of his outward appearance.

'Your hair is a shade darker and you're leaner and perhaps taller, but that could be due to you leading an active life before you were injured.'

'I wouldn't know whether I look like him or not; there are no portraits of my father left at Linaire House and I don't really remember what he looked like.'

That was the bare formalities out of the way, so Colm tensed, waiting for an order to stay away from the Winterleys from now on. God-send the man had not found out about Verity's misadventure or the roles he and Miss Winterley took in it on that night he was trying so hard not to remember.

'You should visit your late father's godmother,' Lord Farenze said. 'She owns a very fine portrait of him taken in his youth and it confirmed all my suspicions about you.'

'And now?' Colm challenged because he couldn't endure sitting here squirming while the man made up his mind whether to dislike him for being his father's son.

Then the ageing butler re-entered, followed by a footman with that wine and Colm had to be patient after all. He watched his glass being filled with rich wine he didn't intend to drink and bit back a sigh.

'That will be all, Oakham,' Lord Farenze said, 'close the door behind you.'

Ah, so they were about to stop dancing about, were they? Colm put his glass down virtually untouched and tried to look a lot more relaxed than he felt.

'I would rather you and my daughter had not met that night at Derneley's, or in the park the next morning, but what's done can't be undone.'

At least Miss Winterley's father didn't know about their disgraceful escapade in Cavendish Square. Colm blanked the thought of it from his mind so his lordship couldn't read it and listened for what came next.

'You have little to offer any woman, let alone my daughter, but you were alone with her for far too long before I turned up to make you respectable.'

'That's true,' Colm admitted carefully.

'Yet you stayed in that library although you knew you were the last man on earth she should be alone with like that.'

'Now there I must argue, my lord. Sir Steven Scrumble proved a worse rogue than me that night,' Colm said bitterly. Having to name that piece of filth as a brother in infamy made him feel as if he was indeed lying down with swine.

'You're splitting hairs, Hancourt. My daughter has fought against the blight of her mother's blown name all her life. If any gossip gets out about her being alone with you in a closed room at Derneley House that night, I'll rip you to shreds.'

'I have already promised to keep silent.'

Deeply offended by Lord Farenze's doubts, Colm wanted to spring to his feet and stalk out in a noble huff, but years of military discipline kept him sitting here and wasn't it true you should know your enemy? There was little doubt Lord Farenze considered him one of those since he refused to take Colm's word for the iron promise it truly was.

'I saw the way you looked at my daughter and you have wild blood in your veins, however hard you try to deny it. If you were still rich as Croesus, you'd have an uphill struggle persuading me to consent to a marriage between you and Eve. You would have to love each other to the edge of reason for me to even think about such a repellent idea. Imagining the public mockery and doubts such a marriage would arouse makes me shudder for my daughter and say that, no, even that would not be enough. Steer clear of her, Hancourt, maybe then I'll admit you're a better man than Lord Christopher Hancourt ever was.'

'I have met Miss Winterley only twice and you really think I see her as a fine opportunity to better myself? I don't recall offering her marriage on such a short acquaintance and you will just have to believe I have absolutely no intention of ever doing so in the future since you don't respect my word of honour.'

'You don't want to marry her?' his lordship asked, sounding as if he was genuinely surprised any young man in possession of his right senses wouldn't want to do so.

He was quite right, of course, but Colm had learnt the difference between wanting something and being able to have it at a very early age and he couldn't argue with the facts. Why would Miss Winterley love him anyway, even if he was fool enough to fall in love with her? He recalled for a dangerous moment how perfectly she had fitted into his arms and how ardently she responded to his kisses, but he was sitting across from her father, for goodness' sake. If the man could read his mind right now he'd challenge him to a duel, or horsewhip him out of the house.

'No, I don't and even if I did I have to admit that if my sister was being courted by a vagabond like me I'd move heaven and earth to stop him as well. I will do my best to avoid your daughter if we happen to meet by chance, Lord Farenze.'

'Oh, no, don't do that. She'd soon realise I've warned you off and insist on conversing with you as if you're the most interesting young man on earth every time you set eyes on each other from that moment on. Don't you know anything at all about contrary young ladies with too much spirit and stubbornness to meekly do as they're bid, Hancourt?'

'Not really, there are very few of them to be found on the average battlefield.'

'There were plenty in Brussels last spring.'

'Not when you had as much to do as we did and so little time to do it in, and certainly not if you are as poor and unconnected as Captain Carter.'

'You're not Captain Carter, though, are you?'

'No, but I'm not quite the Duke's nephew yet either.'

'You can't escape the bed you were born in,' Lord Farenze said as if he was trying hard not to hold his breeding against him, but still unconvinced he was any better than his father at heart. He watched Colm with his grey-green eyes suspicious and very guarded indeed for a moment, then seemed to make up his mind to trust him so far and not much further. 'My wife has invited your uncle and aunt to Darkmere to view our collections and for her Grace to paint whatever she chooses,' he admitted rather grimly. 'I couldn't rescind her invitation when I realised his Grace's nephew has been included in my lady's hospitality, since your uncle and aunt seem reluctant to part with you so soon after they nearly lost you at Waterloo.'

'Oh,' Colm said, almost silenced by the novelty of actually being wanted by family for once in his life. This certainly wasn't the moment to feel almost unmanned by the idea and he scrambled round for an excuse to stay away of his own accord, but his latest adversary was too far ahead of him.

'As a public declaration of peace between Hancourts and Winterleys it could hardly be bettered, so I expect you to accept my wife's invitation to Darkmere, but be very careful how you conduct yourself when you get there.'

'Of course, Lord Farenze,' Colm said stiffly, thinking he would almost rather be back with his regiment on a forced march.

'I am sorry to be so blunt. Eve's happiness and peace

of mind come first with me, but I am ashamed of offering hospitality with one hand and snatching it back with the other. If not for my daughter, I could like you very well and, according to a man who knows more about most people than they probably want him to, you're a brave man and a good officer.'

'I thank him for his good opinion,' Colm said, wishing he could go to Darkmere Castle as anyone but Colm Hancourt for a foolish moment.

'I'm glad we've had this talk. Now my wife can go on peace-making and you will have to endure the sharp edge of my daughter's tongue once she finds out how neatly you deceived her. I hope I can rely on you to infuriate her even more?'

'I think you can be quite certain of that, my lord,' Colm said glumly.

A week later Farenze House was closed up and the knocker had been taken off the door. Colm noted the blank unlived-in look of the place when his uncle's carriage swept past at the start of its own long journey and he rode behind as the Duke of Linaire's almost noble nephew on a horse Captain Carter could only dream of. Colm watched the ponderous coach navigate the busy streets, then gain the Great North Road with mixed feelings.

He was Colm Hancourt again for the first time in years, but he had little control over his destiny.

For the next few days he tried to forget their ultimate destination and enjoy the tour of the greatest houses and collections in the land before they ended up at Darkmere Castle. At first all he noted was mud and the biting cold, then the quiet beauty of the late autumn landscape stole his heart. He didn't suppose dire poverty felt better in Britain than in the war-ravaged lands he'd quit with a sigh of relief after the first, fragile peace was made and Bonaparte went to Elba for a nice little holiday before Waterloo. It wasn't much to boast about, but a British pauper could aspire to more than he was born to and stand some chance of achieving it.

This particular Briton had gone from fabulous fortune to nothing much at all, so he'd done it the other way about, but he was privileged all the same. He was the Duke of Linaire's nephew and dressed as a gentleman. He had a good horse to ride, warm clothes to wear and the luxury of sleeping in the best inns when they were not staying in some of the finest houses in the land. This was a chance to learn more of his own country than a London childhood and eight years in the army allowed until now.

He rode out on a crisp November morning a week or so after leaving London as courier to his uncle and aunt and wondered at the meandering route they only seemed to decide a day at a time.

Wherever they were going he had settled into being Mr Hancourt again, he reflected, as he got a lower bow from the landlord of the Swan and Whistle than Mr Carter would have done. Life was less dangerous than it had been as a humble ensign, lieutenant, then captain of the 95th Rifles. Colm once swore to manage without a family who saw him as an embarrassment, but eight years of war had tempered him. He managed a self-deprecating grin at the thought of that angry resolution and hoped he was a better man than he was when he invented Mr Carter.

But for Miss Evelina Winterley he might even be content and it would be so much better if he could forget her until she was under his nose again, but somehow he couldn't. He had too much time riding ahead of the ducal carriage to think right now. While Miss Winterley should have vanished from his thoughts after her father's warnings it was impossible to forget a lady of character and grace to order. He caught himself smiling at thin air as if she was smiling right back. Just as well he was riding ahead of his uncle and aunt today and not by the side of the coach because this way neither of them could ask what he was grinning at.

He groaned quietly. This was nonsense, wasn't it? He had nothing; he wasn't quite nobody, but what sort of a gentleman lived off his wife's dowry and his uncle's charity? Not his sort, he told himself against the wild thunder in his blood that turned hot and primitive at the thought of having Miss Winterley as his wife. Her father was right and even if she wanted him right back that would fade when the sneers and whispers made her wonder what sort of a fool she was to wed the penniless son of her mother's last lover. He didn't love her; they had only met three times, for heaven's sake, so how could he? This stupid feeling that they were perfectly designed to fill the dark and empty places in each other's lives was a snare to avoid at all costs. Longing for a woman he couldn't have would drive him mad. He could stop himself wanting what he couldn't have if he worked hard enough. If he put his mind to it and perhaps wasted far too much of his meagre savings on a mistress, he could stop himself longing for impossible things and forget how urgently he wanted Miss Winterley that night at Warlington House and ever since.

Lord Farenze had made it very clear he was to arrive at Darkmere as the Duke's nephew and act as if he had no idea Miss Winterley ever met a librarian in a dusty book room, or a lowly clerk in the respectable confines of Green Park. Colm thought the man was worrying without cause. He hadn't seen any signs she even liked him in the lady's lovely turquoise gaze. The sneaky idea that if his lordship was worried about his daughter's feelings he must have good reason to be banished somehow. Yet he only had to think of their first meeting in Derneley's neglected library to become that tongue-tied idiot again and as for that confounded kiss...

Best not to think about that. What else was there? At that dangerous point the yard of tin sounded and he turned round to see a groom waving at him to stop.

'Colm, dear boy, we were supposed to turn off at the last crossroads, but you're so deep in thought we missed it. Anyone would think you were Wellington busy planning a battle,' Aunt Barbara said when he was in earshot.

He'd been thinking of Miss Winterley most of the morning then and wasn't it a good thing her father didn't know? 'I am a clod, your Grace,' he admitted with a sheepish grin. 'We could take the next turning and get back to Berry Brampton as best we can.'

'I'd sooner find somewhere Rooksby can sweep round so we can head back rather than risk being jammed down a narrow lane,' the Duke argued mildly.

'I should be paying attention,' Colm replied, feeling a fool for letting Miss Winterley get between him and his duty yet again.

Chapter Ten

'I quite thought the Duke of Linaire would be here by now,' Eve said to her father as they rode back to Darkmere in Verity's wake one day in early December. Chloe had given up riding until her latest baby was born now and Verity wanted to spend as much time as possible with her beloved aunt. Verity's life was changing and she was poised on the edge of womanhood. Eve shivered at the thought of that night at Warlington House and feelings she didn't want to think about ran through her as Carter's kiss felt so vivid on her lips it was almost as if she could still feel the warmth, strength and excitement of his touch with all her senses. Verity wasn't the only one confused by the war between mind and body as she tried to come to terms with a new reality.

'The Duke said they were to call on friends and fellow scholars on the way,' Lord Farenze replied, seeming oblivious to the battle she was waging against a heady memory. 'Are you bored with our company then, Eve?'

'No, but it will be awkward for you to meet Lord Christopher Hancourt's son under your own roof, won't it, Papa?'

'Maybe I already know him,' her father said with that closed expression she had seen a little too often lately.

'What's he like, then? Goodness knows what he's been up to so far, it seems a deep dark family secret.'

'Goodness might know, but you'll find out soon enough.'

'I wish you'd stop being so mysterious and tell me about him.'

He shot her a sceptical look, as if he'd like to get inside her head and have a good rummage about. 'I shall let you judge for yourself.'

'Why do you seem to dislike him already? You were living apart from my mother when Lord Christopher Hancourt became her lover.'

'Maybe I can't forgive his father for being such a confounded idiot then?'

'There are so many of them in the world according to you, Papa,' she said sweetly. 'What was so special about that one?'

'You think I'm a grumpy bear?' he said, neatly avoiding her question.

'I think you might be if you hadn't had the sense to marry Chloe. She usually laughs you out of your dark moods now and I'm very grateful for the improvement in your temper.'

'If my temper is so uncertain, I like to think my daughter is shrewd enough not to provoke it too often.'

Eve couldn't tell if he knew how disturbed she was

by Mr Carter. He should have faded more with every mile they travelled from London, but it was as if she had brought the fogs and gloom of the capital with her to Darkmere and him as well. Try as she might she couldn't get the wretched man out of her head.

'I did say it improved when you married Chloe, didn't I?' she teased lightly enough.

'So you did.'

'I shall risk it and ask again why you hated Lord Christopher for running off with my mother so much then.'

'It's complicated.'

'And you still think me too young to hear the full story, I suppose? To you I'll always be so; isn't it about time you realised that I need to know?'

'I'll discuss it with you after you wed and can understand the contrary passions of men and women better. The truth is I don't really want to think about your mother and her last lover at all. If Lord Christopher Hancourt ever thought she would bring him joy, I suppose I ought to pity him, though.'

'You acquit me of any stain from my mother's sins, but seem reluctant to give his son the same immunity, Papa.'

'I never said I was logical about it,' he said austerely.

Eve almost gave up on the subject to stop that bleak look silvering his eyes whenever he thought of his first unhappy marriage.

'Hancourt is more of a man than his father was, but I don't want him near you, love. I know how young men think and feel, I was one myself once upon a time.'

'I have no intention of encouraging Mr Hancourt as more than a simple acquaintance.'

'Far from simple, I suspect.'

Eve rolled her eyes at the grey sky over their heads and waited for something more worthy of her father as an excuse. 'I have no intention of falling in love with the man, or is he still a boy? He can't be very much older than I am.'

'You must judge for yourself, but I wish your stepmother had been a little less generous with her hospitality for once.'

'I'm hardly likely to fall in love with Lord Christopher Hancourt's son at first sight, so you're worrying about things that will never happen, which isn't like you.'

Her father still looked troubled as they rode along the Northern Avenue towards the more workaday side of Darkmere and the stables. 'I only ever want to do what's best for you, Eve,' he said at last.

'Anyone would think Mr Hancourt was going to ride up the drive on a knightly charger and carry me off across his saddle brow. How astonished the poor man would be if he knew we even considered him as an impassioned suitor for my hand. He's never even set eyes on me and I don't inspire that sort of romantic passion in a young man's heart, thank heavens.'

'Only because you have never met one who could wake the passion under the careful control you assume in public,' he said a little too seriously.

'Don't worry, Papa, I shall lock myself in the Sea

Tower and throw away the key if I begin to harbour even one warm feeling towards Mr Hancourt.'

And once the week or so the Duke and Duchess of Linaire were due to spend here was over, they need never see Mr Hancourt again, Eve decided as her personal groom hurried up to help her out of the saddle and Papa's attention swung back to his wife.

'I think it's sweet the way he fusses over her,' Verity objected when Eve whispered Chloe might not welcome her husband's anxiety until she had finished being unwell for the day when they met later. 'For years she had to be strong and self-sufficient for my sake and she deserves to be doted on by your papa.'

'She does and I'm so glad she dotes on him as well,' Eve said. 'Would I could love and be loved like that,' she added with a sigh. 'I'm not the sort to inspire such a grand passion in a man.'

'Nonsense,' Verity argued loyally. 'It just takes longer to win your good opinion, but I am shallow as yonder puddle and don't think true love is for me.'

Eve suspected Verity's infatuation with the youngest Louburn brother was responsible for that declaration and the accompanying grimace. It was good that Verity had realised how much danger she was in that night, but Eve didn't want her to wear a hair shirt.

'As if Chloe would let you be a careless butterfly even if you were that way inclined. Stop belittling yourself.'

'I've good reason to be wary after I nearly landed us both in the basket that last night in London. Now we're home and the world fits as it should again, I can't imagine why it mattered so much to see Rufus that night. It wasn't as if he was leaving for far-off lands or about to marry someone else; marriage is clearly the last thing on his mind.'

'I doubt he has very much on that at the best of times, but I expect your parents' love affair led you to expect something truer and deeper of first love than it can usually bear, Verity. I know your mother was barely half a year older than you are now when she fell fathoms deep in love with your father. You had a very different childhood, though, and Chloe always put your welfare first so you don't need to escape a lonely childhood and an uncaring father. Captain Revereux adores you and can never wait to get home and spend time with you. Find a decent man to fall in love with and remember your mother and father paid a terrible price for loving so passionately and so young. Even the thought of you suffering like they did makes me feel quite faint.'

'Please don't turn into a hysterical female for my sake then, for I can't have been in love with Rufus Louburn to have forgotten him so quickly and I promise not to imagine myself in love with a handsome face ever again. So stop frowning and come and play with the babies; I swear little James has grown a new tooth since yesterday, so no wonder he was fretful last night.'

Would that logic and determination were strong enough to stop a woman falling in love, whispered the secret Eve, under her good sense and virtuous reputation. *Be quiet*, the everyday one ordered and hurried after Verity before the reckless creature could come up with a scathing reply.

* * *

'Fine sight, hey?' the Duke of Linaire asked as the coach stopped so they could wonder at the famous prospect of Darkmere Castle ahead.

'Indeed,' Colm replied, 'caught by the afternoon sun like that it makes me wish I could paint.'

'Would that I could as well,' the Duchess observed ruefully.

'Come now, m'dear, I never came across a lady who could hold a candle to you at watercolour.'

'I want to paint as I see, not as I can,' she objected, her gaze sharpening as the sun caressed the famous old fortress and the last rags of autumn leaves left on the noble trees planted to shelter it from the worst of the wind shone russet and gold.

'We've lost her again, m'boy,' the Duke said with an indulgent look at his wife. The Duchess collected her sketching equipment, then he jumped down to help her out of the coach. 'I shall tell Farenze you'll be along when the muse deserts you, my love,' he added as his wife's maid joined her with a resigned nod to say she would get her mistress up to the castle before daylight faded completely.

'Hmm? Yes, that would be as well,' the Duchess said absently, making rapid pencil strokes in her sketchbook to capture Darkmere with the low winter sun on it and an angry sea and sky behind.

'I hope Lady Farenze is as tolerant as she seemed in London,' the Duke said with a last proud look at his Duchess before they went on without her.

'Since she asked me to come here with you, she must be,' Colm said ruefully.

'Nonsense, lad, you have to meet them sooner or later. I suppose we'll soon find out if her ladyship's forbearance extends to my bookishness and your aunt's painting. We rely on you to do the polite, my boy; you do it so much better than we ever could.'

'Then we had best not unpack too hastily.'

'Don't be such a defeatist, lad; you and Farenze have more in common than either of you realise.'

His daughter for one, Colm thought gloomily and doubted Miss Winterley would ever be a bond between them.

Lord and Lady Farenze welcomed the two guests who turned up without a blink. The Viscount even seemed mildly amused that the Duchess of Linaire had absented herself before she could even arrive and Lady Chloe was too good humoured to take offence where none was intended.

'I have learned to love this wild and glorious place and often wish I could paint it myself,' she told them when they turned up at her door a duchess short. 'I lack both skill and talent with watercolour myself and am in awe of those with both. I should love to see your wife at work, your Grace, and promise not to be offended if she would rather not have a spectator. A true artist must be respected.'

'I am sure my wife will be delighted,' the Duke said and exchanged a wry glance with Colm at the thought of Barbara's contempt for would-be artists who only wanted to talk of their own efforts. *Polite dribbles of paint on expensive paper*, the Duchess dismissed the correct and soulless watercolours that usually caused a young lady to be thought accomplished.

'I don't suppose she will, but if I promise not to make silly observations and sit still, maybe she will rescue me from being kept indoors and coddled half to death,' Lady Farenze said with a militant look for her husband.

'You may have to clean brushes, sharpen pencils and act artist's assistant, Lady Farenze,' Colm warned, as he concluded rumour was right and the lady must be with child again. 'My aunt never intends to be a tyrant, but forgets everything but the next mix of colour and stroke of her brush once she is at work.'

Chapter Eleven

A whisper of movement on the edge of his senses and Colm saw Miss Winterley pause in the doorway of what looked like a family sitting room to glare at him. For a moment he thought she was going to rip up at him for letting her believe Mr Carter was a real man. He was a real man, Colm decided, in a hot daze at the sight of her so passionately angry he wondered candles didn't light spontaneously in their sconces all around her. Very real, he discovered, as all the enchantment he'd been trying to argue himself out of for so many miles flooded back. He wanted to step forward and greet her very personally, ask if she'd thought of him as constantly as he did about her and please excuse all his deceptions. They were not alone, though, and she didn't look in any mood to listen even if they were.

'Good day, your Grace, welcome to Darkmere,' she said with genuine warmth. She let it drain away when she turned her unique blue-green eyes on Colm. 'I suppose you must be Mr Hancourt. How do you do, sir?'

she said, so icily indifferent that the hand he hadn't even known he was holding out to her fell to his side.

This was the guarded and coldly aloof young woman he had spied from a distance that first night at Derneley House and he wondered if he would ever crack the ice he could almost see forming in the air between them again. Unlikely—she didn't hate him that night and she certainly looked as if she did now. She might sound cold and look it, but the fury in her eyes was hot and hasty—if there was a vat of boiling oil handy he'd be very warm indeed right now.

'Miss Winterley,' he returned with an elegant bow he didn't know he had in him. Something tender and tentative shrivelled under that Ice Queen stare and he was her parents' guest after all, even if her father had put stern limits on his hospitality back in London.

'I hope you had a comfortable journey, your Grace?' she asked his uncle with a sweet smile.

Colm had to admire her acting, even if the fierce guard she put on her fury made him wonder if he would ever know the real Eve Winterley. Why did he want to? She was Pamela's daughter and that divided them efficiently as a wall. He had to control his unfortunate sense of the ridiculous as he imagined Miss Winterley building it herself, setting stones and hurrying the masons along lest the barbarian invader come back. It wasn't funny being her enemy, though, and he saw hurt as well as fury in her turquoise gaze. Nothing could have sobered him more surely, not even Lord Farenze's hard gaze reminding him of that promise he had made to keep infuriating Miss Winterley. Right now she looked as if she would like him to leave before he'd hardly got over the threshold, so at least his host should be happy.

'Very comfortable, thank you, my dear,' his uncle said genially.

'I'm so glad the Duchess has found something worth painting already,' she went on greeting his uncle as if Colm didn't exist. 'After seeing some of her paintings when I was in London I thought she would enjoy our magnificent scenery.'

Colm wondered if he was invisible and decided Miss Winterley had even better ways of humbling an errant gentleman than that icy glare she treated him to just now. Why had he ever worried about her among the less scrupulous rakes of the *ton*? She could wither the worst of them with a pointed stare and that air of charmed ignorance that he even existed as she chatted about the landscape.

'You must be a fine diplomat to have persuaded my wife to let you see her work when you were last in London, Miss Winterley,' Uncle Horace said absently and Colm followed his gaze to the open door of the library and wondered if he might wander off to inspect it much as his wife vanished into the castle grounds. Serve the infernal woman right if she was left stranded by his bookish uncle before she could trot out her next platitude, he decided disagreeably.

'My father will tell you I rarely give up until I get what I want, your Grace, but I hope you will ignore him,' Miss Winterley joked with a fond look at her father and no sign that the Duke and Duchess were unwelcome, so it was probably only him she wished a hundred miles away.

'Can't do that, m'dear. Your father might not let me have the run of his library if I'm rude to him,' the Duke said with the wry smile that made him endearing, despite his limitations as a duke and guest who hated being lionised.

'So, how does it feel to be yourself again, Mr Hancourt?' Miss Winterley's coolly ironic murmur came as they followed her parents and guest of honour upstairs to the rooms the Duke and Duchess had been allotted, before Uncle Horace could plunge into my lord's library.

'Very odd, Miss Winterley,' he answered honestly. 'I was Carter so long I almost forgot about myself.'

Her sidelong glare told him he'd better not think that was an excuse for deceiving her. 'Why did you invent him in the first place?' she asked distantly.

'Grandsons of dukes don't serve in the 95th Rifles, Miss Winterley. I would have been out of place.'

'And the scandal would follow you?' she challenged as if he was a coward to hide behind that alias so long.

'Yes, of course. You know as well as I do that it goes everywhere with me,' he said bleakly.

'Which is why you clung to Mr Carter after the war was over and he could be safely pensioned off, I suppose?'

She sounded so indifferent they might have been discussing a stranger. Colm hoped the Viscount was listening and approving of the void that now gaped between his least wanted guest and the daughter of the house. Or did he know how much of a challenge that icy façade of hers was to a red-blooded male? Colm was torn between a longing to drag her into the nearest empty room and kiss her until she forgot all about Carter and his sins and everything else and this thorn in his pride that argued he should limp back downstairs and ride away from a place where a man of his birth would never be truly welcome.

'Not entirely. My uncle wanted me to bring his new purchases safe back from Derneley House and I could hardly go there as my true self, could I?'

'I doubt it would have been very comfortable, considering who you really are, but Lord Derneley is hardly in a position to argue with your uncle, is he?'

It would have been damned *un*comfortable to live under that particular roof as himself, Colm reflected, but he couldn't argue with the daughter of the house when he was only supposed to have met her minutes ago. So he gritted his teeth and supposed it was another way for her to punish him for being who he was.

'The view from here is reckoned to be one of the finest in the Borders,' she pointed out helpfully as he paused on the half-landing to rest his knee before limping up the rest. She knew he was struggling and had given him a chance to pause even though she still looked furious with him. It seemed that Miss Winterley was an enemy in a million and how he wanted to be disarmed by her, but he didn't think she would accept if he threw his rifle at her feet and her father might even shoot him with it.

'Don't pity me, Miss Winterley,' he made himself say brusquely instead.

'I don't,' she said with her chin raised haughtily and her eyes on the admittedly wonderful view up the Darke Valley from the wide range of leaded windows.

Uncle Horace was being gently but firmly shepherded up the next half of the wide staircase and into a fine suite of rooms allocated to the ducal couple by his hostess. Colm hoped he could retreat to his own room soon and lick his wounds, then he might be able to reassemble the Duke of Linaire's nephew in good time for dinner. Even furious with him and chilly as a Northumbrian snow storm, Miss Winterley made him feel as if she showed up in full vivid colour and her father's castle and all its inhabitants were somehow at a distance from them both. Which would never do, he reminded himself, and tried to pay more attention to his host and hostess as they caught up with them.

'Most comfortable,' the Duke said, looking a little awed by the elegant splendour made ready for him, as if someone might denounce him as a fraud at any moment and send him to an attic nobody else was using. 'I do hope Colm isn't too far away, my lady? My wife thinks the lad's leg bothers him more than he will admit, so we'd rather not have him run up and down the stairs of one of those fine towers of yours, Farenze, if you don't mind? I dare say there's enough room in this splendid suite to lodge him in here as well if you're cramped for space.'

For a moment Lady Farenze looked startled at the idea she might not have enough room here to barrack an army. 'You are our honoured guests, your Grace. Mr Hancourt has been allotted the Silver Room just along the corridor,' she said with the poise of a natural hostess and years as housekeeper in a noble household.

'I am grateful for it, my lady,' Colm said sincerely and caught a sharp glance from his host, as if his words had an edge he didn't intend.

He silently cursed his father for running off with another man's wife—whatever the state of their marriage at the time—and putting this perpetual barrier between him and the Winterley family. It looked as high as the castle walls at the moment and he felt too weary and battered to try to scale it again right now.

'Mr Hancourt is such a dashing gentleman,' Eve's friend Alice Clempson remarked after dinner the following evening.

'He is well enough, I suppose,' Eve said warily.

She hadn't forgiven him for deceiving her so completely yet and their neighbours were finding her relations with Lord Christopher Hancourt's son so fascinating she could scream. Still, she must try and forget about him. As the granddaughter of an iron founder, Alice wasn't considered good *ton* by some of those neighbours. Eve wondered if it might be a good idea to borrow the air of weary sophistication Alice assumed as a defence against their critical gaze right now. Then they could both sit here and ignore the stares of the curious together, as if they had no idea they were being watched.

'If his father was even half as handsome and romantic looking as the son is I can't blame your mama for finding him so irresistible,' Alice said with what sounded suspiciously like a besotted sigh.

'You mustn't say such things to me, Allie,' Eve was shocked into saying.

'Miss Mendaville-Rouste is making enough noise to drown a cathedral choir. Someone should tell her mother the girl can't play two right notes in succession.'

'Well, you still can't say them, even if nobody else can hear you for that infernal thundering on Chloe's poor pianoforte. I hope we don't have to have it restrung or whatever it is they do to pianos.'

'You really aren't musical, are you, Eve, dear?'

'No, but neither is Miss Mendaville-Rouste.'

At least they were talking about the wretched girl now and not Mr Hancourt, Eve thought with a sigh that was lost under the racket the determined pianist was making. How could her usually clever and tactful friend say such things about a man Eve was doing her best to take no notice of? She managed to ignore him for most of the day without actually being rude and came down tonight determined to show the world she was *not* like her dam. It was easy to resist being charmed by Lord Chris's son *and* to seem deaf to the gossip his presence was stirring up in the area. She did very well throughout dinner and tea in the drawing room afterwards, despite one or two impudent comments from the sillier young ladies and some who were old enough to know better.

'All this must be such a strain for you, dear Miss Winterley...'

'What a true gentleman your dear papa is to make

such a public display of peace between your family and Mr Hancourt's after what happened, my dear.'

Worst of all was: *'I think it's such a very romantic tale; those two headlong lovers galloping off into the night to meet their deaths in eternal togetherness.'* This from one poetically inclined young woman Eve was tempted to slap. She managed a sickly smile instead and handed the silly creature a second cup of tea, whether she wanted one or not. A hasty visit to the ladies' withdrawing room in a little while would serve the sentimental idiot right and might teach her to think twice before she spouted such nonsense next time.

'We could still be overheard,' she cautioned under cover of the Haydn sonata Miss Mendaville-Rouste had gone on mangling even now the gentlemen were back in the room.

'I doubt anyone can hear themselves think with that row going on, let alone listen to us. Nobody can stop the silly girl when she's got the bit between her teeth,' Alice said with a glare at the pianoforte where the well-bred and talentless Miss Mendaville-Rouste was thundering on with steely determination.

Eve shot a furtive glance at Colm Hancourt and wondered how long she could ignore his manly presence without offending the Duke and Duchess. One thing was certain: she could never watch him as openly as Alice was when Eve gave her a disapproving glare.

'He has a limp,' she pointed out half-heartedly.

As if that would blind any rational female to his hawkishly masculine features, unruly tawny hair and supple height. As for his gold-on-brown velvet eyes…

She shivered and caught herself on a reminiscent sigh. No, meeting his wary gaze full on was not to be thought of right now. Mr Hancourt could lure her into a world Eve Winterley couldn't afford to explore and as for a repeat of that kiss…it wasn't delight she felt as she recalled the warm shivers running all over her sensitised skin that night when he kissed her as if he meant it and looked at her afterwards with a brief, intimate smile in his eyes before glaring at the Louburn brothers as if he'd like to run them through for just looking at her the wrong way. She only shivered now because she was afraid she was more like her mother than she wanted to be, of course.

'And who knows what wounds Mr Hancourt might have that we cannot see,' she added almost to herself. Was she trying to convince herself or Alice that she had better taste than to admire or even—heaven forbid— lust after the son of her mother's last lover? And this Hancourt male was a proven liar as well.

'Whatever they might be, that slight halt in his step doesn't trouble me. It makes him look dashing and then there's that scar, that turns him from the usual sort of fit and healthy gentleman into something of a pirate, don't you think?' Alice went on blithely. 'A very handsome and well-behaved pirate, of course.'

Eve only just stopped herself glaring at her friend because she could enjoy the luxury of eyeing Mr Hancourt without a flurry of excited comments from her fellow guests sweeping round the room like an autumn gale. Alice could size up the lying toad as a potential husband and decide she liked him well enough and never mind his scars, his limp or his lack of a fortune, and his imitation of an almost humble clerk Alice didn't even know about. It was true, though; Alice and Mr Hancourt might suit each other very well. Oh, dear, she could have eaten too much of the fish course at dinner because there was that sharp sick feeling deep inside her again that must not be because her friend and the Duke of Linaire's deceitful nephew could have been made for one another.

'I doubt he'd enjoy being likened to one of those, however civilised,' she said tightly.

If Alice did decide he would make her a suitably gentlemanly husband and Mr Hancourt agreed, Eve sincerely hoped they would move a long way from here, so she wouldn't have to watch them be deliriously happy together. She felt horribly unworthy of her clever, generous friend as she struggled with a sneaky idea Mr Hancourt could have changed her own life in so many ways, if he wasn't Lord Chris's son. And a liar and deceiver, and a cold fish who walked away from a woman after kissing her until she didn't know if it was night or day. Give her a few more minutes and she was sure she would be able to produce a dozen more reasons why he was as far from her ideal lover as it was possible for a man to be. And if he had wanted to be that lover he would have come to her after that kiss and admitted who he was, wouldn't he? The fact he had not proved he was an adventurer and a liar and had probably left a trail of broken-hearted women stretching all the way back to Portugal behind him when he moved through Europe on the Duke of Wellington's coat-tails.

'It seems to me you aristocrats suffer from the circumstances of your birth every bit as much as we parvenus at times,' Alice said with more insight into Eve's contrary feelings in her steady blue eyes than Eve wanted to see. 'Mr Hancourt is as hemmed in by who his father was as Papa is by his father being the village blacksmith before he made his fortune as an iron master. Your polite world isn't so different from the one we humbler beings have to find a way through, is it?'

'No, not that different at all,' Eve admitted and ordered herself not to watch Mr Hancourt pretend he was deaf as he sat beside the Duke and Duchess of Linaire. He was dressed in immaculate evening garb and looked very worthy of the honour as all three of them took pride of place as guests of honour. Which only proved how deceptive appearances could be.

'Mama and Papa would like me to marry a true gentleman. Mr Hancourt would fill that bill nicely, don't you think?' Alice speculated with a nod at the dratted man as if Eve might not have noticed him sitting there bold as brass and twice as handsome.

'He doesn't have a fortune of his own,' Eve whispered back.

'I don't think that would be an obstacle, do you?' Alice asked with a wry smile and of course the Clempsons had more money than they knew what to do with and one child to spend it on.

'He is a proud and aloof man,' Eve said unwarily.

Alice raised an eyebrow and shot a significant glance at Colm, who was now busy coaxing the very shy young woman he had partnered at dinner to converse with him.

He was trying to include her in the circle of not quite fledged young ladies and gentlemen who usually ignored her as too quiet to say boo to a goose. How dare he add kindness to all the other reasons Eve had to regret the old scandal that stood between them? Never mind the scandal, he'd told her he was someone he was not and he let her think they might be friends if they were born a little more equally. And they had been born that way, after all. The difference was she had stayed in her privileged place and he had been deprived of his by Lord Christopher and her mother. She recalled the vast fortune Lord Chris and Pamela ran through before they died and felt guilt slide under her shield of righteous fury at the wretch who had deceived her so easily in London. Was part of it because a sneaky voice in the back of her mind argued he would have told her who he was if he wanted to be more than Mr Carter ever could be to her? It seemed shallow to be glad that if they should ever, by the slenderest and most unlikely chance, happen to love each other they might marry if they could only get past his silly pride. What an unthinkable idea, what madness had come over her? She didn't want to marry him and if he felt even a spark of love for her he was very good at hiding it. He sat there like the prize exhibit at the fair and all the silly chits in the area sighed over his scar and limp and mysterious past and little Miss Browne was probably fathoms deep in love with him now he'd been so gently encouraging. Eve and Mr Hancourt were as far apart as ever and she was glad, of course she was.

'He doesn't look high in the instep or particularly

chilling to me, Eve,' her so-called friend said as she shot him a glance that seemed far too warm and approving to Eve. 'Indeed, Mr Hancourt seems quite genial and looks very intelligent so I expect he will make some lucky female an excellent husband.'

'I doubt he'd live easily on his wife's fortune,' Eve said almost under her breath. It wasn't a warning to Alice as much as a reminder to herself not to see him as a suitor. Not that he'd shown much sign of wanting to spend five minutes talking to her since he arrived here with his aunt and uncle, let alone finding the time and effort to offer her marriage. The fact she would have frozen him into an ice sculpture if she could, then walked away as if he might contaminate her if he had tried to speak to her privately was neither here nor there.

'Love might reconcile him to being poorer than his wife in the end, don't you think?' Alice said as if she was far more of a romantic than Eve thought.

'I try not to,' Eve replied with a stern look to say this topic was worn out.

'One day you will fall fathoms deep in love with a fine mind and a handsome face and throw your bonnet over the windmill, despite all your resolutions to be coldly logical about the whole business of marriage, Evelina Winterley. Don't you shake your head at me and frown as if I've suggested you might get scurvy. Nobody is immune to loving and needing another human being almost as dearly as their next breath. Your parents certainly are not and neither, I am thankful to say, are mine.'

'You wish to make a love match, then? Nobody

would think so from the way you just assessed Mr Hancourt's assets as a potential husband.'

'I am open to the possibility of falling in love with a man of his looks, bearing and proven ability as a leader of men, that's all. Given my position in life and his as the only grandson of a duke so far, I would be a fool not to be. That doesn't mean I intend to fall in love with him, but at least *I* can see him as he really is. Perhaps those of us who lack my objectivity should think twice about their prejudices?'

'I really don't know why I ever thought I liked you,' Eve said with a huff of annoyance and she was glad a temporary lull in the poor, mauled sonata for dramatic purposes meant neither of them dare say much until it began again.

Chapter Twelve

For a while Eve simply sat and simmered and did her best to ignore her mischief-making friend. Alice was saying what most females in the room were thinking. Mr Hancourt *was* handsome, clever and well born. He had no fortune, of course, and had been forced by his circumstances to take paid employment as his uncle's secretary and whatever else it was he did. Still, he was nobly born and respectably occupied and if the world found out what he'd been doing for the last eight years he would be lionised. Eve sighed under the cover of the final crashing chords of Miss Mendaville-Rouste's musical disaster and decided life was far too complicated.

'That was quite delightful, Miss Mendaville-Rouste, but you must be quite worn out,' Eve's stepmother stood up and announced firmly. 'I shall call for more tea to revive you and I'm sure your mama will insist you rest after your labours.'

Mrs Mendaville-Rouste was perhaps more sensitive, or less tone-deaf, than she appeared when her daughter took over the pianoforte with such verve and so little talent. She nodded and beckoned her eldest daughter to sit by her proud mama. Eve watched the charade with cynical eyes and concluded Mrs Mendaville-Rouste knew the Viscountess Farenze had more power and status among the *beau monde* than she could dream of, despite her much-trumpeted blue blood and Mr Mendaville-Rouste's ancient name and equally ancient manor house. Less powerful families than her own must think twice before inviting Mrs Mendaville-Rouste and her eldest daughter to any entertainment that could include music, however amiable Mr Mendaville-Rouste and his son might be. Eve speculated on an upcoming outbreak of broken instruments, or the woodworm, afflicting genteel houses in the area, until some worthy and deaf gentleman carried off Miss Mendaville-Rouste to his distant hearth and kept her there until she got over the notion she could play anything more complex than a penny whistle.

'Your stepmother is a wonderful woman, Miss Winterley,' Colm Hancourt observed softly from behind her and made Eve jump, then look round furtively to see if anyone else had heard him.

Where was Alice when she needed her? Watching smugly from across the room as she deftly helped Chloe with the re-introduced tea things and handed out cups with such grace and deftness it was almost a weapon in her battle with the local dowagers. Her friend wasn't taken in by a handsome face after all, then, Eve concluded, as she nodded helplessly when Mr Hancourt indicated the empty chair next to hers and raised his eyebrows in silent question. The dowagers soon lost interest in her supposedly impudent friend and shifted in their seats to watch or listen to whatever Eve and Mr Hancourt might have to say to each other instead.

'True,' she managed to say calmly enough although her heartbeat had speeded up ridiculously for some odd reason, 'and never more so than when she selflessly rescued us all from our headaches.'

'That's not all she rescued us from. My aunt was within seconds of marching up to the pianoforte and slamming the lid on the wretched girl's fingers if it was the only way to stop her. She has a true artist's love of the beautiful and that was nothing of the kind.'

'I suppose we ought to make allowances,' Eve said half-heartedly, since her ears still felt persecuted and now her breathing was oddly congested as well.

Impossible to blame Miss Mandeville-Rouste for that when the cause was sitting right next to her. She shot Alice another sidelong glare to demand rescue, but the scheming wretch pretended not to notice.

'I really cannot imagine why,' he argued.

What had they been talking about? Oh, yes, making allowances for the Mandeville-Rouste girl. What a good thing one of them had a firm grasp on reality.

'Miss Mandeville-Rouste is doing nobody any good and putting off every available suitor for miles around, unless I miss my guess. But how frustrating it is for some of your guests that we were not put in the centre of the room instead of my aunt and uncle. We could be so much more easily overheard and commented on like figures in a masque,' he drawled with a politely blank

look of enquiry at the middle-aged lady who was trying so hard to listen to their every word that she was
nearly falling off her chair.

Eve suspected it was his cold stare that made the
woman blush and move further away rather than any
sense of shame. He probably had no idea how effective
that chilly glare could be and she shivered at the memory of it sending ice down her own backbone that first
night at Derneley House.

'Since you have buried Mr Carter on some foreign
battlefield, our neighbours must be wondering what
you have been doing with yourself all these years,' she
murmured and encountered a lazy warning in his brown
and gold eyes not to give him away that made Alice's
words echo in her still-aching head.

He truly was a brave and intriguing gentleman,
wasn't he? And a lot more dangerous than she had let
herself realise at their first two meetings. She looked
for the limping and oddly dazed-looking clerk she encountered in Lord Derneley's library in this assured and
elegant gentleman. Mr Carter had disappeared and she
wondered why she regretted him. Mr Hancourt had a
confidence Carter lacked, for all his daring deeds on
the battlefield. This version of the man wore his new
clothes with quiet elegance and looked as if he might
have got his scar and limp during an illicit duel over a
lady's reputation.

'Thank you for the warning, Miss Winterley. My
uncle has perfected a look of blank incomprehension
I am doing my best to copy. It serves him very well in
the face of awkward or impertinent questions,' he told

her with an almost smile that must have their would-be audience perching on the edge of their seats again.

'My friend Miss Clempson would say he can do that because he's a duke and you might get away with it as the grandson of one,' she managed to reply. Alice might have blushed if she was here instead of across the room, pretending not to see Eve's silent pleas for rescue, but she refused to feel guilty about using her so-called friend as a decoy.

'Miss Clempson is obviously as perceptive as she is lovely, I must cultivate her acquaintance.'

'Please don't,' Eve said impulsively. 'Miss Clempson is more easily hurt than she would have the world think. She has to walk a fine line in local society, given her supposedly humble birth.'

'Almost as fine a one as you and I do, Miss Winterley?'

'And only we know how thin that is, Mr Hancourt.'

'I do have the benefit of being a male, don't forget,' he pointed out as if she could when the fact of him next to her seemed burned into her senses.

How could she not remember he was acutely masculine from the tip of her toes to the last hair piled up on her head? She felt a flush of heat unthinkably deep inside her and threatening to overwhelm her in public, and that was exactly the sort of giveaway she couldn't afford.

'As such, my reputation can endure more strain than a lady's under the same circumstances,' he added, as if she might not have noticed she was about to blush and stammer while he stayed perfectly cool and collected.

'You have your father's example in front of you to argue with that idea, Mr Hancourt, just as spiteful reminders of my mother's sins will check me if I forget to be proper for more than a moment,' she said stiffly.

'I doubt you ever do that,' he said dourly and he didn't mean it as a compliment.

'I did at that horrible masquerade,' she admitted to her fan.

'That wasn't unwariness, it was love for a girl you think of as your little sister,' he said in a low intimate tone that set her nerves jangling.

She didn't want him to admire her for protecting those she loved. She didn't want him to understand her either. Even as a friend Colm Hancourt would be dangerous, but they could never be anything as simple as friends.

'I should never have left Lady Derneley's ballroom alone that first night, despite the rip in my gown, and I ought to have seen how restless Verity was before that horrid masquerade,' she said all the same. 'I'm used to the idea I must take more care than any other female I know to keep my good name, but in the future I shall guard Verity's as well.'

Why was she telling him this when she had been so determined to ignore him once she knew who he really was?

'My sister suffers much the same way, although her circumstances are very different.'

'Is she Miss Carter?' she asked, certain Miss Hancourt had endured far worse than she had without a protective family to shield her.

'She chose another name and don't ask me to give her away when she has a living to earn, Miss Winterley.'

'You don't trust me, do you, sir? Why would I harm a lady I have never met, particularly when we share in a scandal that's none of our doing?'

'You won't deliberately cause mischief, but what you don't know you can't give away by accident.'

'How kind of you to trust me so far and no further.'

'War has not made me kind,' he said bleakly.

'I doubt it changed you very radically. It seems to me a man is kind or unkind by nature and war brings out what was in him all along.'

'So you think me one of the unkind ones?'

Reluctant to let him know about her real thoughts and feelings towards Mr Carter-Hancourt, she eyed him cynically. A hint of hurt in his eyes made her sorry she'd baited him like that because she was still angry with him for deceiving her. He was a sensitive and lonely man under his various masks. For a dangerous moment she wanted to take his hand and offer her warmth and some of the human contact he'd lacked for so long. Quite impossible with their eager audience, of course, and he might pull away even if she forgot them and that would be one humiliation too many.

'I suspect being one of the kind ones made you hate what you had to do at times.'

'You're right,' he said, the memory of those things bleak in that changeable gaze of his.

How had she not let herself notice his deepest thoughts were reflected in his eyes before now? Maybe they hadn't been; perhaps he had never let her see them before. 'Then I'm glad the war is over and you came home.'

'So am I, now,' he said with such warmth in his eyes she really ought to avoid them from now on.

'Yes, your uncle and aunt are very pleased to have you with them, are they not? And all our local beauties are lining up to sigh over your piratical looks and mysterious past. If that has been repeated at every stop on your journey here you must be very glad not to be with the army now, sir,' she teased, when she had been sure they would always be worse than strangers now the truth was out.

Who would have thought Miss Winterley could joke with Mr Hancourt with half the neighbourhood looking on and her hurt at being deceived still raw? She looked around where those neighbours were, still wishing they could hear every word.

'I expect their doting relatives are lining up horse-whips to use on me right now, since I'm so ineligible,' he said ruefully.

'That would make you more irresistible to them,' she said lightly and she heard him groan at the idea of a pursuing pack of eager young ladies.

How dare he be so different from most young gentlemen she met? He didn't seem the least bit flattered that he looked like a hero to most of the young ladies he came across. It would help her forget Mr Carter's gruff strength and his kiss if only Colm Hancourt was an idler or even a deliberate charmer. He really was no help at all, she decided, and it was high time they parted as well. Stay together much longer and gossip would go round the area like wildfire, so she made herself rise to her feet and dipped a curtsy to the graceful bow he'd acquired with his new clothes.

'And here comes my darling stepmama. I trust Miss Mendaville-Rouste is recovered from her exertions on our behalf, Mama Chloe?'

'I think so, dear,' Chloe said with an insincere smile at the nearest listeners. 'I doubt the rest of us will get over them for at least a week,' she added in a hushed whisper for their ears alone.

Eve concluded her stepmother liked and trusted Mr Hancourt more than she wanted her to, since she had let him hear her private thoughts. Luckily he went to speak to Alice and looked more at ease with her than the giggling misses waiting to flirt with a duke's handsome nephew. They were soon drawn into a knot of young ladies and gentlemen noisily playing parlour games and Eve noted how much better Alice fitted in than usual. He really was kind and she hoped it was only kindness that made him insist Alice was included in every pleasure on offer. The idea of her friend wed to a man with so much pride and so little money made her fear for Alice's future happiness. She was concerned about her friend's welfare and Colm Hancourt would hate to depend on his wife. Even if Eve was rash enough to want him herself that would lie between them like a castle full of stumbling blocks and Alice's fortune dwarfed her own marriage portion.

'I like your Mr Hancourt, Eve,' Chloe announced happily and jolted Eve out of her troubled thoughts.

Eve met Chloe's violet gaze and frowned, then shook

her head to discourage her from saying such things. Chloe let her gaze linger speculatively on Mr Hancourt's half-tamed golden-brown locks currently so close to Alice's beautifully dressed blonde head and Alice did look comfortable at his side. A true friend would forget her own tumultuous emotions and be glad of a chance her friend could be happy with him. Not sure she was that saintly, Eve did her duty as daughter of the house for the rest of the evening without once telling the ladies probing for juicy gossip to go hang, but the effort made her headache thunder more fiercely than ever.

At last parents began to signal their offspring it was time to go home and Eve told herself off for being so glad the young women she had grown up with were carried off to rest. They would have to make do with their usual supply of young gentlemen when Mr Hancourt left the area and she felt a nasty little dip in her stomach at that reminder he would be gone in a few days. She frowned as one of those very young gentlemen bowed and managed to seem even less tempting than usual.

'G-goodnight, Miss W-Winterley,' the boy stammered, then almost ran after his parents with whatever he meant to ask unsaid.

'I feel honoured to have won a mere frown now I've seen your gorgon's glower, Miss Winterley,' the cause of her ill manners muttered as the last of the guests left and she realised she hadn't made her escape fast enough.

'Goodnight, Mr Hancourt,' she said severely.

'You could try to sound as if you mean it, ma'am.'

Ma'am? How dare he make her sound like an antidote? 'I wish you every second of slumber you deserve,' she said so carefully he should know he would not have many then.

'We will have to talk some time,' he warned, 'unless you have changed your mind about putting the past behind us?'

'Did I say I wanted to do that? And I'm not a gorgon.'

'I said you had a frown that would do credit to one, not that you resemble one in any other way, Miss Winterley,' he assured her solemnly.

'Our opinions of each other are irrelevant.'

'Which is probably as well, don't you think?' he asked with a weary smile.

'I do my best not to at this hour of the day,' she replied with an air of boredom that was a lie since being with him seemed to revitalise her. She would be counting the hours until a lazy dawn if she wasn't careful.

'Then you should seek your bed and rest,' he said, mock concern and something a lot more dangerous in his eyes and why had she ever thought him kind?

'If only my father's guests would do so I could,' she said grumpily. Being rude betrayed the fact he disturbed her so much her temper was constantly on edge and she had been determined to be coolly indifferent to him tonight. The bittersweet memory of one brief, disturbing kiss, snatched to add to their disguise as husband and wife, brought weak tears to her eyes for a disastrous moment, but she shook her head and refused to let them fall.

'May I hand you your candle then, Miss Winterley?'

he asked with a graceful flick of his long-fingered hand towards the patient footman waiting to hand them out and go to bed.

'Of course. My father and Bramble will be in as soon as the last of our guests are safely on their way home, Hastings, so you may go to bed at long last.'

'Thank you, Miss Eve. I can't say it won't be welcome tonight.'

'I'm sure it will, so please do as Lady Chloe said and leave the rest until morning,' Eve said, then went upstairs as fast as she could without extinguishing her candle, a rather mocking 'Goodnight' echoing in her ears from Mr Hancourt.

Chapter Thirteen

'Please sit down, Hancourt,' Lord Farenze said the next morning with a wave at the chair on the other side of his desk.

'Thank you, my lord.'

The dreams Colm had had last night made him angry with his mind for the fantasies it indulged in when he wasn't looking, so he hated to think what Miss Winterley's father would have to say about them if he knew. He met the man's almost-smile and waited for his host to say what he wanted.

'I suppose you think me rude for summoning you here like this?'

'You have something to say and I am here to listen, my lord.'

'You don't give much away, do you, Hancourt?'

'Not if I can avoid it, Lord Farenze.'

'It's all right, I didn't ask you here to warn you off again.'

'Thank you,' Colm said tightly.

He felt as if he was turning his back on something unique, but he would ignore this need to spend any moment he could contrive in Miss Winterley's company. They didn't have the mutual need, courage and passion to seize the present and damn the past. They were not in love and they would have to be fathoms deep in that to find a way round the obstacles that lay between them like razor-sharp rocks waiting to scupper them.

'I thought you would want to know what I learned from my late wife's diaries, since you found them and have a valid interest in parts of them.'

Colm wondered what good could come from Pamela's incendiary outpourings, but kept silent and waited.

'I have read them and the papers her landlord sent here after her death,' Lord Farenze said stiffly. 'There are questions about your father's affairs nobody seems to have picked up when he and my first wife died together and some secret he refused to reveal even to Pamela and she found that very irritating needless to say. I have presumed and asked a friend to find out when your fortune went missing and if some of it might be recoverable so many years on.'

Colm hated the idea of someone else knowing the full depths of his father's folly, but was almost convinced Lord Farenze meant well, as long as Colm avoided his daughter.

'You think me interfering?' his lordship asked with a cool look.

'I'm not sure I want to know how my father wasted my money. I don't want the old scandal woken up again and would not have thought you would either.'

'The man I speak of is so close mouthed he hardly lets his right hand know what the left is doing.'

Colm thought through the formidable set of noblemen this man belonged to. Sir Gideon Laughraine trailed a bigger scandal than even Colm had behind him, but the one-time lawyer was said to know more secrets than the whole of the government put together. If he was the man Lord Farenze was refusing to name, Colm had little reason to fear his father's secret would leak out by accident.

'I don't want my sister to suffer any more than she already has from our father's idiocy,' he admitted gruffly.

'Yet if there's a chance of recovering a competence you must take it. I doubt a lady spirited enough to rescue her brother from a battlefield will quail at some ancient gossip surfacing if it puts you both back where you should have been all along.'

'I don't know how you knew about what she did this summer; I hope you won't expose her to gossip.'

'I admire her too much for facing the slaughter after Waterloo for your sake to do that. You must be very proud of her.'

'I am, she is a sister in a million,' Colm admitted.

'So you should read my late wife's papers without prejudice for her sake.'

'I'll try, my lord.'

'Nicely non-committal. There's only one key to the Italian cabinet in your room,' Lord Farenze said as he handed it over. 'Don't mislay it or leave it in the lock.'

'Neither of us would want your first wife's papers out in the world, but they will keep me neatly out of your daughter's way until the Hancourts leave Dark-mere, won't they?'

'Eve is always my first consideration.'

'My sister is mine,' Colm said, but Nell had looked after herself *and* him this summer and he was beginning to doubt she would give up her independence, even if he had everything back his father took from him by some unlikely twist of fate.

'The day someone lays your first child in your arms that will change,' his lordship warned as if that explained everything.

Colm supposed his host was right when it came to his firstborn and he ordered his stupid imagination not to show him any more images of Eve Winterley wearily smiling at him from their bed as a nurse handed him *their* firstborn. It was a twist of the knife that made him want to rub his belly just to make sure there wasn't one sticking in him.

'Maybe,' he said and took the key Lord Farenze offered.

It took him two days of snatched hours to read everything, since the entire neighbourhood was vying to entertain the Duke and Duchess in their midst. In the time left over from dinners and dancing parties and sightseeing trips Colm plodded through every word. When he sat down to read he had to call on all his self-discipline not to sit and dream of what might have been, if this woman had never met his father. The more he read, the less he believed the jewels were lying about somewhere waiting to be discovered. The instant he heard of Pamela's scandalous demise, Derneley would have plundered the house where Lord Chris kept his mistress for any remnants of Colm's fortune to bankroll his own wild lifestyle with.

Colm paced the airy guest room he'd been allotted with a letter in his hand he would love to rip up and throw on the fire. It was obvious how Derneley kept his head above water so long. When he thought of all the waste and dissipation his mother's jewels must have financed Colm wanted to strike the man down, then dance on him. How had he not seen the obvious before? But he supposed he had no chance to grow up knowing which of the *ton* were sharp as knives and who was rackety and wild, or light in the upper storeys. After his stay at Derneley House Colm knew very well that Derneley cared for nothing but cards, brandy and loose women. It would never occur to Lady Derneley to argue Pamela's jewels rightfully belonged to Colm, but Colm hated his eldest uncle anew for what he had let happen because he was indifferent to, if not plain neglectful of, Lord Chris's children. Pamela was right for once; jealousy lay at the heart of it, Colm decided hotly, wondering how the last Duke let such a petty emotion twist him into the mean-spirited man Colm remembered.

He frowned out of his window at the gathering clouds and wondered if the gems Pamela loved so much had been cut up and reset to crown the Empress Josephine or even her martial husband, since they disappeared a year or two before he crowned himself Emperor of France. He grimaced and wondered if the old legend that the rubies were cursed was true and perhaps he and Nell were better off without them.

Which left the diamonds as his father had had no time to hand them over to his greedy mistress before they left England. They would buy a small manor and dower Nell, if his eldest uncle hadn't given them to his mistress as Pamela claimed. Even the most discreet and retiring kept woman would have worn the confounded things now and again though, wouldn't she? Whispers she had them would leak out, since legend said they were too spectacular to go unnoticed and his early memories of his mother wearing them agreed. If the last Duke had kept them, how dared he preach of the poverty and shame Lord Chris had left his children while he robbed them of their last chance of security?

For a moment Colm wanted another battle to fight or a wild horse to tame as a way to wear out his frustrated fury. Or perhaps he should gallop off to Linaire and demand access to the safe in his elder brother's private apartments that Uncle Horace had no desire to move into. They wouldn't be there, because open possession would mean his eldest uncle admitting he was a thief from beyond the grave. Any chance of seeing the diamonds again seemed like a mirage as he stared out of the lofty windows of this elegantly furnished room. Did he really want to drive himself mad chasing one of those?

Chapter Fourteen

Eve found out how humbling it felt to be less interesting than her dead mother when her father cunningly gave Colm Hancourt access to Pamela's papers in a way she couldn't share. Perhaps she was more like Pamela than she wanted to be, since she had this urge to rage and sulk until both the managing idiots admitted she had more right to see those diaries and letters than anyone else. Not that she *wanted* Mr Hancourt to consult her about his lost fortune and neither did she want to enslave a lover as her mother did every man she ever met so far as Eve could tell.

She wandered over to the windows of her favourite sitting room to stare into the driving rain at the restless grey sea being lashed against them by a fierce storm. Her mood fitted the day to perfection, but she must pay more attention to those around her and forget about Colm Hancourt. And as for that wretched, ridiculously haunting kiss they had exchanged in London, it wasn't even as if he meant to kiss her, she told her inner siren crossly. He had done it to pretend they were a man and wife looking for a little illicit privacy on a mad and mysterious night when everyone was masked. How could she feel so hot and confused by the very idea of that intimate encounter so many weeks after he'd turned away from her as easily as if it was only a means to an end?

'Is Miss Revereux's papa expected to join her for the Christmas season?' Alice asked her so casually Eve tried to forget her own blue devils and look harder at her friend's averted face. Of course, Alice must have a *tendre* for the gallant captain. How could she have missed that for so long?

'I am sure he will do his best to spend it with his beloved daughter, even if he has to row in a ship's boat up the Channel by himself,' she said as she recalled all the little signs she'd missed that Alice longed for a man she thought she couldn't have.

She was a fool not to have seen it sooner—pretty, clever Alice had neatly dodged a pack of eager suitors and fortune hunters over the years and done it so well nobody realised how odd it was that she hadn't married years ago. So how did Verity's father feel about Miss Clempson? He learnt to hide his feelings in an even harder school than Colm Hancourt, but was he indifferent to Alice? Something told her he was not, but thought he ought to be.

'He is touchingly devoted to Verity, isn't he?' Alice said so carefully Eve was sure she was right, if feeling stupid not to have seen how the land lay long ago.

'I don't think there's anything he wouldn't do to

make sure she's happy, even when it means seeing less of her and leaving her with us when he's away.'

'He's endured a great deal for love over the years, has he not? Lady Farenze is so lovely I suppose her sister was a rare beauty as well and he will never look at another woman as he must have done at his wife.'

'You only have to look at Verity to see how lovely her mother must have been, but I suspect Lady Daphne's character chimed well with the Captain's as well. Papa and my stepmother are very definite people and suit each other to the finest degree. I dare say Captain Revereux and his Lady Daphne loved as fiercely, however young they were at the time.'

'And a man who once felt such deep and passionate love might never settle for a lesser one after losing his wife so tragically and at such a young age,' Alice murmured so softly Eve wasn't even sure she was meant to hear.

Adam Revereux was a warrior and a man of real substance. Eve regarded him as an honorary uncle to match his daughter as her sister of the spirit, but her friend must see him in a different light. Trying to adjust her ideas about both parties, she realised Adam Revereux could only be about four and thirty and Alice was almost four and twenty. Of course Alice saw him as a handsome hero and Eve had just been mentally bemoaning the lack of potent single gentlemen to distract her from Colm Hancourt. Why wouldn't Alice look hard at the one under her nose as often as he could get to Darkmere to spend time with his daughter?

Eve preferred less dour and aloof gentlemen herself.

One a decade younger than Captain Revereux, and at the same time tried and tested by war and experience, appealed as that hard-edged commander never could. A man with unruly golden-brown hair that constantly disobeyed his attempts to keep it in military order and eyes every shade from defended dark brown to sparkling golden merriment when he remembered he was young and glad to be alive. The Eve she was trying to push into a corner and ignore sighed for her chosen hero and stuck out her tongue at the woman living in the real world, where she had no right to prefer Colm Hancourt to any other man and so many reasons not to.

'Maybe a person loves differently a second time, but that doesn't mean it must be a lesser feeling,' she finally managed to say and hoped it was what Alice wanted to hear. She certainly wanted to believe it herself, because if it wasn't true she might be in for a lonely life.

'I suppose I could be happy with the respect and companionship of a husband if he was content with me. It's more than most young women in my position expect from marriage. My parents want me settled and happy with a family of my own, but they will be disappointed if I don't wed above my station,' Alice said with a resigned shrug. 'Love is probably too much to ask.'

'Why would a husband *not* love you, Allie? You are clever and lovely and easily as accomplished as any of our neighbours. I like you a lot more than most of them as well, which must make you a paragon of all the feminine virtues, don't you think?' Eve joked in an attempt to lighten the atmosphere, lest they both sit here being brave about gentlemen they couldn't afford to love.

Wanting was a different matter; she couldn't seem to stop doing that so much her body felt as if it had taken on a life of its own the day she met Colm Hancourt and now went its own way, despite her resolution to stop wanting any more of his hot and mind-stealing kisses and this time with nobody watching.

'Good afternoon, Mr Hancourt.'

Colm hesitated, then decided he couldn't pretend not to hear and hope she would pass on when this was the only shelter easily available. 'Good afternoon, Miss Winterley. You should have stayed indoors and paced the long gallery rather than come outside in this.'

'Being used to a daily dose of bracing northern air I felt in need of some before dark. This is only heavy mist by our rough standards,' she said with a wry smile that did unfair things to his insides.

'It looks like rain to me,' he grumbled with a jaded look at it lashing past this colonnaded summerhouse he dearly wished he hadn't sought refuge in now.

'Aye, it does know how to rain here, which is one reason we normally spend this time of year in Somerset, but my father misses Darkmere and Chloe is happy where he is. I hope to persuade them I have no wish to spend the next Season in town and would far rather be here when my next little brother or sister is born.'

'If you can convince them they will be content to stay,' he said and wondered how he managed to sound cool when he was so hungry for her it hurt. It felt private and intimate in here watching the rain and cut off from the real world. Lord Farenze's warnings were so much thistledown in the wind with her standing far too close and his inner savage roaring for more than a stumbling conversation about the weather and her plans for next Season.

'I love it here,' she said with a glance out at the down-pour that looked almost affectionate, as if she realised it meant privacy as well. 'I spent my first sixteen years living at Darkmere most of the year. How can I not when it's rugged and beautiful and my home into the bargain?'

'It is a magnificent sight, even in the rain,' Colm conceded with a glance at the view of Darkmere Castle even a fine landscape gardener couldn't tame.

It stood rugged and undefeated against a lowering sky and the wild roar of the waves at its feet he could hear even from here. A tamer family might have re-treated from the thunder of storms that churned up the sea under the curtain wall night after night, but he sus-pected the warrior race she stemmed from gloried in the constant battle of sea and rock-hard shore. The Winter-leys probably regarded it as their family lullaby. Even as the product of a far tamer line, Colm felt the tug of primeval nature the Winterleys had breathed in since they were born. If he could sense something wild and restless in the air today, how could he expect Eve Win-terley not to? She had been feeling and probably fight-ing the unlimited passion of it all her life.

'It's a lot colder here than it is in the south,' she said as if the battle of reason over feeling was almost won for her. He wanted to yell out loud it never would be while she held such heady passions inside her that to kill them was an affront to nature. 'Even my father has been heard to admit the weather can be dour and relentless, so if my stepmama finds it too much we will decamp for the winter, I suppose.'

'Your people seem very happy to have the family here for Christmastide and I dare say spring even comes here some time before July.'

Now he was the one being polite and impersonally light-hearted. Even as the words left his lips the wild energy in the cold, wet air, the feeling fire was flowing through his veins and calling out to the same heat in hers was as real and primeval as the heavy beat of the waves against the shore. In this shadowy little shelter from the worst the elements could throw at them the battle between reason and unreason, the possible and the impossible but infinitely desirable still raged unspoken between them. Lucky he had so much experience of the fear and exhilaration and sheer terror of war, then, because this time he was fighting himself and part of her she didn't want to admit existed.

Miss Winterley shrugged and looked as if she didn't quite understand why he asked her if family came before her own wants and needs. He felt a stab of envy at her conviction kin were more important than everyone else and reminded himself not all families were like his. He had learnt to live with what was and what a timely reminder she was as remote as the moon. He couldn't reach for her and kiss her with a pinch of honour left to him.

'What were the winters like in Portugal and Spain?'

she asked as if she had no idea he was on the edge of a wildness close to the unleashed elements.

Yet there was tension in the very air that said she knew and felt it too and this was her way of keeping it under control. He tried to follow her lead. Those days seemed so long ago and yet so close it was as if he had just disembarked from a troop ship and couldn't quite grasp the new life he was stepping into. Men he thought of almost as brothers were dead; or with the regiment; or doing their best to fit the puzzle together of family and friends who didn't know how it felt to live each moment as if it was your last.

'In winter quarters we acted in plays, kicked up the odd lark, and did our best to keep the men occupied with shooting practice and any sports we could persuade them to take an interest in. It was an uphill battle with most. If they could get hold of liquor, drink their days and nights away and cavort with the local women they were content, if nigh ungovernable. In some ways Old Nosey is right about them being the scum of the earth, although most fought like demons. They were capable of heroism and even compassion, when not disgracing the uniform they wore and making me ashamed to be a British soldier, but I should not share all that with a lady.'

'Oh, stuff! Am I to pretend I'm blind and deaf to the world around me? I refuse to not listen and not see and hope to blast such silly expectations of me out of the water.' She paused, shot a look at him that said she suspected how grim and haunting some of his memories were, even if she had plenty more to say on the subject.

She still turned the subject. 'Rumour has it the Duke of Wellington loves the chase and hunted as often as possible—did you join in?'

'He and his staff did go out whenever they could, but only a few Light Bobs had horses of any sort, let alone beasts fine and fast enough to keep up with the beau's entourage.'

'That must have been galling,' she said carefully.

Colm wondered if he was too touchy about his strange status as not rich enough for the *ton* nor plain enough for a secretary. 'Not really, my parents preferred London to the country, so my sister and I didn't grow up longing to join in the chase as we might have if we spent more time at Linaire Park. It's a privilege I am happy to have been denied after hunting men for too long.'

'You ride as if you were born in the saddle.'

She had noticed how he rode then, had she? Devious Miss Winterley, he silently accused as he recalled her queenly indifference to him when she rode ahead of the pack on those sightseeing expeditions and left him to his fate as squire to more nervous lady riders. 'Trust my father to make sure his son could ride, even if he was less proud of my love of books and scholarship.'

'I dare say he couldn't understand the lure of learning when his own father and eldest brother despised it so deeply; your uncle has my sympathy.'

'Mine, too, now I know him better. As a child I heard tales of my father's useless scholar brother and thought he sounded more interesting than the rest. My eldest uncle raged about Aunt Barbara whenever he heard her name mentioned and she sounded much more fun than my other aunts as well. I admire them for ploughing their own furrow and leaving the rest of the family behind to wear themselves out with rage and endless arguments. Nothing he could say or do would alter things one iota and I suspect my Uncle Horace is more of a realist than the rest of us.'

'Whereas I suspect the Duke regrets not being here to fight for you and your sister when Lord Chris died and left you two at the mercy of his brother.'

'He would have wasted his breath and serenity and my uncle would still not have let him have any say in what happened to us.'

'And you were already too proud and stubborn to ask for his help? Be careful, Mr Hancourt, one day you might wake up and find yourself so alone you are no more than a rocky outcrop of humanity marooned in the midst of a desolately empty sea.'

'Like a latter-day Robinson Crusoe in the cold?'

'You can make a jest of it, but it sounds a very lonely existence. Be careful of hugging your past ills so close they blind you to the joys you could have in life, sir,' she said and something in her stormy gaze made his heart plunge, then race as the elemental forces around them seemed to crackle and shimmer and he heard a real peal of thunder over the harsh rhythm of the waves this time.

'You know how stupid of me it would be to expect more.'

'And you never take risks, do you, Mr Carter?' she taunted, knowing he had done so every day of his military career, but that wasn't the sort of risk she was talking about, was it?

'You don't know me,' he told her gruffly.

'You don't know yourself, so how can I?' she said and refused to take the warning.

'You won't want to know this, then,' he said gruffly, reaching for her as heat flared between them despite the December rain. The half-worn-out blast of the sea's fury on to the rocks below Darkmere stirred something forbidden and desperate in him and he was so weary of fighting it.

'Dare,' she ordered provocatively, no longer cool and composed Miss Winterley, but the warm and passionate Eve he longed for every night in his dreams.

What else could he do in the face of that but let go of his chains? He shaped her close, breached the chill and felt her warmth with a shiver that ran over his whole skin like fire. They shared heat body to body against the seeping cold of damp air salty from the sea. 'Lovely, reckless fool,' he chided as he gazed down into her challenging green-blue eyes and spoke the words against her mouth. Sharing air only added to the heat, however wet and cold it was outside. How could he care right now who might happen on them, then stumble back into the lowering afternoon upon finding out what Miss Winterley and young Hancourt were doing to pass the time?

'Yes,' she murmured by way of encouragement.

He was so strung out with hot curiosity he broke first. He bridged the final gap between them with a kiss that healed yet burned like wildfire at the same time. Haste, heat, fury, excitement, and a pinch of doubt, roared through him in a heady tangle he couldn't begin to sort out. Then she kissed him back and that wild rush of feelings melted into just her, just them.

'Closer,' he urged until they shifted together so the back wall of the summerhouse stopped them. He braced against it to keep her from the cold hardness of it and they were locked together now as if they might dissolve walls and pillars and damp December with their own version of summer heat and never mind hard angles, chilly marble and the ever more ferocious storm outside.

'Again,' she demanded back and he spared a moment to marvel at the insatiable recklessness of her as he shaped more of her delicious curves to him, sure enough of his damaged knee with all this solid masonry at his back to draw her up on to her tiptoes and feel the blessed suppleness of her against his body as she stretched sensual and catlike against his longer limbs and thundering heartbeat. She felt like silk and moonbeams and at the same time as real and supple and alive as if she was the embodiment of all womanhood as her name suggested.

'Eve,' he whispered reverently, then plunged them straight back into a passion he had never before dared imagine with another, even deeper kiss.

He was rampant by now; he tried to shelter her from the blatant fact of his manhood rigid and desperate for a virgin the last whispers of reason reminded him he could not have. A little feminine mewl of protest and she shimmered her body closer still, blasted that last shred of caution clean out of him and denied his never into an urgent maybe. Deepening his hungry kiss against her eager mouth, he felt every inch and sinew that marked him from her dissolve in a white-hot blaze. Was heat, need, possession or sheer madness first and foremost and which was his and which hers? Why would they want to know? Best if she didn't ask questions while he still had a faint rag of sanity to hang on to. Still he plunged his tongue into the depths of her mouth and she met it and played and parried and demanded right back, as if she had embraced this madness completely and wanted to know every inch of him intimately at this very moment.

He felt her curiosity, her dangerous wonder about the heat and need burning deep inside her and his heat and more obvious need against her. He groaned and heard all the warnings he should have sounded before this happened in his need as she shifted her long and slender limbs again. The beast in him roared and he had to clench his fists against the intriguing hollow at the small of her back to stop his hands lowering and moulding her neat buttocks as they strove towards risking a climax Miss Winterley and Colm Hancourt could not afford to reach.

'We can't,' he said his voice rusty and reluctant; the words making his throat ache at having to say them even this softly against the heat and reality of her sweet, teasing, daringly bold mouth and all the promises they couldn't make each other.

'I have to argue with that statement, Mr Hancourt,' she said as she lowered one wickedly wondering hand to shape the undeniable fact of his need and passion for her where it reared its eager length between them and made him a liar.

Once she gave, she gave everything, didn't she? She knew this was impossible just as grievously as he did, but she still refused to let him get away with pretending he didn't want her to the edge of madness and made him face the truth. The fact she trusted him so much humbled him and made him realise how vulnerable she had made herself. For a woman who spent her life doing her best to avoid scandal she was courting one right now and that made her braver than he was. Could he be more than a passing passion for a reasonably fit and healthy young male? He physically shook with the effort of not making that question irrelevant and taking everything she had so recklessly offered.

'We could,' he admitted in a voice so rasped with that admission he hardly recognised it as his.

She shivered with the awe of it, he could see that in her eyes, even if he didn't dare read more in the wide, dazed depths of the blue-green mystery looking back at him. He knew her so well and yet not at all. Even as he stared down at her spellbound and on the edge of something life altering, he saw her come back to the real life all around them and Mr Hancourt and Miss Winterley being heedless and wild together. Which would never do; he saw the fact of who he was reaffirm itself as her gaze sharpened and the misty blue of her passion-blurred gaze faded to sharp Winterley green. She had thrown off the spell and somehow he could not. He felt as if part of him was being ripped out and might bleed all over the fine resolutions he'd made never to let another human being hurt him again the day his eldest uncle told him his father was dead and he had no home and no fortune but what the latest Duke of Linaire chose to give him and he chose to give him very little. This wasn't about him right now though—it was all for her. He felt enough for Miss Eve Winterley to care more about her hurts than his own.

'But I never want to need this as desperately as my mother did and you don't dare love me insanely, the way your father loved her,' she said huskily, sounding so unlike her usual cool, clear self he knew it was an Eve no other man had heard, even if she was saying things he didn't want to face right now.

He clung to that with a sort of desperate, selfish possession; the owning of that once-in-a-lifetime intimacy for only a second or two was more than he had ever expected. *Let yourself rest here just for a moment*, the lover he might have been whispered, and he intended to gloat over it while he had the chance, *the chance of this is all you can have. One day she will rediscover this Eve for the man she can wed and bed and respect and how I wish he'd envy me the first sounds and sight and scent of her that he can't have, but won't know he's missed. He will have every other moment as her husband that I can't, but not this one.* Which only went to show how unworthy of her he really was, he told himself sternly, and prodded his conscience back into life.

'That sounds like a problem with no solution to me,' he admitted grimly and all the dank chilliness of the month and the place and the brooding bulk of Darkmere Castle in the rain lined up to shout *No* to the sensual meeting their bodies still longed for as they clung to each other as if they couldn't bear not to feel their heat and all the chances they were about to let go. An essential part of him he'd almost hoped was dead yearned for her with a want that seemed to go on for ever. Perhaps he was Lord Christopher's son in every way after all, he reflected bitterly as frustrated need jagged through him as hard as the French bullet that hit him six months ago.

Chapter Fifteen

'Eve Winterley! Whatever are you thinking of?' Lady Chloe's usually mellow contralto voice rose almost to a squeak from the other side of the fine curtain of rain and then she was in here with them. There was no need to wonder what the world thought of them kissing in the rain, it was there in her ladyship's pale face and wide, shocked eyes.

Eve pulled herself out of his arms at last and turned to meet her stepmother's horrified gaze. Colm tried hard to force his will on his body as he stood where she left him, like a piece of wreckage cast up by her wild northern sea. His heart stuttered with something he told himself must not be love when Eve deliberately stayed in front of him to hide his blatantly aroused state from her father's wife. Nobody had protected him so rashly since his mother died and that realisation threatened a hard place he didn't even know he had. To feel Eve put herself between him and Lady Farenze's appalled stare made him feel wild emotions that threatened to burst out in unsayable words and deeds that would make Eve's choices narrow unforgivably. He couldn't do that to her, so he tried hard to control unchained Colm while Lady Chloe's face revealed her search for words powerful enough to express her shock and disquiet.

'Probably what every healthy and unattached female thinks when she looks at a handsome young man,' Miss Winterley said as airily if they had been discussing the weather, or what they might have for dinner. She was Miss Winterley again now; warm, wanting Eve had been put in the corner until she said she was sorry.

'Well, you can't think any of those things about him,' Lady Chloe said with a helpless shrug and a gesture at Colm that said so much a lady like her did not want to speak out loud. 'What if somebody else saw you, Eve? You were kissing Mr Hancourt, nobody could think you reluctant the way you snuggled in his arms and gazed up at him spellbound like that. Your reputation would be in shreds right now if anyone but me had caught you and I can't bear to think what your father would say and do if he stumbled on you instead,' she added with a horror-struck shiver. The fear in her eyes at the thought of her husband duelling with a sharpshooter made Colm feel guilty and wonder if such terror might endanger her unborn child.

'I'm quite sure Mr Hancourt would offer for me if things were that dire,' Eve said soothingly, looking as if she thought he'd have to be horsewhipped to do so. He wanted to protest he could think of nothing he'd like better than to marry her right now, if she wasn't so horrified by the idea and he wasn't as poor as a church mouse.

'I would, that is I will. Will you marry me, Miss Winterley?' he heard himself ask like a simpleton.

'No, thank you, Mr Hancourt. My stepmother is not going to gossip and I refuse to wed a man who doesn't even want to love me,' Eve Winterley said with a bitter irony that lashed at his heart, because it sounded as if he'd really hurt her and he thought it was she who didn't want to love him.

'You are a Winterley, Eve, and I know by now every one of you is born reckless and bold, despite the years you spent pretending to be the exception, but I'm shocked at you, Mr Hancourt,' Lady Chloe scolded as if she couldn't quite cope with her stepdaughter's bleak logic and found it easier to blame him. 'I thought you far more honourable than your father until this very moment.'

'I'm quite shocked myself,' he admitted unwarily and felt Eve stiffen, as if she thought he was disowning their hasty, soul-branding kisses when they felt as if they'd altered him right down to the bones. 'Miss Winterley is everything a man could ever dream of in a wife, of course,' he added as if some demon was prodding him to make bad worse, 'but I can't make her marry me,' he said to her now rigid back. Even through her cloak and the gap rapidly growing between them he felt her fury at him for being such a clumsy great idiot and his father's son.

'We exchanged a curious kiss when trapped here with nothing else to do, Mama Chloe. Right now I really can't imagine why; maybe I wondered how the world might look if I actually liked you, Mr Hancourt,' she informed him regally, without bothering to turn round and glare at him.

'You do know I would never condemn you to wed a stray gentleman you happened to kiss so lightly, Eve?' her stepmother said earnestly.

Colm felt the dart her ladyship probably didn't even know she fired hit home and cursed opening his secret self to Miss Winterley's scorn. He must get that Colm back into the cage the idiot would just have to live in from now on and like it. Such joyous vulnerability was out of character and would soon wear off, he assured himself bleakly, but deep down he knew he was lying. Bidding Eve and Colm a final goodbye and a *No, never* would hurt for the rest of his life, but he'd do it for her sake. He straightened his shoulders and thought chilling thoughts before he was fit to step past Miss Winterley and meet Lady Chloe's bewildered gaze. She was far too much of a lady to look lower and remind them how eagerly he and Eve had been trying out that 'impulse' for size before she chanced on them anyway.

'Of course I do, darling.' Eve's queenly gaze softened for her stepmama. 'It took you ten years to wed my father for love. How could I expect you to push me into a lesser marriage because Mr Hancourt and I were silly enough to explore a fleeting urge when we were trapped here by the rain?'

'I doubt any gentleman likes to be dismissed so lightly, but for both your sakes I hope you were truly curious about that impulse and nothing more?'

'You arrived in good time, my lady, so I presume that will be that? What with me being who I am and Miss Winterley being a lady of high birth, good character and comfortable fortune,' Colm said flatly, deciding the best thing he could do was remove himself before any more distress was caused.

A stiff bow in Eve's direction and a slightly more graceful one for her stepmother and he left them to decide what to tell Lord Farenze. He'd seen enough of Lord and Lady Farenze to know the lady would not keep such a secret from her lord and Eve would not ask her to. Now he must wait for an order not to darken his lordship's doors again, or to eat grass before breakfast with him.

'You know how foolish it was to kiss Mr Hancourt where anyone might have seen you, Eve. I'm sure I don't need to tell you again how shocked I am,' Chloe said as Colm Hancourt's stiff-backed figure limped into the driving rain.

Eve could hear the lingering astonishment and horror in Chloe's voice and spared a moment to regret Chloe had come upon them when she did for her own sake, not just because she felt cold and forsaken standing here watching Colm limp off to brood alone. He hadn't taken the path back to the Castle, so he must be heading for the cliffs above the raging sea Eve could hear thundering against them from here. She hoped he'd be careful and realise how dangerous Darkmere was for the unwary on a day like this, then sighed for her own stupidity. The man had survived troop ships crossing the Bay of Biscay in winter; who knew how many skirmishes and pitched battles; forced marches and desperate retreats over far worse terrain than any peaceful England had to offer, and then there was Waterloo. He didn't know this sometimes wild and capricious coast, though, and part of her seemed to have gone with him, to stand at his shoulder and fret over slippery paths and shifting soil. How was a man as proud and prickly as Colm Hancourt going to look out for them as he should when his thoughts were occupied with what they had not quite done today?

'Papa is sure to have warned him about the cliffs and the danger of losing his footing in the rain,' she reassured herself softly.

This time she actually felt her stepmother's acute mind focus sharply on her as she wondered how deep the damage had gone between her stepchild and the stubborn, bungling great idiot of a man. Right now Chloe must be thinking she should have kept Colm away from Darkmere, rather than invited him here as if he were a harmless youth. Anxiety for his safety nagged at Eve like a sore tooth and argued she should not have been so bitter and angry when he fumbled out that forced proposal. If she hadn't lashed out at him in hurt and frustration he would have gone to find her father to make that ridiculous offer real and he wouldn't be out there on the cliffs in a raging storm right now.

'And before you ask, no, I don't know what I feel, Chloe,' she added absently. Those devastating kisses must be shut in a corner of her mind to think about after she had coped with here and now.

'I might be able to help you,' Chloe said, an unexpected thread of laughter in her voice. 'Such feelings can creep up on you all unwanted and unlooked for, but pretending they don't exist is a waste of time.'

Chloe was obviously thinking about her own gruff, tardy and reluctant suitor from the faraway look Eve had become familiar with—Papa and Chloe always wore it when they were thinking about each other and wondering why they had been such idiots for so long. Then Chloe's acute violet eyes focused on her and Eve fidgeted at the thought of all the uncomfortable questions that would probably come next.

'I suppose if you take his father and your mother out of the equation, Mr Hancourt *is* a brave and honourable man,' Chloe said as if logic had overcome her initial shock. 'Don't look at me as if I've grown two heads, Eve; you must like him to have done what you did with him this afternoon.'

'I really don't see what that's got to do with the price of fish,' Eve muttered.

Whipping up her own fury at his clumsy proposal and unspoken rejection of all they could be to one another might block out this feeling she had lost something crucial to her future happiness this afternoon. He kissed her as if she was all he ever wanted in a woman, then limped away with that tight, closed expression she recognised from the night she met Mr Carter. How dare he make her feel so confused and shaken and confoundedly empty as she did right now, standing here agonising about whether to follow him or stay with Chloe?

'You weren't exactly struggling in his arms, my love,

and you must know your demons if you want to banish them,' Chloe cautioned with an anxious look down that sodden and rain-blurred cliff path as if she was afraid Colm meant far too much to her stepdaughter as well.

'As you did, I suppose?'

'Refusing to admit our feelings cost your father and me so much I can hardly bear to look back at all those wasted years.'

'But this is different and you saw how completely Mr Hancourt was himself again when he walked away. Neither of us can change the past.'

'So it's as well you don't love him then, isn't it?' Chloe said with the stubbornly practical logic Eve usually valued, but didn't feel in the least bit soothed by right now.

'Except if he wasn't Lord Chris's son, I think I might,' she admitted on a long sigh that did justice to this grey and sodden day.

'Then he wouldn't be the man you could fall in love with in the first place, would he?'

'True, a Lord Chris with all his flash and glamour and selfishness would never do for me. He was the perfect mate for my mother though, wasn't he?' Eve said bitterly, thinking the worst crime those two ever committed was happening now.

Their shades were standing between her and a man of such depth and character it was impossible not to want to be closer to him somehow. Because of what they did, she had to say goodbye to a *perhaps* that could have been wonderful. Because of them Colm didn't trust himself to love Pamela's daughter.

'I think they both deserve to be forgotten,' her step-mother said as sadly as if she knew exactly what Eve was thinking and it was impossible to make life easier for her.

The fact she wanted to made Eve love her more and she forgave Chloe for coming on her and Colm a little too soon for the tortuous ache of unsatisfied need that still ground inside her. It felt like a warning she might never recover if she thought too hard about what had happened, and what had not.

'Yet as long as Mr Hancourt exists they never will be and I refuse to live in their shadow any longer,' she said practically.

That was it, then, she would soon be her old sensible self again and might even be safe from feeling too much once again. Except she doubted folly worked backwards like that. This tender ache inside said being sensible never felt as glorious as being reckless and headlong and… Her supposedly clever mind took over at that point and told her not to listen to her inner wanton.

'Your mother and Mr Hancourt's father are so firmly lodged in both your heads I wonder if you can see past them,' Chloe surprised her by saying and now she had to revise her prejudices through her stepmother's eyes.

'Then you think I exaggerate?' she asked, the shock of wondering if she was the person she thought she was jarring through her for the second time today, joining the tension of watching that dratted cliff path in the hope Colm would come back down it and relieve her mind of its greatest anxiety to date.

'No, what they did and how they died was dreadful,

in both senses. But that was fifteen years ago and this is now—your life, Eve, and not theirs. If you did happen to love Mr Hancourt it would be hard for you to be watched by the gossip mongers all the time, but it would be worth it, believe me.'

'Luckily we don't love each other,' Eve said flatly, feeling as if she was the one standing on an imaginary cliff looking down at awe-inspiring stormy waters, as she suspected Colm was doing in reality right now, and refusing to even consider that disaster. 'Do you think he'll be safe on a rocky path with a bad leg and all that spray and rain buffeting at him?' she added unwarily.

'Since you don't love him, why would you care?' her cunning stepmother asked and anyone would think Chloe wanted her to love the stubborn great idiot.

'He is a guest here, of course I care about his welfare. Think of the scandal if Lord Chris's son fell into the sea from a cliff near Darkmere and drowned.'

Even saying such a terrible thing out loud made her want to scream a denial at the gods and rush after him, pull him to safety and rage at him for taking such a risk with himself in the first place.

That Eve whispered, *To hell with any risk that we might compromise each other once and for all by returning to Darkmere sodden and storm-wild together with our clothes so wet we might as well be naked.*

The real Eve still wanted to be with him, but she cursed her doubts for not falling away in the face of the tragedy it would be if Colm Hancourt fell to his death from those rocks because they wouldn't have each other as lovers, despite that life-changing kiss.

'Think of his poor uncle and aunt rather and he's more than his father's son to the rest of us now we've met him. We had best go back to the castle and send out a rescue party, don't you think?' Chloe said practically.

'Yes, I thought he would come back when he saw how wild it must be out there, but he's not going to until someone talks some sense into him, is he?'

Eve sighed at her own cowardice for not admitting how desolate she would be if anything happened to him and set out with her stepmother through the gloom of the December afternoon as fast as she dared with Chloe's pregnancy and this terrible heaviness in Eve's heart to slow them down. For some reason every step she took away from the cliff path and Colm felt heavy and wrong, as if she was the only one who ought to go after him and risk what he was risking. They were both too stubborn to let themselves take that last step into loving one another together, but he was lodged so firmly in her head and heart it felt as if any fate that befell him would stay with her for ever as well.

She felt... Eve paused her thoughts and wondered if she even knew how she felt about this tangle of emotions fighting for breath inside her. She felt desperate, she finally realised with a shock of horrified honesty. So she made a breathless apology to Chloe, then ran ahead as fast as she dared go. It would do Colm no good if she slid into the nearest muddy hollow and hit the ground at speed and needed rescuing herself, so she concentrated on remembering every path for hazards and sped on with heart racing and a suspicion she cared more about Colm Hancourt's well-being than was good for either of them.

* * *

Standing brooding about things he couldn't change wasn't doing any good, but Colm couldn't seem to uproot himself and tamely plod back to the castle in order to get out of this infernal rain. That would mean facing the world as if nothing much had happened and it had. The hypnotic boom of furious waves pounding the sternly indifferent rock Darkmere was built on beat in time with his busy heart and made him wish he had even a thread of poetry in him. He thought it a blessing he lacked the sensitivity of a poet as he struggled to live the life his eldest uncle and the Almighty had laid out when he was little more than a child. Now unformed words beat in his soul and he'd love to shout them at the angry sky, launch fury back at the mighty sea and defy stars he couldn't see through the depth of rain in the clouds and an early dusk.

Damn fool, he railed at himself instead. *Careless, reckless fool.* The feel of her in his arms still haunted him, as if *Evelina Winterley* was printed on his skin. To open himself up to so much pain, such needless hurt; didn't that make him as guilty of stupidity as their parents? He had made the idiot's move that let her inside his barriers and she walked into Fort Colm as if she belonged. He left her behind now with an effort that still tore at him like a wound, but she was still doing something strong and deep to him he dare not define. Part of him wanted to get away, to ride into the storm, mud, danger and darkness; a saner part refused to put his horse through so much and so he stood here like a monument to folly and glared down at the pounding sea.

A vast wave broke on black rocks that seemed even further away now it was almost dark. The mighty surge of spray even reached up here as a wave broke on the cliff edge to soak any part of him not already drenched in salty fury. He shook his head like a wet dog and roared back at the storm in wordless outrage. All this majestic madness was going on around him and he was so wound up in Eve Winterley and wanting, needing, demanding things he could never have from her. Even vast, angry nature seemed smaller than the maelstrom inside him. Pain stretched from his head and heart to his gut and shook him with a powerful longing he didn't even want to think about.

By now discomfort should have driven her out of his head, but she was still there. Still unattainable, still herself, still uniquely alive for him as no other woman ever would be now, thanks to her. If the ancient, capricious gods of Olympus still ruled the world he might think his birth offended one of them—Poseidon himself perhaps, the cross-grained old thunderer of legend.

'What the devil are you doing out here, you young fool?' his host demanded, sounding almost as furious as that imaginary god of the sea.

'Being a damned fool,' he shouted above the storm.

Lord Farenze shook water out of his own rain-plastered dark locks and motioned Colm impatiently inland. 'Grab my hand and make very sure you don't slip and pull both of us to our deaths. I have no mind to chase you into hell for taking such a risk,' he said dourly, but still held out that hand and defied Colm not to step away from the cliff edge and the towering spray sniping at them from so far below he was dizzy and a little sick at the thought of the rocks waiting if he put a foot wrong and Eve's father made a hasty grab, then plunged in after him.

Feeling the locked agony of standing too long on his bad leg and waving the man away, Colm flexed his abused limb until it felt strong enough to bear his weight again. He backed slowly away from perdition, ignoring the angry lord at his back until they were safe and could yell at one another in relative peace.

Chapter Sixteen

'Why?' Lord Farenze demanded. 'Why did you take such a stupid risk?'

'It wasn't much of a risk until you came,' Colm replied, sounding like a sulky boy even to himself.

'You're not immortal, despite managing to survive more battles in your short life than most men have nightmares about in three-score years and ten. What about your sister and aunt and uncle? For some odd reason they seem fond of you. How do you think they would feel if you lost your life for the sake of an urge to dare the devil?' The angry Viscount paused and shot Colm an even more furious look through the increasing gloom and lashing rain. 'It *was* only recklessness, wasn't it?' he added, looking as if he'd land Colm a facer if he'd been working himself up to launch into the abyss and end his time on earth.

'I survived death in battle too many times to court it lightly now.'

'Nice to know you're just an ordinary looby and not a coward then.'

'I should save your praise until you hear why I *am* out here,' Colm shouted over the receding thunder of the waves as they walked cautiously away from immediate danger through this incessant rain and the ever-thickening gloom.

'Never mind that now, we need to get warm and dry and call all the other wet and cold men looking for you back in before you have them on your conscience as well.'

'You should have left me to take my chance with the sea, idiots like me rarely come to harm.'

'And have the world whisper I did away with the son of my first wife's lover one dark night on the cliffs of my sinister northern stronghold?'

'I refuse to let every turn in my road lead me back to them,' Colm railed uselessly against fate, then shook his head and signalled that he could match whatever pace the Viscount set and wanted to get those searchers in too, since it was his fault they were out there in the first place.

'I doubt even they were this mad,' the man said grimly and set such a punishing speed neither of them had breath to argue.

Colm had to add several cans of hot water to his bath water before he felt even close to warm again. Now he was fighting the last hint of a chill in his bones to re-assure his uncle and aunt all was well with him. Aunt Barbara had put aside her latest picture to concentrate on him like a hen with one chick. Uncle Horace used the excuse of escaping her fussing while he helped his nephew strip off his soaked clothes and climb into the bath as if he was a boy again. Colm watched them with rueful affection now and decided he had family beside his stubborn sister after all. He might not have much in material terms, but their love and respect was priceless to someone who had walked alone as long as him.

'Better?' Aunt Barbara demanded once he was dressed and furnished with a brandy. Only when he finished the fiery spirit did he finally feel warm again.

'Yes,' he agreed with a sigh.

'Then you had best have good reason for giving us such a fright, lad,' his uncle told him sternly. 'And your aunt will lose her temper if it isn't up to scratch.'

'I kissed Miss Winterley,' he admitted baldly, then wondered if he was still in a state of shock to admit it out loud. No point pretending it wasn't a calamity and, if he was about to be evicted from Darkmere, they ought to know why.

'Oh,' said his uncle blankly, as if he understood why Colm had to stand on a cliff edge in the middle of a storm and brood now.

'Was the young lady shocked and angry, or frightened half to death, perhaps?' his aunt asked him sharply.

'Not at the time, although I suspect she may be by now.'

'She didn't fight you off or demand you desist immediately?'

'No, she did neither of those things,' Colm said carefully, trying not to revisit the way she had reacted to his kiss in this quiet room with all their attention centred on him and something deep and painful in his heart he'd best not think about.

'She put her face aside as soon as she was able to and treated you with frigid disdain, perhaps?' Aunt Barbara persisted and he had to control an urge to shout *no*, then go and find Miss Winterley to rage at her for not doing exactly that.

'No,' he answered as blankly as he could manage.

He felt confused and on edge, but there was no point blaming Eve. He couldn't let himself believe a woman like her could love a man like him. With his father's example in front of him he wasn't sure he knew what love was anyway. He didn't want to ignore the rest of the world or wrap Eve up in a cocoon where he could worship her all day and every night and to the devil with everyone else. He could still see people around him and responded to them perhaps a little more than before he met her. So he couldn't possibly be in love with her, could he?

And what were her feelings about him? Maybe the passion that exploded between them in that confounded summerhouse had made her hate him. She feared her own desires; he knew that because she guarded her true self so fiercely. Now he knew about the passionate, desirable, vulnerable creature behind that careful shield of hers he could quite see why. Again, he wanted to find her and shake her, then make her listen when he told her she was her own woman and totally desirable in her own right. She had no need to look for her mother in herself and say a polite, *No, thank you*, to a side of her she had kept walled up for too long.

Not that he wanted her to go about the countryside kissing any fool who forgot to ask her if she minded, of course. The thought of Eve in another man's arms made him wish he'd stayed on that cliff until the fierce night cooled his ardour *and* his temper. He had to get away from Darkmere, he decided with a shudder. The frown of concern on his uncle's face after that giveaway shiver brought him back to here and now and reminded him he was trying to look warm and recovered from whatever ailed him. Calm and collected might take longer.

'If Miss Winterley did none of those things I conclude she kissed you back,' Aunt Barbara broke the near silence in this comfortable fire-lit room to quiz him.

How could he admit that a young lady he wasn't going to marry had done anything of the kind, even to his aunt? Somehow he couldn't quite lie to her either.

'Ah, so she did exactly that,' she said as if his silence explained everything.

Colm wondered what she was up to when she looked quietly satisfied with the results of digging about in his most tender places. Aunt Barbara knew perfectly well he was no fit mate for the daughter of the house. The best thing he could do was leave now he'd made such a damned fool of himself, so why was his aunt happy he must struggle to forget Eve Winterley and those fiery, unique kisses? He had been almost ready to admit this part of his family liked him as well.

It was beginning to dawn on him how much he had changed these last few weeks. He'd dreamt of living secure and respected in a quiet country house so often when the Duke of Wellington's army waited on the verge of battle, but was that really all he wanted out of life? On retreat from unbeatable odds, when any sort of home seemed a million miles away, he would dream his sister was restored to her proper position in life in that neat little manor house and he was free to court a quiet and contented wife to share it with them.

In the real world Nell would be bored in a month and their respectable neighbours would still look down their noses at the progeny of the most scandalous lord of his generation and avoid them. Colm's faceless dream wife would have grown shrill and a lot less content when the gossips mulled over the past and speculated how long it would take him to fall in love with a painted hussy and run off with her. Ah well, none of it would happen now and he was sure his grandfather's fabled wealth had been spent, whatever Lord Farenze said to the contrary. Even the jewels had gone to fund Derneley's extravagant lifestyle, so the fact it was all a castle in Spain didn't matter now. As long as his uncle was alive Colm had work and a chance to invest his salary and make his own money. He was the grandson of a nabob; he ought to have some of Joseph Lambury's fabled luck and cunning in him. It was high time Colm Hancourt became his own man—he was beginning not to like the one his father and eldest uncle made him into.

'Miss Winterley is not at all like her mother,' he said carefully into a thoughtful silence. Eve had a generosity of spirit, an untapped warmth and joy that argued she was the very opposite of her faithless, heartless dam.

'Perhaps you should explain that to the young lady herself,' his uncle said with a weary sigh, as if he was tired of tiptoeing round the subject. 'And why do you take your father's sins on your shoulders, Colm? Chris didn't feel the burden of them, so why do you?'

'Probably because he didn't,' Colm admitted after thinking carefully. 'Miss Winterley's mother refused to own up to a single flaw, let alone the cartload she rejoiced in, but because of those two heedless idiots Miss Winterley and I cannot afford to look at each other as we did this afternoon.'

'Why ever not?' his aunt challenged, looking as if she would shake him if she could reach. 'Because society says so? That's no reason not to do whatever needs to be done in the real world we live in day by day, Colm. Society is only for best and God judges our actions, not them. It's high time you stopped letting your father and Augustus spoil your life and as for the opinions of shallow idiots who never did a proper day's work in their lives, I can't believe you listen to a word they say, let alone allowing them to dictate whom you can or cannot love.'

'Best not let those idiots hear you, my dear,' the Duke of Linaire said placidly, as if he agreed with everything else his wife said.

Loving Eve, if she loved him back, would risk cutting her off from her family and secure place in society. Even if he wasn't Colm Hancourt, he was still a nobleman's secretary, not the match her family must have hoped for all her life.

'So you think I let the gossips rule my life?' Colm said, wondering if his aunt wasn't right.

'Not just them, but you were too young to fight what

my brothers did after Chris died,' his uncle put in sadly. 'They bundled you off to some charity school, then the army without giving you a chance to make sense of any of it, so I suppose it's little wonder you got things out of proportion. Yet you endured all that and emerged a hero and I don't know how to make you see yourself as you really are.'

'I'm no hero; all I did was survive.'

The thought of all those who did not made Colm shake his head and frown at the fire. None of them felt anything now, not the warmth of a fire, or the elemental passions of the storm raging outside the castle walls. He sat here warm and cosseted and feeling guilty about Eve and they were in the cold ground. Somehow the thought of what they had lost so young made the weight on his shoulders feel heavier than when he only had Eve to feel empty and protective and wretched about.

'You shrug off that description and claim other men behaved better in the Peninsula and during that terrible business last summer, but your aunt and I have come to know you, Colm. A good man stands in those shoes you fought so hard not to have, along with the few clothes fit for my nephew we nearly had to force you into when you finally came home.'

'Thank you for them and I admit Carter was a mask I hid behind.' The business of killing and surviving had gone on so long Colm refused to think beyond Carter and his next march or the best shot to take with the Baker rifle no true gentleman would carry as he skirmished with his men beyond the main army.

'I suppose you were too busy staying alive to be Colm Hancourt at the time,' his aunt excused him.

'There was plenty of time to think when we were in winter quarters, too much at times, but I refused to do it,' Colm admitted.

'At a time like that a young man needs to get through the next fight, not worry about things that might never happen,' his uncle said and Colm realised these two would always find an excuse for him.

'You may be right, Uncle,' he said lightly. He was lucky to be loved by three good people, but the reason they were having this conversation in the first place almost robbed him of joy. 'I can't replace one fantasy with another though, can I?'

'You could if you loved the girl,' Aunt Barbara argued.

'We Hancourts make such a poor fist of love it's probably best if I don't attempt it,' he said with a weak attempt at a smile, 'I'm sure the lady agrees.'

'Oh, I don't know, I once met a stubborn idiot who wore a hair shirt that didn't belong to him either and I fell deep in love with him, despite his bad habits. Who is to say who will appeal to a young lady weary of the ordinary sort of fool she can meet every day on the marriage mart?' the Duchess of Linaire summed up the younger gentlemen of the *ton* with magnificent contempt.

'Thank you, Aunt Barbara.'

'Don't mention it, my boy,' she said smartly, rose to her feet and tucked her hand in his elbow when he did the same, then she nodded as if it was the right thing to do when the Duke of Linaire stepped back to let his family precede him.

So they went down to dinner and whatever declarations his aunt and uncle made about his place in their lives with that touching gesture, Colm was no more than a duty acquaintance for the notice Miss Winterley took of him. Everything they almost were this afternoon made Colm wonder if he might choke on the fine dinner he worked his way through as if his life depended on it. Refusing port and painfully polite conversation in the drawing room afterwards, he retired to his room to brood about young ladies who kissed as if their hearts were in every ragged breath and racing pulse, then sat down to eat their dinner a few feet away and ignored him as if he was part of the furnishings.

'We'll have to stay until Monday, my boy,' Colm's uncle told him the next morning when he suggested leaving as soon as everything could be packed and ready. 'If we scramble off on a Saturday we must stay at an inn tomorrow and it will seem as if we fell out with the Winterleys. Since we came here to mend a quarrel, we can't set tongues wagging again and if we leave on Monday we might even seem sensible if we're not careful.'

'I could paint something special on our way home. An icy waterfall, frozen in its tracks would do nicely,' his aunt said with a dreamy smile.

'The boy's not a miracle worker, Barb, and it'll be too mild to freeze a millpond this side of the New Year,' the Duke argued.

'Will it? What about the Pyrenees, then?' she asked Colm half seriously.

'At this time of year they are bitterly cold, treacherous and unfit for man or beast after so many years of all-out war.'

'Maybe the Alps would be better,' she said with a thoughtful frown.

'Perhaps next year,' the Duke said as if he meant it and Colm only just bit back a groan.

Now Bonaparte was truly beaten travellers had no limits except the depth of their pockets and the strength of their nerves. If his aunt and uncle chose to travel he would have to go with them and never mind this feeling he'd seen quite enough of the world to be going on with. He couldn't let them be exploited by renegades and rogues posing as couriers or interpreters to the unwary as British travellers flocked over the Channel after so many years pent up on their own island.

Somehow the thought of being hundreds of miles and several countries away from Eve Winterley made him feel cold to his bones and that was ridiculous. Staying here another two days with that passionate encounter looming over him like the sword of Damocles should horrify him. He had two days to feel sheepish and silly under her father's vigilant gaze and take in enough of Miss Winterley to last him a lifetime. Best if he avoided her then; he didn't need any more images of her to haunt him as if they had truly become lovers.

'Aunt Barbara, can you endure company on one of your sketching outings this morning?' he asked, rather desperate to avoid Eve and her family until he could ride away from this place she loved so much.

'Of course, I haven't caught the sun on the sea as I'd like and it looks as if we shall see more than a glimmer of it this morning at long last. We might as well find out if you remember anything you learnt about drawing as a boy while we're out there,' she agreed happily, but could he really afford to open himself to another way of feeling when he had so many of them to cope with already?

Chapter Seventeen

'I have lived at Darkmere most of my life, but still don't understand our weather,' Eve told the Duke of Linaire as they strolled down to the beach below the castle in placid sunlight later that morning.

'It is a fine day after that impressive storm last night,' the Duke answered with the vague smile that hid his true thoughts about yesterday quite beautifully.

'The wind from the sea is cold though,' she persisted, determined to talk about the elements as they took the gentlest path to the sea with a small procession of servants picking their way down it some distance behind them.

'You really don't need to worry about my wife, Miss Winterley. I may seem preoccupied to a busy young lady like you, but I make sure Barbara is well wrapped up before she goes outside. She's too eager to be out and about to bother with aught but her paintbox if I don't watch her. She will be glad of that coffee and soup your people are carrying so diligently by now though, for all she claims not to notice anything but the scene in front of her when the muse is upon her and the light just right.'

'The Duchess is a dedicated artist,' Eve observed, cross with her own inability to go beyond the obvious this morning. The simple mechanisms of every day got you through bigger things and what had happened yesterday seemed almost too big to think about right now.

'She is and I'm proud of her. It's as well neither of us enjoy the state my late father and brother always insisted on though. We couldn't afford it and we're far too old to learn after years of going our own way. We did well enough with my wife's portion and our earnings after my father cut me off when I ran away from an arranged marriage and wed Barbara instead.'

Now why did she think that was a veiled reference to Colm and who her family thought was a suitable husband and who wasn't suitable at all? Not that Mr Hancourt would offer again and she wouldn't accept him if he did. So why was the Duke quietly letting her know love was more important than money and family expectations?

'What a hard man the last Duke was. He stood by while his father treated you so coldly, then he rejected Mr Hancourt and his sister after their father died,' she said impulsively then she thought a little harder about what she had said. 'I'm so sorry, your Grace, your brother has hardly been dead a twelve month and I dare say you are still mourning him.'

'Oh, no, I don't pretend to be grief-stricken. Gus did his best to control us all while he did what he pleased and pretended to be saintly as an archbishop. My youngest brother's actions were deplorable and I'm very sorry for the shadow they have cast over your life and my nephew's, but I liked Chris a lot more than my other two brothers.'

'He wasn't a very reliable parent though, was he?' she said, thinking how lucky she was her father had put her welfare ahead of his own.

'I can hardly imagine a worse one, Miss Winterley,' the Duke replied quietly. 'But at least my wife filled the dark corners in *my* life with her verve and imagination. Would my nephew could be as lucky in a wife, if he'd only get on and marry one.'

'I suppose most of our kind wed for the sake of a family and connections,' she managed casually. The thought of Colm loving and marrying another woman stung her bitterly. She felt wrapped up in darkness on a day when low December sun slanted down on a sea blue-grey and silvered in the sun with the sky serene and clear above it and yesterday's storm and fury impossible.

'I hope you don't expect so little from marriage, Miss Winterley,' the Duke said a little too seriously.

Eve stayed silent, struggling with how she might feel if Colm married a rich young woman who considered him too fine a catch to get away. Thinking about heiresses made her consider Alice and understand her friend's rather wistful cynicism about the world. If Alice had really loved Verity's father from afar all these years, how painful it must be to love a man who didn't seem to have noticed her. She didn't want Alice to give up on her dream and settle for someone poor and well connected like Colm Hancourt. Eve wanted him too much herself to make that idea at all acceptable. She struggled with the dilemma of trying to stay away if one of her closest friends married the man she longed for so much, try as she might to ignore him. Now she and the Duke were picking their way over the rocks newly rearranged by the storm as the path began to broaden out and she should stop worrying who the wretched man might marry and watch her step. Excellent, she would learn to be grateful for that storm yet.

'Your papa and stepmother seem blessed in their marriage, so mutual love cannot be that rare among the *ton*,' the Duke persisted gently.

'Ah, but I have my mother's poor example to make me a doubter, your Grace,' Eve said with a would-be careless shrug. 'I would as soon not wed at all as waste my life searching for a perfect lover and never find him.'

'You fear the marriage bed will wake similar demons in you to the ones that drove your mother then?' the Duke asked a question nobody else had ever dared.

Eve gasped in shock and was very glad the servants had fallen behind to flirt and laugh with each other out of earshot. Even Chloe would think twice about asking her that and it was outrageous of the man to even mention such a possibility, but the memory of how it felt to burn in Colm's arms whispered was his uncle right? Did her shame and contempt for Pamela stand in the way of accepting one of the eager young men who asked her to marry him? No, she decided, as she conducted a mental review of her suitors and couldn't consider being intimate with a single one without a shudder.

Her next silly idea about wedding and bedding Colm instead sent a shudder through her that had nothing at all to do with being cold.

'Perhaps,' she said at last, because how could she take offence and storm off when the idea of being scandalously close to this man's nephew and enjoying it as much as she had last time crept into the least-visited corners of her mind and settled in as if it belonged? He seemed so concerned for Colm's happiness and well-being it would feel hard and brittle of her to snap a ladylike denial, then stalk off in a huff.

'You seem very much yourself to me, Miss Winterley,' the Duke went on gently. 'So why do you allow your mother's past sins to shape your future?'

It was a fair question, considering they had wandered so far from the nothings that usually passed for polite conversation. The Duke's good intentions practically shone out of the brown eyes she suddenly saw were very like his nephew's and far more acute than he let most people know.

'Your particular demon looks the opposite of Pamela Verdoyne's to me,' he continued. 'Could it be you risk loving the right man too much, my dear? The first Lady Farenze wasn't capable of love and it was my brother's tragedy to love her even so, but your father and stepmother's story proves there are very strong passions in the Winterleys and I doubt you're immune to them. Don't let the life you could have with the right man slip through your fingers simply because your mother died with her lover a decade and a half ago.'

Silence fell between them and how could she fill it

with neat little observations on the day and the scene in front of them now?

'It isn't what we do that sometimes haunts us like fierce ghosts; it's what we don't do,' the Duke added soberly.

She watched his gaze focus on the shore now they were past the last curve in the cliff path and she finally saw the Duchess of Linaire sitting next to her husband's stubborn nephew. She should have known, she decided, wanting to glare furiously at the devious man who brought her here as if he had no idea how she and Colm were together yesterday. Yet how could she condemn the Duke when he was clearly a good man with a bad conscience about his nephew? She let the tug of simply looking at Colm off the leash for a weak moment. Standing next to a man who had already seen too many of her secrets, she still let herself appreciate the way sunlight picked out the gold in Colm's unruly mane and outlined his lithely powerful shoulders and lean hips. His gaze was fixed on the wonders of nature with a fierce intensity Eve let herself know she wished was focused on her instead. He had no idea she was here; that she could stand spellbound by such a vigorous young man when he forgot to be humbled by war and life for an hour or two. The footmen and maids catching up with them at her back would see how her eyes lingered on Colm Hancourt's finer points and vivid presence if she wasn't careful, so she wrenched her gaze away from him and gave her companion a look of queenly reproach.

'Is Mr Hancourt your ghost, sir?' she demanded, but

he had brought her here and asked outrageous questions, so she had the right. 'If so, he haunts you and not me.'

'Ah, but the boy hasn't left Darkmere yet, has he?' the Duke said, as if he knew gaps would yawn in her life the very moment that happened.

She almost wished Colm really was plain Mr Carter, except then he wouldn't be himself and she wouldn't have this fear gnawing away inside her that the Duke was right. She *would* miss the wretch when he left, as if someone had cut away a vital part of her and the rest was limping on as best it could. She refused to be the woman he wished he didn't want, though. He refused to fall in love in his father's footsteps and she had too much pride to chase after a man and make him want her as her mother would have done, so thank goodness she didn't know the full complement of pleasures a woman could ache for in a man's arms. Yesterday afternoon they had stopped, or been stopped, in time for marriage to be a choice and not a necessity, so she chose to let him ride away.

'Monday will remedy that,' she said coldly. 'Since my stepmama tells me you are leaving us on that day, your Grace,' she added and she shouldn't be hurt Chloe heard about it before she did. Her stepmother was mistress of Darkmere Castle and had every right to know when their guests were going home.

'Yes, I think we must before more damage is done,' he replied with a frown of concern for his nephew that made Eve squirm. 'I failed him as a boy, you know. His sister as well, although my mother did live long enough to make sure young Eleanor went to a school where she could be happy. She considered a boy the province of the men of the family, unfortunately, and I was hiding on the other side of the Atlantic. I let my brother take out his fury on two helpless children, Miss Winterley. Somehow Colm and Nell managed to grow into two of the finest beings I know, despite the efforts of their family to ruin their young lives, but they did so on their own.'

'I'm sure they don't see things that way,' she said uneasily.

'I did say they were fine people, didn't I?' he insisted with gentle tenacity, then smiled and seemed to realise he was being an awkward guest. 'On a bright and hopeful morning like this one old misdeeds should not cast such long shadows.'

'Yet still they do,' she said with bitter resignation.

Now the Duchess had seen them and Eve wondered what kindly meddling to expect from Colm's next partisan relative. She ought to be thankful his sister was not here to take over once the Duke and Duchess had finished with her.

'Ah, coffee and soup, how very welcome. And you have been so careful with it that I dare say there will be enough for all of us,' the Duchess said to the footmen as they solemnly set out stools for the quality to sit on and the maids laid a cloth and cutlery on the biggest one before decanting soup into rougher bowls and mugs than usually graced a lord's table.

Impossible to sit stiffly aloof while everyone enjoyed an impromptu luncheon on a beach in December, cocooned against a cold wind from the North Sea and warmed by the sun still shining so serenely the cloud and tempest of yesterday might have been a dream, but for the forbidden tingle in her belly whenever Eve met Colm's eyes by accident. Impossible to dismiss that as imaginary when she could feel his touch echo through her again simply by being within ten feet of the wretched man, with enough chaperons handy to satisfy a convent nearby.

Once the food was eaten and the coffee flasks empty, the servants sat and enjoyed a few moments' rest on sun-dried boulders. Eve had to stay here or look as if she was avoiding the Hancourts, but she eyed the maids and footmen heading back to the castle in a merry gaggle rather wistfully. The Duke seemed hell-bent on interfering today and next he insisted on taking his Duchess for a walk to shake the stiffness out of her legs and get her truly warm again. Soon they were out of earshot, yet close enough even to satisfy Eve's papa no more mischief could be done.

'It seems we must talk, Mr Hancourt, your uncle is almost insistent upon it.'

'I'm rapidly finding out he can be very stubborn under his act of the mild-mannered scholar,' Colm observed with a distracted smile as he watched his aunt and uncle and refused to centre his brown and gold gaze on her.

'He's quite right, of course; it *is* foolish to pretend yesterday didn't happen when we both know it did. It was a moment of madness and that's all. So there, I have said it and now we can forget it ever happened. If we don't, the good our families did each other by this visit will be wasted.'

'And we can't have that, can we?' he asked gruffly and Eve felt as if Mr Carter was back and had little to say to the daughter of a viscount.

'No, it would waste a great deal of effort by my parents and your aunt and uncle to put the past behind us,' she said briskly and wondered why she cared which of his masks he was wearing today.

'It's not though, is it? The past, I mean,' he added as if she might misunderstand and heaven forbid she thought he was talking about their long, sweet kiss in the rain.

'If we take yesterday out of consideration it is. From now on our families can meet and be at ease with each other, if we forget that particular idiocy.'

'What if I can't forget?' he demanded roughly, as if the words forced their way out of his mouth against his better judgement. 'What if the memory you kissed me back so passionately got inside my head like a burr that won't go away however hard I try to rip you out of my mind, Miss Winterley?'

'That's not a flattering comparison,' she said with a weak attempt to make light of things that felt wrong even as she said it.

'Damn it, woman, why should I flatter you? I didn't want that folly to happen any more than you did. There's no future in us feeling anything for each other and whichever way I turn I always end up wanting and never having. I thought I was used to being Lord Chris's son and living with that lack every day of my life, but it's all you see when you look at me, isn't it? My father and your mother. So be careful how you tweak my tail, Miss Winterley, because I'm not sure I'm quite as tame and resigned to it as I thought I was.'

'I didn't intend any of it to happen,' she whispered because saying it out loud seemed dangerous. 'Chloe wanted peace between us all and her intentions are so good. Anyway, I had no idea you were not a Mr Carter but a Mr Hancourt when she asked me if I minded your aunt and uncle and their nephew coming to Darkmere for a week or two. If I had known he was you, I might have gone to stay with my Uncle James and Aunt Rowena and saved us the ordeal of sitting here trying to be civil today.'

'My aunt and uncle wanted to bridge the gulf as well and we have made it bigger. We might as well be Capulet and Montague for all the good we will ever do each other, Miss Winterley.'

The way he said her family name hurt as if he'd aimed a fist at her heart. The Duke's warning not to throw love aside went directly against her father's wariness about Colm and that balance felt too hard to think her way around right now. She had to keep the chaos of feelings she didn't want or understand at bay somehow and that meant making sure the unsayable never got said.

'Then we must learn not to want each other,' she said and tried not to look at him again. She might find him too vital and grumpy not to want more from him than words could say if she did. He didn't trust love and mere passion would never be enough for her, so all they could do was hurt each other more.

'Do make me a map of that, then,' he demanded urgently, as if she was the one refusing to let go of her prejudices when she felt it was the other way about.

'When I have one myself, I will send it to you.'

'I spent all morning trying to draw one and look what came of that.'

He thrust one of the little books of drawing paper she had seen the Duchess take out of her reticule and make lightning sketches on at her, then he strode away, as if only by removing himself from her presence could he breathe freely. Insulted that he wanted to get away from her so urgently he couldn't stay to be seen to part friends by anyone who might be watching, she held the little book at arm's length, as if it might explode and stared at his retreating back. She told herself it didn't matter if he loved her or loathed her, he was the most infuriating and stubborn male she ever encountered and she almost wished she hated him.

Chapter Eighteen

'In a month or two this will be no more than a half-forgotten nightmare, Evelina,' she whispered to herself as Colm disappeared round the headland and her hungry eyes couldn't follow his halting gait any longer.

How dear a dream he could have been, she acknowledged in the privacy of her own head. She smiled to herself at his stubborn refusal to admit his leg still hurt barely six months on from Waterloo and all the terrible danger he had somehow survived that day. Any other man would cosset himself and use a cane to ease the stiffness that must plague him badly today, after that reckless dare against the churning sea and her father last night on the cliffs. Colm Hancourt was far too proud and obstinate to do anything of the sort, she accused him crossly, as she turned her gaze back to the sea, where the sun still shone on playful little wavelets, distant cousins of the wild ones that thundered against the cliffs as if they meant to tear them down last night.

There, he'd left his borrowed sketchbook in her hand

with a driven invitation to look at it and she was wasting her time watching him go away as if every second she could still see him was precious. She eyed the book dubiously, expecting to see furious lines and harshly scored portraits of this place she loved so dearly, despite its capricious moods. Well, she defied him to spoil Darkmere for her and opened it anyway. Oh, Heaven, how could he do such a thing to her and then stump off as if he couldn't wait to get away from her? She stared down at first one page, then another and another of quick images and one or two more finished drawings of nothing but her. Except how could it be her when he seemed to see her as her mirror had never shown her to herself? There was Eve Winterley looking pensive and a little bit sad; here she was smiling as if greeting the most precious person in her life; now she was frowning and here looking offended.

Her heart jarred, then galloped as she came to the final page and found out he'd drawn her a picture of yesterday—Eve undone. She admitted the truth of that image to herself as he shot down hers of a lady who had only let herself forget who she was for a few moments. She looked soft mouthed and heavy eyed, a world of possibility in her kiss-swollen lips and avid gaze as she stared back at the man who had woken her up to so many things she wanted to cry just looking at herself. This was the chance they must never risk again, the Eve and Colm she longed for yet dreaded with all the caution in her after growing up not just motherless but with Pamela's example to say, *Don't take her path through life. Never allow the scandalmongers to whisper in corners about you as they still do about her.*

How she would miss the lovers this drawing showed her. Even now she felt as if half of her life had gone with them and she would always be less than her full self because she would never be the woman in his drawing again. It hurt, but the Duke and Duchess would soon complete their tactful circuit of the beach and she had to meet their acute gazes as if she hadn't seen this portrait of herself as she might have been, if only Colm let himself love her. So she tucked the little sketchbook into her shawl and turned to greet them with a social smile.

'I see my nephew has flown the scene,' the Duke said by way of greeting.

'He is such a restless soul at the moment. I think he could make a fine artist if he would only sit still long enough to apply himself,' the Duchess observed with a sad shake of her greying but still handsome head.

Eve wondered how brilliant Colm might have been if he had application since that little book seemed to burn her inside its sensible wool wrappings as she met the lady's eyes as serenely as she could. 'Mr Hancourt must be used to a very active life, considering his occupation these last few years,' she said blandly.

'All the more reason to calm down and fulfil his potential now he's home,' the lady said forthrightly.

She would miss the Duchess, Eve realised. The Hancourts were nothing like the proud and snobbish people her childish imagination had painted them when she learnt of her mother's nightmare death at her lover's side. She tried to imagine the sort of man Lord Christopher Hancourt must have been coolly, but it was no good. She couldn't be dispassionate about a man who deserted his children and spent their inheritance on his selfish and greedy mistress. He would be a soft version of Colm, without his son's bone-deep integrity and with a flashier version of his son's quiet good looks. Eve suddenly realised her father had recognised Mr Carter as Lord Chris's son when they were still in London. She would have words with him about that, but for now she went back to the differences between Colm's father and his son. Lord Chris would lack the rock-like chin and stubborn courage of his only son, but have an easy charm and a way with the ladies Colm lacked. Colm was much more trustworthy though, wasn't he? He hadn't run off with anyone's wife so far either, but this wasn't being dispassionate, was it? She put all the strength and integrity on Colm's side of the balance, weakness and neglect on his father's.

'What was Lord Christopher Hancourt like?' she asked the Duchess after the Duke had wandered back to the castle and his beloved books.

'From what little I remember of him before Horace and I fled London and his family, Chris was much like any other spoilt youngest son who refused to grow up.'

'He was a decade older than his son is now when he met my mother though, wasn't he? And he'd been married and had children,' Eve said, feeling she needed to understand how his father's desertion changed Colm's life.

'You won't get an impartial opinion of them from

me, Miss Winterley; if you're looking for one of those, you must go elsewhere.'

'Any interest I showed in your nephew would stir up gossip enough to deafen us,' Eve said stiffly.

'Then trust the evidence of your own eyes, girl, and stop letting the actions of a pair of long-dead fools cloud your judgement.'

'I have two little half-brothers, your Grace. What if the next child my parents produce is a girl and I go about proving the gossips right? My bad blood will taint a little sister, or even put off the girls my brothers might one day want to marry if I am not very careful about any risks I take with my good name now.'

'Can you really intend to live your life chained to a set of maybe happenings years in the future? Or let it be dictated by the past? Your mother had no blood in common with your brothers and sisters and there's little to connect her to you but the bare fact she gave birth to you. I pity you if you intend to let Pamela Verdoyne's shade overtop you for the rest of your life.'

'How can I not have a care when she was so notorious?'

'By living your own life—there is no better proof I can think of that you take after your father and not your mother. With Colm the sum went the other way, but it adds up to the same total: he is not his father and you are not your mother. All you two have to do now is see yourselves as you really are, before you miss out on a happy life, together or apart.'

Which was all very well, but, even if she wasn't her mother's daughter, Eve would still flinch from loving a man so self-sufficient even he didn't seem to know what he was feeling most of the time.

'Ah, Hancourt,' Viscount Farenze observed as he looked up from some ancient estate map later that morning and met Colm's eyes with a cool challenge in his own. 'I wondered when you were going to explain what happened yesterday.'

'I am sure you already know, my lord,' Colm said, standing stiffly on the other side of the desk even when the man waved imperiously at the chair opposite his own. 'Lady Chloe has a clear-minded command of most situations she stumbles across and will have described it to you in detail.'

'So, what do you intend to do about it?'

'I will meet you whenever and wherever you choose, my lord.'

'And that would damp down any gossip about you and my daughter quite wonderfully, wouldn't it?' the man asked with the cynical irony he was once famous for. 'You could pick your spot and put a bullet through me wherever you choose. I know what a fine marksman you are held to be by your peers, Hancourt, because I made it my business to find out all I could about Captain Carter of the 95th Rifles, so please don't try my patience by pretending otherwise.'

'Another sign I am no gentleman, don't you think? As if you really needed proof,' Colm said quietly. No ordinary infantry officer would dream of carrying a gun at the head of his men instead of his sword. Only among the Rifles did an officer occasionally do so, but it was considered eccentric even there.

'You're a young fool if you think I'll meet you. I have no mind to become a murderer when you send your bullet into the nearest tree, so keep your challenge and I hope it eats into that prickly conscience of yours when you next feel the need to kiss a man's daughter you have no intention of marrying.'

'I shall not,' Colm said stiffly.

'What, develop a conscience or kiss disappointed girls?'

'The kisses, of course.'

'You trust your will to triumph over base nature a little too easily then, lad,' Lord Farenze warned him as if that kiss was nothing more serious than a moment's misjudgement on his part.

'I have nothing to my name but a few decent clothes provided by my uncle and a Baker Rifle there is very little use for in civilian life, my lord. I am in no position to keep a wife and family, so I must learn to keep my more unfortunate longings under strict control in future,' Colm said, like some spotty youth who was ready to launch himself on any halfway-willing female simply because she was one.

'Isn't that something you should have remembered before you kissed my daughter?' this slippery lord demanded.

'Yes,' Colm said, driven to brevity by the lie he was a knave who had been caught kissing a desirable young lady he couldn't aspire to marry.

'Don't be a fool, lad,' the Viscount surprised him by

saying on a sigh. 'We both know you are mature beyond your years and little wonder, so please don't treat me like a flat and pretend you feel nothing for my daughter but a little misplaced lust you will both get over quickly.'

'I could never be that deluded, my lord.'

'I don't want to know the deepest and darkest secrets of your heart, Hancourt, but please don't imagine I would agree if you demanded Eve's hand in marriage. I told you in London only the most dedicated and determined sort of love between you would make me let you marry her and you don't look like a man who thinks the world well lost for love.'

'I am not my father,' Colm said, hanging on to his temper by a whisker.

'Which is the only reason I'm not brandishing a horsewhip at you like the indignant father out of a bad farce right now; Eve is not like her mother either.'

'Well, of course she isn't,' Colm said impatiently. 'She is the most extraordinary young woman I have ever met,' he caught himself saying and felt a foolish grin on his face at the mere thought of her.

Yesterday afternoon she watched him with so much in her turquoise eyes he'd hardly dared breathe. No, best not to think how she looked after that kiss in her father's company, he remembered, as enchantment threatened to make a fool of him all over again.

'And the world had best be ready for a shock when she finally steps out of my late wife's shadow,' Lord Farenze said.

'I expect she will dazzle it. I promise to do my best

to avoid your daughter from now on, my lord,' Colm said stiffly.

'Ah, but what if she seeks you out?' the man challenged.

'I learnt to retreat in good order as well as to advance in the Light Division,' Colm admitted with a self-mocking smile.

'You're a stiff-necked young idiot, Hancourt, but I suppose you're young yet and might learn to do better if you live long enough.'

'Thank you, my lord,' Colm replied and took it as permission to go away and leave the puzzling Lord Farenze in peace.

Breakfast was served a little earlier than usual on Monday to allow the Winterleys' guests to depart in good time to reach comfortable lodgings before dark now that it was so close to the shortest day of the year. Colm wondered if it was more tactful to take a tray in his room, but when did tactfulness become cowardice?

'How wonderful, here's a letter from Papa,' Verity Revereux said as she danced into the room and took her seat, holding out her cup for chocolate as Eve took her stepmother's place as hostess, until Lady Chloe felt equal to greeting the day. 'Would it be very rude of me to read it, Uncle Luke?' she asked with a hopeful look towards the Duke and Duchess, since they were more likely to tell her of course not and she must read it as she was clearly longing to.

'Yes,' Eve said austerely and Colm felt small for hoping her pale face and lack of breakfast conversation gave away a disturbed night almost as hellish as his own had been. 'But no doubt you will do so anyway.'

'I do hope he will get here in time for Christmas, so you are quite right, step-cousin of mine. You have a letter from Sir Gideon, Uncle Luke. It looks very long as well, so what a good thing Lord Laughraine franked it so as not to bankrupt you,' she said with a solemn face and mischief in her eyes at the idea any Winterley need worry about paying for a letter, especially when a member of the Lords.

'I have been waiting for his answer to a question, so I hope you will forgive my appalling manners as well, your Grace?' he asked the Duchess, who waved a hand to say of course and went back to discussing the Lake poets with Eve and the Duke.

Colm sat and brooded about his latest glimpse of family life. Verity had got over her youthful infatuation with the youngest Louburn very quickly and was happily absorbed in her father's letter just as if she had never taken that false step into adulthood. The resilience of youth struck him as he visualised the pale, pensive and woebegone girl he saw at the Warlingtons' masquerade only a few weeks ago and felt older than his rightful four and twenty. He wouldn't bounce back from whatever he felt for Eve Winterley like that. Somehow he doubted he'd ever be able to put his hand on his heart and say he felt nothing for her. He gave himself the luxury of furtively watching her as she discussed poets and poetry with his aunt and uncle. She was such a passionate creature under all that cautious coolness she used on the outside world and the sad thing was she didn't even realise it. How would she fare with the polite and careful husband she thought she needed? He shuddered at the thought of her trapped in the safe little world she thought she wanted to find and wondered if he was such a bad bargain after all.

She would be miserable with that paragon, he concluded gloomily. He frowned at his half-empty plate and felt what he had already eaten threaten to curdle in his gut at the very idea of her half living her life because of a pair of long-dead strangers. That was all they were, those dead lovers; strangers who once faced a choice between their children and their own wants and needs and took the easy one. Neither had a right to shape their children's lives or who they loved and how much, yet somehow they still did.

Colm felt the injustice of it bite deeper than ever as he slid another glance at Eve Winterley and almost wished he'd never set eyes on her. The desolation she would leave in his life threatened, but how could she be happy married to him if her money paid for everything? Sitting at my lord's breakfast table, Colm let himself know that he loved Miss Evelina Winterley. He sighed and thought how joyful most men could be about such a realisation, but they had the means to keep a wife, or knew that there was nothing between them but love and hope for a better future. Either a man and his wife had nothing or everything together. In his mind that was the equality of marriage and loving Eve made him even more ready to walk away from her.

'Well, I'll be…' Lord Farenze suddenly exclaimed, then stopped just in time and looked about him as if he had forgotten exactly where he was for a moment. 'My apologies,' he said abruptly.

'You didn't actually get as far as saying anything awful, Papa, but whatever is the matter?' Eve said anxiously.

'I have some surprising news from Sir Gideon,' her father said absently, as if that news and whatever he felt he must do about it lay heavy on his mind.

'Is Lady Laughraine unwell, or my dear little godson? Or is there something wrong with the new baby, or Lord Laughraine perhaps?'

'What? No, no, of course not. Sorry to alarm you, love, and they are all well. There is nothing like that for you to worry about.'

'Then what is it, Papa?'

'Nothing bad, or at least I don't think so, but it's not my news to tell. I think some of you may need to hear about it in time all the same,' he muttered as if conducting a debate with himself. Eve couldn't recall seeing her father this torn and uncertain about anything since shortly before Chloe agreed to marry him. 'Yes, there's been too much concealment and lying already. If you would join me in my book room as soon as you are done here I shall be obliged to you, Mr Hancourt, at least then the rest of it will be up to you.'

'I can eat no more, my lord, so I am ready now. We must be away by mid-morning if we are to stand any chance of reaching Durham before dark,' Colm said warily, as if he was uneasy about anything her father had to say to him at Sir Gideon Laughraine's prompting.

Feeling as if all the certainties of life were shifting

around her, Eve watched in silence as her father and Colm left the room together. Colm was nearly as tall as her powerful father and, despite the halt in his step, looked almost as dangerous as he loped at the side of the mature man of power her papa had only truly become when he wed Chloe and learnt to be happy at long last. Despite all the differences in age, wealth and status between them, Colm wasn't diminished by Viscount Farenze as so many *ton*nish gentlemen were in comparison. His lithe strength and leaner build hinted at potential not yet fully explored and picked him out as younger and less certain of his own worth than the Lord of Darkmere Castle, but Colm was very much a man for all that.

Chapter Nineteen

After a few minutes passed rather flatly in the breakfast room a footman came in and muttered something to the Duchess, then the Duke of Linaire and they left the room as well. Now only Eve and Verity were left sitting in ignorance of what was going on and Verity was too preoccupied with her crossed and recrossed letter to notice the strangeness of it all. All this mystery must have something to do with the past if Uncle Gideon had got involved. Eve felt panic rise at the thought of what he might have uncovered and Colm was finding out at this very moment. Her fingers tightened involuntarily on the remnants of a piece of toast she was still holding for some odd reason and turned it to a handful of dry crumbs before she could order them to stop.

'If I did that I would be told to go to my room and not to come back to the breakfast table until I learnt manners,' Verity told her as she eyed the pile of breadcrumbs Eve let fall to her plate as if she had no idea where they came from.

'Why would you do anything of the kind?' Eve said hollowly, trying to cope with the awful suspicion Colm meant far more to her than he should.

'Because I was upset that a handsome and heroic gentleman whom I liked and admired a great deal more than I was willing to admit was about to ride off as if he meant nothing to me, perhaps? Or maybe I might wish I was going with him, but lacked the courage to say so?'

'Stop! You have no idea what you are talking about,' Eve said, on the verge of tears as she heard all Verity was saying and nobody else had the gall to say out loud. Not that it made any difference. She couldn't go after Colm and tell him her life would feel bleak from the moment he left Darkmere.

'You think not? I was old enough at the time to know Aunt Chloe and your father nearly turned their backs on love because of things their families did or didn't do years before. You were as keen as I was back then to see them united and happy together as they have been these last five years. What happened to you, Eve? Did you listen to the scandal when the world found out who my aunt truly is and what my mother and father went through at the hands of her family? All the head shaking and tut-tutting in the world can't change a thing. It's just words and those who matter don't take any notice of them; I should have thought you were clever enough to work that out for yourself by now. I know your mother left you with your father so she could dance off and do whatever she wanted, but that wasn't your fault and it isn't Mr Hancourt's either.'

'I know that.'

'Then why are you punishing him for something he had no say in? Your mother didn't desert you for his sake. Mr Hancourt was just a boy at the time and he certainly had no say in any of it.'

'That's absurd and unfair; I'm surprised you can even think such things about me, let alone say them out loud.'

'Maybe I don't want to see you grow sad and a bit too brave for the lack of your love in your life as my aunt did for your father? Ten years is a terribly long time to waste pining for a man for the want of a little truth-telling. Then there's my own father wasting his life longing for a lady he thinks too young for him as well, even though he hasn't bothered to ask if she agrees with him. I don't intend to be such an idiot with so many examples of what not to do in front of me. I love you like a sister, Eve, so how can I *not* say you are being a fool? And please don't pretend you have no idea what I'm talking about.'

'Well, that certainly told me, didn't it? But don't forget you're the one who ended up having to be rescued from Warlington House dressed in a pair of breeches, Verity Revereux, and not me.'

'Nobody will be able to accuse me of being fainthearted though, will they?'

'I don't think any of us will ever be that foolish.'

'A blind trust, you say?' The Duke of Linaire said with a dazed look on his face.

Perhaps realising shock had stopped Colm's tongue, Lord Farenze nodded for him. 'A very well hidden one, your Grace,' he said. 'Sir Gideon Laughraine seems to think he would have had an even harder time finding out the details if the trustees were not in such a puzzle as to how they were going to discharge their final duties on the day your nephew turns five and twenty when nobody else seems to know it exists.'

'And Christopher truly set it all up and managed to keep the woman he was so besotted with from finding out, all to make sure my late brother-in-law couldn't get hold of Colm's inheritance if anything happened to him in France?' the Duchess said as Colm tried to take in this astonishing turnabout in his life and fortune.

'Yes, because apparently the last Duke was the one with debts and an expensive mistress to keep. He used Lord Christopher's personal fortune to pay his creditors off, then told the world how feckless and extravagant his little brother had been before he died. Although the Lambury Jewels are still missing, I'm afraid, so Lord Christopher still gave them to my late wife when they were not his to give. Gideon says that when the late Duke found he couldn't break the trust he put the tale about that everything was gone and refused to do anything for you or your sister. I can't pretend my first wife wouldn't have done her best to spend everything Lord Christopher had and your fortune as well if she could have got her hands on it and lived long enough to spend it, Hancourt, but she didn't and the rest of it is still intact.'

'The rest of it?' Colm said in a voice he hardly recognised as his own. 'So my Grandfather Lambury's entire fortune will truly come to me in a few weeks?'

'Apart from the not insignificant loss of the Lambury Jewels. Even the diamonds have disappeared, despite the fact my first wife doesn't seem to have lived long enough to wheedle them out of your father from her complaints in her diaries.'

'I think Derneley had the rest cut up and my late uncle probably did the same with the diamonds, since he must have found them after my father died,' Colm said, still struggling with the idea he was going to inherit a huge fortune in six weeks and, somehow more important, his father might have loved him after all. 'Derneley should have gone under years ago and he's stayed afloat far too long, you see? Apparently he set off to France on the excuse of finding out how his sister-in-law really died when the Treaty of Amiens was signed.'

'You think he took the jewellery my wife cozened out of your father with him and sold it piecemeal to the highest bidder?' Lord Farenze asked.

'Probably,' Colm agreed with a shrug.

'Then I should recompense you. My wife stole it and her sister's husband has lived off it all these years.'

'No, a gift is just that, so I will not take your money if you try, my lord.'

'Don't look at me, Farenze, it's no business of mine,' Colm's uncle said with a shrug. 'Colm is a gentleman of fortune now; he can do whatever he wants.'

'Except I own nothing much for another six weeks, Uncle Horace,' Colm reminded the Duke with a wry smile. 'Lord Derneley is no relative of yours, my lord, so you have no right to his debts. A legal document shall be drawn up renouncing any claim on you and your heirs for the Lambury Jewels, or their value. I'm not a greedy man, Lord Farenze; one vast fortune is quite enough for me.'

'At least you and your sister can take your place in society and your pick of several estates to make your home,' the Viscount said uneasily.

'If I can persuade her to do any of that I shall think myself lucky,' Colm said ruefully. It would be an uphill struggle to persuade Nell to leave her four noble waifs, but at least she could never be cast out penniless now. Convincing her it was downright peculiar for the sister of a rich man to earn her bread might take him some time, but the urgency to protect his little sister from the harshest aspects of poverty was fading for the first time since their father had died. He had no idea how tightly that need had wound him up until it was gone.

'And Sir Gideon believes my late uncle knew that this trust existed?' he asked.

Silence. He looked up and saw something uncomfortably like pity in the eyes of all three.

'I conclude everything I will inherit in six weeks reverts to the dukedom if I die before I'm five and twenty?'

Odd how painful it felt to find out his late uncle and guardian bought him a commission in the most dangerous regiment he could think of in a time of war and blithely sent him off to die, so he could get his hands on the Lambury fortune he had always begrudged his nephew.

'I do hope he is rotting in hell,' his aunt said so softly her words seemed all the more potent. 'I have to trust God to judge him, because if he was in front of me now

I wouldn't hesitate to put a bullet in Augustus's black heart,' she concluded with a defiant glare at her husband and her host to tell them she meant every word.

'You'd have to find it first,' Uncle Horace said darkly, then the hint of a smile lit up his gloomy countenance, 'and you couldn't hit a haystack at ten yards, my love.'

'True, and after you tried so hard to teach me when we decided to cross the Atlantic as well. It's just as well I never did get pursued by a bear, isn't it?'

Colm laughed and love for these two extraordinary people lifted him out of the dark place his other uncle's villainy had threatened to push him into. He was truly blessed in the family he had now and the past was dead and done with, wasn't it?

'Gus had a mean soul, for all he grew up as heir to our father's honours and the fortune they both spent so lavishly,' Uncle Horace went on. 'I didn't realise how mean it was until I got back to England and found out what he had been up to while we were away. Poor Chris was the youngest of us and always did as Gus and my father bid, so it must have come as a shock to them when Chris fell in love with such an unsuitable female, begging your pardon, Farenze, and she taught him to rebel. He would have handed the bulk of your maternal grandfather's fortune over until then for the sake of a quiet life. That must be why Sir Joseph Lambury made sure Chris couldn't inherit it through your mother, Colm, and why he didn't leave much to your sister for fear she'd be sold off for a share of her marriage portion. So you see, Lord Chris Hancourt was a better man than any of us thought him and I owe him an apology for believing he could behave so carelessly he'd risk leaving his own children with nothing a year to live on.'

'He wasn't a saint though; he still died with another man's wife at his side, but are you really trying to say loving the first Lady Farenze put courage into him?' Colm asked his uncle with an apologetic glance at her one-time husband.

'He learnt guile from somewhere, since he made such clever arrangements for your future before he went on that mad journey. I expect he wanted everything neatly wrapped up before he embarked on a life of wild adventure,' the Duke said as if he'd been given his little brother back this morning as he really was as well.

'True, and it's a shame your father underestimated Augustus's malice and cunning, Colm, but he outwitted him in the end,' Aunt Barbara said pensively. 'The last Duke was cruel and selfish and the world is a better place without him,' she added and nobody argued. Colm thought it a sad memorial, but after such a betrayal of the man's own brother and two vulnerable children the man deserved no better.

The Hancourts departure was delayed by the momentous news from Sir Gideon. Eve's father mumbled some nonsense about apologies to be made and accepted when he lured her into his book room after dinner that night, then he left her alone with Colm. She sighed and shot a longing look at the door he had left open a bare inch as a sop to propriety. It was obvious what this was by now and it wasn't an apology for that heart-stopping kiss. Or at least she hoped not, because that would be an insult to something that had been impulsive and true and deeply passionate and she didn't want a mumbled *sorry* spoiling it.

'You don't have to ask me again,' she told Colm flatly.

'I don't have to ask you what?'

'To marry you.'

'I believe it's usual for a young lady to wait to be asked before she turns a gentleman down.'

'Well, now we don't have to endure the embarrassment of you asking me, since I won't marry you however often you ask.'

'I might be convincing,' he said ruefully and there he was again, the man she could so easily love if she let herself—or if he let her. 'This time I might have a poetic speech ready to dazzle you into accepting me and making my life worth living.'

'You might have,' she replied and how hard it was to resist him when he was almost the light-hearted, teasing beau he could have been if he'd never had to be Mr Carter first.

'I could be about to sweep you off your feet,' he continued the farce of being a willing suitor, then seemed to realise he had already done that by kissing her until there wasn't a single coherent thought in her head but Colm Hancourt the other day. 'Or plead with you to excuse my fumbled attempts to show you how much I adore you last week and let me try again with a little more restraint and refinement. So you are wrong, you see, Miss Winterley. I am here to apologise, even if I hope you will accept me as well as my very sincere sorrow for losing my head and kissing you as I have longed to from the first moment I laid eyes on you in Derneley's library.'

'You hid it remarkably well, then,' she said sceptically. 'I quite thought you despised me on sight.'

'I regret giving you such an untrue idea of how I felt about you then. I am not very good with words and have too much experience at hiding my feelings from the world. Indeed, I am not very good at knowing what I feel myself at times, let alone showing it to those I care about.'

Eve decided he was a lot better at it than he thought, then reminded herself most men had urges and passions she still didn't fully understand and she had yet to see any sign he felt anything more for her. 'You had last night and all day today to propose to me, yet you waited until you found out that you truly are a man of fortune before you tried again,' she accused him.

'I did,' he admitted, tight-lipped and unreadable as ever again.

'No doubt my father informed you he knows that you kissed me and you told him you had no desire to wed me. Since you two did not sneak off to fight some silly duel at dawn you must have agreed that you were unsuitable and I suppose you undertook to remove yourself from the Castle forthwith. Am I right so far?'

'You are; how did you know?'

He looked so pained and betrayed by the idea she and Papa might have been talking about him behind his back that Eve felt her hand get ready to touch his tense jaw and remind him how human they both were.

She put it behind her back and gripped it with the other one because she really didn't want to marry a man who didn't want to marry her.

'I know my father. I thought I was beginning to know you, Mr Hancourt, but you put a full stop on that when Chloe came upon us kissing in the rain, didn't you? How fortunate that I said no to your grudging offer the first time,' she added as she saw what almost looked like hope in his eyes before she said she was glad she had said no when the blood was still hot in their veins and his kisses a wonder on her lips. No, he didn't want to marry her and she wasn't going to be talked into it now that he was rich enough to afford any wife he chose.

'I was too poor to afford a wife until today,' he confirmed her worst fears so coolly she was tempted to shout, *no, you weren't, you just didn't love me.* Luckily she bit back her fury and faced him with nearly as closed an expression as his own.

'You don't trust any woman enough to want the sort of marriage I do and I refuse to be a burden you shouldered, a duty your conscience won't let you escape.'

He looked as if she had stuck a knife in him for a moment. There was a flare of powerful emotion in his eyes before he shook his head and argued, 'I shall be deeply honoured if you will agree to be my wife, Miss Winterley, and can promise never to see you as a duty or a burden, because nothing could be further from my true feelings towards you than that.'

She almost softened, almost took the spark of hot gold in his eyes at face value, but she had been deceived like that before, only last week in fact. How could she share the rest of her life with a man who could shut her out the moment he thought she was getting too close to the real Colm Hancourt?

'If you had said so the night after you stood and raged at the storm for trapping you in the summerhouse with me and leaving you time and chance to want me for a while I might have believed you, sir. This far on from that day I do not.'

'I could not support you then,' he protested as if that was an excuse for refusing to make a life with her and to hell with hows and whys.

'I have a good dowry and a manor of my own, it would have sufficed for me, but I suppose a duke's grandson thought it contemptible.'

'No, what I thought contemptible was the idea of me living off my wife. What sort of a man would it make me if I had to ask you to make me an allowance? How do you suppose a husband lives with himself if he has to ask his wife if she would prefer to be a secretary's lady, or try to find out if he will be accepted as a no-body in her home instead and batten on her for the rest of their days?'

'I don't know; how do you suppose a wife could live well in such a marriage when she knew her husband resented every penny of hers that stood between them? So you are quite right, you see, Mr Hancourt, we want different things from marriage and simply would not suit. Thank you for your dutiful proposal and I think I will pass on it once again. A very good night to you, sir.'

'Eve, don't,' he burst out almost as if it hurt to see

her go with so much hurt and misunderstanding between them.

'Don't what? Don't feel hurt or let myself feel battered by your insistence on still being Captain Carter, even if you call yourself by another name? Don't want more from a man who belongs to nobody and wants nobody to belong to him? Don't imagine there is a real person under the stiffness and resentment you have built over the years against your hard lot in life? Very well, I won't. Goodnight, and I hope you find some joy in your new life, because there seems precious little in the old one to me.'

Deciding she had endured enough of being asked to marry a man who looked as if he would rather be having his teeth pulled, Eve finally brought this painful interlude to an end by leaving him standing there like an austere and rather well-dressed statue, since he didn't have the grace to leave her in possession of the field with an insincere smile and a relieved sigh because she said had no to him yet again.

'Don't ask,' she told her father, who was hovering as if he might be getting ready to send for his best wine to celebrate her nuptials with a man he would have ordered her not to marry only yesterday. 'I can't believe you just did that. How could you change your mind about him because he's rich today and was poor yesterday?'

'You truly think so little of me, Eve?'

'Yes…no—oh, I don't know,' she said unsteadily, suddenly on the edge of a storm of tears nearly as catastrophic as the one outside on the night she last kissed Colm Hancourt.

'Chloe informed me I was wrong to try to stand between you and a man who might love you, and never mind how much or how little you had to live on. I stamped about a bit and argued a lot, then finally had to admit she's right. You must make your own decisions about who you marry, love, and I am sorry I ever tried to keep that stiff-necked young Galahad of yours away from you.'

'He's not mine, Papa, and *you* didn't keep us apart, he did. Now I'm going to bed,' Eve said so she didn't have to burst into overwrought tears with Colm silently listening from inside her father's book room where she'd left him. 'We can talk about it in the morning when I might be able to tell wood from trees,' she said, gave him a quick peck on the cheek to say she almost understood, then ran upstairs to her room without sending for Bran to help her undress. 'I never, ever want to see that idiotic man again,' she informed her reflection in her dressing mirror, then went and locked her bedchamber door before anyone could come in and tell her this would pass and her heart wasn't breaking and how the devil did they know?

Colm stood as if he'd been frozen to the spot and listened as the sound of Eve's light steps faded away down the ancient stone corridor not even the wealth of the Winterleys could make other than stark and echoing. There was no point wondering if the constriction in his chest was brought on by hearing her words to her father or too much rich food on a tense stomach at dinner because he knew it was far worse than that.

'You made a right mull of that, Carter,' he whispered into the chilling air of his lordship's book room and hoped the man had gone away and wasn't standing outside nodding his agreement.

Colm almost smiled as he imagined the colourful language of some of his former commanding officers if he failed in a mission for them as spectacularly as he had at this one. For all the lives that depended on him getting it right back then, this felt like a worse disaster somehow. He had wrecked his chances of a better future *and* made her despise the passion that had torn at him heart and soul from the first moment he set eyes on her. Why the devil couldn't that letter of Sir Gideon Laughraine's have come either a few days before it had or a few days after? If he had only known he was about to be rich, he would have begged her to marry him with every word and action he could come up with the instant Lady Chloe found them together in the summerhouse. At least Eve couldn't have said he was cold then. Even the memory of how she felt in his arms, what it felt like to feel her lips soften under his, then kiss him back made his heartbeat thunder and that tightness seem more like a great hand squeezing his heart now, when he let himself know it would never happen again; not now he'd made her think proposing to her again was only an untidy end her father would insist on being stitched back into place before he could leave here unencumbered by a wife.

Did the ridiculous female think he was about to go off to London this spring and find a substitute because she wouldn't wed him? If so she was deluded and didn't understand him at all. So why did she matter so much, then? It should be a relief that she'd turned him down again, but instead it felt as if a bullet had slammed into him and was lodged somewhere a lot more crucial than the last one had been. Not that it made any difference, since she said she never wanted to see him again and sounded as if she meant it. He'd better oblige her and leave before she could glare daggers at him across the breakfast table tomorrow. He didn't think he could look back at her as if it didn't hurt any more, so persuading his aunt and uncle he must leave early to smooth out the kinks in their ducal progress would occupy some of the hours that must creep by before he could set out on that self-appointed task with the dawn. Since he wasn't going to sleep he had to find a way to occupy the rest of his last hours at Darkmere. Fantasising about how it would feel to be Miss Winterley's husband and polish every hour of the night with the joy of loving her and doing his best to persuade her to love him back would get him nowhere except shut up in the nearest madhouse.

'Your Mr Hancourt has gone ahead of his uncle and aunt to arrange for changes of horses and beds for the night, Eve,' Verity said next morning as if nothing very momentous had happened.

Eve knew her too well and saw the sly glance at her face to see how that news affected her and somehow managed to blank her shock and surprise. 'He's not my Mr Hancourt and must have gone very early, for I heard nothing,' she managed coolly enough as she helped herself to food more or less at random and wondered how she could not have known he wasn't here any more by instinct alone. Suddenly her home felt vast and lonely without him and that was absurd; she loved Darkmere and her family was here, so what more could she want from life?

'I suppose your room is on the wrong side of the castle for you to hear anyone ride out from the stables,' Verity went on with a cheerful relentlessness Eve found almost unforgivable right now.

He was gone though. She could plan the rest of her life without him and he would be fully occupied with putting his huge assets into stern military order and reviewing his assorted properties. She wouldn't put it past him to take on the task of dragging the ducal lands and grand houses into the nineteenth century at the same time. By the time he finished all that *and* bullied his sister into living the life of a lady of birth and fortune at his side, Eve would have time to find a true gentleman, marry him and get on with making a family of her own. Colm Hancourt wouldn't matter a jot by then, so why did it feel as if more of her was being torn apart with every mile he rode from Darkmere?

'Your Mr Hancourt seems a very proud man. It will be a challenge to get him to come back now you have made him go away,' Verity said as she eyed Eve's odd mix of breakfast food as if she knew how bereft she was feeling because the wretch wasn't even under the same roof as her to quarrel with.

'He's not my Mr Hancourt and you're the last person

in the world who should urge me to think twice about a fine masculine figure and a handsome face.'

'Ah, so you're ready to admit he's handsome at last, are you?'

'Of course he is, if you like austere gentlemen and not human ones.'

'And you do, Eve Winterley, or you wouldn't be pretending to eat that mess.'

Eve wanted to shout, *Stop, he's gone and he won't be coming back and I might have made a terrible mistake, but he's still gone and he still won't be coming back*, but she frowned at her plate instead.

'I don't love him and he doesn't love me,' she told it dolefully, refusing to meet Verity's gaze and let her see how much it hurt to admit she had killed off any chance Colm would love her back last night, even if she was silly enough to have let herself fall in love with the blundering great idiot in the first place.

'So why do you look as if the sky has just fallen on your head then?'

'Maybe I have the headache after facing your impertinent questions over the breakfast table every morning?'

'Or you have the heartache and won't admit it,' Verity said. 'Oh, well, if you truly don't want Mr Hancourt maybe he'll wait until I'm old enough to marry him. I won't worry about ancient history when I look for a husband and he is very handsome.'

'By the time you're out he'll be in hiding from the husband hunters or already married to one,' Eve said gloomily and went off the idea of breakfast altogether.

Chapter Twenty

⟨⟨⟨ ❦ ⟩⟩⟩

For weeks Eve felt as if part of her was standing aloof and glowering while she tried to go about her daily business as though nothing had happened. The Eve who went wild in Colm's arms, the one who yearned for him so passionately butted in every now and again to remind her how empty her life and her bed felt without him. So she did her best to get lost in the solemnity of Christmas, then the headlong delights of Twelfth Night and the celebrations of a day when life turned upside down and lords and ladies waited on maids and boot boys.

On the other side of all that merriment she sat in her sitting room in one of the towers and stared down at the sea where waves roared and rain dashed against the glass as nature lost her temper again. It reminded her so vividly of that afternoon Colm kissed her passionately, then stamped off and risked everything he was to rail about who they were against the raging sea, that she could almost feel his arms around her again as she snuggled deeper into the cushioned chair and yearned for comfort that wouldn't come.

Mr I-Don't-Need-Anyone Hancourt once wanted her so urgently she cursed him now for not taking the final step and making them lovers that stormy day. If he had been as lost in need and passion as she was that afternoon, he couldn't have helped himself and Chloe's coming on that particular scene would have made it impossible for her to refuse to marry him. He could have got her with child and they would have been wed by now. He would be here with her, lounging on the bed next door with a stray cat smile on his face and remembering heat in his gold-shot eyes. They would flare into a blaze of need if she turned her head and gave him a siren smile as she rather thought she would, if he was here.

She wondered how many society beauties had beat a path to his door since they found out he was about to become very rich indeed. Her fingers curled into claws as she thought of their insincere simpering and greedy eyes on the man who ought to be her lover right now, if only she had the sense to let him seduce her. The Colm Hancourt about to celebrate his true coming of age would make a fine catch for any eager husband hunter and how dare they lay hungry eyes on him when he was…

No, he *wasn't* hers, was he? She had no right to begrudge them a single look or smile from her Mr Carter. She might be the one who wanted him when he had nothing and did his best to pretend to be nobody, but she was also the idiot who let him go. Now he was rich and a superb catch on the marriage mart, she finally let herself realise Captain Carter had been her passion *and* her true love. So why was she staying here and letting the darling brusque idiot be lost in the indecently rich grandson of a duke. Gruff and defended Mr Carter would fade more and more every day as Mr Hancourt gained assurance and learned his way round a new world without her around to remind him of the wounded soldier she first met at Derneley House that eventful night she'd thought so disastrous at the time. It had turned out to be the most important night of her life, but did she love a man who no longer existed?

Coward, she accused that attempt to get herself off the hook. Either she loved him or she didn't and never mind what he called himself. As the gap between them stretched out more painfully every day she was more certain she loved him and less hopeful he loved her back. It was mawkish to sit here and mourn a future they might have had, so she took a deep breath and went downstairs to take up smiling and laughing and pretending to be delighted with her life once again.

And it was truly wonderful that her best friend after Verity had just agreed to marry Captain Revereux and he and Alice seemed so determined to be happy together at long last. So perhaps throwing yourself at the man you loved and making sure he had no excuses left about being too old, or too cynical, or too long at war was the way to win your way to a happy ending after all. Eve wondered if her friend had been as shameless with her lover as she wished she had been on that early December afternoon she remembered with such doting fondness with hindsight. She hoped so, because they deserved their chance at happiness and Alice would make the slightly melancholy captain happy at long last, but he had better reciprocate and forget all that nonsense about being too old and jaded for such a young and vivacious lady.

What idiots men were, Eve decided, as she pictured the scene when Alice told her over-gallant beau exactly what she thought of his gentlemanly scruples and grinned. She could just imagine him open-mouthed and dumbstruck as the usually self-contained and rather flippant Miss Clempson told him exactly what she wanted from him and why and refused to be dismissed as too young to throw herself away on the likes of him.

So Papa had done everything he could to avoid loving Chloe for ten years, Alice took far too long to rebuke Captain Reverreux for making her decision for her. Was she really going to sit and stare at the sea until Colm came to his senses and finally admitted they might have been made for one another? They might both be old and grey before then, so could she seek out *her* love and never mind the risk of a rebuff that would sting until her dying day? Seeing where patience and resignation got a woman, she began to think she might have to, before one of them went mad with longing for the other.

'Happy birthday, my boy,' the Duke of Linaire toasted his nephew with an exquisite Sèvres coffee can the morning of Colm's twenty-fifth birthday.

'Indeed, and I wish you many happy returns as well, Colm, dear,' his aunt said with a sly, questioning look that asked if he was quite as happy as he ought to be the day he became one of the richest men in England.

'Thank you,' he said with a guarded smile as he gathered his own breakfast, then hid behind his own cup of coffee as best he could.

'It's a shame young Eleanor is so determined not to leave her post and run one of the houses your trustees invested in,' the Duke said with a sad shake of his grey head.

'And that Miss Winterley was so steadfast in refusing your offer of marriage.' The Duchess walked in blithely where angels feared to tread. 'You will be driven half mad by fortune-hunting young ladies and their mamas from this moment on, I'm afraid, Colm. It would be so much better if you were engaged to marry a lady who has no need of your fortune before you brave the *ton*,' she finished innocently.

'I am not about to do the Season like a giggling debutante, Aunt Barbara,' he replied rather shortly.

'Then there is sure to be a plague of carriage accidents, lost puppies and badly twisted feminine ankles near any house you decide to live in if you don't settle on a wife soon,' his uncle warned happily, as if it was not a worry to him that Colm might end up wed to a designing female when all he wanted was the one who wouldn't marry him if he came wrapped in gold.

'I still won't marry them, so they might as well save themselves the trouble.'

'Might have to,' his uncle said with an uneasy glance at his Duchess this time, as if the joke had gone too far. 'A man needs contact with his neighbours if he's to make any sort of life for himself, be he rich or poor.'

'I shall have to put the tale about that I wed a ravishing Spanish lady and have carelessly lost her somewhere along the way then. That should hold them off; not even a husband-hunter would try to wed a bigamist.'

'I think you may be underestimating some of them,' his aunt said gloomily.

'Give up whatever scheme you're hatching, love,' Colm begged her wearily. 'Miss Winterley would rather marry the stable boy than tie herself to me. Please face that fact and let me get on with living my life without her. There's a good duchess.'

'I hear that Revereux is getting married again,' the Duke said with a shifty glance at Colm. He might have looked a little harder at his not-that-vague scholarly uncle if the wild notion that Revereux was about to marry Eve hadn't stormed into his head and made him feel as if he'd been shot again.

'Yes, and whatever is that deluded girl thinking of?' the Duchess put in. 'He is over a decade older than she is and even more stiff-necked and battle-hardened than you, Colm.'

'I'm only five and twenty,' he snapped back and wondered what difference that made when he felt nearer to a hundred right now.

Revereux was rich from the prizes he and his crew had captured during his career as a dashing frigate captain, then commodore in charge of his own fleet. A tried-and-tested hero whose golden looks had been refined by war and hardship *and* he trailed a tragically romantic past behind him, so, little wonder if he was irresistible to a much younger lady. Oh, and his daughter was Eve's best friend. What more could a sensible, well-born and unforgettably attractive female want in a husband? Nothing, he decided gloomily, put down his coffee and frowned at his breakfast as if it had been made from husks.

'Her family are unsure about the match apparently, but I dare say they can be persuaded to announce the engagement before everyone goes to town this spring,' his aunt reflected as if she hadn't noticed his revolted expression and sudden loss of appetite.

'He's too old for her. How the devil does she think he will make her happy?'

His uncle shrugged and looked uncomfortable. Colm wondered if he had shouted in his fury that Eve Winterley should give herself to a man who would never treasure her unique qualities as he would. She was too unique to play second fiddle to a long-lost love, too vulnerable under that careful guard she kept on her heart. How could she accept anything less than complete love and commitment from the man she intended to spend a lifetime walking next to? The very idea of such a marriage for her made him shudder and wish the bullet that left its mark on him had been an inch or two lower after all, so he need never have met her and lost her to another man.

'It is a good enough match on both sides and solves a great many dilemmas for both families, although I can't say I envy any girl of her age for having to bring out the man's daughter one day. That child may look like an angel without wings, but Verity Revereux will be a handful for any chaperon, let alone one barely half a dozen years older than she is herself.'

'Why the devil does it matter to me who she marries?' Colm muttered under his breath. They must have heard him since they both seemed uneasy as they eyed him with what looked horribly like compassion.

'It is not a sin to fall in love, Colm,' his aunt told him gently.

'That depends who you fall in love with,' he replied dourly.

'And you have control over that, do you?' his uncle put in, as if he heartily disliked of the notion such a mighty emotion could be turned on and off like a tap.

'No,' he admitted wearily. 'I have no hold on it at all. I may be new made, but Miss Winterley still doesn't want Lord Christopher Hancourt's son and I still don't blame her.'

'Then I shall do so on your behalf,' Aunt Barbara told him with a fierce glare to say she wasn't done yet, so he had better not interrupt. 'I hope you don't really intend to stand by while she promises herself to another man. The girl might be almost as stubborn and hot tempered as you are, but she loves you, Colm.'

'Then why would she marry another man?'

'Perhaps you ought to ask her that question yourself before it's too late? How terrible if she wed another man before you two realised you might have been put on this earth to love one another. She is not like her mother, who seems to have been able to transfer her passions from one man to another with hardly a pause, but only imagine how you will both feel if she marries another man and you two find out too late that you love each other. If you don't think that was a hair shirt to your father now you know he was not the hard-hearted monster his eldest brother painted him, you are not the man I think you are either, Mr Carter.'

'Oh, him,' Colm said, all the years that humble fool spent soldiering fading to nothing as he recalled standing staring at Miss Winterley like a mooncalf that first night. That idiot could afford to love a lady he would never aspire to marry; it was being Colm Hancourt again that had wakened impossible needs and feelings in him and set them both on a path to potential disaster. 'At least that looby is properly dead and done with this time.'

'Is he, my boy? I truly hope not,' his uncle said and had the last word because Colm gave up pretending to eat his breakfast, threw his snowy napkin down on the table in disgust, then stormed out of the room to brood in peace. His aunt and uncle were so intent on telling him things he didn't want to hear that they could hardly blame him if he couldn't sit and listen to any more of them on his birthday.

Chapter Twenty-One

'I can't give you the best bedchamber, sir, as it's already been took. Nor the second-best neither, nor even one of the rooms over the tap. It's all this snow, d'you see? It come in like the lion it did, just when we all thought the worst of the winter was over with. There *is* our Joe's room, I suppose. He can turn in with the lads over the stables if you want it.' The landlord looked doubtfully at the tall figure who had tramped in from the stable yard looking more like a snowman than a benighted traveller.

'I don't mind the loft if your son is averse to it; I've slept in far worse places in Spain. All I need is shelter and a good billet for my horse until this infernal storm has abated and then I can go on my way again,' Colm said absently.

'You was an officer, once upon a time then, sir?' the man asked, looking a little less uneasy about his latest visitor now he'd heard him speak.

'Yes, now can I come in and rid myself of this snow and some of my wrappings?'

'Right you are then, sir,' the innkeeper said and stood aside at last.

'Out of the way, Fletcher,' a large woman demanded when the landlord stood and gaped while Colm shook the worst of the snow off his shoulders, then stepped into the taproom. Sizing up her latest guest with shrewd eyes, she made a silent gesture at his snow-encrusted hat. Colm obediently shook off what snow he could outside and was finally allowed in to take his boots off under her stern gaze.

'Fine workmanship,' she told him. 'Shame to risk ruining them by being out on a day like this one.'

'Indeed,' he said, amused by this mismatched couple now he was out of the driving snow and bitter wind and his horse was safe, warm and fed.

'That's a good hat as well.'

'One of the best.'

'So if your purse isn't heavy enough to pay your shot, we'll keep both until it is,' she said as if it was natural for a landlady to ask for proof he could pay before he took another step inside her pristine inn.

'I would have my work cut out walking away and earning more barefoot in all this, but I have means enough for my needs,' he said and dug in his pocket for a guinea. 'This for a seat by the fire and a down payment on the room your husband says I can have at your son's expense,' he added, because he wasn't fool enough to let her know he could buy and sell her inn so many times over it would make her head spin.

'He'll bide with the lads and be glad of it.'

'Good, now I would dearly like to feel the heat of that fire.'

'Take your coat off then, I'll not have all that wet-ness messing up my fireside, guinea or not.'

Colm did as he was bid and felt the woman's assessing gaze on the well-cut coat and modest waistcoat underneath and was glad he'd insisted on Scott as his new tailor, since the quiet elegance of his work seemed to impress her. At least one woman was taken in by his fine new feathers. He fought his frustration at not getting closer to the one he wished to impress before all others. No point trying to outface his horse and forge on against the odds, but he'd hoped to reach Northampton today and he was still twenty miles away. Revereux wasn't an impulsive youth though, they wouldn't marry in indecent haste, or so he told himself as the drive to go on even in the teeth of the weather plagued him once again. He had to be patient and not stump back out into a blizzard to hire the first horse anyone was fool enough to lend him. Hadn't he learnt anything from Wellington? Patience, steady resolution and the long game often won in the face of very stiff odds, but now he was fighting time itself.

'Oh, my,' a diminutive woman who looked vaguely familiar gasped at the sight of him dishevelled and weary from the road, but she left the room in a hurry with her head down before he could take a proper look at her.

'It don't look that bad to me,' the landlord muttered as he gazed at the scar on Colm's forehead as if it was a disappointment to him.

The cold had made his leg ache like the devil so at least his limp passed muster. A gruff coachman made room for him on the bench beside the fire and the landlady became almost maternal as she insisted rum punch would do more to keep out the cold than French brandy, even if they were at peace now and she supposed folk could drink the stuff if they really had to.

Sipping the spicy mixture gratefully, Colm stretched his bad leg to the warmth and almost managed to relax at last. He had nearly nodded off when the landlady began to berate her husband and the inn staff so loudly in the kitchens that they could hear her through the walls. Apparently some fine lady had changed her mind about dining in her room and wanted to come down to the coffee room after all.

'And we're neck deep in folk now and most of them must eat dinner in the tap if the gentry want my coffee room. Give me a nice quiet lawyer's clerk or a farmer or two any day, for at least they can't afford to keep changing their minds.'

She emerged to harry the pot boy and innkeeper as they moved most of the tables out of her best room and chivvied her guests to fetch their own chairs and benches if they wanted to sit down to eat their dinner. Colm sat and watched while the cramp gradually eased out of his misused leg and he resigned himself to yet another day on the road after this delay to try it even further.

'You can take yourself off in there out of the way and wait for the young lady and the reverend gentleman and his wife, since you're quality make as well and I can't keep the place empty just for her highness to dine in state,' the landlady told him once he'd thawed out enough to offer his help.

He limped off to do as he was bid so they could all eat before midnight. No doubt there was another fire in the coffee room and he didn't care where he ate. A rustle of movement from within told him the lady was a lot less tardy than her hostess thought she was and had probably heard all the fuss and carry-on as the public rooms of the inn were rearranged at her whim. He prepared himself to be polite to some spoilt young woman who changed her mind at the drop of a hat and then stopped in his tracks when he realised exactly who she actually was.

'Eve, but how...I mean why? I don't quite know what I do mean any more,' he greeted her clumsily as the shock of seeing her when he'd longed for her so desperately for so many miles took his breath away. Fatigue and hope made him stumble and hastily right himself after her gasp of horror when she saw him looking so travel stained and weary. 'That is, Miss Win—' Fingers he had so longed to kiss all that way pressed his lips together and silenced the rest of whatever it was he'd been going to say. So he simply stood and breathed in the fact of her, the closeness and the wonder of her; here, when he thought he had a hundred more miles to go before he was anywhere near her, and a tough naval commander to fight before he could make a last desperate bid to walk with that hand in his whenever they could get it there for the rest of his life.

'I told them my name is Winter,' she whispered as

if everyone else in the building was listening to what they had to say to each other, when the old oak door had closed itself behind him and they were alone here in the low-ceilinged room and the premature dusk of a snowbound afternoon with only firelight to guide them.

'I can't let you do it,' he burst out as soon as she took her hand away. Shock at the unexpected sight of her, his weariness and the longing he'd fought for so long finally loosened his tongue. 'He doesn't love you like I do. He can't love you even half as much, or he would have offered for you long ago and even if he does, he's not the right man for you and you can't marry him.'

'Colm, I really have no idea who you're talking about, but you're quite right,' she said on a soft laugh that sounded not very far from tears. 'Nobody loves me like you do and I shall never love anyone else as deeply as I love you.'

'Eve, oh, my darling, I love you so much I can't even think straight,' he whispered and sank his forehead down to meet hers, stared into her eyes since he would never get enough of the sight of her and kissed her ravenously.

Or at least he would have done if he wasn't dizzy with cold and the delicious shock and relief of finding her here and still his Eve and not Captain Revereux's. Lack of breath nearly made him swoon even as her mouth moved under his in a tender kiss, then her lips kicked up in a glorious smile he could feel rather than see as she made a tiny distance between them to whisper, 'Idiot, you're nearly frozen to death and exhausted into the bargain. Did you ride here from Linaire Park *ventre à terre* to prevent me marrying this gentleman I didn't even know I was engaged to?

'Do you know I rather think I did,' he managed to murmur as the fact of her truly began to sink in at last and joy fought a battle with his wobbly leg and won long enough to get them to the ancient sofa by the fire without him dragging them both down on to the floor because he couldn't bear to let her go.

'I used to picture the wild young lover I was going to have one day doing that when I was a girl,' she said as she settled against his shoulder with a very contented-sounding sigh and Colm grimaced at the difference between that image and his own unheroic almost collapse. 'He was nowhere near as handsome and dashing as you are, though,' she said with a beaming smile as if she truly believed it and who was he to disillusion her?

'And I used to dream of you to distract me from battles to come and cold nights on bare mountains with no rations or baggage.'

'Hmm, I suspect you dreamt of lovely Spanish *señoritas*, but we'll pretend you didn't as long as you stop doing it from now on.'

'No, truly I dreamt of marrying the love of my life and loving our children together while I waited to find out if I was to live or die that day. It was that or run away, so you see, you have kept me from disgracing myself all these years.'

'Did I indeed? Well, I shall choose to believe you, even if Pamela Verdoyne's daughter as a wife would be your worst nightmare.'

'Not once I'd actually met you it wasn't,' he said

with a stage leer that made her chuckle deliciously and wasn't it a delight to laugh with this woman who had turned his life inside out and upside down and made him like it that way?

'I love you, Eve,' he said seriously as soon as he could wipe the foolish grin off his face because she was here with him and all that cold and loneliness had been worthwhile, and his journey through a snowstorm to find her before she wed Revereux had been as well, which reminded him, but first he had to convince her he really did love her after all that shilly-shallying. 'Not Pamela's daughter or Lord Farenze's beloved eldest child, but you, my darling, you're my one and only love.'

'You do say the nicest things, Mr Carter,' she told him solemnly.

'And how you did dislike that plodding fool that first night.'

'No, I didn't, I was just better at pretending than you were. I love him as well as Colm Hancourt. You won't forget to be him as well now you have a new life, will you?'

'I can't cut myself up into neat pieces and be one man here and another there. If you really do intend to marry me, you might regret I was Carter once upon a time. I have nightmares and a few memories I find hard to forget even now I'm home and Colm Hancourt again.'

'From now on you will have me to wake you and talk to until the dreams fade, Colm, and of course you remember that other life, why should you forget it?'

'Ah, love, you take my breath away,' he managed to murmur shakily, because how could he be suave and collected when she was here, now, with him and loving him right back?

'And there I was hoping you had recovered enough to kiss me again,' she told him with the most inviting pout he'd ever seen and what else could a gentleman do but oblige a lady?

'Well, I don't know where we're supposed to put a real live lord,' the landlady informed them as she bustled into the room without seeming to notice her most inconvenient guest until now had just been kissed breathless by the limping gentleman she shooed in here to get him out of her way. 'Everyone will just have to move round and your coachman and groom will have to sleep in the stables, Miss Winter. For all this one here said he'd be content there if he had to, we can't have that, what with him being a gentleman and that leg of his giving him gyp and all.'

'I'm sure they will make the best of it,' Eve said as soon as she could get a word in, but the landlady had whisked herself away without waiting for an answer.

'Of all the places we could choose to seduce each other this is possibly the worst, love. Before she comes back and tells us royalty has rolled up and we all have to sleep in the barn, will you promise to marry me?' Colm asked urgently, his dear face so painfully anxious and eyes every bit as intense and intriguing as she dreamt of them night after night as he made love to her in her wildest fantasies that she almost forgot to answer.

'Yes, of course I will, Colm—you and no other. Now do you promise never to leave me alone for so long again? Then you can hurry up and kiss me again before Papa comes in and starts acting like a bear with a sore paw because I put him to the trouble of chasing after me in weather not fit for man nor beast.'

'What a happy reunion this promises to be, but I promise. And you can come with me even if I decide to search for the source of the Nile or the tears of the last dragon. I will be such an overly attentive husband you will soon be wishing…'

'Never say I shall want a lover, Colm. I would rather stay single all my life than marry even you and expect to do that,' she said very seriously.

'I was going to say you would be wishing me at Jericho. And don't you think I know that about you, love? I will do my best all our lives to make sure we never stop loving one another, but you will be as true as steel even if we do. Hush,' he said when she drew breath to argue that was impossible. 'Before your father gets here to breathe fire at me again for wanting his daughter immoderately, can we vow to take time to fall in love with each other all over again at this time every year? Being besotted as husband and wife in a nice little snowstorm like this one is a much better idea than our parents' peculiar way of going about things, don't you think?'

'Oh, Colm, I do,' she replied with a smile that felt blissful and smitten and amused all at the same time. 'It sounds wonderful,' she said and kissed him this time because he was far too gallant to risk it when her father was in the same inn and about to glower at them until he had properly thawed out.

'Good evening.' A plump lady dressed in a dark blue

wool gown with a snow-white collar interrupted that kiss from the doorway just as it was about to get very interesting indeed. 'I see that you two already know each other, or at least I hope so. In my younger days a lady never kissed a gentleman so enthusiastically unless they were very well acquainted indeed.'

'We are going to be married,' Eve said with a misty smile.

'Are you now? In my younger days a *gentleman* asked a lady's father for his permission before they announced their engagement to the first person who happened along,' Viscount Farenze commented over the lady's shoulder.

'Papa, you're cold and cross and you know perfectly well Colm asked to marry me weeks ago,' Eve said, not sure if she was glad to see her father or not for once. His presence meant there was no chance Colm would find his way to her bedchamber tonight and she badly wanted to be his lover, now they had got all that nonsense about the past sorted out. *Ah, well*, her wild inner Eve sighed. *It won't take for ever to marry him if we get on with it before Lent. Then we can be improper every night for the rest of our lives if we choose.*

'That was when I knew you would say no,' her father said glumly.

'Well, I changed my mind,' she announced, hearing such joy and happiness and surprise in her own voice that she nearly laughed for sheer delight and relief. She was going to be so happy with Colm. After all they put one another through since that night they met in Lord Derneley's library it seemed such a wonderful surprise it was a shame her father wasn't delighted for her as well.

'Be very sure of it this time,' her papa urged her, with a challenging glare at Colm and a worried frown for her that almost made her forgive him.

'We have to be, sir,' Colm argued so she wouldn't have to, 'we love one another and there would be no point enduring all the gossip and speculation our marriage will cause if we did not mean it.'

'Aye, well, I might remember I like you when I can feel my toes again and have found out if all my fingers are still in place. Right now I need a good fire, something warm to drink and a good dinner before I feel well disposed towards you or anyone else, Hancourt. I apologise for entertaining you with our family arguments, madam, but I expect you understand how these things will fall out willy-nilly, even in the best regulated families and mine has never been one of those.'

'I have four grown-up daughters of my own, sir,' the lady admitted with a placid smile. They exchanged names, were joined by the lady's unworldly husband and fell into a discussion of the most unlikely weddings the Reverend Stow had presided over during his thirty years as a parish priest.

Eve wondered how her grand dash south, Colm's knightly quest north to rescue her from some marriage that never existed except in his head met in the middle and turned from high romance into this. She didn't care what it could be classed as, she decided, as she slipped her hand in his under the table. The delightful feeling of being able to share such contact with her lover for the first time in her life felt huge and generous and very much like the beginning of a totally new life. Here was her mate; she had found him, the one man in the world exclusively right for her. Her silly, selfish mother spent her life looking for love, then didn't even recognise it when Colm's father fell at her feet. At least Pamela's daughter had enough sense to learn from her example.

'I love you so much, Colm,' she whispered when Mrs Stow diverted her father's attention long enough to slip a murmur past his sharp ears.

'I love you too, Eve,' he replied softly, 'but if you don't eat your dinner your father will probably call me out and the landlady will never speak to either of us again,' he added with a nod at her almost full plate.

'That's so unromantic,' she accused and wondered how she could have been so hungry when she got here after that interminable journey in the teeth of the snow-storm still raging outside.

'I know, but eat your food, love, we'll feast on one another when we're wed.'

Chapter Twenty-Two

❦

'I thought they'd never go,' Colm told his wife grumpily when he opened the door between their grand bedrooms. Eve stopped gazing anxiously at herself in the peer glass and scuttled into bed, pulling the covers over her scandalously exposed body. 'Even now we're wed at last I was almost expecting to find your father in here waiting to make sure we only intend to read sermons to each other all night long if he finally leaves us alone. I swear there was never a stricter chaperon to an engaged couple than he has been this last fortnight and your stepmother and my aunt were nearly as bad.'

'They love us and want us to be happy,' she said with a shrug that agreed they had endured a long and aching wait to be man and wife at last, or at least it had seemed like it at the time.

The trouble was all the hope and love and confidence that got her through the wedding ceremony so blithely was beginning to wilt. There had been a wedding breakfast, a family dinner and a wedding ball to get through since then and Colm was right, her father had been so strict with them since they agreed to love each other for life that they hardly dared steal a kiss from each other during the weeks of their engagement. She knew Papa was determined to show the world how different this was from the last Winterley and Hancourt left-handed connection, but it had made her nervous about tonight. By now she suspected most affianced couples who loved each other would have found a way to prove that love to each other somehow and never mind the conventions. Not so for her and Colm though; they had been as closely guarded as if they were the only heirs to their respective kingdoms.

'Lady Chloe is the best of mothers-in-law, Verity is a scamp and I'm glad her father's new wife will stay in the area once they marry because she will need all the help she can get with the minx. Your Bran is a treasure and loves you like a mother, but please, love, can we lock them all out now? If one more person recalls a last piece of advice they simply must give you on your wedding night I shall very likely break down and cry.'

'I can't quite imagine stern Mr Carter in floods of tears somehow,' she replied, relaxing a little as she recalled that stiff-necked, intriguing gentleman and realised how much Colm had changed since they first met, even if she loved Mr Carter as well as her official husband.

Knowing his father had loved him and been almost as badly treated by the last Duke as Colm, he had lost that fearsome self-sufficiency he used to convince her he didn't need her for far too long. Thank heaven she had seen through it to the real man and now he was letting the deep feelings and heady passion underneath it show. The fire in his brown and gold eyes was unmasked as he met hers now and even his limp seemed better. Her Colm was younger somehow, less burdened. So how could she be scared of her wedding night with this lithe and handsome man who loved her so much he had learnt to defy the past and seize a bright future with her? Any other man and this would be terrifying, but he was Colm: her love and her lawfully wedded husband. She watched him prowl towards the bed with hardly a trace of a limp and was awed by the fact they had made it to being man and wife against all the odds.

'What if I snore, Colm?' she asked suddenly, the appalling idea springing into her mind from nowhere in particular.

He laughed joyously and how good that sounded. There had been so little for him to be light-hearted about until so recently it almost made her cry to think of him being so self-contained and alone for so long. They must laugh a lot in future to make up for the past and love enough to chase the last shadows from his eyes.

'I suppose I shall learn to endure it,' he said solemnly as he came closer and looked at her with a heat in his eyes that said he was wondering how to get those covers off her with the least possible delay. 'I had to when we were in winter billets or camping in the field. Can you imagine how much noise an army full of ruffians makes in its sleep? No? Just as well, but my first sergeant could outdo the artillery, so I don't think you could ever come close to his nightly performances even if you do.'

'His poor wife,' she said as she gazed at her husband and recalled how lucky she was he had survived so much to tease her like this tonight.

'Yes, she would have been, if he had had one,' he murmured with a sadness that told her the man did not survive.

'Poor man,' she said, refusing to look away and pretend she had no idea war killed good men and bad indiscriminately. Theirs wasn't that sort of marriage; she wouldn't allow it to be.

'Yes,' he replied quietly.

'I want to be your everyday lover, Colm, not some fragile lady you put in a box marked wife and feed sweetmeats and pretty words,' she told him seriously.

'As if I would dare,' he said with that old wry smile she realised was put on to defend his tender feelings. 'We make each other real, Evelina Hancourt,' he added with a more piratical version of it and how had he pushed back the covers without her even noticing? Now he would see the almost-not-there nightgown and peignoir the Duchess gave her in such plain wrapping paper Eve was surprised the stuff didn't combust with embarrassment.

'Could we work on being more so right now, do you think?' she whispered as his eyes dwelt longingly on her outrageously outlined body and the hot gold sparks in them enchanted her so much she forgot to blush.

'Do you know, I think we could,' he replied and traced the folds that filmy fabric had fallen into first with his eyes, then a whisper of his index finger that sent shudders of longing through her and never mind how this would go. He was sure and intent on her pleasure more than his own, so it would be wonderful whatever happened.

'More,' she invited with a long sigh that stuttered as he deepened that feather touch and played with warm, eager curves under thin silk. She pushed away the last of the bedclothes to kneel up and meet him kiss for kiss, exploring touch for touch. 'My Colm,' she muttered into his mouth as she sat back on her heels to look up at him and wonder. 'My husband,' she added with another butterfly kiss on his waiting lips. 'My lover.'

'Love,' he said as if more words were beyond him.

So he took over that kiss instead of her and it became deep and hungry. She met him with everything she had to give back and found more when he cupped her needy breasts and her nipples peaked to hard nubs that he greeted with exploring fingers and an approving hum. She arched backwards and thrust up against his touch, eyes heavy and lips open on a moan of sensual approval. Heat shot through her as his hot gaze met hers and promised riches she hadn't dared dream of until this moment. He bent to take one of those begging nipples in his mouth and play with it. All the bones in her body seemed to turn to honey when heat blazed through her as if it might burn them both up and still never be satisfied. Something close to pain ground inside her and she moaned softly to tell him that she didn't know how she could feel so much and not break.

If it wasn't for the fact that he was shaking with need and nerves she might feel exposed and vulnerable when he slid the last whisper of soft silk off her and she was naked. It only took a reproachful look at his fine waist-coat and breeches for him to get out of them so fast she wondered if officers practised dressing and undressing in record time before they went to war. That fast idea faded away as she saw the marks of war on his body even as she wondered at the intriguing differences be-tween satiny male skin over taut muscle and bone. He was lean and toned as a greyhound, and every nerve and sinew of him was eager for her as that hound would be for the chase. Even so, her loving eyes lingered on his poor damaged knee, up to a healed slash on his upper arm, then, worst of all, a wide graze that came so close to his heart it made her own thump in dread of what had almost happened to him on some faraway battlefield.

'Oh, love, look what your evil uncle nearly did to you,' she gasped and traced the path of that old wound across his chest.

'Nothing,' he said with a smile that wanted to reas-sure her, but went a little awry, as if he was wondering about a hard world where he died of it and neither of them would ever know how it felt to love another this deeply as well. 'He meant to do me ill, but made a man of me instead. Can you imagine how soft and despicable you would find me if I had grown up as the pampered heir to a vast fortune? Yes,' he said with a sly grin Mr Carter would be proud of, 'so can I.'

'Don't you try to divert me, Husband. Doing good by accident will not help your eldest uncle at the Day of Judgement,' she said with a severe nod to say Colm might forgive that wicked aristocrat his sins but she never would.

'I am who I am, Eve. That was little enough as far as you were concerned the night we first laid eyes on each other,' he teased her.

'If not for Mr Carter, I might never have let myself love you, I will have you know, Colm Hancourt,' she informed him as militantly as a woman could when she was stark naked with the new husband she loved desperately and wanted even more. 'You would have had to work far harder to charm me if you had lived as your true self all those years. Money doesn't buy everything, you know.'

'It bought me a marriage licence. I'm very fond of that piece of paper and my new wife, but if she doesn't stop her tongue and let me love her I might have to ask the Bishop for my money back tomorrow. I am very careful with my investments now I actually have some at long last, you know.'

'An investment, am I?' she demanded, running a finger softly down his throat and feeling his Adam's apple work as she slid further down and settled at the bottom to count his pulse. Then she explored the supple flex of his muscular torso and the tight masculine nipples that made a tiny echo of her own still-aching ones. He jerked as if she had burned him, so she repeated the caress he had tortured her with just now. 'Is that value for money?' she said with a sly look sideways at his flushed face and hot, unfocused gaze.

'Do that again and you'll have been robbed,' he said huskily and broke his leash, at last, passionately kissing and caressing her until she moaned for more.

There, his sensitive touch on places she hadn't known

she had until tonight tipped her over a dizzying edge. She shouted for him as she went, protesting at the loneliness of being love shot and at the end of the world without all of him. Then he was there, riding the breathless joy of it with her, both within and without her, all around and as gentle as such a desperate lover could be when he finally took her. Another landscape she had never expected to see spread in front of her as she reached it with him hard and rampant inside her and the fleeting pain and strangeness of that invasion a pause on the way. He held himself at bay for her sake, waited to tip her into delirium where all she wanted was for him to go with her. How had he known it was easier for her to take him as she fell into that new world of sensual pleasure? She stuttered a delirious sigh into his heaving chest as he bowed almost upright in the extremes of it all as they soared together into a final climax.

'I think I love you even more now than I thought I could, Colm,' she gasped as he let himself rest for a moment against her softer curves and slender limbs, feeling her with every inch of his body against hers like a full body kiss.

'And I love you, Mrs Hancourt, so very much. I never thought I would have one of those, by the way—a wife. I was certain I wouldn't the day I rode away from Darkmere and you didn't even get up early to stop me.'

'It took me far too long to find out that love matters far more than what people think or say about us, didn't it? There's no need for you to look so smug either, since you thought money mattered more than love to me for far too long. I can't believe you left me alone so long after that obstacle was out of the way either.'

'I thought you might decide that I only asked you to marry me because I can now afford a wife and we were caught kissing each other by your stepmother.'

'I almost understand that, so I must be in love with you.'

'I hope so, considering how thoroughly we just made love to one another.'

'We did, didn't we?' she said with a reminiscent sigh. 'Have you ever felt like that with another woman, or am I a fool to ask?'

'It's your wedding night, woman, you have the right to ask any question you feel you need answering. That one will be, no; not even a shadow of it. We kicked up almost as great a storm in here as Mother Nature is working on out there.'

She listened to the wind lashing rain against the windows and dreamt of summer anywhere with him, maybe even with the promise of their child growing in her belly as they strolled along the avenue here at Darkmere to the first place they nearly made love. This time they might dare even further in the warmth as they nearly did in the full fury of an even wilder storm on that December day.

'Soft southerner,' she murmured as he pushed himself up, rolled over to pull her into his arms and twitched the covers back into place over them now that the blazing fire had died to a glow and neither of them wanted to be parted long enough to make it up again.

'Guilty,' he said and wrapped his arms closer, so this

time she was the one body on body, learning him avidly as she wriggled herself as close to him as she could get.

'That's not all you are guilty of,' she murmured as she felt his sex wake again beneath her.

'Ignore me; we have all the time we need to learn about each other now, love.'

'We have and isn't that a luxury?' she said sleepily as she thought about that day she sat and truly thought about the years stacking up wearily on each other until she met her maker, if she let this one chance of love pass her by. 'You are my best minutes and hours and days on this earth, love. Without you I would have existed until I didn't; with you I love and am loved and I know we are far more together than we ever were apart.'

'And you only have to be in a room to stretch my senses and lift my heart, my darling Evelina. Whenever we argue, we will have to take out the wild promises we made tonight and make them true again, for we will argue, my love. Sometimes you will ask yourself why you ever put yourself through the ordeal of loving a stubborn idiot like me.'

'What will my answer be?'

'That you couldn't help yourself, any more than I could. We might as well tell the sea outside this window to stop thundering and the wind not to throw rain at us as if it wants to get through glass and stone to us as not admit we loved each other almost from the first moment we met.'

'You were such a gruff bear of a Mr Carter as well, were you not?'

'And you such a proud and defiant Miss Winterley

you dared a Hancourt to want you from the moment he laid eyes on you.'

'I thought you despised me, especially after reading my mother's diaries. Your Uncle Augustus would have been a better match for her, don't you think?' she said idly as she realised they had both been as stony hearted as each other. 'Your father sounds as if he had a generous heart after all.'

'The last Duke and your mother would have driven each other mad with greed and selfishness. Now let's forget about them both and live, my love, for I've had enough of my life being governed from the past, even if you have not.'

'I have, but what about your sister, Colm? Wasn't she the reason you felt you had to stay unwed and save up for her dowry? Now you have settled enough money on her to satisfy the greediest of suitors and she still intends to be a governess. No fine gentleman will be able to meet her and realise what a very fine wife she could make him.'

'I'm sure Nell has told you she can look after herself by now, if she had time before she insisted on returning to her charges when the ink was barely dry on our marriage entry, of course. She certainly told me so when I offered to hire a whole school full of mistresses and the finest chaperon I could find for the infernal brats if only she would come home and live with us.'

'Mr Hancourt hates not to be in charge of his troops, doesn't he?'

'Never having been in control of his sister or his

wife to start with, he will have to get used to not being anything of the kind.'

'Sometimes he worries too much about control and refuses to let go of his at the most frustrating times,' she informed him with a provocative wriggle.

'No, go to sleep. There will be time for us to love each other senseless again when I get over the strain of having a wild ex-virgin in my bed.'

'There will never be enough time for that,' she chided even as she felt her eyelids grow heavy and the exquisite novelty of sleeping in her lover's arms call to her for the first time. 'But I do love you, Colm.'

'And I love you more than I ever dreamt I could love,' he whispered and kissed the top of her disarranged hair, since she was still on top of him and it would be a shame not to. 'If ever a man found treasure beyond price when he wasn't even looking for it, I did the night I met you in Derneley's dusty library, my lovely, lovely Eve.'

'True,' she told him and twisted to look up at him with a smug smile. 'I met you and dreamt of gruff and limping heroes all night long. Now I don't have to dream, because I've got you in my bed,' she said with a contented sigh.

'And I've got you in my heart,' he whispered and how could she cap that? She couldn't, so she went to sleep to the steady beat of her lover's heart and she didn't even have to dream of him any more, because he was here.

* * * * *

THE GOVERNESS
HEIRESS

Chapter One

'I would rather be outside, too, Lavinia, but you said it was too cold to learn as we walked this morning. Now we're inside you still won't listen,' Eleanor Hancourt said sternly. 'Remind us how many rods make a furlong.'

Nell's eldest pupil went on staring out of the high schoolroom window and it took Caroline's nudge to jolt her cousin out of a daydream. 'Archbishop of Canterbury, Miss Court,' Lavinia said triumphantly.

'We have moved on from Plantagenet kings and troublesome priests, Lavinia Selford. British history was this morning.'

'Oh,' said Lavinia listlessly. 'Well, it doesn't matter, does it?'

'Kindly explain how the fate of Kings and measuring God's creation are unimportant, Lavinia,' Nell said softly, although she wanted to let her temper rip.

'Because I don't care. Knowing such rubbishy stuff won't get me a husband and a fine house in London,' Lavinia replied defiantly.

'Being a well-bred mother to his children will be enough for you, then?'

'No, he will adore me and when I make my debut I'll dance and have fun while you sew for the poor and read improving books out loud of an evening.'

Nell mentally conceded the girl could be right about the dullness of their current lives, even if everything else she had to say showed how immature Lavinia was. It *was* dull in this half-closed-up house at the back of beyond. Even she, the girls' governess, was only three and twenty and sometimes longed for more and now it was temptingly within reach. Except nobody else really cared if they were happy or miserable, so long as they didn't cause trouble. So she would have to stay until the Earl of Barberry came to take responsibility for his wards and the estate, but that seemed about as likely as pigs learning to fly.

Her authority felt fragile even after two years teaching the man's orphaned wards, but at least he wasn't here to challenge it. He had never been here to see if she was doing her job properly. He hadn't even bothered to meet his young cousins during the decade he'd been head of the Selford family. The Earl left the country as soon as he heard his grandfather was dead and had stayed away ever since. Even two years on from being brought in to try and drive knowledge and ladylike behaviour into the Misses Selford, Nell was too young for such a role. Now she was an heiress to add to her puzzles, but she could think about that when Lavinia wasn't as slyly confident she was going to win their latest battle.

'I am well born and pretty and I have a good figure and a fine dowry,' the girl listed smugly, the difference between them sharp in her light blue eyes.

'A true gentleman requires more than looks and a large collection of vanities in a wife,' Nell replied coolly, pushing the unworthy argument she was well born and a lot wealthier than her eldest charge to the back of her mind. 'A talent for flirting and dancing won't fascinate the fine young man you dream of marrying when every second debutante has that as well. Wit and charm, a sincere interest in those around her, a well-informed mind and a compassionate heart make a true lady, Lavinia. Youthful prettiness fades; do you want to end up lonely and avoided since you have no conversation or common interest to keep your husband at your side when you are no longer as young as you were?'

'Oh, no, Vinnie, imagine how awful it would be to end up like that lady who stayed at the manor last year. The one who bored on and on about imaginary illnesses and how hard her life was until her husband went out of his way to avoid her,' Caroline exclaimed with genuine horror.

'What sane gentleman would marry an empty-headed creature for aught but her money?' Caroline's elder sister Georgiana added with a sideways look at her least favourite cousin.

'That's enough, Georgiana,' Nell said firmly.

Lavinia was the daughter of the last Earl's eldest son and senior in status and years, but what did that matter when all four of the old Earl's granddaughters were stuck here in the middle of nowhere? None of them could inherit the earldom and Nell counted herself lucky that she could only imagine the last Earl's fury when his youngest son made a runaway marriage to Kitty Graham, still whispered of as the loveliest actress of her generation. Hastily doing some mental arithmetic, Nell supposed Kitty and the Honourable Aidan's son hadn't mattered to his paternal grandfather for over a decade. The fifth Earl's eldest son had a robust heir and never mind if his wife refused to share his bed after the boy was born and she declared her duty done. Since the lady was the daughter of a duke the old Earl didn't challenge her until the boy was killed in some reckless exploit at Oxford. Then he'd ordered his heir to mend his marriage and even the Duke agreed, so Lady Selford gave birth to Lavinia a year after she lost her son and was declared too fragile for further duty by the doctors. According to local gossip, the lady turned her back on her baby daughter and returned to her family. Nell marvelled at her indifference, but Lady Selford died when Lavinia was seven and Nell doubted the child had set eyes on the woman above once or twice.

At least Georgiana and Caroline seemed to have been loved by their parents, but a sweating fever killed Captain Selford and his wife and Nell imagined the girls had had a stony welcome from their grandfather, since the servants still gossiped about how bitterly he resented his granddaughters for daring to be born female. Only Penelope had escaped the fury of that bitter old man by being born three months after the Earl died, but as a posthumous child of his third son she had been his last hope of keeping the offspring of an actress out of the succession. The latest Earl of Barberry had carried off the family honours in the teeth of his grandfather's opposition then, but the sixth Earl had done precious little with them. Nell supposed it was better for the girls to grow up without another angry lord glowering at them when he recalled their existence. Lavinia's old nurse once told her how the old Earl cursed whenever Lavinia crossed his path, so little wonder if she grew up imagining a rosier future for herself. Nell hoped the girl would make a good marriage, but misery awaited her if she wed the first young man who asked her to so she could escape her lonely life.

'Forty, Miss Court,' Lavinia said casually at last.

Nell wondered what she was talking about, then remembered the rods and furlongs. 'Very good, Lavinia. So, Georgiana; how many feet in a fathom?'

'Even a land sailor knows there are six and we were at sea until Papa died.'

'You and your stupid sister insist on telling us about him all the time. As if we care,' Lavinia said, quite spoiling the novelty of joining in a lesson for once.

'Then why don't you go and count your rubbishy ribbons, or gaze at your own ugly face in the mirror for hours on end, since you love it so much? At least then we won't have to look at your frog face or listen to you rattle on about who you're going to marry this week, Lavinia Lackwit,' Georgiana scorned as tears flooded Caroline's wide blue eyes at the thought of what the two sisters had lost when their parents died.

Nell felt sorry for Lavinia when even little Penny glared at her for upsetting the most vulnerable of the cousins and all three looked as if they'd be glad if Lavinia disappeared in a puff of smoke.

'Georgiana, that's an inexcusable thing to say. You

will stand in the corner until I say you can come out.
Lavinia; apologise to your cousin, then copy out the
One Hundredth Psalm twice in a fair hand. Maybe
that will make you humbler about your own short-
comings and a little kinder to others, but your guardian will be displeased to hear you refuse to make any
effort at your lessons and fall out with your cousins.'

'He doesn't give a snap of his fingers for any of
us and I hate this place and all of you as well. You're
always such good little girls for your *darling* Miss
Court and she's only a servant when all's said and
done. You make me sick. I hate you all, but I hate
Cousin Barberry most. Why should I care what he
thinks? I doubt he remembers we exist,' Lavinia
railed at the top of her voice, stamped her feet as
if words couldn't express her anger, then ran out of
the room on a furious sob. Nell listened to the sound
of her charge thundering downstairs and the garden
door slamming with a sinking feeling in the pit of her
stomach that her day was about to get even worse.

'I hope she took a shawl,' Caroline said with a
sympathetic shiver.

'And I hope she didn't,' nine-year-old Penny argued vengefully.

Georgiana flounced to the corner she'd been ordered into with a sniff and a contemptuous glower
and Nell tried to do what came next instead of feeling defeated.

'Georgiana, stay there for ten minutes without saying a word or pulling faces at Caroline and Penelope. I shall ask Crombie to sit with you. Caroline and
Penelope, you can read quietly, but you will *not* tease
Georgiana or speculate about Lavinia. As soon as the

ten minutes are up you may read as well, Georgiana,' she told her charges as calmly as she could.

Seeing how impatient Penny's one-time nurse was about being fetched away from her comfortable coze with the housekeeper, Nell knew they wouldn't be allowed to riot in her absence. Now she only had to worry about organising a search for Lavinia with the daylight already fading. She gave orders for all the available staff to comb the gardens and parkland, then went outside to search her own section of the shadowy gardens.

Fergus Selford, Earl of Barberry, rode into the stableyard of Berry Brampton House for the first time in his life and found it strangely deserted. He hadn't expected a fanfare on the arrival of an errant earl nobody knew was coming. Or much of a welcome even if they did, but it felt a bit of come down to stable his own horse. He owned the dratted place from cellar to rafters, yet he'd settled the tired animal in a convenient stall and retrieved his unfashionable boat cloak from the tack room before he met a single soul.

'We're not expecting visitors, so if you're the new land agent you couldn't have arrived at a better time, although you're three weeks late and we had almost given up on you,' a rather pleasant contralto voice told him from the shadowy doorway. 'I saw the lamp and heard someone moving about in here as if he had a right to be here. All the stable boys are supposed to be out looking for one of my charges so I came to see if one of them was shirking. Now you're here we need all the help we can get before Lavinia hurts herself or one of us falls into the ha-ha. You can help me search, since you'll get lost if you wander about on your own and we'll have to find you as well.'

'If you've managed to mislay one of the Selford girls that's your problem,' Fergus told her gruffly, blaming his shabby cloak for her mistake. He was almost inclined to tell her who he was and that he employed her to take care of his wards, so why should he bother himself with a search for one of them when he was weary and uncomfortable and didn't want to be here in the first place?

'It'll be yours if the Earl finds out we couldn't keep one of his wards safe because you refused to help.'

'Is she mad or just simple? It has to be one or the other since you believe she'll do herself a mischief in his lordship's private grounds.'

'Miss Selford is a bright and spirited young girl who has trouble keeping her temper in check. A trait I sympathise with at this very moment,' the governess said through what sounded like clenched teeth.

Now why was arguing with her in the semi-darkness more stimulating than flirting with sophisticated beauties? He heard her take a deep breath and she seemed to call on the reserves of patience his wards hadn't already tested to the limit. Reminding himself he was here to do his duty, not amuse himself at the governess's expense, he ordered himself to stop provoking her and get on with it.

'Never mind, we'll find her without your help and I suppose you wouldn't be much use anyway,' she said haughtily. 'If you can exert yourself long enough to cross the yard and find Cook, I expect she will feed you, then direct you to your quarters. I wish you joy of the land steward's house, by the way. You should have told us you were coming—since you are so tardy we had given up on you and abandoned the attempt to make it more welcoming.' Even in the gloom he could see the glare the Amazon shot him before she turned to march back the way she came.

'Stop,' he ordered and she turned as slowly as an offended queen. He wanted to kiss the temper off her lips for a shocking moment. She would slap him and quite right, too, and he hadn't come here to prove that every hard word his late grandfather had said about him had turned out to be true.

'No, I'm busy,' she said and strode towards a path he could only just see in the fast fading light.

'Two pairs of eyes and ears will be better than one in this gloom,' he said as he caught up with her, bowed ironically and indicated she carry on leading the way. 'You know where you're going,' he explained, beginning to enjoy himself now he had such a prickly lady to annoy and this new disguise to settle into.

He told himself he wouldn't have thought of such an impersonation until she thrust it on him, but *not* announcing who he was to a household he never wanted to inherit in the first place was too tempting to turn his back on. As a ruse for finding out what was going on without putting the entire neighbourhood on alert that the new Earl was home at last it could hardly be bettered. Pretending to be the land steward would save him the huge effort of being the sixth Earl of Barberry and he could spy out the land, then decide if he could endure being here. Perhaps it was as well the Moss boy, who he'd lined up to act as land steward, had backed out of this post for an easier one since his lack of backbone had forced Fergus to come here, but taking up his inheritance in the teeth of the late Earl's bitter opposition still rasped his pride somehow.

Everything the Selfords had worked so hard to keep from a whore's son, as they so charmingly called him, was his, but it felt like a hollow victory. After living on his own terms in Canada for almost a decade the rules of a polite little English society felt petty. As a heedless and rather angry young man he had been determined to defy his grandfather and all those who made his time at Eton and Oxford a mixed blessing. There was always some aristocratic sprig ready to deride him as grandson of Lord Barberry on one side and an Irish gypsy on the other. None of them would believe he never really wanted the titles and lands hanging around his neck like a millstone, so he'd left the country when the old Earl was barely cold in his grave. There were so many things he could do elsewhere, so many adventures to have, but he'd been doing his best to ignore the voice of his conscience and his mother's pleas to come home ever since he'd fallen in love with the vastness and promise of the so-called New World. Another thing he could blame being Earl of Barberry for, having to leave a place he could have made his home if not for all the responsibilities he'd been so intent on running away from ten years ago.

Still, as Moss he could learn what he wanted to know, then go away again if he chose to and nobody here would even know he'd been. He ought to thank the woman striding along the path ahead of him as he stumbled in her wake like a rowing boat chasing a stately galleon.

Now what *was* her name? He was ashamed to find he couldn't remember it, despite the quarterly reports she insisted on sending him of the state of his cousins' health, happiness and progress, or lack of it. Still, she was the latest in a long line of governesses who'd all insisted on writing to him about their woes with the Selford girls when they were paid handsomely to deal with them. Just as well this one had no idea who he was, because he paid little attention to her meticulous lists of how Miss Lavender or Miss Patty, or whatever they were called, were progressing when his lawyers sent them on. Thousands of miles away he'd had to trust that his senior lawyer knew what he was doing when he'd insisted that young girls needed someone youthful to care for their happiness as well as teach them to paint screens and sew samplers, or whatever young ladies did until they were old enough to marry. Considering this female had carelessly mislaid one of his wards, he was beginning to wonder about the fellow's wisdom and sanity right now.

'Where are we going?' he asked as he followed Miss Whoever into a generous old orchard.

'If I told you it would mean nothing, unless you've been studying estate maps before taking up your employment?' she said with too much irony for his taste.

'I'm here now, aren't I?' he said defensively.

'And only three weeks late as well. How very diligent, Mr Moss.'

'That discrepancy is between me and my employer.'

'And he doesn't sound the most patient or tolerant

of them. In your shoes I'd be careful how I conducted myself, now you're here at last.'

'Is that a threat?' he asked, with what his half-sisters said was his most annoying sneer. Annoying or not, it was wasted on this woman. She was peering at what looked like a tall hutch in the twilight as if he didn't exist.

'An observation,' she said absently. He felt like a fly so trivial it wasn't even worth slapping him. 'Don't get too close,' she warned and he instantly wanted to.

He was beginning to sympathise with his absent ward's need to escape her governess's authority. Then he got too close and an angry buzz shot past his ear. He stepped back hastily as the persistent little creatures took exception to him but, annoyingly, left the governess alone as if she belonged here and he didn't.

'I did warn you,' she said with *I told you so* in her voice.

'What is this place?' he asked gruffly.

'A bee house, of course,' she said and followed him away as if nothing about this place troubled her, which it didn't, he supposed—she wasn't the one in danger of being royally stung.

'Oh, of course, and what an ideal place for a runaway schoolgirl to hide.'

'Lavinia is a fanciful creature and local lore insists the bees be told whatever happens in a household if they are to be part of it.'

'And they really want to know when a girl is out of sorts with her governess?'

'It was a possibility. Now maybe you'll go back to the house and ask for your dinner so I can get on,' she said as if tired of indulging him.

'While you wander about in the dark and risk life and limb? Even I'm not that much of a yahoo, Miss… Who are you anyway?' he demanded irritably, glad now he hadn't remembered her name and given himself away.

'Miss Court and I'm not in any danger since, as you pointed out just now, we are in his lordship's private grounds. And I'll get on a lot faster if you leave me be.'

'No, if the wench has done something to herself in the dark you can't carry her, great girl of fifteen or sixteen as she must be.'

'How do you know the age of my eldest charge?'

Curse the woman, but now she sounded suspicious. Fergus searched his memory for lies he'd already told her. Even the son of a country squire would know enough to guess how old the Earl of Barberry's wards must be now.

'Everyone knows Barberry was left with a stable of female cousins when he inherited,' he said and even managed to sound plausibly impatient. 'The old lord's quest for another male heir is hardly a secret and if those girls were old enough to be presented they wouldn't need a governess, so even the eldest cannot be out yet.'

'Clever,' she said flatly and why didn't he think it a compliment?

Chapter Two

~~~~~~

They reached the end of the orchards and the interfering female found a wicket gate out into the park
as if by instinct, or perhaps she came here rather too
often in the dark, a jealous impulse prompted Fergus.
The notion she was so familiar with his grounds because she came here to meet a lover and flit through
the moonlit park at the idiot's side for a stolen idyll
goaded him to the edge of fury for some odd reason.
He hadn't even seen her properly yet, but she sounded
just the sort of woman to order some poor besotted
idiot to dance attendance on her in the dusk so they
wouldn't be caught courting and risk dismissal. He
employed the woman to look after his cousins, he
told himself uncomfortably. She should be keeping
a close eye on his little cousins, not planning to run
off with a local curate or farmer's son even her family might consider a misalliance.

'Where are we going now?' he demanded rudely,
but he'd ridden all the way from Holyhead and felt as
if he was entitled to be a little out of temper.

Miss Court might have a lover lurking nearby *and*

she was being rude to the very person she ought to impress if she wanted to keep her post. Was he more impressed by his title than he thought, then? No, he didn't want to be an earl today any more than he had ten years ago. Miss Court made him feel like a grubby schoolboy who hadn't washed behind his ears even as his inner demons tempted him to kiss the wretched female and find out if she was as headlong and determined a lover as she was as a rescuer of wild girls in the semi-darkness. And it *would* be nice to find a way to make her stand back and take notice. Not that she'd waited for him to fight his inner demons back where they belonged. She was almost beyond reach by the time he realised he didn't want to be left here like the last lame nag in a stable. He speeded up and almost fell over a tree root in the shadows.

'Devil take it, woman, will you slow down?'

'No. You didn't want to come in the first place, so I don't understand why you won't go away. I should never have made you come, you're no help at all.'

'If the girl doesn't want to go home, you won't be able to drag her back,' he pointed out rather sharply.

Had she paled at the idea of having to force her errant charge to obey her? Hard to tell in the gloom and why should he care if she endured the role of governess or loved it? Catching himself out thinking like the spoilt aristocrat he'd sworn not to be, he wondered if his half-brother was right and he was as arrogant as any Selford in his own way.

'Hush,' she whispered. 'Do you hear something over there, on our right?'

'No,' he said in a normal voice, telling himself he

was bored with looking for unruly schoolgirls who didn't want to be found.

'I *wish* I hadn't bothered to find out who was lazing about in the stables when the lads were supposed to be looking for Lavinia,' she informed him crossly and strode into the night yet again.

'The wages of curiosity,' he called, then scurried after her like a tardy footman before she could disappear. 'Where are we going?' he asked when he almost ran into her standing still under a tree as if she could hear her way to what she wanted if she tried hard enough. She was warm and rather delightfully curved and he felt passion thunder through his senses until he reminded himself the woman was his cousins' governess and he was her employer.

'*Will* you go away?' she demanded as if she was oblivious to him and his unruly masculine urges, then she started off again without giving any indication where she was heading.

'No,' he said, grabbing the back of her cloak and holding on when she did her best to snatch it away. 'Tell me, or I'll shout a warning we're on our way.'

'Can't you hear the poor girl, you blundering great idiot? She isn't going to run in that state,' she whispered furiously as she towed him forward by his hold on her cloak.

He wondered how he'd managed to miss it as well now; self-preservation, he decided ruefully. Noisy sobs and the odd pathetic little moan carried on the cooling air as the girl fought for breath against all that sorrow. Fergus wished he'd left the governess to cope with a soggy storm of tears and almost melted into the darkness as Miss Court ordered. On the one hand, he would be obliging a lady, on the other he'd be a coward. He let go of Miss Court's cloak and meekly followed in her footsteps.

'It's me, Lavinia,' Miss Court said so gently he wondered if he'd been wrong to class her as an irritable she-wolf in petticoats when she'd first loomed out of the darkness. 'You must be hungry and cold, and you sound as if you need a shoulder to cry on.'

Fergus could make out a Grecian-style temple. As they emerged from the trees he saw the first stars reflected in the lake beyond it and wondered how it would feel to meet Miss Court here for a twilight tryst. Exciting, a forbidden voice whispered in the back of his mind and he uneasily tried to ignore it. He didn't even know the woman; even if he did it would be wrong to lead her on when he was really her absentee employer and never mind this odd feeling of connection to the wretched female.

'Oh, Miss Court,' the girl gasped and Fergus backed away when an overgrown schoolgirl pelted down the steps of the summer house, then flew into her governess's arms with such force he stepped forward to steady the woman and never mind feminine tears and his dread of a *scene*. 'I'm so sorry,' the girl managed to gasp out between sobs. 'I don't think I'll ever learn to behave properly or keep my temper as you say I must.'

'Hah!' Fergus muttered darkly. He felt Miss Court stiffen beside him and knew she must have heard him, but she *had* lost hers with him several times and if she was going to pretend to be a pattern card she should get her emotions under better control.

'Never mind that now. I'm so glad you're safe, even if you are more than a little bit woebegone. And it's getting dark and chilly, so why not come home and be pampered a little for once? We can talk about your troubles when you're feeling better. I only want the best for you and, whatever your cousins say when you all lose that fiery Selford temper, they love you, Lavinia. At times I'm even quite fond of you myself.' Miss Court ended with a laugh in her voice that made Fergus smile in the darkness, so he wasn't at all surprised to hear a watery chuckle from the drooping young lady snuggled in her governess's arms as if they'd never had the argument that probably caused this fuss in the first place.

How unworthy of him to envy the girl and wish he was enjoying all that warmth and welcome. Miss Court was a lady and he certainly wasn't a land steward. He hadn't even met the woman in the clear light of day, he reminded himself hastily and if this was what pretending to be Moss did to him, he might have to reconsider the plum she'd handed him when she'd made that hasty assumption about who he was. He could have been anyone, he condemned her with a frown it was as well she couldn't see. Who knew what sort of rogue could be stumbling about in the dark silently lusting after her if he hadn't found her first?

'Thank you, but I do wish Mama hadn't died, Miss Court. There's nobody left to love me,' Lavinia confessed in a whisper and reminded him they had a very effective chaperon and Miss Court had only ever seen him as an extra pair of eyes and ears to help her find her charge.

* * *

Nell knew how it felt to be lonely, but at least her brother had always loved her, however determined their eldest uncle might be to keep them apart. 'All the wishing in the world won't bring her back, I fear,' she said gently, 'but soon you'll be able to show the world how a true Selford lady behaves and what a shame to waste it on the first callow youth to pluck up the courage to ask you to wed him.'

'Heaven forbid,' Nell thought she heard muttered with heartfelt sincerity by the annoying man behind her. She turned around with Lavinia in her arms and the silence that met her glare was so innocent she knew she'd heard aright.

'Who are you?' Lavinia demanded and Nell didn't correct her manners for once because he didn't deserve any better.

'Miss Court will tell you I'm the new land steward,' he said in the lazy drawl that made Nell's palms itch.

'And are you?'

'So it would seem.'

'You are a very odd person if you need someone to tell you who you are, isn't he, Miss Court?'

'Mr Moss seems quite deaf, the poor gentleman. He certainly takes no notice of anything I say.'

'You don't look very old, sir,' Lavinia observed sagely.

Nell had to argue with herself before she corrected her gently. 'Remember what I said about it being impolite to make comments on the odd behaviour of others, Lavinia?' she said, but Mr Moss saved the girl an apology Nell hadn't quite demanded.

'I could lie and say I'm a mere stripling of five and fifty, I suppose, but it's hard enough being Methuselah without making things any worse, Miss Lavinia,' the rogue said with such self-mocking laughter in his voice Nell wanted to smile, briefly.

'Now you're teasing me, sir, and, as you don't seem offended by what Miss Court insists are my bad manners, *are* you telling the truth about yourself?'

'Oh, I never do that,' the new land steward said brazenly. 'If you choose to believe me, I'll admit to being one and thirty, Miss Lavinia. If you don't; I'm five years less because even we gentlemen have our vanity.'

'Since he has confessed to being a work of fiction, maybe we should add five years to the total and make Mr Moss quite an elderly young gentleman instead, Lavinia,' Nell said lightly, wishing he could see her best frown through the gloom. She wondered how he managed to irritate her so much when they'd only just met; it was a special gift, she decided, one she was glad most men didn't share.

'You have my sympathy, Miss Lavinia. Your governess makes *me* feel like a small boy with a dirty neck and I thought I was grown up until we met.'

'Miss Court is a wonderful governess and a very kind person, Mr Moss,' Lavinia surprised all three of them by saying earnestly.

'Thank you, my dear,' Nell said, giving her most challenging pupil another hug and draping most of her cloak around her shivering shoulders. 'But we must get you inside before you take a chill. Never mind Mr Moss and his poor opinion of anyone who doesn't fawn on him as if he was your guardian and not the Earl's new land steward, we must scurry home as fast as may be now I've found you at last.'

'And I have travelled far today, so let's hope my manners will mend after a good night's sleep. The lawyers tell me I have a great deal to do if things are to be run smoothly here once more,' Mr Moss said in what Nell felt sure was a rather kind attempt to divert Lavinia from the last of her sobs and the convulsive shivers that followed them.

'They're right,' she replied as calmly as she could with the chill reaching both their bodies now. The cold was biting even through her sensible gown with Lavinia wrapped up in most of her cloak. 'Your predecessor should have retired sooner with such a large and complex estate to manage,' she went on, mainly to distract herself from her own need to shiver and in the hope it would take Lavinia's mind off her physical woes as they had to pick their way back over roots and rabbit holes in the ever-deepening twilight.

'Poor man,' Lavinia said and Nell heard the shake in her pupil's voice and pushed their pace as hard as she could without one of them falling flat on their faces.

'Aye, and if you're not set on catching a chill in order to be thought interesting for the next week, we'd best get you home faster than this, Miss Lavinia,' Mr Moss said and hefted the girl into his arms when they paused for breath.

'Gracious, you're very strong,' Lavinia said breathlessly.

'I'll run ahead to warn everyone you're on your way if you will direct Mr Moss, Lavinia? You should be safe with him, by the way. He has atrocious man-

ners and a misplaced sense of humour, but he made
no attempt to molest me on the way here,' Nell managed to say brusquely and scampered away before
either of them could argue.

'Why, thank you, Miss Court,' Fergus muttered as
he eyed the darkness in her wake.

'She is a very definite sort of person,' Lavinia said
with a catch in her voice that told him she was fighting the last of her tears.

'Here, let's wrap you up in this cloak since she's
left it behind. If you can face her wrath if you catch
a chill, I'm not sure I can and don't get us lost, will
you? I don't know the way even by daylight.'

'How thoughtless of Miss Court,' the schoolgirl
in his arms said sleepily and Fergus suspected he'd
have to get them back as best he could, dark or not.

What a good thing he didn't lead the sort of life
most idle earls about town did, he decided, finding a
path through the woods almost by instinct. Slight as
this girl was, he was weary from his journey and she
was almost an adult. He was oddly touched when she
fell asleep in his arms, but wasn't it as well she didn't
know who he was? His wards probably regarded him
as a devil incarnate. He changed his hold on the
Selford sleeping so trustingly in his arms and marvelled at the toll too much emotion could take on
a young lady. Memory of how it felt to be torn between childish simplicity and the need to find your
own way in the world made him feel sorry for his
young ward.

His mother had dealt with his rebellious and confused younger self with her usual common sense and

his stepfather would shrug and take him on one of his adventures whenever he got out of hand. Saints, but he was lucky, wasn't he? Not for him the starch and disapproval of a Miss Court; or the memory of parents who saw their own child as a failure simply because she was born female. His mother would have loved him if he had been born a dumb, cross-eyed lunatic, but at least Lavinia's governess hadn't ripped up at her. Indeed, Miss Court seemed truly concerned that the girl felt she had to sob out her woes alone. The woman could stay until he found out more about her, he decided grudgingly. Now he would take the role she had thrust at him by mistaking him for Moss and what better way to find out if he could trust her with his wards until they were ready to be brought out in polite society? Then he could go somewhere he would like better and forget Miss Court and his stupid reactions to her in the dark.

What with racing back to the house, making sure the stableyard bell was rung to signal Miss Lavinia was safe and organising a welcome for her, Nell should have no time to think about rude and disobliging Mr Moss. So, of course, she thought of little else while she ordered a hot bath for Lavinia and a warming pan for her bed. Then there were the other girls to reassure that their cousin was in one piece and being brought home safely. The stir of the man's arrival with Lavinia seemed oddly muted and Nell went to peer over the wooden banister of the staircase leading to the nursery wing. Why did the sight of Lavinia fast asleep in his arms make her heart ache so?

Puzzled by her own emotions at the sight of the girl

cradled protectively in a stranger's arms, she ran up to Lavinia's room to announce she was on her way. 'We'll forget a bath and get her straight into bed as she seems to be fast asleep. The new land steward is on his way upstairs with her right now.'

'He's turned up at long last then, has he?' Mary said, showing more interest in the steward than she ever did in her young mistress. 'He must be much fitter than old Mr Jenks to carry Miss Lavinia here, then have breath enough to bring her upstairs.'

'Only just,' the man himself announced ruefully as the butler shepherded him into the room as if he was important. Mr Moss had impressed someone tonight then, Nell thought ungratefully. No, some were too impressed, she decided, as she watched Mary making sheep's eyes at the newcomer. The buxom little maid seemed to have forgotten she was employed to look after the young lady they must now try to get into bed without waking her up.

'Thank you, sir. Mary and I will manage now,' she told the man coolly as he gently sat his burden in the comfortable chair by the fire.

'I know I'm in the way now, Miss Court.'

'Goodnight then, sir,' she said repressively.

'I fear not; the housekeeper has insisted I stay here for dinner while my house is being hastily got ready for occupation. It seems it was got unready and left cold when I failed to arrive at the appointed time.'

'You *are* very tardy,' Nell said shortly.

'But also sharp set after such a mighty journey,' he told her with a knowing grin, then sauntered out as if he owned the place.

* * *

'Insufferable man,' Nell spluttered when the door was shut behind him.

'He's very handsome, Miss Court,' Mary said with a longing gaze at that very door, as if wishing might bring him back.

'Not really,' Nell said as she tried to decide why he was so uniquely attractive.

Not wanting to discover the secret of it, Nell set about undressing Lavinia as gently as she could and shot the maid a sharp look to remind her of her duty. Between them they coaxed Lavinia to raise her arms so they could strip off her muslin gown, stockings, indoor shoes and flannel petticoat without rousing her fully.

'Let her sleep in her petticoat this once,' Nell said as they each put an arm about the girl's waist and walked her over to the bed. 'She needs rest more than food right now,' she warned and put a finger to her lips to tell Mary not to argue until they were out of earshot.

'What if she wakes up hungry later?' the girl whispered when they were out in the corridor with the door almost shut.

'I must persuade Cook to make her something that won't spoil. If she sends your dinner up, will you listen for her while I go downstairs? If the poor child has one of her nightmares I don't want her to be alone.'

Nell could sense the young maidservant wanted to argue, but it was her job to look after the eldest Selford girl. Mary probably wanted to giggle with her fellow maids at the thought of such an exciting addition to the local pool of bachelors. Nell would stay and watch Lavinia's slumbers herself if she didn't have three other charges and a disturbing stranger to keep an eye on. Mr Moss might regret accepting the housekeeper's invitation to stay to dinner while she scurried her staff over to his house to give it a hasty airing. Or at least he might when he found out Nell was in the habit of instructing her pupils in the art of fine dining and good manners and he would be a tame gentleman to practice on.

Chapter Three

'Mr Moss has gone upstairs to wash and shave. Parkins showed him into the Red Room and sent Will to wait on him,' Penny told Nell when she went along to the night nursery to make sure her youngest charge was ready for the meal ahead.

'Are you sure you don't want to move into a proper grown-up bedchamber, my love?' Nell asked to divert them both as she caught Penny's sash and hauled her gently back into the room to be made as neat and presentable as she already thought she was.

'No, I like it in here and Crombie is next door if I have a bad dream.'

'Sooner or later you'll have to become a young lady,' Nell said as she brushed Penny's wavy nut-brown hair to shining perfection. It struck her that Penny might well be the most sought-after Miss Selford one day, for all Caro's potentially stunning looks. As Penny was nine years old at least Nell could put off worrying about her future for a while.

'Not until I'm too big to have a choice,' Penny said with a grimace of distaste.

Nell knew it was wrong to have favourites, but she secretly doted on her youngest pupil. She pronounced Penny perfectly turned out even for dinner with a strange gentleman now and reminded her that her manners ought to match her appearance.

'Of course,' said Miss Penelope Selford with a solemn nod and a hop, skip and jump to show how excited she was by even this much company.

Memory of how it felt to be the daughter of a scandalous lord had kept Nell here, trying to fill some of the gaps in the girls' narrow lives, even if they were lonely for a very different reason. Now her brother Colm's fortune was restored and her own dowry doubled by her father's efforts to protect his children before he died. She wondered what Mr Moss would make of a governess with a handsome fortune and a scandalous father. As the third son of a country squire he might court her for her fortune, whatever he thought of her and her blighted family name, and that was another reason Nell refused to join Colm and his new wife for the upcoming London Season. Fortune hunters. Even the thought of men pursuing her solely for her money made her shudder with dread. Then there was the unscrupulous lecher who had been trying to force her sister-in-law to marry him on the very night Eve and Colm met. Nell knew she would find even less determined ones difficult to fend off and she didn't understand how to do it without a fuss, as Eve had learned to during her rather trying three years as a single society lady with that same scandal hanging over her. Nell had spent most of her life in the company of women and girls, so how would it feel to be put on show for the poorer gentlemen of the *ton* to decide if they could endure marrying her for her moneybags? Appalling, she decided with another shudder and snapped back to the here and now with a sigh of relief.

'Are we going downstairs soon, Miss Court?' Penny asked. 'Mrs Winch will not be happy if you leave her to make sure that Caro and Georgie behave like proper young ladies in company.'

Nell shot a look at her own reflection in the small mirror. She was neat enough in a dark blue stuff gown and at least her hair had stayed in place. It took a legion of hairpins to keep it neat and she had no intention of making a special effort so that would have to do. Mr Moss would have to endure the sight of her everyday clothes. How silly to have a vision of dazzling him in a fine silk gown with her hair arranged to flatter instead of disguise her charms. Even if she had such a gown she wouldn't wear it for Lord Barberry's land steward.

'We had best hurry before they go down without us,' Nell said and braced herself for the ordeal ahead, wishing they could have nursery tea in the schoolroom and retire betimes instead of having to meet Mr Moss again today.

Before they went downstairs she had to make Georgiana remove the pins from her hair, then take off her late mama's second-best pearl necklace and do up the buttons of her gown all the way to the top. Drat him, but the man was disruption in breeches, she decided with a long-suffering sigh. As she plaited the girl's tawny mane neatly she tried not to be disturbed by the idea of dangerous adult company herself and sincerely hoped he was less intriguing by the light of several wax candles than he was in the dark.

Oh, confound the man, she decided when they finally got downstairs; he looked every inch the gentleman. How on earth did a lowly steward afford to have his coats made by a master tailor? Scott had crafted her brother's fine new coats and was a firm favourite with former military gentlemen. Perhaps Mr Moss had engaged Weston instead, but that midnight-blue superfine coat wasn't the work of a provincial tailor. Nor did his snowy linen and spotlessly sleek knee breeches seem quite right on the younger son of a country squire. Nell frowned as her charges meekly curtsied to him, rendered almost speechless with awe for a few brief moments as they took in the splendour of their unexpected guest. There was something very much out of kilter about a hired man appearing here in clothes that must have cost most of his annual salary before he had even begun to work for it.

'Good evening, sir,' Nell managed coolly, as all the reasons for his unexpected style clamoured in her head and she couldn't find one that didn't spell trouble. 'Miss Georgiana, Miss Caroline and Miss Penelope Selford, meet your guardian's new land steward, Mr Moss.'

'Good evening, ladies,' he replied with a courtly bow. Now thoroughly out of sorts, as she worried about the reasons Moss had left his last post, Nell had to whisper a sharp aside to Caro and Georgie before they remembered their manners and returned his greeting.

'You look very fine, sir,' Nell said as her eyes met

his and he seemed to mock her conclusions some besotted lady had paid for her lover to appear every inch the gentleman in her company. She wished she had someone ready to whisper good conduct in *her* ears and tried hard to ignore a sharp pang that couldn't be jealousy. Why didn't she have the wit to invent a headache and excuse them all this supposedly quiet dinner with his lordship's new land agent?

'My godmama pays my tailor's bill once a year, so I can present a better appearance than a younger son is usually able to do,' he replied smoothly.

Nell looked for mockery in his acute blue eyes and met bland innocence, but did she believe him? No, yet she could hardly challenge him in front of the girls. She gave him a polite, insincere smile and waved the girls to sit on a sofa the other side of the fire from their unexpected guest. She didn't approve of him looking so at home by his employer's fireside, but the Earl didn't want it, so she had no real reason to object. If he took advantage she would deal with him in private, but she suspected he was far too subtle a man to do anything so obvious.

'Were you waiting for your new clothes to arrive before you came?' Penny asked innocently. Nell was ready to rebuke her, but Mr Moss shook his head and smiled at her youngest pupil.

'A land steward needs gaiters and homespun more than a fine coat and expensive boots, Miss Penelope, but the Earl had another use for me so I did as I was bid. I hope my workaday clothes turn up on the carrier's cart soon, because I certainly can't ride about the countryside in my town finery if I wish to be taken seriously as Lord Barberry's steward,' he said.

Nell hoped the girls didn't notice his mocking look in her direction, as if he'd read every doubt in her mind about that tall tale. He could have as many lovers as he needed to keep him in style, so long as he didn't impart his dubious morals to her pupils, she concluded, with a militant frown he ignored with annoying ease.

'That would be sensible, considering the dire spring we have endured so far,' she agreed as if she almost believed in his doting godmother instead of a foolish lover.

'I promise to be ill dressed and muddy next time we meet, ma'am. You Misses Selford have a very conscientious governess. I doubt you get away with putting a foot wrong without her knowing about it almost before you do.'

'Miss Court is kind and looks after us very well,' Penny said loyally.

Even Caroline nodded and Georgiana looked as if she was disappointed in him and Nell would have hugged them all if he wasn't looking.

'I'm sure she does all a good governess should,' he approved with a sly smile Nell didn't trust one bit.

'Thank you, Mr Moss,' she said calmly, although it sounded more of a challenge than a compliment. 'I do my best.'

'And who can ask for more?' he asked and she wasn't sure she could endure much more of being laughed at by an estate manager who looked more like a society rake without telling him exactly what she thought of him.

She couldn't do anything of the sort, but his questionable standards of behaviour felt like a betrayal and what was between them for him to betray? Nothing; she was Miss Hancourt and he the son of a country squire with a living to earn and never mind any side benefits he had fitted in along the way.

'I feel quite famished tonight,' Caro said quietly.

Nell was concerned enough about her least garrulous pupil to look for signs of girlish infatuation in her eyes. No, from the spark of anger when she eyed the man warily, Caro was trying to stop this exotic newcomer mocking her governess. It warmed Nell's heart to think shy Caro wanted to defend her from this puzzling stranger.

'I expect dinner will be served as soon as Mrs Winch is able to join us,' she said with a fond smile at Caro to say she was excused the minor faux pas of admitting to hunger in public.

'Lavinia will be very sharp set by morning,' Penny said cheerfully.

'I asked Cook to make something cold for her to eat if she wakes up hungry,' Nell said with a slight frown at her youngest pupil to warn her not to gloat about Lavinia's exhausting bout of tears.

'Good, because she really can't help it,' Georgiana said earnestly.

'I know, Georgiana, and I'm sure Penelope will forget what her eldest cousin said in the heat of temper, especially if she wishes to take dinner with us tonight,' Nell said firmly.

'She said…'

'There are faults on all sides,' Nell pointed out. 'Your cousins were rude to each other and the slate is clean now, unless you would like to do penance for your own hot words and uncaring sentiments?'

'No,' Penny said with a sidelong look at her cousins to confirm she would be an idiot to work out a grudge against Lavinia when the alternative was dinner and far more exciting company than usual.

'Miss Court the peacemaker, who would have thought it?' the company said as if he had every right to pass judgement on her.

'And Mr Moss, the peace breaker, what of him?' she replied so quietly the girls couldn't hear when she crossed the room to find Parkins and get him to tell Mrs Winch dinner was overdue. The lady's services as chaperon to her and her pupils felt more important than whatever was delaying her and the sooner this meal was over the better.

'Oh, him. He's a rascal,' Moss murmured when she was on her way back to the stiff-backed chair as far away from him as she could get and still feel warmth from the fire. She had taken it because she disliked him, she reassured herself, and gave a little nod of confirmation she hoped he'd take so badly he wouldn't tease her again.

The girls needed practice at polite dining and proper topics of conversation when gentlemen were present and she would usually admit she needed more adult company. As a single lady who might end up alone and at her last prayers, the whole neighbourhood would assume Miss Court was doing her best to marry any spare bachelor who came along. No doubt everyone in the area would assume she was intent on catching the wretch now he'd turned out to be vigorous and well looking. The thought of speculative eyes watching them at church every Sunday made her shudder. The last thing she intended to do was break her heart over Moss and she doubted he had one to break if she was so inclined. She would stick to the schoolroom or wait for the paragon who might inspire even half the love and passion in her as her brother Colm and his new wife Eve had for one another.

In public the newlyweds acted like a very proper young couple. There was no sitting gazing into each other's eyes and sighing for a bed and just a bit more privacy for them. Yet they showed how much they loved each other by small glances and little touches. One always knew where the other was without having to watch every little movement and, whereas most people grew heavy eyed and weary the later it got in the day, those two glowed with delicious anticipation of being alone again at last. Nell had never seen two people so silently and discreetly delighted at the idea of being wrapped up in the night when nobody else would expect them to be polite for a few precious hours.

Something told her Moss would never let his cynical detachment drop long enough to allow a female that far into his life. What would she find if he did offer to share it with her? A hardened heart and calculating mind? Or perhaps, a protected heart—because he had such a tender, ardent spirit under all that cynicism? *And look where misplaced love got your late father,* Nell reminded herself, resolving to get on with real life before it got out of control.

A suitably bland topic of conversation eluded her. She doubted Mr Moss would let the mild amusement of speculating who the new rector of Great Berry might be run for long. It was impolite to wonder who was up or down in local society when he didn't know them; which left the state of the nation or the arts. Nell opted for the latter until Mrs Winch finally tore herself away from other duties and they could go in to dinner and get this difficult evening over with the sooner.

'I'm so sorry,' Mrs Winch said breathlessly as she hurried into the room a few minutes later. 'One of the maids has managed to scald herself *and* tip half the fish course on the floor,' she murmured in Nell's ear before greeting their guest graciously and signalling to Parkins it was time to announce dinner was served.

Nell hoped that part of the meal went to the pigs, however spotless the kitchen floor was before it fell. And what would Moss make of the simple dishes they were used to in the Earl's absence? The girls were too young for elaborate sauces and the clever touches of a French chef and Nell and Mrs Winch were happy with Cook's beautifully cooked but simple meals. If the man usually took his dinner in the sort of company his evening attire indicated he must, he'd be disappointed. He seemed to enjoy it though, so perhaps he really was a simple man in dandy's clothing. If so, his godmother's folly in outfitting him so splendidly was no kindness when he must earn his own bread. Why, he could sit down to dinner with the Earl and not be outshone and what a mistake that would be in an underling.

How had she got from hoping her food had never been on the floor to worrying about the social niceties of Moss's wardrobe? The man was old enough to look after himself and if he chose to ride around the country fine as fivepence or dressed in the meanest homespun it wouldn't matter to her.

'Surely a fine novel can outshine the shady reputation of its kind, Mrs Winch?' she intervened in the conversation she had started earlier, before Georgiana could recite a list of those she had read and enjoyed. That might reveal the fact Nell had allowed her to read books many would consider unsuitable for a young girl.

'A fine novel might, but the occasional triumphs are lost in the morass of sensation and fantasy,' Moss answered before the worthy but upright lady could condemn the whole genre and Georgiana might argue hotly for her most-loved examples and let out their secrets. 'I have neither the time nor patience to work my way through stacks of three-decker novels to find the occasional gem. Poetry and plays are an established form and I can trust time to sieve out the worst and keep the best of them,' he added as if dropping stones into a pond just for the pleasure of making ripples.

'Some might say that makes you a lazy reader, sir, but I hope you will concede that Dean Swift and Mr Defoe tower above their imitators,' Nell argued because she couldn't seem to help herself.

'I grant you those excellent examples, ma'am, and Sir Henry Fielding's works, although these young ladies must be ignorant of all but *Amelia* now society thinks the rest improper, which says more about society than Sir Henry if you ask me.'

Hiding a smile as Mrs Winch tried to decide if she should argue, Nell shot Georgiana a warning look. It had seemed a good idea to let her read *The History of Tom Jones* as well as *Amelia* at the time, to show her the world wasn't always kind to an innocent abroad. Luckily Lavinia had no interest in any but the popular novels Moss was being so scathing about, so Nell needn't worry she would let Mr Jones's name out unwarily. Caro was worried enough about what lay outside the gates of Berry Brampton House not to burden her with such vivid misadventures.

Luckily talk soon moved on and Nell could relax while they argued for this or that favourite poem. It was a chance to listen instead of having to instruct her pupils. The elder girls seemed much like any on the verge of womanhood and, considering what a pair of hostile little savages they were when she'd arrived here, Nell was proud of them. Penny was confident enough to sit and listen when she had nothing to say, but Nell couldn't rest on her laurels. Even Penny would soon feel the changes in mind and body that transformed little girls into women. The others were well launched on that stage when Nell arrived and she tried not to shudder at the memory.

For once Mr Moss was a welcome diversion. He was a strong man, she decided after a few furtive glances at him to take in what the shadows hid earlier, long-limbed and oddly graceful, despite his air of suppressed energy and to-hell-with-you manner. Something about him recalled Lavinia for an instant, but she looked again and thought it was a trick of the light. They both had intensely blue eyes, but he was dark as the devil and Lavinia was fair and the shape of their faces were quite different.

And what did an almost-handsome man think of the governess? That she was a middling sort of person and quite unremarkable, she concluded. Her once angelically fair locks were halfway between gold and brown and her eyes were plain brown. She was neither tall nor short and even at seventeen Lavinia outdid her in womanly curves. All Mr Moss's worst fears must be realised by candlelight, not that it mattered; once he settled into the agent's house he'd be in such demand among local society they would not meet except by chance.

It was no small thing to be land steward to the Berry Brampton Estate and, as the Earl did not live here, some of his status would fall on Mr Moss. Genteel young ladies would badger their fathers and brothers to call and invite him to dinner or an informal party so he'd soon be too busy charming the local beauties to dine with four unfledged young ladies, their plain governess and Mrs Winch. The Selford cousins were above his touch and Nell beneath it. What if he wasn't Mr Moss and she wasn't Miss Court, though? With a fortune like hers he could buy his own estate to manage. Revolted at the idea of being courted for her money, Nell decided if she ever married it would be to a man who loved her for herself. She came out of her daydream to find the others all but done with their meal and Mrs Winch more than ready for a cup of tea and half an hour nodding by the fire.

'Parkins will bring in the port, Mr Moss,' the lady said. 'It's time we left you to it and Miss Penelope looks half-asleep and ready to say goodnight.'

'It is early for the other young ladies to retire, don't you think, ma'am?' he said as if he was the master here and not his man.

He must have seen Caro's wry grimace at the thought of another early night and Nell couldn't let herself be charmed that he seemed to be trying to save

Caro and Georgiana from dull routine. It seemed a simple act of kindness, but was anything about him truly simple?

'Mrs Crombie is waiting to take Miss Penny up, Miss Court,' Parkins told her when he came in with the decanters, treading the fine line between housekeeper and governess with his usual impassive gloom.

'Are you happy to take that sleepy head of yours up to bed?' Nell whispered to her smallest charge.

Penny nodded and smothered another yawn behind her hand. 'I'm half-asleep,' the girl said with a smile that won Nell's heart anew. 'I know you must stay and help chaperon Caro and Georgie, so goodnight, Miss Court. Goodnight, Mr Moss,' she said with a curtsy to gladden any governess's heart. She kissed Nell, wished her cousins goodnight and seemed likely to tumble into bed and sleep as soon as she was undressed.

Chapter Four

❧

Fergus watched pupil and teacher bid each other goodnight. The dragon seemed almost soft-hearted so perhaps Poulson wasn't as far abroad in his judgement as he'd first thought. Of course, she was still too young for the post and two years ago could hardly have been long out of the schoolroom herself. Take away the spotless wisp of lawn and lace perched on her shining golden-brown curls and he could take ten years off the ones he'd first put in her dish. Her assured manner and limited patience fooled him at the time, but a very different person was revealed by candlelight. This Miss Court might pretend to be at her last prayers, but her mouth gave her away. It was less certain than he imagined when he met her in the gloomy stables. The young lady under the front of a no-nonsense governess had soft and expressive lips to go with her pert nose and brown-velvet eyes. Miss Court was a shade under the average height for a woman and slim as a whip, with the sort of slender yet intriguing womanly curves even a blue stuff gown made high to the neck couldn't quite conceal.

A connoisseur of feminine beauty might not rank her a diamond of the first water, but she would be very pretty if she threw away that dire gown and ridiculous cap. It wasn't right to long to discover the vulnerable and generous woman under her would-be stern exterior. He usually liked his lovers buxom and bold and wished his mistress was nearby to visit when the need arose, because it might arise right now if he wasn't very careful where his thoughts wandered in Miss Court's presence.

'I promise to restrict myself to one glass, ladies,' he said as Mrs Winch and her chicks rose, looking uncertain about this whole enterprise. As well they might, he told himself sternly. He blinked away a vision of the lovely young woman under Miss Court's armour and stood up politely.

'Very well, Mr Moss, we shall see you shortly,' Mrs Winch said.

He caught a sceptical governess look from him to decanter and was tempted to live down to Miss Court's low expectations and get roaring drunk before he staggered into his smallest drawing room and gave himself away as the owner of all this faded glory. He wasn't prepared to do that, he decided, and if the truth ever came out he must remember to thank the starchy female for the disguise she'd thrust on him, because he wasn't sure he wanted to be 'my lord' now he was here. His grandfather might have found the vast portrait of a Cavalier ancestor and family an aid to good digestion, but he did not. The Baron Selford portrayed so skilfully had an arrogance that must have had recruits rushing to join the Parliamentarian Army in order to escape his tyranny. A master painter had caught hints of rebellion in the man's son and heir and a sidelong glance from the old lord's lady said she didn't blame her eldest one for wondering if he wanted to die for the same cause.

God forbid any child of his would ever look at him with such cool dislike in his eyes. If it wasn't for his uneasy conscience about shirking his duty as Earl of Barberry for so long, he'd turn tail and catch the next tide to Ireland and his stepfather's comfortable home. No, he had a chance to observe his estate and mansion as he never would in his own shoes. He girded Mr Moss's loins and took him back to the Small Drawing Room by proxy.

'Do continue, Miss Caroline,' Fergus said as the piano playing stopped the instant he pushed opened the door. 'I am very fond of Herr Mozart's sonatas, at least when they are played with such a delicate touch,' he added and the obviously very shy girl smiled and carried on.

He had expected his cousins to be haughty and aloof, but they were brighter and more thoughtful than most of their kind, which he put down to their own spirit and Miss Court's influence. According to Poulson's reports, the laziness of a junior partner he had dismissed the moment he found out how negligent he'd been meant these girls had had little real guidance before their young governess arrived to try and bring sense, order and a little compassion into their lives. Once more he found himself oddly drawn to the young woman who sat as far away from him as she could. The sooner he was installed in the land steward's house and busy about the estate the better. Miss Court and Mrs Winch had his wards and his house in order and it was high time he could say the same for the land, and that would keep him out of Miss Court's way until it was time to go away again or reveal his true identity.

'Do you think Mr Moss will like the steward's house, Miss Court?' Caro asked Nell sleepily as they finally went upstairs, at long last.

'I'm sure he will and he can't stay here with us. That would be dreadfully improper in the Earl's absence, or even with it now I come to think about it. For either gentleman to move into Berry Brampton, we would have to leave.'

'I suppose so, but it's such a long time since Mr Jenks decided to retire and live with his daughter. I know the house was cleared out and dusted when we were told a new steward was coming, but that was weeks ago. The whole house could be damp after this dreadful weather and all sorts of things might have happened while it was lying empty, don't you think?'

'Not if I can help it,' Nell said with a weary sigh. 'If Mr Moss couldn't send a message to warn us he was coming, at long last, he must accept the fact his house needs airing before it is quite comfortable. Mrs Winch will have kept an eye on the place, so I doubt it will be as difficult to sleep there as you imagine. Mr Moss will not find the land in good heart, though. I suppose I should have found a discreet way to let his lordship know how bad things were before Mr Jenks admitted his sight was failing and left.'

'Oh, no, Miss Court, Jenks said he owed it to Grandfather to carry on managing the estate and he was so loyal to the family we couldn't betray him, could we? He has such old-fashioned ideas—perhaps it's as well Jenks had to go all the way to Yorkshire to live with his daughter so he can't argue with everything Mr Moss wants to do,' Georgiana said with a wise nod that left Nell trying not to smile at her unusual interest in estate management.

Georgiana enjoyed a combative relationship with the local squire's eldest son. One day it might grow into something more and Nell thought them well matched. Persuading Lord Barberry that the heir of a mere squire would make a good husband for one of his wards would be a challenge, but not one she need worry about now Georgiana was fifteen and the lad a year older.

'Yorkshire is not so very far away,' she teased gently as she urged the sisters upstairs to the modest room they insisted on sharing, despite the many splendid bedchambers in this grand old house.

'It is as far as Mr Jenks is concerned,' Caro put in and smiled her thanks when Nell loosened her laces and helped her out of her simple round gown, then began brushing Caro's thick blonde locks while their maid undid Georgiana's gown.

'You can't help wondering why he agreed to go there in the first place though, can you?' Georgiana observed with a frown and Nell wondered if it was odd that the man had finally left in such a hurry.

'The love of family can lead us to the most unexpected places,' Nell said with a shrug and a last look around. Becky had everything in hand and her charges looked so tired they should sleep soundly. Wishing them all a good night, she went to check on Lavinia and found Mary nodding in the dressing room.

'Miss Lavinia hasn't stirred all evening, miss. I've never known her so quiet or so little trouble,' the maid admitted sheepishly.

'You might as well go to bed now, Mary. If Miss Lavinia was going to take a chill, we would know by now and no doubt you'll hear if she wakes up and needs you in the night,' Nell told the maid with a nod at the truckle bed already set up in the narrow little room for her to sleep in and still be close if Lavinia needed her.

'Thank you, miss,' the young maid said dutifully.

Nell wondered why nobody found it odd Mary was Lavinia's age and yet a maid had to be far more sensible and self-disciplined than the girl she was employed to wait on. 'This isn't a fair world,' she murmured when she shut the door on her responsibilities for the night. 'You ought to know that by now.'

She was only three and twenty herself and had taken responsibility for four young girls when she was barely of age. Looking back, she wondered why Mr Poulson picked her from the list of mature and experienced applicants for this job and decided it could only be because she wasn't either of those things. Add Miss Thibett's hard-won praise for Nell's five years spent as a pupil teacher at her school and she supposed Mr Poulson thought she would understand her charges better and perhaps grow up with them. She recalled her giddy, schoolgirlish rush of excitement when she'd met Mr Moss's deceptive blue eyes for the first time tonight and wondered if it might not be better if she knew a little more about men and their odd quirks and unlikely preoccupations.

Nell had grown up apart from her brother and she wondered why aristocratic gentlemen were so harsh with dependent children as she recalled the servants' gossip about how little time the last Earl of Barberry had for his female grandchildren. Her uncle certainly didn't have any for her. Parting her and Colm when her brother was old enough to be sent to school at eight years old was cruel. The more she pleaded with her uncle for one holiday a year or even Christmas together, the less he was inclined to grant them even a day. The memory of being desperately lonely in her late uncle's house made her shudder even now. She'd cried herself to sleep for months after Colm had gone away and memories of how it felt to be alone and unwanted in an echoing house was one reason she'd agreed to apply for this job when Miss Thibett suggested she should. The thought of four lonely and abandoned girls got her here when Mr Poulson chose her for the post of their governess and memories of being unwanted by her own family made her grit her teeth and stay, although she wanted to run as far and as fast as her legs would carry her as soon as she met Lavinia's hostile glare and realised the younger Selford cousins took their cue from her and had very good glares of their own.

Was she sorry she had stayed now? It had taken months of patience to wear their hostility down, but she truly wanted the best for them. She recalled the feel of poor Lavinia sobbing in her arms and letting out so much pent-up unhappiness and at least she understood her a little better now. If she didn't have responsibility for these lonely girls she might have agreed to join Colm and Eve for the coming Season in London, though. Maybe there she would have found a gentleman quiet and steady enough to marry and make the family she'd always longed for with. Oddly enough an image of Moss interrupted her daydream and mocked her with a cynical smile. He might be right, if he was actually here and knew what went on in her head, because by the side of him her paragon did sound dreadfully dull.

With thoughts like that jostling about in her head wasn't it just as well she wasn't about to join the polite world as Miss Hancourt, heiress and elderly debutante? She stared into a mirror softly lit by the candle in the nightstick. Imagining what the so-called polite world would say about her behind her back made her shiver. They would laugh and call her a quiz, she decided, and glared into her looking glass as if they were already on the other side being airily amused by her.

Her father was wild Lord Chris Hancourt, lover of the most notorious woman of her generation and her partner in reckless death when they'd raced to a party in a land at war with Britain. What would Moss make of her shady history if the truth came out? Never mind him, the Earl of Barberry would dismiss her, heiress or not. The mud that stuck to her father's name would finish his daughter's career as guide and mentor to young girls. She hated the thought of all the snide whispers that would do the rounds wherever she went if she did as her family wanted her to and tried to ignore them for a Season.

In a decade or so, when Penny was old enough to

be presented as the last of the beautiful Selford orphans, it might be time to consider what she would do
with the rest of her life, but until then she had a job
to do. Nell unpinned her flimsy cap, managed to un-
lace her dull blue gown without the aid of a maid and
sat at the dressing table to unpin her hair and brush
it the vast number of times Miss Thibett had always
insisted on to transform it into a shining, silken mass
that fell heavily about her shoulders and reached as
far as her waist.

Was this the true Nell at the heart of Miss Court's
dreary plumage? The girl looking back at her seemed
far too young to be the guide and protector of four
vulnerable young ladies. She looked too uncertain to
resist the charm and experience of a gentleman who
wasn't anywhere near as humble as the third son of a
country squire ought to be. Her brown eyes were soft
and dreamy as she stopped brushing and felt the silky
thickness of those tawny waves tumbling around her
like a shining cape. Her workaday locks felt sensuous
and heavy and a little bit wicked against her shift, as
if a lover might loom out of the soft shadows of this
familiar room and run his hand over the silken ripple
of it at any moment, then whisper impossible things
in her eagerly listening ears.

Nell shivered, but it wasn't from cold; the hand
she pictured adoring and weaving a sensuous path
through her thick pelt of shining hair to find the
woman underneath was firm and muscular, but gentle
and a little bit reverent. The owner of that hand was
intent on her, his blue eyes hot as he watched the way
her creamy skin looked through fine lawn and a veil
of glossy golden-brown hair that didn't feel ordinary

any more. As she went breathless with anticipation his touch would get firmer and his gaze even more intent and wickedly sure she was ready for more.

No, here she sat, shivering with hot nerves and anticipation—like the caricature of a frustrated, dried-up spinster governess, longing for a lover in every personable man she met and never finding one to watch her with heat-hazed eyes as he stepped into her dreams and took them over. Nell snapped her eyes shut, squeezing her eyelids so tight it almost hurt. Then she took up her comb to part her heavy locks, ready to make plaits for the night ahead and forget imaginary lovers of any sort. She swiftly wound it into two thick tails of hair without looking at herself in the mirror, her fingers deft and driven to tighten the silky mass as her thoughts raced. Argh, but that hurt. She couldn't sleep with hair that pulled at her scalp like a harsh saint's scourge for sinful thoughts. She must begin again and pay attention to what her fingers were up to this time. That was it, her hair was tied easily enough for sleep and just tight enough to remind her to sin no more, even in her dreams.

Now for her formidably proper nightgown. Plain and buttoned sternly to the neck, made up from warm and practical flannel, it was a garment without a hint of sensuality. Let anyone find a hint of seductress in such a respectable get-up and she'd shout her true identity from the rooftops. She gave herself a severe nod, knelt to say her prayers and begged to be delivered from such silly fantasies, then got into bed. Staring into the night, she ordered herself not to dream of dark-haired, piratical gentlemen who could raise such silly fantasies in a spinster's heart without even trying as she snuffed her candle and hoped for quiet sleep against the odds.

In a faded corner of the great city of London another member of the nobility was finding it impossible to sleep. 'Thought I'd never get away from the jackals, Lexie,' Lord Derneley told his wife as he settled into a grim corner of a wine cellar in this rotten old house on the Strand with a sigh of relief. It might not be much for a man born to splendour and great wealth, but at least it wasn't the Fleet Prison.

'So did I, my love,' she whispered back, as if their creditors might manage to hear them even down here if she wasn't very careful. 'Lucky for us that my Aunt Horseforth is such a misery nobody will believe you're here. I think she expects me to be an unpaid companion and skivvy for the rest of my life,' she added gloomily.

'She's a dour old trout, but it's the only port we have in a storm. At least everyone knows she can't abide me and wouldn't have me in her house if she knew I was here. I could always come out of hiding and scare her into an apoplexy.'

'No, no, Derneley, don't do that. Her grandson will come down from Scotland and put me out on the street before she's cold if you do and you'll starve to death down here without me. There's nowhere else for us to go now the creditors are after you as if you murdered someone instead of taking their horrid loans when we ran out of things to sell. Heaven knows I got nothing but snubs and refusals to acknowledge they even knew me for my pains when I tried to visit my friends,' she said mournfully and even her selfish, careless lord looked humble and almost defeated for a moment, before his true nature reasserted itself.

'Have you found anything worth selling yet?'

'No, her grandson's man of business has everything locked up that isn't already in the bank. He doesn't trust me,' she said, sounding very put out.

'If we could only lay hands on a few hundred guineas we can slope off to Italy and at least be warm while we think what we're going to do next. Right now I can't even afford a decent bottle of wine, for if there were ever any in here someone drank it years ago.'

'If only Lord Chris hadn't deceived poor Pamela so badly we'd have all the Lambury Jewels in our possession now and none of this would have happened.'

'Except if he wasn't dead she wouldn't be either and if you think we'd have got a single jewel out of her, you're more of a fool than I thought. Chris was a lot more cunning than we gave him credit for being once she'd got him under her spell though, wasn't he?' Lord Derneley sounded almost admiring for a moment. 'Who would have thought he'd be able to palm her off with paste versions of the emerald and sapphire sets after she had the rubies tested to make sure they were real the moment he handed them over.'

'Everyone said the rubies were cursed and it turned out to be true, didn't it? My poor sister was dead within six months of wheedling the wretched things out of him. And he never even pretended to hand over his wife's diamonds to her, so he must have put them somewhere for that horrid little girl to find.'

'We could make far better use of them,' her lord

said thoughtfully, 'but nobody said a word about the Lambury Jewels turning up when young Hancourt came into that blind trust thing, did they? You could be on to something, Lex,' he added and his wife stared at him in wonder.

'You mean *we* could find them?' she said.

'I daren't show my face, but that tough your sister used to play with when Chris wasn't looking might track them down for you if we promise to share.'

'No, he's dead and I was too frightened of him to go anywhere near him if he wasn't. I might be stuck upstairs waiting on my nip-cheese aunt most of the time, but I suppose I could find out when they were last seen if I get her talking about the old days long enough, but are you sure we'll be able to find them, my love?'

'Why not? And we have nothing to lose, do we?'

'No, we've already lost it,' her ladyship said gloomily, the fabulous wealth her lord inherited the day he came of age seeming to haunt her for a moment. 'They only let me leave Derneley House in what I stood up in *and* they searched me for anything valuable before they even let me do that,' she remembered mournfully.

'You can keep a ring and one of the small necklets when we sell the rest,' her lord said almost generously.

'Thank you, my love,' she said meekly.

'Hmm, it might work, but Hancourt's too tough a customer for us to get anything out of him and he knows us too well.'

'Yes, and he must be dangerous with all those scars and fighting in all the battles he survived when Gus Hancourt sent him off to be killed in the army,' her ladyship said matter of factly, as if she saw nothing very wrong in the late Duke of Linaire's heartless scheming to gain his nephew's fortune.

'Cunning as well—think how he deceived us. He was only a secretary when he came to Derneley House to take my father's books away. He must be hiding that sister of his somewhere though, because she certainly ain't doing the Season, is she?'

'No, I would have heard. Aunt Horseforth may not go out much, but she corresponds with half the old dowagers of the *ton*.'

'I dare say the Hancourt wench is as plain as her mother was then, or he'd have insisted she came to town by now.'

'I wish Pamela never met their father, but she and Chris would have had far more beautiful children together if he'd been able to marry her.'

'You're the aunt of the wench Hancourt married though, ain't you? You must call at Linaire House when she and Hancourt get back from the north and make sure he feels a pressing need to write to his sister. That way we'll be able to find out her address and somehow get her to lead us to the jewels. Chris must have realised how plain she would turn out to be and he knew a man needs a good reason to wed an antidote. Lady Chris could never have hooked the son of a duke without the Lambury Jewels and the old man Lambury's fortune as bait. The diamonds would set us up nicely and the old man gave them to Chris's wife after the marriage, so they weren't part of the settlements and he could leave them to his daughter if he wanted to.'

'You're so clever, Derneley,' his wife said with an

admiring sigh. 'I can't imagine how I'm to make that horrid boy of Chris's so worried he'll give her address away by writing to her, though.'

'Oh, really, Lex, do I have to think of everything?' her lord said sleepily and waved her away so he could sleep after a strenuous day of escaping his creditors and looking for new money to waste.

Chapter Five

'Oh, do stop the carriage, Binley!' Georgiana shouted before Nell could check her. 'Good morning, Mr Moss.'

Nell managed a sickly smile for the man who had been haunting her dreams.

'Good morning, Miss Georgiana, Miss Court,' he said politely.

'But we are keeping you standing in the rain, Mr Moss,' Nell said in the hope he'd agree and hurry on without further ado.

'A mere drizzle, Miss Court. We land stewards have to accustom ourselves to the whims of the English weather.'

Now why did she think he was mocking himself as much as her this time? 'All the same it is another cold and dreary day—can we take you up as far as Brampton Village?' she offered as politely as she could manage when she didn't want to be shut in a closed carriage with him even for that long.

'That is very kind, ma'am. My horse is being re-shod so it will save me a half-hour's walk to collect him from the forge,' the man said cheerfully and Nell bit back a protest she was being polite and didn't mean it.

At least he sat with his back to the horses, but that meant she must look at him instead of feeling his muscular male limbs next to her and it was only marginally better. He had acquired more suitable clothes in the three days since he appeared out of the night to plague her. In practical leathers and countryman's boots and coat he should be quite unremarkable, but somehow he was nothing of the sort. His linen was spotless and his plain waistcoat was cut by a master, but it wasn't his clothes that made him stand out, it was the man underneath them. His masculine vitality seemed almost too big for a confined space and Nell felt she couldn't even breathe without taking in more of him than she wanted to. And she didn't want to, did she? Her doubts about that had been creeping into her dreams. Every morning she had to tell herself they were nightmares when she woke up with those fading rags of unthinkably erotic fantasies shaming her waking hours. How was she to look him in the face with the thought of them plaguing her with impossible things?

'The others are sewing with Mrs Winch this morning,' Georgiana informed him happily. 'I share Maria Welland's music lessons and Miss Court comes with me to have tea and a comfortable coze with Maria's Miss Tweed while our teacher shouts at us in French.'

'You unlucky creatures, no wonder the other Misses Selford prefer their embroidery frames.'

'Lavinia has no ear for music; Madame says she would rather—'

'Never mind her exact words, Georgiana,' Nell interrupted hastily, having overheard the lady's agonies before she'd declared Georgiana the only Selford girl with even the suggestion of a voice and refused to hear the others sing ever again.

'I was only going to say she would rather teach cats to sing than Lavinia, Miss Court,' Georgiana said with such mischief in her eyes that Nell would usually have to laugh, except she refused to do so in front of Mr Moss.

'Well, don't,' she said crossly instead. 'Lavinia can't help being about as unmusical as possible without being tone deaf.'

'I know and she does embroider exquisitely,' Georgiana admitted. 'She can paint far better than the rest of us as well. But that's why we're out and about on our own this morning, Mr Moss,' she went on with an expectant look at him that said it was his turn to recite a list of engagements for the day.

'I am engaged to meet several of your guardian's tenant farmers at the market in Temple Barberry, so I shall have to hurry there as soon as my horse has his new shoe, Miss Georgiana,' he replied obediently.

Contrarily, Nell felt excluded as they chatted about the market and how most farmers were gloomy about prospects for the harvest, whatever the weather. They conceded this was a very peculiar spring and this time they were right to be pessimistic. Being brought up in London, and then Bath, Nell had had to learn even to *like* the countryside when she first came here and she was the first to admit she didn't know its ways and habits as well as her pupils. She felt like a town mouse as Georgiana and Mr Moss happily discussed the difficulty of sowing crops and getting them to grow when it was cold and the skies so grey nothing seemed likely to thrive. Sunshine was now needed to make it all work and Nell felt she might be withering for the lack of it herself by the time the carriage rolled into Brampton and pulled up at the smithy.

'You seem unnaturally quiet this morning, Miss Court,' Mr Moss observed as he gathered up his crop, hat and a leather case that must contain tenancy agreements or leases, or some such dry stuff it was as well not to be curious about.

'I have nothing to say, Mr Moss. I am an urban creature and know little of agriculture and country lore.'

'Then it was rude of me to bore you with them.'

'Not in the least, sir. I hope I can still listen and learn as well as hold forth about what I do know.'

'Then I shall send over one of the agricultural reports on this county for your further education, ma'am, since you want to know it better.'

'Only if you are not using it, sir,' she said coolly. She could imagine nothing more likely to send her to sleep so perhaps it would have its uses.

'Oh, no, I'm a quick study when a topic interests me and the state of land is important. I suppose that's one reason my wider family disapprove of me and mine,' he said, then seemed to regret his frankness and his expression was closed and formal as he jumped down and gave them a fine bow, before waving goodbye to Georgiana and nodding stiffly at Nell as the carriage drove past on its way to the Wellands' manor house. Why would a country squire regard his interest in the land as undesirable? Mr Moss might not be able to inherit the family acres, but not all younger sons were destined for the army, the navy or the church. Becoming a land steward was a perfectly respectable ambition in a gentleman of slender means. On a large estate like Berry Brampton the position was often filled by a junior line of the family who owned it. So why was Mr Moss so defensive about his chosen way of life?

By the time Brampton Village was behind them at least Georgiana had stopped speculating about Mr Moss and the reception he would get from the notoriously close-mouthed farming community, so that was a relief, wasn't it? Hearing her most lively pupil shift her attention from the steward to what her friend Maria might have been about since they last met might make her head spin, but Miss Welland's sayings and doings were a much safer subject and she let her pupil chatter on unchecked. It didn't matter how well or badly the man got on with his family, he was here, at last, and Nell hoped the injustices and oddities Jenks had closed his eyes to on the estate would come to an end. Anyway, she could hardly condemn Moss for being so late to take up his post when she had deserted hers twice in the last year. Governess or not, responsible for the girls as she was with no resident guardian to look out for them when she was gone, nothing could have stopped Nell finding her brother after Waterloo and, six months later, attending his wedding to the love of his life. It had been a joyous marriage ceremony, despite the time of year and the rough weather and terrible roads. At last Colm had looked as joyous and carefree as a man of his age, birth and fortune ought to when he stood up so proudly to wed his unexpected bride. The last marriage in the world anyone would have predicted for the children of the Hancourt–Winterley scandal and there they both were, as shiningly happy as any couple Nell had ever met. It felt strange coming back here from Darkmere Castle and those bright celebrations to be Miss Court again and pretend nothing had changed. Until Mr Moss arrived she'd been plagued by a feeling this world seemed dangerously unstable after the bustle and common purpose in Lord Winterley's northern heartland. If she left Berry Brampton House as her brother and sister-in-law wanted her to, what would become of the girls? Without a competent manager, the estate had been like a rudderless ship in these hard times. The war was over, but the whole country sometimes seemed about to plunge into chaos as they floundered from one crisis to the next. Now her worry about the lack of a strong man to keep all steady here was gone, she realised how uneasy she'd been before he arrived.

Mr Moss was an unlikely protector of a pack of schoolgirls, but he would still do it if he had to. The footmen and butler were tall and strong and the formidably respectable Mrs Winch gave the household gravitas, but nobody else had the status of my lord's land steward. She didn't have to like him for it, though. He had sat opposite her and talked to Georgiana of matters she didn't understand, then offered to lend her a book. Well, she'd read the dratted thing if that would stop him doing it again. As for that habit he had of calling her *ma'am*—there might be more exasperating ways to address a lady not yet four and twenty, but she couldn't currently think of any.

'Mr Moss was right; you are quiet today, Miss Court. Do you have the headache?' Georgiana asked as the carriage turned towards the next village and the Wellands' neat manor house.

Not yet, Nell thought, *but I soon will have if I brood about the impossible man for much longer.* 'No, but I couldn't get a word in when you two were chattering nineteen to the dozen.'

'Papa always said my tongue ran on wheels when we were little…' She paused and looked out of the small carriage windows at the dull grey sky before sighing heavily. 'I know I was only a child when he died, Miss Court, and I was so lucky my parents loved me and Caro, but will I ever stop missing them, do you think?'

'Now that really is a hard question.'

'I know I shouldn't pry into the feelings of my elders, since you told me so, but do *you* still miss your mama and papa?'

'At times; although my mama died when I was little more than a babe, so I don't really remember her, and my father was more often away from home than in it during the last few years of his life. I do still miss him though, yes. I found it very hard to be parted from my brother when he was sent to school as well, so I'm glad you and Caroline are together and can share your feelings as well as your memories. Lavinia and Penny love you both as well, however little they choose to show it at times. I suppose the pressure on the heir to produce a boy was so strong in your family that Lavinia has always felt herself at a disadvantage and she is unsure of herself and a little jealous of those who seem to be more fortunate.'

'I will remember that and try to make allowances, but you don't like to talk about yourself, do you, Miss Court?' Georgiana responded with a direct stare that made Nell feel she was the younger of them for once.

She had hoped nobody would notice her habit of turning the subject and not giving anything away about her past that she didn't have to, but Georgiana was a lot more perceptive than most people realised. 'I'm not a very interesting topic,' she replied warily.

'Now there you are quite wrong, Miss Court. Mr Moss finds you as much of a mystery as we Selfords do. All the time we were talking about farmers and cows and fields at least half his attention was fixed on you.'

'No, it wasn't. He thinks me an antidote and was very happy to talk to you this morning instead of me, so please don't start imagining otherwise, Georgiana. Your matchmaking efforts are unwelcome at the best of times and Mr Moss would laugh himself hoarse if he could hear you now.'

'Which would be very ungentlemanly of him, don't you think? Although I doubt he would; he seems a kind man under that teasing manner of his.'

'I don't think we know him well enough to say if he is kindly or not yet, Georgiana, and if I did want more to do with the gentleman than I have to because we work for the same employer he'd be horrified. I doubt I ever came across a gentleman less likely to be in search of a wife than that one and I'm certainly not the woman to make him change his mind.'

'If only you would wear something that doesn't

make you look centuries older than you truly are and throw away that silly cap, he'd soon make a liar of you. He's a single gentleman and you're an unattached lady; what would be so terrible about him taking an interest in you as a person instead of a governess, Miss Court?'

'The fact I have a job I enjoy, despite the occasional bouts of nonsense my pupils indulge in. It's impertinent of you to even ask that question as well and some governesses would punish you severely for it. I don't want to hear any more of such silly speculation from you or your sister and cousins on the subject and I have no desire to marry the man. Even if I did, neither of us earns enough to be comfortable if I had to stop work. I don't think your cousin, the Earl, would be pleased to hear you plotting to deprive him of one or other of us either, do you?'

'I suppose not, since he hasn't even bothered to meet us and, now his estate will be run as soundly as his house, he can stay away until we're ready to be married off. I dare say he'll come home the instant the last of us leave for London.'

'Lord Barberry will probably find himself a wife and need his grand home sooner than that, my dear. Penny is not ten years old and will not be marrying for another ten if I have anything to say about it.'

'You think eighteen is too young for a young lady to wed?'

'I think not many young ladies have seen enough of the world to know what marriage will entail by then. A woman should be able to love and trust a man before she commits all she is and can be to marriage and I hope you are mature enough to make an informed choice when the time comes.'

'You have little time for the Marriage Mart, then?' her pupil asked as if she was still more interested in Nell's future than her own.

There were odd little corners in all four of her young charges' hearts. Nell hoped against hope they would find happiness when they became part of the pairing off into brides and bridegrooms the *ton* organised for their young twice a year. 'I always thought that such a repellent term and hope you won't use it in public, but in private I admit there seems little difference between the sort of market Mr Moss is off to observe this morning and this habit of selling off well-bred young ladies to the highest bidder. Marriage is more than bargaining for titles or money and so many other things ought to be taken into consideration. I shudder to think how huge a shock it must be to innocent young things who end up married to a virtual stranger.'

'Me too, so don't worry, Miss Court; the Earl probably wants to marry us off as fast as he can, but I'm not minded to oblige him. Caro is quite stubborn under her quiet manner as well and we all know Penny has a mind of her own. Lavinia is the only one of us eager to wed in a hurry, but Lord Barberry will find the rest of us a much bigger challenge, if he ever bothers to meet us.'

'Best if he stays away perhaps, at least until you are old enough to argue for your chosen future.'

'True, so you had better keep sending him pages of boring reports on our excellent progress as pattern cards of dutiful obedience, Miss Court.'

'How did you know about…? Oh, you dreadful girl. Now you've made me admit I've been lying to the man since I stepped over his threshold.'

'Tut, tut, Miss Court, what a dreadful example to us Selford girls. No wonder we're going to disappoint our cousin when he finally deigns to meets us.'

'True, now all I need do is persuade Lavinia to frustrate him as well and perhaps the wretched man will sit up and take notice. If he bothered to come and meet you he'd soon realise you have feelings and hopes he has no right to trample over so he can be rid of his responsibility all the sooner,' Nell declared too forthrightly and was glad when they reached Welland House and she could stop her tongue saying outrageous things without permission from her sensible governess's brain.

Chapter Six

Fergus watched the carriage he had ordered from afar to make sure his wards travelled in comfort draw away and sighed at his own idiocy. Being here incognito had proved distinctly uncomfortable so far. He'd had no idea until he'd pretended to be Mr Moss how much he enjoyed the comfort he could expect as a gentleman of wealth and importance, even when he went under an alias. Instead of the best bedchamber of the best inn he had to endure an old-fashioned house with chimneys that smoked and windows that let in nearly as much chilly spring weather as they kept out. Not that he spent much time there, he supposed philosophically. His days were taken up with walking fields with his tenant farmers, inspecting tumbledown cottages and all the obligations Jenks had neglected. It was a wonder he wasn't in for re-shoeing instead of his horse, he decided, with a rueful glance at his once spotless and very expensive riding boots.

'He looks to be in fine fettle again,' he told the smith and enjoyed a genial argument over the slightly inflated price the fellow wanted to charge because

Fergus was new to the area and might be fool enough to pay it.

Having won that battle, he reviewed the bigger ones he must fight before he left here, with or without admitting who he was, as he rode to Temple Brampton. So far his predecessor's failures as land steward seemed understandable, given old Jenks's failing eyesight and other infirmities. The man had lied about his age from the day Fergus inherited the estates, but he should have come here and judged it for himself. Jenks claimed to be not quite sixty when a report on this estate was made for the new Earl ten years ago, so he could have found the old rogue out years ago, if he wasn't still so sore about being the heir his family had moved heaven and earth to keep out of his grandfather's shoes. Jenks probably was capable of carrying on a decade ago, but why hadn't he admitted that he was failing sooner? Now Fergus had to undo all the abuses the old man was too weary to notice were happening under his nose and drag the whole estate into the current century.

He frowned at the horizon and hoped he recalled the route into the nearest town from the sketchy estate map his new housekeeper had found when she turned out the long-disused front parlour. Jenks used the framed map as a makeshift fire screen, but he knew the place like the back of his hand and had no need of it. Fergus sighed wearily and wondered if he would ever overcome the prejudices of his grandfather's tenants. At the moment he was too busy learning the differences between land here and land everywhere else and getting the estate back in proper order to confront them as his true self, but the sooner he found a suitable replacement for young Moss the better. At least then he could decide if he was ready to admit to being Earl of Barberry or not and stay or go as the fancy took him.

Which brought him back to the puzzle of the last ten years. He'd begun them a furious young lord with a burning need to put as much distance as possible between himself and Berry Brampton and all he was never supposed to inherit. Wrong and irresponsible of him to stay away, but he had been absorbed in his new life and all but forgot this other one for too long. His fascination with a new world kept luring him on to explore the Canadian wilderness until he was entangled in the lives of those who sought to tame or live with its trackless wildness.

He'd stayed too long and got caught up in a senseless war between the United States and Britain, so how could he slide out of Canada like a coward when both nations were fighting over it and the native tribes losing more than any people should? His mouth set in a bitter line as he thought of friends who'd lost homes and families and turned into killers. Now there was a ceasefire rather than peace he could mourn and celebrate a land he had come to love. During those ten years he had lived through many adventures; loved a wild and generous woman and lost her to a better man; then fought against men his instincts screamed should be comrades and not enemies. The whole war felt like brother fighting brother and soured the promise of the new world he'd fallen in love with as a rebellious and angry boy. He'd learned so much and spent those years living and loving and exploring as Mr Ford, a man of modest means, but a stern voice he'd tried to ignore had been whispering he should go home ever since he'd got there.

So what now, Fergus? Now you're here at last and still not your true self?

It wasn't quite home though, was it? he excused himself. His stepfather's rambling manor felt like his real one, but it would go to his half-brother Brendan one day. Fergus Selford had far grander houses and even more fertile acres to call his own. Yet the temptation to not quite commit himself to Berry Brampton and the life of an English nobleman had been too strong to resist when Miss Court offered him an easy alternative. Every day that went past showed him what a coward he had been that night and how far he was from calling this place home.

Then there were his wards to consider and how had he managed to close his eyes to their needs for so long? They were little more than babes when he'd turned his back on them as if him having to be the Earl of Barberry was their fault. He *was* the reason at least two of them existed though. Lavinia would never have been born if the true heir hadn't done something so reckless that he'd died in a hastily hushed-up scandal and her parents had reluctantly reunited to try to put him out of the succession and produced a daughter instead of the longed-for son and replacement heir. Fergus suspected Georgiana and Caroline's parents had made a love match, but from all accounts little Penny's birth was something of a wonder. Even in Ireland there were whispers that the old Earl's third son was not interested in the fair sex, yet the man wed some accommodating girl at his father's command then died before his child was born. The old lord hadn't been able to hang on to life long enough to be disappointed yet again, but silly, immature Fergus Selford had still walked away from a babe only days old when he left Britain, knowing he was the new Earl of Barberry after all and be damned to every Selford who thought he'd ever lusted after his grandfather's coronet.

Well, he could sit here on his fidgeting horse and feel more and more guilty about what he'd done and not done ten years ago, or do his best to get a true picture of all that needed to be done here before he admitted who he really was and got on with doing it. The past was done with, now he must get on with finding out what could be salvaged from such youthful idiocy. The girls were safe with their fierce young governess and protector for the time being and he would make sure they stayed that way. There was so much to do he barely knew where to start. At least Miss Court cared about her charges and he could go on leaving her to that while he got the measure of them.

He glanced at yet another stand of woodland that ought to have been thinned and coppiced years ago. A fierce frown knitted his brows and he imagined his mother telling him they'd stick like that if he wasn't careful. His hard gaze softened as he pictured Kitty, Lady Rivers, ordering him to solve his problems instead of puckering the perfectly good brows she and his father had given him at great personal cost and giving himself premature lines.

'Yes, Ma,' he'd murmured, then chuckled at an image of quiet and respectable Berry Brampton under the onslaught of his nearest and dearest, intent on protecting it, and him, from all invaders. The fact they were the biggest invaders of all would pass them by, but at least his half-brother was five and twenty now and capable of keeping a still tongue in his head if he absolutely had to. All Fergus needed to do was persuade Brendan to do just that and they could both be in and out of here a lot sooner than if he had to work alone. If it could be done without having to admit he was the Earl of Barberry until he was ready, then so much the better.

His horse jigged at a crow flapping raucously out of the woods. They were nearly at Temple Brampton and none of the problems he'd been brooding on since parting from Miss Court and Georgiana needed solving today. He'd tried to be an idle gentleman when he got back from Canada, but now he'd spent time with his mother and stepfather and visited the finest tailor in London he needed to be busy again. He ought to be happy with at least a decade of neglect to make up for and, less than a week after arriving, he hardly recognised the man looking back at him out of the pitted and watery old mirror Jenks had made do with when he shaved of a morning.

Which reminded him, he must put repairs and modernisation of the land steward's house at the top of the long list he was assembling. He'd never keep a real replacement for Jenks longer than a few days if he didn't. It might not even take that long for the next candidate to decide his old-fashioned and neglected quarters were not up to scratch. He imagined Miss Court looking down her rather fetching nose at him for putting his own comfort first, but if he was really going to do that, she and her precious girls would be out in the cold looking for respectable lodgings right now. There, he was thinking about his wards' governess again and he had far too much to do to bother himself about the stubborn woman. He rode to the Angel Inn, handed over his horse to be pampered after his cold ride here, then strode inside to find paper and whatever ink the landlord could come up with in order to write to Brendan without delay. At least with his half-brother around he wouldn't have time to brood on how different his life would be if he really was Edward Moss and Miss Court was her usual prickly self. She might be a good match for the third son of a country squire but he was an Earl, like it or not, and way above her touch.

'Don't get up, dear niece, although you must tell that delicious young husband of yours to have words with his uncle's butler. The impudent wretch insisted that you were not at home. I told him I am your aunt and even then he tried to leave me in the hall like some common servant.'

'Aunt Derneley,' Mrs Colm Hancourt said coldly, 'what do you want?'

'Must I want something? You're the only family I have left,' the faded lady said in a die-away tone that implied she probably wasn't long for this world.

'And I'm so dear you stood by while my mother tried to kill me with neglect in your own house when I was a baby? Add your scheme to make money out of me last autumn and even you ought to know by now that you can't rely on that accident of birth to get you a welcome under this roof.'

'What a hard-hearted creature you are,' Lady Derneley said with an elegant sniff into her lace-trimmed handkerchief. 'So like your father.'

'Yes, I'm very proud to agree with you, for once,' Eve Hancourt said with a sceptical glance at her supposedly weeping relative.

'He drove her to it, you know? With his stiff-necked pride and that ridiculous expectation of his that she would agree to live in that dreadful Gothic castle of his miles away from civilisation for months on end. Poor, dear Pamela. She swore there wasn't a party to be had from one week to the next and she was used to living at Derneley House and there was never a dull moment with us in those days. No wonder the poor child pined away for some life and laughter, shut away as she was in the wilds of Northumberland with only proud and stuffy Winterleys and all those wretched sheep for company.'

'I have no interest in my mother's excuses for leaving my father; if you've come here to plead her case, then you're twenty years too late.'

'No, I mustn't do that, must I?' Lady Derneley said rather distractedly. 'I doted on my little sister and miss her to this day, but I can tell that you were only ever told hard things about her.'

'Perhaps there were only hard things to say,' Eve said warily.

'Not from me. She had such energy, such charm and wit,' her aunt explained and her faded features warmed into a shadow of the girlish loveliness that netted her such a dashing young husband nearly three decades ago. 'And she was such fun.'

'At least one person loved her then,' Eve said gently.

'Lord Chris Hancourt adored her, don't forget,'

Lady Derneley objected, then covered her mouth with a delicately gloved hand as if to remind herself nobody under this roof would want to be reminded of that uncomfortable fact.

'Good afternoon, Lady Derneley,' Lord Christopher Hancourt's son said smoothly from just inside the door of his uncle's newly refurbished drawing room. 'Are you receiving this afternoon after all then, my love?'

'You know very well I'm not, Husband,' Eve said with a smile of welcome.

'Then how may we be of service, Lady Derneley?'

'Since Winterley has forbidden any of you to help poor Derneley you cannot, but I don't see why I shouldn't visit my niece,' the lady replied, sniffing delicately at the thought of her lord in hiding from his creditors.

'My wife might have welcomed one in the past, but you're more than twenty years too late,' he said implacably.

Lady Derneley started as if she'd found a viper in her reticule instead of a handkerchief. 'Pamela was my sister; how could I go against her wishes?'

'Because she was wrong in every way I can think of. Is there anything else?'

'No…that is, yes,' the lady said as she shredded her lawn and lace handkerchief and avoided Colm Hancourt's level gaze. 'We are family. It's our duty to show the world a united front,' she said like a well-rehearsed child repeating her catechism.

'Your husband is still under the hatches, then?'

'Yes,' she admitted baldly.

'I'll give you a cottage on one of my estates and a

pension if you agree to live apart, but Derneley's not having a penny piece of mine or Eve's.'

'How can you be so mean? You have so much.'

'He tried to sell Eve into slavery for the sake of a share of her dowry and *you* schemed to leave her alone with a contemptible rogue last autumn. You're lucky to be offered so much, madam. I'd let you join Derneley in the sponging house but for my wife's tender heart. You are her mother's sister, although most nieces would turn their back on you after what you tried to do to her.'

'I refuse to be parted from my husband for ever,' the lady said in a quavering voice.

'Then I'm sorry for you, but Colm is quite right, Aunt Derneley. I won't pay a penny towards your husband's upkeep. He did his best to trick me into marriage with a monster and even if I could forget what he did, Colm never will. If you change your mind our offer of a home for you alone still stands, but until then I wish you good day.'

'You'll regret this; family should stick together. You should remind your sister how badly it looks when one does not do so, young man. It does none of you good for the wench to stay in the countryside now she's an heiress and can catch some sort of husband, even if she is a quiz and too long in the tooth to take properly. Rumour has it she's ugly as sin or not as virtuous as she ought to be and hiding her in the country now she has a fortune in her dower chest won't help. Derneley says they're taking bets in the clubs on which of those reasons for her staying away is most likely.'

'I'm amazed he's welcome anywhere in St James's,' Colm said.

Eve frowned at her aunt for prodding her husband where he could be most easily hurt, through his family. 'Goodbye, Lady Derneley,' she said coldly. 'Despite your spiteful gossip a letter to this address will suffice, if you ever decide to take up our offer.'

'And one to my aunt's house will tell me that you have recalled your duty to me, Niece,' Lady Derneley replied, then swept out of the room as if she was still a rich and secure peeress and not the wife of a fugitive bankrupt.

'She'll have to walk back to the Strand; her carriage was seized by her husband's creditors weeks ago,' Eve said.

'I'm not sending her home in one of my uncle's carriages or your new town chariot, love. Derneley probably thinks we'll tow him out of River Tick if he drowns in it showily enough and he's not having a penny after what he did to you.'

'She seems determined to drown with him, though.'

'Then let her; at heart she's as cold and unscrupulous as Derneley. She would have let you die as a babe and schemed to get you raped and forcibly wed the night we met. If you hadn't foiled that plan, I'd have had to kill the brute to free you and look where that would have got us.'

'We probably wouldn't have met at all,' Eve said with a shudder.

'Unthinkable,' he said and took Eve in his arms to reassure them both they had and were now blissfully happy, despite the Derneleys' worst efforts.

'You must write to your sister though, Colm,' she said hesitantly as soon as she had breath to spare.

'Aye, I must,' Colm replied with a frown that emphasised the scar high on his forehead and might make him look almost saturnine to someone who didn't love him to distraction. 'I'm not sure Nell will change her mind and come to town for the Season because of the scandalmongers though, love, she's more likely to dig her heels in and snap her fingers at the gossips than listen to what they have to say about her.'

'Then maybe you should hint how satisfying it could be to prove them wrong. She is a Hancourt, after all, and therefore stubborn as rock.'

'And you think we're all like that, do you, Wife?' her own particular Hancourt asked softly. Eve did her best to reassure him she liked him exactly as he was and they forgot the Derneleys and even Colm's sister for a blissful hour or two.

Chapter Seven

Nell carefully folded her brother's latest letter and put it in her writing box to read again when she had time. While she was genuinely fond of the Selford girls, such snatched moments were more precious than gold. She was glad Colm was content with his new life and had his darling Eve to share it. He deserved such happiness, but she did feel lonelier at times when she compared her life with his. It made her feel guilty to sit and long for the sort of love Colm and Eve had found together. She had made a useful life here, but sometimes the longing for a lover and family of her own was so strong it felt almost like a physical pain. Ridiculous, she told herself sternly, she had chosen this existence. The fortune she inherited the day Colm was five and twenty gave her alternatives she never dared dream of until now, but she was still here.

If the former Duke of Linaire had been as good a man as the current one Nell would have been the wealthy and pampered Miss Hancourt all her life, or maybe even Mrs Somebody or Lady Self-Important by now. In that life her gowns would be of the finest wool, silk or velvet; she could wear a jewel-bright spencer jacket or pelisse. She preferred the simple graceful lines of gowns fashionable at the start of the century and an image of herself reclining gracefully on a fine *chaise* appeared in her head, despite the reality of her drab wool gown and tightly bound hair. She would look charming and seductive as she gazed at her chosen lover, like an engraving she had once seen of Madame Récamier as painted by Baron Gérard. Her watcher; the man who commissioned this fantasy picture, now *he* would want her so urgently his brilliantly blue gaze would be almost molten with heat as he gazed past the artist as if he wasn't even there and soon he would dismiss him and make love to his wife until…

Until nothing, Eleanor, the voice of her stern conscience interrupted, followed by Caroline's voice calling her back to reality.

'Miss Court, where are you?'

'Up here, Caroline,' Nell finally made herself reply even as she remembered why she had stopped reading Colm's letter and blushed rosily.

In that other world her husband had looked a lot like Moss. Why on earth was she taking the man into her fantasy world when she didn't even like him? She sighed and waved that very different version of him smiling mistily at his lovely, fashionable wife a sceptical goodbye.

'Here I am,' she said, after a look in the small mirror on the landing outside her room to make sure her improper thoughts about the land steward didn't show.

'Oh, good, because the strangest thing has happened, Miss Court.'

'I am on pins to know what it is, Caroline.'

'A gentleman has called and he is asking for you or Mr Moss.'

'And why is that so strange?'

'Because he says he's our cousin's half-brother.'

'Which cousin does he claim to be related to, then?'

'Why, our guardian of course; the Earl.'

'Goodness,' Nell heard herself say faintly and wondered what on earth she was supposed to do with such an unlikely visitor and whether he had come here to test the ground for his very tardy half-brother.

'He seems very polite and he is really rather handsome.'

It got worse, Nell decided, with another panicked glance at her reflection in that scrap of looking glass. Nothing to show her front of a calm and competent governess was as fragile as glass today, she decided with a sigh. But wasn't Mr Moss trouble enough without this latest disaster? If they had to contend with the Earl's younger brother as well, Nell almost wished the Earl was here to take command of his own household for once. Although if he were, she supposed she and the girls would have to take up residence elsewhere. Even Mrs Winch wasn't enough to stop the gossip if the elusive Earl of Barberry, his wards and a young governess lived under the same roof without a stern and aristocratic chaperon to squash any hint of scandal.

'Never mind handsome,' she muttered as she hurried after her much more eager and rather awe-struck pupil. 'What on earth are we going to do with him?'

'Good afternoon,' the young man waiting in the small drawing room greeted her with a smile and rather a gallant bow, considering she was only the governess.

'Good afternoon,' Nell managed faintly in reply and blinked owlishly at their 'really rather handsome' guest. She tried to recall her manners as she managed not to gape at him openly and wondered if it might be a trial for a young man to be born so dazzlingly good looking. Not that he didn't seem perfectly at ease with his golden hair, dark eyes and all the other outward perfection of an Adonis in breeches and a superbly cut riding coat.

'When Miss Caroline said she would fetch her governess I was picturing a stern grey lady with twice as many years in her dish as you, Miss Court.'

'We governesses come in mixed ages and I believe we can be found in all the usual variety of heights and temperaments as well, sir.'

'Maybe you do, but I haven't come across one I wanted to spend *more* time with until today.'

'Flattery will not do you any good with me, sir— rather the opposite, in fact.'

'That wasn't flattery,' he said with such an admiring look Nell was tempted to find another mirror and make sure she hadn't been turned into a ravishing beauty by a passing fairy godmother on the way downstairs.

'I beg to differ and if I am to remain here until the last of your brother's wards is old enough to be out of the schoolroom we must do better than this, sir. Please treat me with respect and spare me such empty compliments in future.'

'They are not empty and I'm not sure I'm ready to admit that my lordly brother and his wards have a right to stand between us quite yet either.'

'Then please hurry up and do so, sir. It will sit very ill with me if you make my task here impossible and I am forced to leave.'

'Since your standards are undoubtedly much higher than my darling brother's I shall concede you take your post as mentor to four young ladies very seriously. Will you not at least tell me your name before I go and get ready to eat humble pie at the inn in Temple Brampton?'

'Can you not stay for dinner, Mr Rivers?' Caroline interrupted impulsively and Nell frowned at the suspicion her shyest pupil was besotted with the man.

'I doubt your governess or cook will thank you for that impulsive invitation, Miss Caroline, but I am grateful for it and very sorry to refuse it,' he said gently and went up a peg or two in Nell's estimation. He seemed genuinely concerned to make sure Caro didn't feel snubbed for speaking out of turn.

'Perhaps another night, Caroline, when we can ask Mrs Clennage and the Vicar to be present and make us all so respectable nobody can talk scandal about us,' Nell said in a probably vain attempt to make Caro's disappointment easier to bear. First infatuation could be painful for a young girl on the edge of womanhood and she was glad Caro wasn't given to melodrama like her eldest cousin.

'Mrs Winch is every bit as respectable as Mrs Clennage and she lives here. Mr Moss dined with us when he first came here, so I really don't see why

Mr Rivers can't have dinner with us as well,' Caro argued stubbornly.

'I doubt my brother's new land steward would be viewed as a suitable chaperon for four young ladies of quality and his employer's little brother by your neighbours, do you?' Mr Rivers asked with a careless shrug.

Nell was relieved to see some of the stardust leave Caro's dreamy blue eyes as she took in the gentleman's arrogant implication that the brother of an earl was far above a land agent in so many ways he didn't need to list them. Such a high opinion of his own consequence would not sit well with Caroline, who seemed to regard Moss as a friend for some reason that escaped her governess.

'I shall make sure I ask if the Vicar and his wife are free to dine with us one evening very soon, Caroline, but perhaps we could ask Mr Moss if he is ready to share his house with a guest yet. If you would prefer staying in the village to riding back and forth to Combe Brampton every day that could be a solution to at least some of our difficulties, Mr Rivers.'

'Mr Moss says the windows in his house don't fit and most of the chimneys smoke,' Caroline said rather sulkily before Mr Rivers could speak.

'Your Mr Moss sounds a very fastidious sort of land agent to me, Miss Caroline. Luckily I'm a hardy Irish peasant and not nearly as finicky about my surroundings as he seems to be,' Mr Rivers said cheerfully in direct opposition to his top-loftiness a few moments ago. 'So long as the roof doesn't leak as well and any ghosts have moved on since he took up residence here, a share of his quarters would suit me very well, if Moss agrees to tolerate my company for a few days while I attend to some business of my brother's that he's too idle to come and see to himself.'

For some reason Nell thought the gentleman was on the verge of laughing even as he tried to sound as if he was having to make the best of a bad job. Did he know more about Moss than he was willing to admit? How could he? He was obviously a gentleman in Ireland, whatever high society had to say about his one-time actress mother behind her second husband's back, and Moss had grown up as a squire's third son from the north of England. A bustle in the hall spoke of another arrival and even when she couldn't see him, Moss's impatient footsteps gave him away before she even set eyes on him. Wasn't it a bit worrying she knew it was him, come to find out what was going on, before she could even see him? She didn't have time to think too deeply before he strode into the small drawing room so abruptly it seemed as if news of Mr Rivers's arrival had interrupted important business and he was eager to be off again.

'Here is Mr Moss, so we can ask what he thinks, can we not, Miss Court?' Caro said brightly.

'We should introduce Mr Moss to our visitor before anything else, Caroline,' Nell reproached her, trying to grab control of this situation back before someone else ran away with it.

Mr Moss was frowning and muddy around the edges when he stalked into the room as if he had a God-given right to say who could stay or go under this roof, as well as his own humbler one across the garden from the great house.

'Yes, indeed,' that visitor said with a mocking

smile at the land steward's hastily wiped riding boots and splashed leathers. 'I've heard so much about you since I arrived that I almost feel I know you already, Moss,' he added with a languidly offered hand.

'Good day, sir, you have the advantage of me,' Moss said gruffly.

'Rivers, d'you know? Half-brother to the Earl of Barberry,' Mr Rivers drawled.

'So he really does exist, then?' Moss asked disrespectfully.

Nell marvelled at his effrontery and wished she could afford to share it. She put the girls' welfare first and kept a still tongue in her head about her true opinion of the absent and neglectful Lord Barberry. This post might be even more of a challenge than it was before rude and abrupt Moss arrived to add a pinch of adventure to their dull existence, but she was beginning to question things that had seemed unchangeable until now. Such as what right did the Earl have to shrug off all responsibility for his wards on to her shoulders? And should she stay here and let him keep on doing it? Not sure she wanted to come up with an answer right now, she waited for two very different gentlemen to finish sizing each other up like a pair of wolves getting ready to fight. They must have reached a silent agreement not to give battle though, because Mr Rivers suddenly grinned like a schoolboy at his potential adversary, possibly in the interests of harmony or perhaps because he needed somewhere convenient to stay for a few days.

'He does indeed,' the Earl's brother said with deep chuckle that didn't do much to endear him to his unwitting host from the look of Moss's austere expression. 'My half-brother is far too big and awkward to be the product of even the most disordered imagination.'

Caroline was staring at the Earl's brother as if he was a fabulous being from another world again, which Nell supposed was hardly to be wondered at. The biggest wonder was she was immune to his looks and charm herself. She was a relatively young and acute female and Mr Rivers was an exceptionally handsome man, so it really was a wonder. Instead of being bedazzled by the Earl's half-brother, Nell's attention kept wandering to the dour and work-stained land steward and not even his mother could call *him* classically handsome without crossing her fingers behind her back first.

'What do you want to ask me, Miss Caroline?' Moss said, with a disapproving glance at the newcomer, as if he was concerned about the dreamy smile on Miss Caroline Selford's face as well and thought the man needed a stern warning not to play with her youthful emotions.

Perhaps he was also wondering if Mr Rivers's arrival would disrupt the smooth running of Berry Brampton House. Nell told herself not to find the idea he cared about Caro's gentle heart touching; the people on the estate might be uneasy and a bit rebellious if the Earl's handsome brother charmed too many young women into losing their wits over him and Moss was here to get everything back in good order as fast as he could. Any distraction from that task was a burden he probably didn't want to even think about shouldering with so much to do already.

'Ah, yes,' Caroline said, as if his question had

shocked her back into everyday reality where she was only thirteen and this god in human form was at least a decade her senior. Nell sympathised, but refused to rescue her shy pupil so Caroline could lapse back into her daydream of being three and twenty and fabulously beautiful instead of thirteen, coltish and terribly shy with anyone she didn't know well. 'Mr Rivers can't stay in the house with us, so we were wondering if he could stop with you at the land steward's house instead, Mr Moss,' Caro finally managed to say in a rush.

'Were you now, Miss Caroline? And you, too, Miss Court?' Moss asked, as if her possible infatuation with Mr Rivers's good looks and charm was a gap in her armour he didn't approve of one bit. As if he had any right to disapprove, Nell chided silently and glowered at him to prove he didn't.

'Mr Rivers is the Earl's brother. We can't expect him to live in the nearest inn, even if his brother does own it and practically every other stick and stone for miles around.' She excused herself as if she needed to, which she didn't, of course.

'He might well be more comfortable there,' Moss said, casting a critical eye at Mr Rivers's impeccable Hessians and exquisite pantaloons. He raised an eyebrow at the fanciful waistcoat which even Nell knew marked the Earl's brother out as a member of the dandy set. Mr Rivers's coat was so beautifully cut that her annual stipend would very likely buy a sleeve and maybe a lapel of it and no more.

'But so very far away,' Mr Rivers drawled, as if Temple Brampton and the Angel Inn were fifty miles away instead of a mere five and even less as the crow flies.

The otherwise polite and sociable Mr Rivers seemed intent on annoying his brother's steward and Nell wondered why, when it had been so hard to get Moss to come here at all that the Earl would surely be annoyed with his little brother if the man upped and left. The younger man didn't seem so impressed by his own looks and attire he was vain or obnoxious with anyone else, so why taunt a man who had to earn his living as Moss had been doing since his belated arrival?

'Shall I ask Mrs Winch to send a couple of maids and the boot boy to help your housekeeper get your house ready for a guest then, Mr Moss?' she offered with a warning glance at their unexpected guest to stop making himself the least desirable one a man could resent having thrust upon him like this. She was beginning to wish Mr Rivers had stayed in Dublin or Belfast, or London, or wherever he was before his wretched brother persuaded him to come here and cause an upheaval for some reason best known to himself.

'If she can spare them, they will be most welcome,' Moss said with a warm smile of thanks that made Nell's knees knock as Mr Rivers's easy grin never would. 'My new housekeeper is a diligent soul, but it took Jenks so many years to neglect it that the house is still hardly fit for his lordship's brother to inhabit.'

'Then we had best go and ask Mrs Winch to order as many of her staff as she can spare to go and help her make it so, Caroline. We must leave Mr Moss and Mr Rivers to become acquainted, since they seem fated to live with each other for the next few days, whether they like it or not.'

'It may even be weeks,' Mr Rivers said sunnily.

'Do you think we all ought to pack up and go to stay at the Angel instead, so Mr Rivers can take up residence here on his brother's behalf?' Caro whispered with a doubtful glance back down the enfilade towards the small drawing room as Nell scurried her away.

'No, Caroline,' Nell said firmly, 'if Lord Barberry wished to live here he would have made arrangements to do so. I think we can safely say this is the last place in the world he wishes to take up residence, since he's not even been to visit you and your sister and cousins once during the ten years he has been your guardian.'

'I suppose so, although Mr Rivers's arrival could argue his brother is softening towards us and this poor old place, don't you think?'

'It could, or maybe Mr Rivers is curious about Berry Brampton House and his brother's wards and has come to see for himself.'

'We're not so bad we need to be inspected like wild ponies, are we?'

'Of course not; you are wonderful girls,' Nell said hastily before the picture of Lavinia in one of her tantrums or a fit of overwrought tears could cast a shadow on that happy picture.

By seeking to distract Caro from the dazzling Mr Rivers she had put doubts about her place in the world into Caro's head again instead. Feeling out of sorts with herself for damaging Caro's fragile confidence by accident, Nell tried to persuade her to charm Mrs Winch into releasing two of her maids and stores as well as bedding from the Berry Brampton House linen cupboards, since Caro was the housekeeper's favourite Miss Selford. Somehow they needed to furnish a room in the steward's house in fit style for the Earl's brother to stay there for as long as he chose. Moss might have to endure patched and sides-to-middle sheets, but Mr Rivers could not be expected to share an upper servant's discomfort when he was obviously used to the best of everything.

Chapter Eight

'Why the devil did you come here looking as if you've never done a day's work in your life?' Fergus demanded the moment he was alone with his brother on their trip from the great house to the one he was making do with for the time being.

'I'm lulling your enemies into a false sense of security,' Brendan returned as if Fergus was an idiot not to see the logic of his plan straight away.

'Which enemies would those be?'

'I don't know; you summoned me here to smoke them out, so you must know more about them than I do.'

'I don't even know if I've got any yet. I only asked you to find out if there's good reason to worry about leaving my wards and their governess virtually alone in that great rabbit warren when I decide to go away again.'

'And you're planning to do that soon, are you?'

'Of course I am; you know I never wanted to be here.'

'Hmm, but how can I guess what you're going to

do next when you're pretending to be your own land steward?'

'As Moss I can find out what's going on here without everyone being wary of telling me the truth. My tenants and neighbours are eagerly lining up to tell me their woes right now and Lord Barberry wouldn't hear the half of it. Why should I look such a gift horse in the mouth when the governess presented me with it before I could even open my mouth?'

'Nevertheless, I'm surprised my dour and upright elder brother is behaving so badly. In your shoes I would have come here ten years ago and to hell with your stiff-necked family and whatever they had to say about me and mine, but you're too stiff-necked yourself to accept what they didn't want you to have. We both know Ma's worth a hundred of every other Selford but you, for all they called her foul names and tried to take you away from her when your father died.'

'And I hope they're rotting in hell for what they tried to do to her, but I still have the care of four young girls on my shoulders and you know how Ma's been nagging me about them since I got home. Now I'm here I know she's right to worry.'

'She usually is, it's one of her worst habits,' Brendan said with a rueful shrug. 'But it's not the girls' fault they were born Selfords, any more than it's yours you were as well. You're going to be busy if you're about to become their true guardian though, Caroline Selford is going to be a beauty and you'll have no peace at all when she makes her debut. I'll give you my expert opinion on the rest after I've met them.'

'If I catch you flirting with any one of them I'll

string you up by your balls,' Fergus said with a fierce protectiveness that surprised him nearly as much as Brendan.

'You'd have to catch me first,' his brother replied with a lazy grin.

'That shouldn't be hard, considering you're too idle to ride here and back from Temple Brampton every day and I've walked and ridden half the county since I arrived. I'm heartily sick of corn and cabbages and can count sheep in my sleep, but I'm fitter than a poacher's dog.'

'Ah, but I only *look* like a Bond Street Beau.'

'And if you ever *look* at my eldest ward the way she's going to want you to, I'll black both your eyes and send her to a nunnery until she's learnt some sense.'

'Like that, is she?'

Fergus felt a terrible urge to wipe the smile off his little brother's face before Brendan could even meet his eldest ward and wondered what the devil had come over him. He felt like the girl's father with a dangerous predator in his sites, for heaven's sake, and he'd never asked to feel anything for these girls who had been thrust upon him along with the title he didn't want either. He wondered if the Fergal Ford of a few months ago would recognise the confused idiot he'd become since he came here.

'Yes, she is,' he finally admitted on a gusty sigh and wondered why it mattered so much to him that Lavinia had the airs and talents of a hardened flirt and turned into a lost little girl the moment she forgot to be so rebellious. 'God knows how I'm going to protect her from the wolves when she'd far rather be gobbled up by the first one who comes her way.'

'Maybe you should let her scare herself on a tame one,' Brendan suggested with the modest look of an expert in the art of flirtation and seducing willing women that Fergus knew was a little too well-deserved for comfort.

'I might, if I thought she wouldn't fancy herself in love with you. I doubt you want to land at the altar with her, but that's what'll happen to you if she throws her reputation away haring about the country chasing after you as she would probably love to do.'

'That's the last place I want to be for a good while yet,' Brendan almost yelped in horror at the idea of marriage to a rebellious schoolgirl.

He followed it up with a colourful curse at the very notion of marriage that made Fergus feel a lot better. At least his sometimes careless brother had been reminded to take care with the confused and confusing young woman Lavinia was about to become. He was doing his brother a favour by warning him off, he reassured himself, as that protective instinct argued any young man who wanted to wed one of his wards had best be close to perfect. If Fergus didn't take him apart for playing along with Lavinia's fantasies, their mother would flay Brendan alive for raising a young woman's hopes if he was reckless enough to do anything of the kind after that warning, then she'd weep because her beloved boy had broken a young girl's heart. Her impressive fury followed by abject misery at any bad behaviour they were forced to own up to could outdo a synod full of bishops saying a stern *No* when they were younger. Yet he could rely on any member of his family to fight for him to the death and Fergus realised how lucky he was now he'd met his true father's family. The more he saw of what his late grandfather had done by putting the succession before everything else, the less he minded being the Selford family outcast. Set against the deep love he had always had from his mother and the patient good humour of his stepfather, the Misses Selford were poor indeed. Miss Court tried to make them feel valued and unique, but even she couldn't blot out their grandfather's contempt for them as mere girls, or his own indifference.

'We're nearly at the steward's house, so kindly remember you're not my brother and we never set eyes on each other until today,' he warned Brendan after the rest of their stroll through the parkland passed in thoughtful silence. He supposed the generous garden of the quaintly foursquare Queen Ann house in front of him ought to say how much the Earl of Barberry valued his land steward, but its current state did the exact opposite.

'What a fine old place this should be, big Brother. You have yourself to blame that it's nothing of the kind, so don't glare at me as if I've been wilfully neglecting it for a decade, Moss,' Brendan said, raising his eyebrows at Fergus's muddy boots and well-worn working clothes as if he couldn't imagine why the brother of an earl had agreed to share the quarters of such an out-and-out son of the soil.

'As if you don't spend most of your days on the gallops looking a damn sight worse than I do now,' Fergus said grumpily, contrarily longing for the fine clothes he'd once thought so disposable as he eyed his brother and wondered if Miss Court was as impressed by them as she seemed to be by the rest of his confounded brother.

'Ah, but that's what I do when I'm in Ireland. We all know what a heathenish place that is, don't we?' Brendan asked as if he didn't love the place passionately.

'Did you do as I bid you and bribe the post boy for a look at one of Hancourt's letters?'

'Of course I did, Derneley,' Lady Derneley replied triumphantly.

Her fugitive lord looked reluctantly impressed by his wife's unexpected talent for subterfuge. 'Good, that was the last half-crown I had; so, where is she?'

'At Berry Brampton House, working for the Earl of Barberry, of all people. I could hardly believe it—that milk-and-water creature in the employ of one of the most eligible men in England. If I was thirty years younger, I'd marry an earl.'

'You're not and he doesn't even live there,' her spouse said impatiently, reverting to his usual bare tolerance of his wife's butterfly thoughts as she flitted from one topic to another without much connection between.

'No wonder the clever little minx doesn't come to London, though. She must be waiting for him to get home so she can catch him by hook or by crook before anyone else can get there first.'

'Shut your chatter, woman. I need to think.'

'Remember, I'm the only one who recalls how life was when we were young and you were handsome and more fun than the rest of my suitors.'

'Aye, and you were a damned fine woman, thirty years ago,' he conceded. 'But that was then, so be quiet and listen to what you must do if we're to get out of here. I can't venture out without being caught by the vultures and put in the Fleet, so you'll have to go to Berry Brampton and get Chris's daughter's papers off her somehow or another.'

'I certainly can't live with my aunt's nip-cheese ways for much longer, so it might make a nice change. I've no pretty gowns and she expects me to sew and clean and even wash my own laundry and cook for us both. You know perfectly well I don't know how to do any of that; I'm a lady.'

'If you don't learn you'll starve or stink,' her lord told her abruptly, 'now listen to what we must do if we're not to be stuck here for the rest of our days.'

'Ooh, no, Derneley, don't even think of it—I swear I'll go as mad as my aunt quite soon if we don't get away.'

Her lord muttered something about that not being much of a leap, then perhaps he reminded himself she was his only ally, because he went on to explain his plan for tracking down the fabled Lambury Jewels and making off with them before anyone worked out he hadn't been able to have them broken up years ago, because Pamela never got the real ones out of her lover in the first place.

'You're so clever, Derneley. I wouldn't marry Barberry even if I could.'

'Seeing you've no money or brains and you can't cook, sew or clean to make up for the lack, it's as well he ain't even in this country to get in my way, then,' her doting lord said under his breath.

'How am I to get to Berry Brampton and do what you say though, my love?' his lady asked, in blissful ignorance of her husband's true opinion of her.

'There must be something left in this dusty old mausoleum the witch or her lawyer haven't locked away. Isn't there anything worth selling?'

'I haven't looked.'

'Why not, woman? How else are we to get out of this mess than by cashing in our assets?'

'But they're not ours.'

'Then you stay here and endure the old woman. Somehow I'll manage this business without you if you're going to be a witless fool.'

'No, no, Derneley, you can't leave me here on my own with her. I'll die without some life about me and my own pretty things, and some new gowns, and hats and…'

'Then be quiet and do as I say,' her lord demanded roughly before her list of requirements could get any longer.

Chapter Nine

By the time her afternoon off came around Nell felt as if she needed peace and quiet even more than usual. She thanked Mrs Winch for the housekeeping lessons she had organised to keep the girls out of mischief in Nell's absence and went out into the parkland armed with her sketchbook. It was urgent with new life, despite the grey and cheerless weather so far this year, but she couldn't seem to find the right place to settle. A stile or tree stump would offer her a subject; she'd open her sketch book and find her thoughts ran on so busily she'd wasted half an hour doodling before she knew it. Sighing impatiently at another drawing of nothing much, she got ready to move again and find some wonder that might finally hold her wandering attention.

'Now here's a dilemma,' the deep masculine voice she told herself she least wanted to hear drawled from behind her.

She turned to glare at Moss, because somehow she couldn't endure being written off as a quiz today. 'You made me jump,' she accused quite unnecessarily; he must have seen her start half an inch in the air. 'Must you creep about like a cat on the prowl, Mr Moss?'

'I do know a true gentleman is not supposed to argue with a lady, but a troop of land stewards could have marched along this path in step with me and you were so lost in thought you wouldn't have heard us, Miss Court.'

'What a nightmarish idea,' she grumbled, then snapped her drawing book closed as she got ready to jump down off the stile and wait for him to pass by.

'You have no time for us sons of the soil, do you?' he said as if he knew the inner workings of her soul and found them narrow and rather petty.

'Your profession has nothing to do with it,' she said, stowing her precious pencils more carefully than usual because she didn't want him to know her face was flushed at his faulty judgement.

The awful truth was he intrigued her and neither Miss Court nor Eleanor Hancourt could afford to be drawn to the Earl of Barberry's land steward. As a governess, she was probably beneath *his* touch. She had to set a good example to her charges and falling at his feet like a besotted schoolgirl would not be one of those. As the granddaughter of a duke and a lady of birth and fortune she truly was, he was an unequal match for *her*. Not that he showed any sign of being bewitched by her, so she needn't worry his tender heart would be trampled by her real status in the world as he clearly didn't have one.

'Why *do* you look down your nose at me whenever we cross paths, Miss Court?' he asked, like a boy taking a clock apart to find out how it worked.

'Maybe I am simply a cross-grained creature, Mr Moss,' she replied primly.

'Hmm, I doubt you're anything as straightforward as that.'

'Of course I am, you remarked on it just now.'

'If you revise our conversation you'll find out I did nothing of the sort. I have the evidence of my own ears and eyes on my first night here to argue with that stiff and unyielding image of a lady who doesn't care for anything but her own comfort. You are a fraud, Miss Court,' he accused, his gaze steady as he met hers with a challenge to argue and prove it.

'Am I?' she asked as lightly as she could when her heart was racing at the very idea he might have found her out and now she would have to tell the truth about herself.

'Yes; you pretend to be stern and unbending to an outsider like me, yet you cherish and protect the girls in your charge so fiercely I suspect you'd walk barefoot across Britain for them if it seemed the right thing to do at the time. If you ever dreamt of setting yourself up as a strict and uncaring educator, you veered wildly off course the day you agreed to take on the welfare of those girls of yours virtually alone.'

'This is plain speaking indeed, Mr Moss. I shall return the compliment and ask what I should think of a gentleman who was outfitted nearly as grandly as the Earl the day you came here, yet you stay in a rackety old house as if you don't care for your own comfort and we're not supposed to find that odd?'

'No,' he said gruffly, as if she had trampled on his pride by pointing out the facts of his life.

'Then maybe I am as ideally suited to my position

here as you are to yours,' she lied. She wasn't born to this sort of life and now as an heiress in her own right again there was nothing ideal about it. He was right the first time; Miss Court *was* a fraud and no doubt he'd be the first to denounce her as such if he ever found out who she really was.

'I don't think so,' he argued. 'Something about you says no to that notion, Miss Court. I wonder if you have a secret you're half-afraid one of us will stumble upon if you don't hold us at a distance?'

'What nonsense. Of course I haven't,' she said briskly, afraid that he might see into her very soul if she let him. The idea that he'd already looked harder than she wanted anyone at Berry Brampton to look made her even more uneasy. She should be eager to get away from him, instead of standing here as if he'd put a spell on her feet so she couldn't make them move until he set her free. 'I was fortunate to receive an excellent education so I can earn my keep by passing it on to Lord Barberry's wards. I'm a simple soul and such fanciful speculation is ridiculous.'

'Hmm,' he murmured with a hint of a smile in his eyes. 'I don't doubt your learning, but a simple soul? You seem rather complicated to me, ma'am.'

'I wish you wouldn't call me that, *sir*. I'm not in my dotage,' she said to try and divert him from his doubts about her.

'Of course not; you're nowhere near it,' he scoffed as if she had managed to irritate him without even trying this time. 'I doubt you're much older than Miss Lavinia Selford. I can't imagine how you came to be appointed governess here two years ago, when you can hardly have been long out of the school-room yourself.'

'Of course I was; I'm a competent and experienced teacher. If I thought *you* had a right to question *my* status I'd refer you to my former headmistress in Bath, as I was a pupil teacher at her school from the time I really was Lavinia's age.'

'I really can't imagine anything less likely than Miss Selford teaching small girls their alphabet. You must have been far too young to teach much at such an age.'

'That's how we schoolmistresses begin. Access to our universities being denied to us women, how else can we learn our trade?'

'Not at seventeen,' he said, as if he knew far more about the education of young girls than she did.

Perhaps he had little sisters, she speculated. Was he too young to have a daughter of his own, but if he had a wife or child he'd have brought them with him, wouldn't he? Nell felt a chasm open up in her heart at the very thought she might have been having hot and forbidden fantasies about a married man. She told herself to stop having them this very minute and it wasn't as if she intended to *do* anything about this feeling that he could be far more important to her than the Earl of Barberry's land steward ever should be. He'd laugh if he could read her thoughts and hastily decline the honour of fulfilling those wicked imaginings of hers, she decided, with a feeling deep down that might easily be regret if she thought about it.

'We do if that's the only way we can pay our fees,' she replied absently.

The horrid thought of Moss with a wife and child

outran Nell's irritation that he doubted her suitability for this post. She'd spent two years battling with the Selford girls' defiant ignorance when three more experienced teachers had declared them impossible before she came. Clearly it was unreasonable to expect a man to take the challenges she faced every day seriously, she decided waspishly.

'What were you doing at such a prestigious school if there wasn't enough money to pay the fees?' he asked as if he knew the costs of Miss Thibett's exclusive school were beyond a penniless orphan. What right did he have to question her, but for some reason she answered him anyway.

'When my grandmother died my guardian said it was foolish to educate me above my station. He informed Miss Thibett that he wasn't prepared to throw good money after bad and that I would have to find work.'

'What sort of guardian was he?' he said scornfully.

For some reason Nell felt her temper strain against the restraint of years. He didn't seem to believe her and this part of her story was actually true. 'Just the run-of-the-mill sort who cared as little how I felt as my current charges' guardian does about *their* hopes and dreams. He was as hard and indifferent to me as Lord Barberry is to four girls who have lost their parents through no fault of their own. They didn't ask to be thrown on his mercy, any more than my brother and I wanted to be dependent on our uncle. As his lordship takes as little trouble as he can over his wards, it seems to me a common enough way for guardians to behave. The Earl gives instructions to keep his charges fed, clothed and alive and as far out of his orbit as possible. No doubt he would rid himself of his wards as rapidly as my guardian did of me, if society would let him turn his back on them and get away with it. So there really must be safety in numbers; four girls cast out into the world to earn a living couldn't go unnoticed as one seems to have done when my guardian decided to disown me.'

'You are very hot against a man you don't know,' he said as if her outburst was personal and not directed at the employer he claimed not to know either.

'And you seem determined to support the Earl against the accusations most of his staff and tenants would throw at him if they dared,' she replied angrily, narrowing her eyes against a rare glimpse of the sun to glare up at him.

'Don't look at me as if I've been supping with the devil, Miss Court, neither of us know Lord Barberry, so how can we judge him? He may feel he's done his best for his wards by stopping away, so they can grow up in peace under your care. No doubt you could teach the instant you left your cradle so he may have done all he needed for them on the day he agreed to appoint you.'

'Don't be ridiculous,' she said stiffly and wished she could break the spell he seemed to have cast on her and walk away. He was mocking her as well as changing the subject and she made herself look into the middle distance while she wondered about Moss and his peculiar failure to arrive here until they had all but given up hope he was coming. His post was one most young men of his birth and station would have galloped here to grab with both hands. 'You clearly doubt I can find my way around a primer, let alone being able to teach them suitably ladylike accomplishments.'

'Spare me a list; my mother's vast numbers of friends line up to provide me with a list of what to expect of a truly accomplished young lady whenever I rashly put my head inside her drawing room of an afternoon.'

'Goodness, I thought you lived in a remote neighbourhood.' Nell allowed herself to be diverted and wonder how big a manor house his father resided in.

'It sometimes seems entirely made up of young ladies who insist on playing pianofortes and flutes very badly, or displaying pages of indifferent watercolours as if they were inspired. Perhaps a man needs to be deaf, short-sighted and oblivious to the frippery nature of most young ladies' accomplishments to be a true gentleman.'

'You are too severe. Perhaps you should consider how it feels to walk in a lady's kid slippers next time you judge one so harshly. A woman may have the acute mind and cunning instincts of a Duke of Wellington in petticoats but, for all the good they will do her, she might as well be born a fool.'

'You long for the smoke of battle and the smell of slaughter then, Miss Court?' he asked with such pointed irony she longed to smack his unfashionably tanned cheek or, even better, plant him a facer in true manly style.

'I doubt any woman does,' she said, her very real memories of the terrible aftermath of Waterloo making her shudder. 'Most of my sex have too much to fear for those who fight and die for our safety to think war anything but a tragedy. We sit at home and hope our loved ones survive, all the time knowing we can do nothing to stop the slaughter but pray for peace. Maybe I chose a clumsy example of how hemmed in and confined the female sex is compared to the masculine one, but how would you feel if every path you chose, every talent you truly possessed and longed to follow up and expand upon was closed off to you by an accident of birth, Mr Moss?'

'Frustrated and angry,' he admitted slowly. He looked thoughtful about his dismissal of half the world though and that was something, wasn't it? 'Do *you* secretly long to join the Royal Society, or mount an expedition to hunt for pirate treasure?'

Nell looked for mockery, but saw only interest in his eyes as she blinked back at him and almost forgot the question. Being alone with him under the budding oak trees lent a dangerous edge to their conversation and she should have bid him a chilly good day and moved on. If they could meet on equal terms, how irresistible he might seem next to the idle fops and rakes of the *ton*. Ah now, wasn't that the timely reminder she needed not to dream of this man kissing her in the shadow of my lord's venerable oak grove? She wasn't only Miss Court and he was Lord Barberry's steward. Even if he could lower his pride to live off his wife's fortune, she didn't know if she could endure an unequal marriage like the one her parents had made. Look what happened when you let your inner dreamer run away with you—one minute you were standing here wondering how it might feel to be thoroughly kissed by a fit and vigorous gentleman you had done your best not to admire from afar; the next you were marching him up the aisle and wondering how you could live together in harmony when your fortune was so much greater than his.

'No,' she replied as if that was all she was thinking of while she considered the biggest intimacies there were between a man and a woman and decided they were impossible for them. 'I don't have a scientific bent or long for wild adventures. Surely even you will admit I've a right to be bitter about the lot of women in our supposedly enlightened times though, Mr Moss?'

'Will I?' he asked contrarily.

'Of course; in a fairer world I could have attended a university if I was clever enough and never mind male or female. A scholar can't have too much scholarship.'

'Now there I can disagree and refuse to feel guilty. Who would want you to spend years hunched over your books until you grow a dowager's hump and need to wear spectacles, Miss Court? Not I, for one,' he said with far too much masculine interest in her currently clear-eyed and straight-backed form for comfort.

'Complimenting me won't change me into a fluffy female who simpers and agrees you know best because you're male, instead of thinking for herself. What if I heard the music of the spheres or found the cure for all ills? No matter if I am man or woman, such knowledge could be of infinite use to mankind.'

'Do let me know when you're close to tracking down either wonder, won't you?' he replied cynically as ever.

Nell knew she was clinging to an argument to shield herself against the glimmer of masculine interest in his eyes and that half-smile of his that threatened to make her heart flip over. She couldn't afford to stare boldly back at him or enjoy the novelty of not being invisible to a vigorous and personable gentleman for once.

'You know very well I'm too busy and too poor to indulge in serious and expensive study,' she said as briskly as she could. Shivers of something she didn't even want to think about were racing up and down her spine.

'And yet I heard this was your afternoon at leisure,' he murmured from far too close and the words on their tongues seemed to have very little connection to the hot thoughts in their heads if the fire in his gaze was anything to go by.

Had he sought her out deliberately? A flush of pleasure and something a lot more complicated threatened to give her away as nowhere near as indifferent to him as she ought to be. 'Yes, it is,' she said breathily and the small freedom of that half-day of leisure tugged her inner rebel to the fore and threatened to tempt her into the impossible after all.

The girls were occupied; she was not expected to supervise or teach them for the rest of the day and there was nobody to frown and shake their heads at the sight of the governess and the steward so deeply absorbed in one another. She remembered Colm and his beloved Eve and the stolen afternoons *they* spent together when everyone pretended not to notice they had sneaked off to their rooms yet again. The unexpectedness of their passionate love still seemed to surprise even them. They would laugh and agree with each other how unlikely their marriage was and wasn't it the most delightful wonder anyone ever came across that the Winterleys and Hancourts were now united by marriage instead of scandal? For a moment Nell longed to visit the same exotically unknown and fascinating territory they went to together with a most unlikely lover of her own.

No, love did neither of her parents any good and somehow she knew her mother had loved the dashing young husband who only wed her for her father's fortune. And after she died Lord Christopher Hancourt blindly loved a wanton, a renegade viscountess who blithely abandoned her husband and child to live the wild life she chose with any personable man who could afford her, until she bled him dry and moved on to the next fool in line. It felt so lonely inside the safe, dry little world Miss Court had made for herself today, though. Nell's father, besotted lover of a notorious woman, dared his very life for Pamela, Viscountess Farenze. Yet even with that warning example of how far Hancourt folly went, his daughter felt the thunder in her blood at the thought of letting all the passion inside her roar. Horrified by her own frailty, she still stood and wondered about the notion she could enjoy being a passing fancy for this man, if only she dared.

How would it feel to be kissed by Moss as if she was lovely, sensuous and desirable? How might it feel to actually *be* those things to a man she wanted so badly it didn't matter about social distinctions or correct behaviour any more? For the longest and most charged moments of her entire life so far those questions sang between them as if she had spoken them aloud. Her lips parted without her permission, his fascinated gaze encouragement enough. Her entire body was aware of itself as never before. Every breath was a novelty as the scent and power and sight of him reached a curious and dangerous place inside her and whispered *maybe*. Had her mouth actually shaped the word to cause his gaze to sharpen on these suddenly rather full and needy lips of hers? His guard seemed to have fallen nearly as far as hers as he looked back at her with sharp interest and something gentler and warmer in his eyes. A curve of almost tender amusement lifted his mouth in a wry smile. Her feet raised on tiptoe, inviting him to lower his head and let wild, reckless Nell Hancourt out of her cage the instant he kissed her…

'Ah, there you are, Moss,' Mr Rivers's genial tenor voice drawled from far too close for comfort. Nell sprang back as if she'd been stung and the land steward stepped away as if he and the governess were always poles apart.

'Indeed I am, sir,' he said blandly with a not very respectful bow, as if the Earl's half-brother was intruding and ought to know better.

'Good afternoon, Mr Rivers,' Nell greeted the newcomer with a hasty curtsy and saw how horrified Moss was by how close they'd sailed to the disaster of being caught together as lovers by this inconvenient gentleman. Well, if he thought it a disaster, Miss Eleanor Hancourt should be congratulating herself on a lucky escape. So why did she feel something rare and precious had been snatched away?

'My brother's lawyer has sent those maps and deeds on, Moss. No doubt he will expect us to pore over them until we resolve the northern boundaries he's so concerned about all of a sudden. Best get on with it as soon as we can, hey?'

'Very well, sir. I'll join you in the muniment room as soon as I've escorted Miss Court to her destination,' Moss said rather shortly, considering the gentleman might get him dismissed if Moss was as awkward and abrupt with his employer's brother as he was with her.

'Miss Court can get there without help, thank you,' Nell snapped because it hurt to be only an obstacle in his path now they'd been brought back to earth so abruptly. 'I am not yet in my dotage, Mr Moss.'

'Indeed you're not, ma'am, but with these rumours of down-at-heel strangers in the area looking for mischief any sensible lady must be wary of roving about alone.'

'Even the governess?' she said bitterly. His refusal to meet her eyes or be other than stiff and correct in front of Mr Rivers felt like a slight, however hard she told herself she hadn't really wanted his sensual attention in the first place.

'Especially her,' said the man who charmed her one minute and disclaimed any interest the next.

'Perhaps we could both escort you, Miss Court?' Mr Rivers asked more politely when she shook her head and stepped back from the man who had her senses so confused they were still yearning for his touch. 'As we're on our way to the estate office anyway it's a good excuse not to talk business until we get there.'

'I'd best agree to be escorted back to my duties then, sir. Mr Moss seems disinclined to move out of my way unless I do,' Miss Court said with her best smile for the Earl's gilded brother and a cool look of disdain for his land steward.

'We had best prove agreeable company then, Moss, since we're reordering Miss Court's leisure,' Mr Rivers said with an odd, mocking look at the man that gave Nell something else to think about as he offered her his arm and they strolled back towards the stately old mansion with Moss following behind like a bad-tempered hound.

'I'm not doing well at my drawing today, so I suppose it is not a hardship to be interrupted,' Nell managed to say lightly enough.

It was the peace and leisure to think that she regretted. Back at the house she was always listening out for the girls; out here she was free to consider the dilemmas her restored fortune and Colm's marriage had thrown her way and now there was Mr Moss and his not-quite kiss to consider as well. The contrary man was stiff and reserved to a fault as she strolled towards the great house at Mr Rivers's side and she decided she didn't understand the opposite sex and didn't particularly want to right now.

'Whatever are you be about now, Fergus?' Brendan demanded the moment they were alone in the ancient muniment room with the stout oak door shut.

'I'm getting ready to read a pile of dusty documents in a room I never saw the inside of until Miss Court thrust the role of land steward on me all those weeks ago and what an idiot I was not to correct her.'

'Don't try and sidetrack me; you've been leading that poor girl astray since you got here. You were about to do something unforgivable until I came along and stopped you.'

'Which poor girl would that be?' Fergus said in the mocking drawl he knew would annoy his little brother most.

He didn't want to be reasoned with about his bothersome fascination with a lady unlike any other he'd come across. So, *did* she seem unique because he wasn't his true self here, or even the modest Mr Ford he'd pretended to be on his adventures? Moss was a working man. Could that be why a much quieter and plainer young lady than he was usually attracted to had come fully into focus and made the rest seem dull and frivolous? Brendan was right, though; it *was* cruel to raise false hopes. Moss could be Miss Court's way out of the life of hard work and responsibility she was trapped by now. Yet she was still so young it pained him to see her frown over Lavinia's antics or look tired and pale at the end of a long day doing her best to teach his wards to at least act like proper young ladies.

'You know perfectly well which lady I mean—don't try to goad me into a temper or change the subject. You can't change the facts. Lord Barberry can't wed a governess and you know it as well as I do.'

'Aye, I do,' Fergus admitted with a heavy feeling in his chest that felt oddly like loss. He couldn't lose something he'd never had and didn't particularly want—Moss was a convenient disguise, but he didn't want to wear his workaday boots for ever.

'Although you pretend not to care a fig for the wider world's opinion of my Lord Barberry, I know you couldn't make a refined and proper lady like that one your mistress and live with yourself afterwards, Fergus. Only imagine trying to meet Ma's eyes over the breakfast table after ruining the girl without your sins being obvious to her and tell me that I'm wrong.'

'You're right,' Fergus admitted reluctantly.

He imagined the brilliance of Miss Court's intriguingly fathomless brown eyes dimmed by shame and an even deeper loneliness than she endured now, if she lowered herself to be an idle aristocrat's plaything. Her current path in life was a hard one, but at least it left her some self-respect.

'Maybe I ought to send for a doctor, big Brother; you can't be well.'

'Worse; I think I might have to grow up,' he said ruefully.

'You mean come here as your real self? Truly be the Earl of Barberry; after you swore not to step into your grandfather's shoes when he died?'

'Hmm, well, maybe one day I might do that,' Fergus half-agreed.

A mental picture of the governess's face when she found out the truth made him squirm at the deception he'd set out on that first night, even if she did offer it up to him on a platter with an apple in its mouth. If he wanted to stay here he'd have to confess sooner or later, but he wasn't sure he could face blank contempt in Miss Court's fine eyes when he admitted to being Earl of Barberry when even the idea of it made him feel slightly sick. No, he became Moss to get a true picture of how things stood here. His lordship could still be fobbed off, so he had at least one good reason to stay as he was.

'This year, next year, some time, never, then?' his

brother asked as if he could read all his basest motives for staying quiet and didn't approve of a single one.

'You think I'm being a coward?' Fergus asked haughtily, wondering if his little brother wasn't right.

'I think you don't know who you truly want to be and it's high time you made up your mind. You've been Earl of Barberry for a decade and refused to admit it whenever you can get away with pretending to be someone else. Until you decide to live comfortably in your own shoes, you'll be a danger to yourself and any stray governesses who expects more of you than you're capable of giving.'

'I hate the fact you're probably right, little Brother. You're five years younger than me and nobody seems to have told you I should be the wise one.'

'Natural genius trumps ageing cynic,' Brendan said smugly, but Fergus knew his brother was worried and why wouldn't he be? He was quite concerned about himself as well.

He had a brother and two sisters a prince of the blood would envy him, as well as a mother and stepfather who'd have gone to the stake to protect him when he was young and vulnerable. His mother even tried to forgive and forget the fact she and her baby could have starved when his real father died for all the noble Selfords cared. She pitied them for refusing to meet her son unless she agreed to relinquish him, but Fergus grew up hating them anyway.

All there was left of the mighty Selford family to be angry with when he inherited were four young girls who would have outranked him if they had been born male. His young cousins were more vulnerable than he'd ever been and he turned his back on them. He'd failed them as badly as his grandfather and uncles did him when his father died. He had a lionhearted mother to love him and they'd had nobody until old Poulson employed Miss Court to be their lioness.

He caught himself comparing Miss Court with Kitty, Lady Rivers, and smiling foolishly at the idea he'd hate to come between Miss Court and anyone she truly cared about as well. The old Earl's dead hand was all that had stopped Kitty dashing to England and gathering his orphans under her wing. That was another vile act to lay at the old devil's door instead of blaming the victims. Fergus was the girls' guardian only as long as his mother had no contact with them that had not been sanctioned by their trustees. And Miss Court wasn't bound to stay here and care for the Selford girls. Any day now a real land steward or curate would do his best to marry her and even the idea of her walking down the aisle and into another man's bed made him feel queasy. Yet as a wife she would be mistress of her own home and mother to her own brood, so why would she stay here and risk an uncertain future when her last pupil left the schoolroom?

All the clever, questing spirit would be knocked out of her if he seduced her because he wanted a woman in his bed, though. It was more than that, he knew it deep down even if he didn't want to. Miss Court fascinated him. He looked for her when he was near the house or in the Brampton villages. His day seemed brighter when he met her out and about with her charges, or busy on some errand in the shabby gig drawn by the placid old horse kept for her use. Although she would greet him stiffly and go on her way as fast as she could, his day improved on first sight of her awful bonnet and dreary pelisse in the distance. Not many ladies owned up to having any brains at all, but she was employed to use hers and had no reason to keep it a secret.

Admit it though, Fergus, his inner cynic whispered, *it's not only her inner beauty you're drawn to, is it?*

Not even Miss Court could completely hide her natural assets under those awful gowns and old-maid caps and bonnets. His mother and sisters could spend hours choosing frivolous hats and poring over fashion plates and he tried to picture Miss Court joining them, but it didn't work, so he must have been right all along—she would never fit into his real life if he was fool enough to pursue her with honourable intentions. He was about to kiss her just now, so he owed Brendan for stopping him committing such delicious folly with his wards' governess.

He spent the hours before dinner deep in estate business so his brother didn't have to. At least then he couldn't wonder how Miss Court's generous mouth would feel under his, if she didn't slap his face for taking liberties and storm off in a huff.

Chapter Ten

Nell let the most recent letter from her brother Colm drop into her lap and stared out of the latticed window at yet another dull spring morning. She wished it would get on and rain, but instead they endured day after day of grey skies and chilly gloom. Local farmers were shaking their heads and making dire predictions about the harvest; seeds couldn't sprout and grow without warmth or water to sustain them and only the crows seemed likely to grow fat this year. Colm said nothing of his own worries about this unremitting gloom in his letter, but between his recently inherited estates and those he oversaw for their uncle, the new Duke of Linaire, he must be anxious as any right-thinking landowner about the dire state of the land. The ducal acres were sadly neglected and Colm's own estates without a true master for a decade and a half, so Nell read between the lines and concluded that Eve had got him to London to enjoy the life of a wealthy and recently married aristocrat for a few weeks to escape all that heavy responsibility for a while.

Nell smiled at the thought of her beloved brother charmed into doing what was good for him by his new wife. Even when he knew she was doing it, he let Eve think she had got her way by stealth because he loved her so much and Eve almost glowed with happiness. Nell sighed and felt guilty about the nag of envy she tried hard not to feel. Colm was long overdue some joy after all those weary years of war their late uncle had inflicted on him by buying a commission in the most dangerous regiment he could discover and insisting Colm join it as soon as he was sixteen.

It must be wonderful to build a family with someone you loved and trusted so truly, Nell thought dreamily. Sometimes she longed for such a love so much it hurt, but she refused to make the Earl of Barberry's land steward the heart of those dreams. Moss would never fall headlong in love with a plain governess and she told herself she didn't even want him to. She sighed and tried to put the wretched man out of her thoughts, but the dull day outside her window offered no distraction from wondering what sort of young lady *would* tempt him. To fend off the shocking stab of jealousy such a smugly perfect female could cause her, she let her mind drift back to her childhood instead. Colm's letter had reminded her how she would read and re-read his every word to enliven the dull days back then. When Colm was sent to school the nursery governess her eldest uncle engaged to keep her out of his way was so stiff and unyielding Nell soon learned not to show her feelings. Tears brought a stern rebuke and an hour in the darkest and most spider-infested cupboard on offer.

Thank goodness Nell was sent to school herself at

the age of eight. She might have gone mad locked in that dull world with her stern governess. Colm's letters and Nell's discovery that Miss Pitch dosed herself with laudanum most nights saved her from the endless greyness of that stark suite of rooms at the top of Linaire House. Tiptoeing down the backstairs once she could hear Miss Pitch snoring, Nell would creep about the largely closed-up house, discovering the luxury of her uncle's rooms; the now shabby watered-silk walls of the ladies' withdrawing room or the leather and velvet of His Grace's State Dressing Room, and her imagination would run riot. She might tremble at the idea of being caught in her uncle's private sitting room even when he was far away, but somehow it still fascinated her.

The last Duke of Linaire never came to London in summer when the city was tired and dusty and stank of too much humanity. Nell wondered if he hoped she would be carried off by one of the epidemic fevers that swept through the capital when heat sweltered in narrow courts and overcrowded rookeries. He was so proud and selfish any hint it wasn't Colm or Nell's fault their father had brought scandal on the family name would have been greeted with blank incredulity. He was a stupid man born to a great title and hadn't cared the snap of his fingers for anyone's comfort but his own.

His next brother, the current Duke of Linaire, was his exact opposite and that was probably why Nell could persuade Uncle Horace to travel to Brussels with her last summer to search for her injured brother on the battlefield at Waterloo. The stench of blood and death and all the appalling sights and sounds would haunt her to her dying day. For most of the day after the battle she and Uncle Horace peered into piles of the sightless dead and tried to avoid looters so eager for plunder they would kill anyone who stood in their way. They asked dazed survivors if they'd seen Captain Carter of the Rifles with desperate hope Colm had survived the carnage. When they were on the point of despairing and going back to the relative safety of the city for the night they finally found him; wounded and already in a high fever, but blessedly alive.

Futile hatred for the last Duke burned in her gut at that terrible memory. The late Augustus Hancourt, Duke of Linaire, might be dead, but she wasn't a fine enough Christian to forgive him for putting her brother in harm's way for eight years of the late war. No… Stop, she couldn't think of the spindle-shanked monster without being sucked under by hatred and fury even now. She refused to let him matter that much, so where was she? Oh, yes, tiptoeing about Linaire House in the dark and never mind her obsession with Moss the steward that constantly threatened to lure her into an impossible daydream of being a poor gentleman's wife and forgetting Eleanor Hancourt altogether.

She could still smell the dust and stale air of that grand town mansion when too few servants were kept on to keep it immaculate in the Duke of Linaire's absence. She could still imagine herself back there, listening for a sign her night wanderings had been discovered. Luckily she was too frightened of the dense shadows of the great city by night beyond the shut-

tered windows to venture outside, but saw some of it
when she stood on a rout chair to peer through a gap.

Sometimes she would creep down the back stairs
to listen to the other inhabitants of the half closed-
up house. The servants kept on to protect it and wait
on her and Miss Pitch would be dozing by the fire or
talking in the smaller kitchen where the housekeeper
baked her cakes when she and the Duke were in residence. Listening to them discuss when the Duke
might return, Nell would wonder why she never went
to Linaire Court, deep in the fertile Midlands and far
away from dusty, smelly London. She had only seen
true countryside from a hackney Miss Pitch hired
to visit her parents in Hampstead on a day when the
maid who had promised to look after Nell for the afternoon took to her bed. The Pitch family lived in
a cottage on the Heath, but seemed happy and less
wooden than their eldest daughter. Nell enjoyed Mrs
Pitch's good-natured fussing, until Miss Pitch bundled her back into another stuffy coach for the return
journey to grey and gloomy Linaire House. After that
the governess seemed to dislike Nell even more and
perhaps a woman forced to earn her living resented
a child born to privilege, even if there were few signs
of it by the time Miss Pitch began her stern rule.

She wasn't doing well at putting the past behind
her and going on with her life as best she could, was
she? Folding Colm's letter to be read again later,
she frowned at the dull grey skies outside again and
blamed Moss. His arrival here had woken something
in her that was better left sleeping. She was content
until he came, even if her duty to her charges was an
excuse not to accept Colm and Eve's offer to stay with

them and live the life Lord Chris Hancourt's daughter should have had all along. That duty still existed, but she wasn't so sure she was the person to carry it out.

She had blossomed at Miss Thibett's school and perhaps her pupils would do better there as well. Once she was here Nell was too occupied with the struggle to get them to learn anything to wonder if she was the right person for the task. It took news that Lord Chris Hancourt was a very different father to the one his eldest brother had painted and the spectacular fortune Colm inherited at five and twenty to make her think again. Miss Hancourt was a catch on the marriage mart again, or she would be if the *ton* knew where to find her. Her father added her more modest fortune to the blind trust he had set up to protect her maternal grandfather's riches from his greedy eldest brother and Lord Chris's last gamble had paid off spectacularly well. Nell had a dowry that put all the Selford girls' portions added together in the shade. Now Moss was here another layer of uncertainty was plaguing her and he'd laugh himself hoarse if anyone suggested she might have a voice in his future, so why was she so reluctant to bid him goodbye if she went to the capital and forgot about Miss Court's duty?

'Miss Court, where are you?' Caro's voice sounded anxious. 'The carriage is at the door and we're all ready for church,' she called and Nell felt guilty about even thinking of leaving Berry Brampton House. Pushing the girls' absent guardian into sending her charges to Miss Thibett's Academy for Young Ladies instead of looking for a replacement governess could be a betrayal and she hastily pushed Colm's letters back into her writing slope.

'Coming, Caroline,' she called and tied the ribbons of her dull bonnet before taking a glance in the square of mirror on the mantelpiece to make sure she looked as dull and unremarkable as ever before picking up her prayer book.

'I was afraid we'd be late. Do you think Mr Rivers will attend church this Sunday?' Caro asked when Nell appeared in the hall. Bad enough that Lavinia sighed over every man she came across without Caro becoming infatuated with Lord Barberry's dashing half-brother.

'If he follows the Roman Catholic faith he will not be able to,' she answered, wishing him and his reluctant host at Jericho right now.

'Oh, no, all his family are Protestant—I asked him.'

'Are they indeed? That makes your family's attitude to his mama even less understandable,' Nell said before she could stop herself.

'That's what I always thought,' Caro agreed quietly.

'I expect they were good and right-thinking people otherwise,' Nell replied and wondered where such clumsiness would take her next.

'Grandfather used to shout a lot and call us girls names. I'm so glad Papa took us to sea with him because Grandfather used to say no girl was of use or decoration and he'd rather be dead than cost a dowry when some fool wanted to wed one of us.'

'Then he needed to beg forgiveness on his knees before he met his maker and was forced to account for his sins. Poor little Lavinia.'

'Vinnie tries to pretend it wasn't so bad being left

here by her mama. It was wrong to leave her child with a bad-tempered old man if she didn't have to though, wasn't it, Miss Court?'

'Between you and me, yes, Caro. You can be very wise sometimes.'

'I'm quiet, Miss Court, I notice things and people often forget I'm there,' Caro said with a shrug that said a little too much about her life here since her father's death.

'Maybe, but not everyone puts what they overhear to such good use. I shall try to be a little more patient with Lavinia in future.'

'And goodness knows, you'll need to be,' Caro admitted with a fleeting hug for her governess that warmed Nell's heart as they walked to the side door to wait for the other girls to finish dressing in their best for church.

'Good morning, Miss Court,' Moss greeted quietly and made Nell jump. She had found out the carriage was about to drive away to the inn yard down the street with Georgiana's prayer book and best handkerchief on board. 'Your footman asked me to give these to Miss Georgiana, but I expect you feel the lack of them more acutely than she will until she has need of them.'

'True, she does tend to live in the moment,' she said absently and wondered why, even blunted by gloves, his touch sent a *frisson* she didn't want to think about through her when he passed them over with a perfunctory bow and a shadow of his usual mocking smile.

'Where else is there?' he observed lightly and offered her his arm.

'There is the future and all the unforeseen consequences leading away from what we do today. Thank you for your offered escort, but, no, thank you, Mr Moss,' she said primly, ignoring his offer to help her into the Selford family pew as if she was precious to him, or many years older than three and twenty.

Much good it did her to refuse his escort, she decided crossly. She could almost feel his amused gaze on the back of her head as he meekly took his place in the lesser box pew allotted to Berry Brampton's upper servants behind this one and all that kept them apart was an inch or two of good English oak. She tried not to know he was scrutinising her best bonnet above the partition as if its fearsome respectability amused him. If Mr Rivers had a lady Nell could remove herself from the Selfords' box and sit with Moss the steward, Parkins the butler and Mrs Winch, housekeeper and her official chaperon. Since that gentleman was young, handsome and free as air Nell had to join him and her charges in the family pew. Somehow Mr Rivers didn't feel a threat to her good reputation. The Earl's little brother was like a large and amiable young dog, not quite fully grown and only half-tamed, but well disposed towards the world and ready to believe it felt the same way about him.

Mr Rivers sang lustily, prayed dutifully and listened as patiently as any man could to Mr Clennage's rambling sermon, so she couldn't blame him for this feeling of being uneasy in her own skin. It was the sound of Mr Moss's rich baritone voice that sent a flutter of prickly consciousness down Nell's back.

Then there was her irrational suspicion his attention was fixed on the back of her head again, despite the day and the place. She sat rigid and uncomfortable in her well-cushioned seat and, try as she might, couldn't recall the thread of the vicar's homily to save her life. And that meant she would have to think of a diversion when Mrs Winch tried to discuss it with her and the girls tonight.

Lingering outside the church door when the service was over was a price a governess must pay for having four young charges with friends to greet and exchange news with, amidst the quieter gossip and making of plans their elders indulged in. Nell felt as if the whole congregation knew how hard she must try not to look at Moss. She made sure they went opposite ways through the groups of parishioners waiting for carriages or husbands, or wives and children. At last she managed to get all her charges shepherded into the largest of the Berry Brampton coaches for the journey home, long after the other servants had left and Mr Rivers and Mr Moss mounted their fine steeds and headed back to the land steward's house for whatever food such fit and healthy young gentlemen needed after a hearty breakfast.

'Faith has been wicked,' Mrs Winch whispered in Nell's ear once the girls were upstairs putting off their bonnets and shawls and finding indoor shoes. 'You had best come to my sitting room and find out what she's been up to, Miss Court, if that's convenient.'

Mrs Winch was a lady superior to most governesses in breeding and status, but Nell's position here was better than most young women forced to earn their own keep. She suspected his lordship's lawyer had made it clear the governess must be treated with respect, so his provisions for the Selford girls' improved well-being were not undone the moment the Nell arrived, suffered a frosty reception and turned tail. She was made of stronger stuff, but it was a relief not to be bullied and ignored by the servants and the family she worked for, as one of the pupil teachers at Miss Thibett's school was when she left to look for excitement. Nell hoped she had earned respect for at least staying in the face of the girls' determination to make her go, but Mrs Winch had never truly unbent towards her. Maybe she thought Nell would presume if she didn't subtly put her in her place now and again.

'Of course, the girls are busy putting themselves to rights and at least none of us need worry about lessons on a Sunday,' she replied and wondered what the girl had done that Mrs Winch could not deal with sternly then forget.

Faith was standing in the middle of the Housekeeper's Room, twisting her apron between her fingers and looking very woebegone. Mrs Winch briskly ordered her to stop ruining her uniform to add to her sins and the girl burst into tears. The housekeeper told her to stop it this minute and to Nell's surprise the young maid did exactly that. Nell wondered if she should try such stern tactics on the Selford girls next time one of them indulged in a storm of tears and imagined Lavinia's scorn or Penelope's surprise and nearly laughed at the wrong moment.

'I could hardly believe my eyes when I caught Faith searching the papers in your writing slope when I went upstairs to check the beds had been properly made. I heard an odd noise in your room and thought the stable cat had got in again, but it was even worse than that,' Mrs Winch said with a stern glare that threatened worse than being scurried outside by the scruff like the poor cat was last time it got ideas above its station.

'I didn't mean no harm, Miss Court,' Faith managed woefully.

'Then why do such an odd thing, Faith?' Nell asked.

'Well, you see, miss, it was because our mam ain't been well, the baby needs medicine and Pa can't get no work.'

'I'm very sorry to hear it,' Nell said and it sounded a tale of woe and all too familiar in these hard times.

'That's no excuse, my girl,' Mrs Winch put in coldly.

'Well, the lady said she'd pay me five pounds if I found what she wanted when I saw her yesterday on my way back from the village,' Faith said defiantly. Mrs Winch glared even more ferociously at her and the girl looked about to cry again.

'What did this lady want you to do in return for such a vast amount of money, Faith?' Nell asked, wondering when this odd tale was going to make sense.

'Your letters and papers and any writing in books I could see apart from what should be in them, miss.'

'Good heavens, what use could any of that be to her?' Nell said, horror at what her correspondence could reveal making her feel quite faint, but nobody outside her family knew who Miss Court really was, did they? And why would it interest them if they did?

She wondered if Faith had bothered to look inside her neatly folded papers before she did her best to steal them and her heart did a panicked rat-a-tat-tat at the idea she wasn't as well disguised as she had thought. Moss would see her as a fine lady slumming while she made up her mind how to play her delayed entry into polite society if the truth came out like this.

'I dunno, miss,' Faith admitted after a pause for thought. 'I wouldn't have agreed to do it, but the apothecary said he'd have us put out on the streets if we didn't pay him. It's only a few bits of paper and a book or two, after all, and we do need the money awful bad.'

'If it wasn't going to hurt anyone, why did this woman want you to steal Miss Court's private letters?' Mrs Winch pointed out with another hard look that said Faith was about to lose her job, whatever Nell had to say about the matter.

The maid wasn't much older than Penny, who seemed so many years away from adulthood the notion of *her* working hard from dawn to dusk seemed ridiculous. Poverty brought maturity long before it was due, Nell decided, thanking God her grandmother hadn't allowed her to be put to work at the same age. And how could she save Faith and her family from being thrown on the parish?

'Perhaps it would be best if we don't let this strange woman know you were found out,' she said, with a warning glance at Mrs Winch to say this was more her business than the housekeeper's. 'How did you meet her?'

'At the Maying, Miss Court. She said she'd come specially to see us dance at dawn and asked if anyone else had read about it in the paper last year. I did, when everyone else was finished with it and it was waiting to go out for the ragman. She said I was a clever girl and walked most of the way back here with us. Then she said she was here to find out something important for the Government and what a pity I couldn't work for her as I was already working for his lordship.'

'Five pounds is too much even for a key to his lordship's strongroom and I'm sure you wouldn't give her that even if you knew where to find it,' Nell said.

The quality of her unknown enemy seemed shoddy as she wondered who would think such an outrageous bribe could go unnoticed if Faith succeeded and her family suddenly paid off their debts. It sounded like the work of a pampered lady, used to casually splashing out large sums of money to get the best service. Might such an exotic creature be behind this odd business? Nell had nothing worth stealing and she shifted uneasily as it occurred to her that a bored society lady might be curious enough about the Hancourt heiress to step outside her luxurious life for a few days to unmask her.

'No, miss, that I wouldn't. Our mam will be fit to be tied when she finds out what I've done as it is.'

'Well, you let her down very badly, Faith. I shudder to think how hard it must be for her to feed your brothers and sisters already and if you lose your job it will be even harder.'

'I know, miss,' Faith mumbled miserably.

Nell reminded herself she was dealing with a child and the woman who had approached Faith to carry out such furtive mischief should take the blame, not an urchin barely old enough to be let out from behind her mother's skirts.

'If I overlook this disgraceful affair and beg Mrs Winch to keep you on, will you promise me not to tell anyone you were caught searching my room? If this lady asks, say you haven't been able to get into my room without being caught and tell me at once.'

'I ain't very good at lying, miss.'

'You seem a little *too* good at it to me, Faith, but perhaps you'd rather Mrs Winch sent you home?'

'Oh, no, miss,' the girl said with an uneasy look at the stony-faced housekeeper. 'We'd be put in the poor house in two shakes of a lamb's tail.'

'I suggest you bear that in mind if you ever see this lady again,' Nell warned with a pleading look at Mrs Winch to persuade her to agree.

'And you'll swear never to do anything wicked again if you want to stay in this house another minute, Faith Roberts,' the lady ordered, presenting the girl with her own bible to make it a sacred oath.

'I swear, ma'am,' the girl said, her hand on the holy book and as solemn an expression as even Mrs Winch could wish on her tear-streaked face.

'Then go about your duties and don't say a word to anyone,' the lady said briskly. 'I shall be watching you like a hawk from now on.'

'Thank you, ma'am, Miss Court,' the girl gasped and bolted for the door before either of them could change their minds.

'Give me one good reason why I should not turn her off anyway,' Mrs Winch demanded as soon as the door was shut behind the shamefaced girl.

'It would alert this woman her plan has been thwarted and I'm afraid she'll try again by some means I may like even less.'

'It's very odd. Have you many enemies who take such a close interest in your private affairs, Miss Court?'

Nell felt she was under as much suspicion as poor Faith. 'I have no idea who is behind this folly, but I must find out if an attack of mania or mistaken identity led her to move against me like this.'

'I don't see how keeping Faith in a position she has shown herself unworthy of will do that.'

'Nor do I at the moment, but it will give us time to think.'

'I'm not sure I want to. We live in dark times, despite the peace, and there are rogues enough in the world without a thief living under his lordship's roof. I hope none of your relatives are Jacobins to account for it if the Government really do need to see your correspondence, Miss Court.'

'You know very well that my brother was an infantry officer for many years and was wounded at Waterloo. I took French leave to find him and drag him off the battlefield, so my family would never side with anyone intent on overthrowing our Government when he put his life at risk every day of his service to his country.'

'True; and I'm sorry to have doubted you, but this is a very strange business. We need wise masculine counsel if we're ever to sleep easily in our beds again.'

'You think I should write to my brother?'

'No, that would take too long. We must consult Mr Moss. He is his lordship's representative and has a strong arm and a clever mind. He may see something in this dark business we cannot. Don't shake your head at me like that; if you wish me to keep that girl on after she agreed to search your belongings for money, I insist you confide in Mr Moss.'

'Very well, but I can't meet a man in private and I refuse to discuss it in front of the girls.'

'Leave it to me,' the formidable housekeeper said with enough iron in her voice to steel a whole regiment of nervous housemaids.

Chapter Eleven

'Whatever can you want with me, Miss Court?'
Moss asked impatiently later that day, once he'd
ghosted into the housekeeper's room and shut the
door very quietly behind him.

'It's not a tryst if that's what you think,' Nell said
defensively.

'Just as well; they're supposed to be voluntary,'
the man said grumpily.

Nell immediately wished she hadn't agreed to this
condition of Mrs Winch's for going along with her
scheme to find out what was going on. Faith badly
needed to keep her place though, so Nell would tell
the brusque, annoying man about the stranger after
her secrets without revealing them to him either.

'It certainly wouldn't be so on my part,' she muttered and thought she saw a hint of hurt in the contrary man's eyes for a moment. 'And I don't want to
be caught in here with the door shut and only you for
company,' she added for good measure.

'Then stop wasting time and tell me what you and
Mrs Winch think so urgent she got me here under

false pretences and shut the door on us like a conspirator in a bad play,' he replied impatiently. After
a militant glare at him for being infuriating, she did
what he asked and told him Faith's odd tale. 'Have
you been through whatever papers and books you
have with you and looked for anything that could
give a clue to this woman's purpose?' he demanded.

'Not yet. I thought her mad and have had no leisure,' she said defensively. Four lively girls and a day
when cards, dancing and games were frowned upon
meant she needed all her ingenuity to keep them from
quarrelling and setting the whole household on edge
of a Sunday. Bad enough that hers, Mrs Winch's and
Faith's nerves were stretched tight without everyone
else catching the ailment.

'Then you'd best hand them over to me so I can
look at them for you,' he said as if it was her only
logical course of action.

'Certainly not,' she snapped, almost overwhelmed
with horror at the thought of her letters from Colm
and old friends at Miss Thibett's being combed
through and all her secrets revealed.

'Then how do you expect me to find out what this
mysterious woman wants and track her down?' he
demanded impatiently, one eye on the door as if he
couldn't wait to leave her alone again.

'I don't; I didn't want to tell you, but Mrs Winch
insisted I must before she would agree to keep Faith
on. I don't want the poor child turned off and her family put out of their house for the sake of a few shil-
lings. In her shoes I'm sure I would have done the
same thing if it meant paying off my family's debts.'

'Then you would have to be put out as well; what's the use of a servant who can't be trusted?'

'A master or mistress can lie and manipulate, but a girl not much older than my youngest charge must be beyond temptation? What an unjust world you live in.'

'It's the same one everyone else inhabits,' he said with a wry smile that almost disarmed her, until she remembered what he wanted and hardened her heart.

'That doesn't mean there's no room in it for change. If we don't want riot and rebellion running rife, then the poor should be less poor and their bread cheaper.'

'Lord Barberry won't be pleased if you impart such ideas to his wards.'

'How would he know? No, don't answer that for I'm quite sure I don't want to know what you say in your reports to our absentee employer. And please don't take me for a fool, Mr Moss. I know debutantes are supposed to be blithely ignorant of the state of the nation they live in and I have no intention of setting the Selford girls up for a fall when their lives are difficult enough already. They can still visit the less fortunate of his lordship's tenants and do their best to see their houses and larders are improved without causing a scandal. Surely even you won't argue his lordship's wards should be brought up in ignorance of how privileged they are? I'm sure the Earl would approve of them being grateful for their comfortable lot in life.'

The irony behind that seemingly obedient and governess-like statement wasn't lost on him. She should remember he was acutely intelligent and might have the ear of their employer, but he'd made her angry with his assumption she'd put radical ideas into her charges' heads then expect them to flourish in the very limited sphere their sex and birth confined them to. She might privately rail against the fact a young lady must seem docile and almost stupid to make a good catch on the marriage mart, but she did want the Selford girls to be happy and accepted when they got there.

'As well for you that I'm Moss and not the Earl of Barberry, madam. He is your employer, yet you speak as if you hold him in contempt,' he said with one of those fearsome frowns that made her search her conscience.

'Reckless of me if you are devoted to his interests. Would you prefer me to pretend he is a good and diligent guardian and will you report me for refusing to lie, I wonder?' she asked defiantly.

'Say what you like about me, I'm not a spy,' he snapped back, then seemed to think about his own words and shook his head as if he had to deny it all over again.

She had certainly tweaked his temper and she eyed him warily. Was she trying to cover her unease at his order to turn over her secrets for his inspection by going on the attack? Possibly, she decided. 'I never said you were,' she said with a weary shake of her own head to admit she might have gone too far. 'Forgive me, this has been a difficult day. I'm tired and let my tongue run away with me.'

'Don't apologise, Miss Court, it's so rare for you to let your true feelings past the stern guard you put around them. I ought to be honoured.'

'You don't look as if you are,' she said with a wry

smile and he chuckled as if she had surprised him yet again.

'Then looks can be deceptive,' he said and suddenly the heightened tension between them had nothing to do with his loyalty to their absent employer and her rudeness about the Earl.

'I'm still not handing you my personal correspondence,' she warned lightly, using their argument as an excuse to head for the door, because now the air was crackling with possibilities that really were impossible and she had to get out of here fast, before his charm overcame her caution.

'Love letters?' he asked, half-joking; almost condemning.

She stopped and turned to eye him warily once more. 'Certainly not, but they are private and written only to me.'

'Something you should remember when you're thinking about the odd events of the day,' he warned, but their voices were stating facts while their eyes were busy elsewhere.

Nell found time to shiver at the idea of those letters in the hands of some malicious rogue bent on harming Colm or his wife. Maybe it was that too-revealing gesture, or the fact she couldn't bring herself to break the contact of their eyes that drew Mr Moss to come closer; whatever it was they were suddenly standing toe to toe, studying each other intently. Nothing her sensible everyday self could say would make her back away and turn the doorknob behind her to break a spell she didn't fully understand. One minute they were about to snarl challenges at each other, on opposite sides of a battle about their noble

employer. The next their almost-argument only added
to tension of a very different kind. If she was going
to be honest with him Nell might admit something
new and reckless walked into her life the night she
met Moss in the twilit stables, but it was best not to
be too truthful when you weren't exactly who you
were pretending to be, wasn't it?

Moss, how absurd to have to think of him that way
when he felt so much closer than a stranger, but it was
all he must be, mustn't it? Whatever he was called
by those he loved, he had proved himself physically
strong and he had an air of power that seemed natural as breathing. Despite his position as a nobleman's
land steward, nobody owned this man; not even Lord
Barberry. She breathed in the outdoor scent of him
and wondered why she wasn't repelled by so much
untamed strength and masculine heat so close to her
it ought to burn such a respectable governess as Miss
Court. For a long moment it felt like waiting for a
force of nature to break over them; she was breathless and in awe of whatever was coming, but shivering excitedly about what it might turn out to be at
the same time.

'Kiss me, you idiot,' she whispered at last and felt
his shoulders shake a little as he laughed softly and it
seemed to warm the very air between them.

'Wasp,' he whispered before he lowered his head
and did just that.

Their first contact lip to lip was almost dis-
appointing—gentle and bland—asking what she
thought about this and waiting for her to remember
Miss Court and Mr Moss, two respectable people
supposedly going about their duty. She responded

with a silent demand for more and that tidal wave she'd been waiting for hit her with even more force now she'd almost forgotten it was on its way. Oh, it was bliss, she thought, as she was swept under it and didn't even want to fight. It was rich and powerful and new and she wanted to stay lost in feeling like this for ever. More than mouth to mouth, it felt as if their whole bodies were kissing, exploring, yearning, owning each other between one second and the next. She shifted in his arms; trying to find her way inside his very skin so she would know everything, see all he was right now, feel at one with him. Sensation burned on sensation in a banquet of taste, touch, scent and small gasped sounds that were all either of them could spare. There was something missing; she prodded her sluggish mind to recall it—ah, yes, *sight*. Opening her dazed eyes was a mighty effort, but there, his were blazing back at her with hot blue fire in his compelling gaze that made him changed and yet so wonderfully the same it didn't matter who they really were. She felt so alive it was as if anything was possible for them right now. If she sprouted a pair of wings and flew out of a window to soar into hot blue skies with him, as if they were a pair of courting eagles, it would feel almost normal. She gasped a huge breath in and wanted to laugh joyously, to squirm ever closer until they saw through the same eyes, felt with the same touch, learnt one another's every last breath and sinew.

His long limbs were the only way a man's limbs should be. The power of the hard muscles under her urgent hands testament to the fact here was no idle beau or nobleman, sitting about his castle in luxury whilst the rest of the world worked to keep him. His rein-calloused hands on her soft curves and narrow waist were bliss, but even that wasn't quite enough for the hungry wanton within. That Nell knew there was more than even this wonder. The everyday one felt the world battering away at her certainty here was her mate, her given man, the one. In protest at this sense not everything was as it should be between them, she explored his jaw line, her hand gliding over supple tanned skin tight on his high cheekbones and down. Who would have thought the feel of a man's beard about to sprout would be the stuff of fantasies under her fingertips as she ran them back down towards his fascinating lips and padded them against his skin? He opened his mouth and suckled on her index finger and she gasped at the wild heat searing through her as his hot blue eyes held hers with a promise to forget everything but her and him for a long, sensuous moment.

Willing to give him that promise back with interest, she fell back against the nearest support her body could find at short notice and felt the cold brass of the door knob at her back. She flinched away as if someone had stuck a knife in her. Heavens above, but they were kissing like lovers in Mrs Winch's very respectable sitting room. She, the governess, and Moss, his lordship's steward, were locked in each other's arms as if they'd been born to love each other. Except she wasn't simply Miss Court the governess, was she? And he didn't love her. Did he? She peered up at him almost fearfully now, unsure if she was delighted or wounded to the heart when he seemed to catch her caution and looked a cool question back at her, despite the sound of his breath coming fast in his labouring lungs and a tremor in his long-fingered hand as he felt the knot in his carelessly elegant cravat for damage.

'I shall leave you to compose yourself, Miss Court,' he said, avoiding her gaze altogether, now he'd put that sensual wildness behind him so completely she wondered if she imagined the impassioned lover of a few seconds ago.

'How can you be so cold, so, so…oh, I don't know… so careless about kissing me and everything?' she managed incoherently.

'Ask me again tomorrow, when we're further from me throwing myself on you and begging for a night in your arms, Miss Court. Right now I'm not quite safe for you to be around; by then maybe I can be tame and Mr Moss again.'

His voice was hoarse and he looked as if it had cost him a great deal to stand back when he'd felt her jolt of shock and instinctive horror at what they had almost done together without love. She wanted to explain it wasn't horror they could have been lovers if they hadn't woken up to where they were in time. Part of her was mortified to say it wasn't that at all, it was because she wasn't being honest about herself, or any of the reasons she was still here being Miss Court instead of Miss Hancourt, with her splendid marriage portion and embarrassment of noble connections. It was the huge lie Miss Court was that stopped her tongue and made her shuffle her feet as if they'd be better off on the other side of this confounded door. A confession trembled on her lips, she even opened her mouth to start it, but he got there first.

'Promise me you will go through your papers as if

you are seeing them through the eyes of a stranger as soon as you can? I can't imagine what you and your family or friends have been up to in order to attract the attention of a felon, but if you don't find some clue why this idiotic female thinks your correspondence is worth five pounds to her, then I will. I won't have the Selford girls endangered because you brought a maniac here and refuse to let me see what makes her think she can bribe and corrupt the servants to get hold of it without answering to me.'

'*You* won't have it?' she asked, startled by the steely purpose in his cold blue eyes now, almost as if she was in league with the woman who wanted to see her letters because she wouldn't meekly hand them over for him to read.

This was the man who kissed her as if his life depended on it moments ago. His eyes had blazed passion and what she took to be even deeper feelings only moments ago, when he gazed at her as if she was the centre of his world. She probably had been as well, for that fleeting instant. Bitterness blotted out her guilt about deceiving him. He didn't care for her, so why should she be uneasy about Miss Eleanor Hancourt and her fine fortune and the distance that ought to set her from the Mr Mosses of this world? None of it mattered, because she didn't matter to him.

'*You* won't let me endanger the girls I spent two years of my life trying to guide and teach to the best of my ability when nobody else cared a snap of their fingers what became of them? *You* accuse me of putting myself first when you have been here little more than a month and know nothing of the struggle I have had to even persuade them to be civil to each other, let alone learn anything? *And* you think me capable of some underhand scheme because someone I have never set eyes on has decided she has the right to single me out as quarry for no good reason? Mr Moss; judge and jury of lords and governesses; mentor and protector of my lord's despised wards and guardian of Berry Brampton's morals—what a fool I was to think you were a man in your own right. You're only a puppet dancing to your master's whims and what a master you chose to caper for; I'd rather sup with the devil than bend the knee to the Earl of Barberry myself,' she finished and took one last, dismissive look at the tall figure of Moss, Lord Barberry's faithful estate manager, before opening the door as coolly as if her hands weren't shaking almost too hard to grip it and stalking out like an offended dowager duchess.

If only she knew, Fergus thought darkly as he listened to Miss Court's petticoats rustling stiffly down the corridor and the fading echo of her soft slippers as she climbed the schoolroom stairs.

She was off to her room, alone and on her dignity, and he felt responsible for that and so many other wrong turns he'd made since he met her. He'd arrived almost ready to admit he was the errant Earl of Barberry and it was her fault he'd been diverted. Her fault he was braced like a trooper about to ride into battle at this very moment. She had no idea how harshly a man roared and ached and tore at his tethers for satisfaction of the sort of urgent, desperate need she'd roused in him just now by responding so passionately to his kiss. If she despised the Earl of Barberry, he *loathed* the man right now. The lord of all this faded splendour would get short shrift from stubborn Miss Court with very good reason. Even if he wasn't the man standing here needing her so hungrily he wanted to lock them both inside her bedchamber until she admitted she wanted him back, then satisfy them both with infinite pleasure, that lord couldn't want a governess.

Except he did and how had he let that happen? Fool, he raged at himself. How could he have been furious with her one minute for refusing to let him see her dratted letters, then step into another world of wanting and needing with her the next? It felt almost as if a cliff had dropped away in front of them and he'd grabbed hold of her eagerly as they both plunged off it into thin air together and learnt to fly. He might as well admit he'd been intrigued by her one moment and infuriated the next since he'd got to Berry Brampton and met her in the gloaming now though, hadn't he? She wasn't like any other woman he'd ever come across and she certainly wasn't a beauty. After ten years wandering the earth as Mr Ford, a gentleman of means but not quite fortune, he'd met enough beautiful women to compare Miss Court's unique features to several patterns of perfection and find it wanting. But it wasn't about symmetry and classical proportions, was it? Not when the woman you were thinking about was Miss Court, governess to the Earl of Barberry's wards and a disaster in petticoats.

He told himself her mouth was too big and her nose was pert and her dark brows too strongly marked and they didn't go with that seductive mass of potentially unruly honey-brown hair she tried to keep under such stern control. The whole shape of her face was wrong as well, he decided, warming to his subject in the hope of breaking the spell she seemed to have him so firmly under right now, beauty or not. Instead of an oval model of classical perfection it was heart-shaped and that firm chin of hers must have been especially formed to defy him—since she'd been raising it to look down her tip-tilted nose at him since the first moment they met. So how was he doing at teaching himself indifference to Miss Court and the delicious feel of her coming vividly alive in his arms when she intrigued him in so many novel ways? Very ill, he decided and began to pace the room like a caged animal as he tried to find a way not to visibly want his wards' governess. He wasn't doing well; this need to teach her to gasp out her wildest extremes of passion under him right now felt so desperate it hurt.

Now, where were all those reasons why that couldn't happen? Ah, yes, there they were; waiting for him to list them and teach himself self-control. One, Brendan was right: he couldn't make her his mistress. Two, he couldn't marry her, even if she would have him once she found out who he really was and how badly he'd been deceiving her all this time. Even if he wanted to play king to her beggar maid, she would refuse him and flounce off in an insulted temper because she despised the Earl of Barberry and was almost reckless about making that fact known to his land steward. An almost tender smile tipped up his mouth as he pictured her blaming him for the fact she must find another place because she wouldn't work for such a charlatan if he offered her ten times her current stipend to stay here. Not that he would, he promised himself faithfully.

Three—or was it four—the only way he could
make this right and not ruin her was to find her another position on the other side of the country from
Berry Brampton when Moss had to ride away as un-
expectedly as he'd arrived. He couldn't stay here and
pretend to be his own estate manager for much longer. It was only ever an impulse he ought to have resisted to pretend he wasn't really *my lord* for a little
longer. Of course he'd learnt far more about the house
and estates than he would have as master of it. Try
telling Miss Court that when she found out who he
really was; she'd be incensed at his deception and
under all her bitter fury would be a deep and abid-
ing hurt. He could picture the mix of contempt and
distress in those depthless brown eyes of hers even
as he thought about confessing to her who he really
was. What a shame he was still too much of a coward to bring this farce to an end right now, before she
was hurt even more badly.

And they would both hurt if he didn't tear himself
away very soon. He'd seen his mother hiding her humiliation at the slights and mockery of her so-called
betters too many times to delude himself that Miss
Court would be accepted as his Countess. Maybe
she was a governess and not an actress, but she was
still poor, vulnerable and working as a servant. He'd
promised himself as a small boy he would never do
what his father did and persuade the best woman in
Christendom to wed him, then die and leave her to
suffer all those sneering comments and slights when
he claimed to love her so dearly. It wasn't a particularly rational way of looking at the world, but the example of that love affair still stood like a stony barrier

between him and a woman he might love, if he truly was Moss and not a very reluctant earl indeed. What if he wed her, then got himself killed, so some distant cousin of his could mock and slight his Countess for not producing a son in time to supersede him and grab the title of Dowager Countess for herself when her foolish lord died? It hurt nearly as much to imagine Miss Court refusing to flinch in the face of such contempt as Kitty had every time someone repeated the last Lord Barberry's spiteful words about her and his own grandfather swore he'd kill her brat before he let him stand in his shoes.

He couldn't go yet, though—Lord Barberry couldn't chase down the woman after Miss Court's papers. He would be too conspicuous as his true self, especially if everyone knew he was here and trying to fit in a place he'd cut himself off from for a decade. He couldn't leave that thread loose and let Miss Court walk off into the world with a villain on her tail either and wasn't it absurd he only knew her by her surname? He wondered what her given one was. Was she a simple Jane or Ann or a complex Clarissa or Augusta? Ah now, wasn't that exactly what he'd promised himself he wouldn't do? No good lingering on her and the fascinating inner self under all the starch. Her odd conundrum had given him a very good reason to be Moss for a little while longer though and wasn't that a relief? He gave himself a mocking grin in Mrs Winch's mirror as he mentally seized that excuse with both hands. Brendan could despise him all he liked for cowardice, but at least as Moss he could creep about the estate unchallenged when the Earl or his half-brother would be remarked on and gossiped about. It was his excuse and he was going to stick to it, because Miss Court might suffer a lot more than a bruise to her pride and a little more knowledge of a man's passions than she wanted if this stranger had good reason to track her down and take her life apart for her own ends.

Chapter Twelve

Nell couldn't see a good reason why anyone would want her letters and what few personal papers she had. Of course there were one or two bad ones, but if someone wanted to blackmail her for pretending to be Miss Court why not simply get on with it? And how would a stranger pick up her deception when she had been here two years without a soul suspecting she wasn't the quiet governess she appeared? It was a small enough leap if anyone found her interesting enough to track down as her true self, she supposed. Colm knew; her uncle and aunt, the current Duke and Duchess of Linaire, agreed to give her time to think about her restored fortune and they were too kind and vague to prod her into the open with a devious scheme they would never consider fair. The Winterley family knew who she was as well, of course, but Colm and Eve had a quiet wedding at Darkmere and the wider public didn't know his sister had been there, so what about her friends?

Her fellow pupils at Miss Thibett's Academy had either become teachers themselves or drifted so far from Nell's orbit they lost contact. Uncle Augustus had insisted she became Helen Court the moment she'd set foot in the school so, even if they wanted to, her friends couldn't betray her secrets. Yes, she was living quietly in the country, pretending to be dependent on her earnings as a governess, but it was a small deception that did no harm. If his lordship was here even a hint she spent time alone with him would have the gossips on the edge of their seats, eager for every detail their busy tongues would make up if it didn't exist. As well the Earl of Barberry was far away, then, so she could cross one disaster off her list.

She sighed and lit all the candles in the branch on her desk for once. Hard to admit to herself Mr Moss was right, but she had to go through all the letters and papers in her writing slope and the locked box of personal belongings under her bed. Looking for any clue that might account for a stranger's odd behaviour would keep her busy. As she pulled the familiar old box out and put the key in the lock she decided it was going to be a long night, but she didn't want to sit and dream of ineligible gentlemen with sense-dazzling kisses and a cross-grained temper until the shock and wonder of his kiss had worn off. She wouldn't sleep with the memory of that wonderful disaster refusing to be dismissed all night long. Might as well make good use of the time, then, and try to track down his wild goose, despite her conviction there was nothing worth finding out about Miss Court, governess, or at least nothing he was ever going to hear.

* * *

Fergus rubbed a weary hand over his eyes and shook his head at his brother's offer to pass more bacon.

'If I had to ride about the place all day long, I'd eat enough to keep several bears alive before I started, but if you want to fall off your horse for lack of food halfway through the day that's your problem,' Brendan told him. 'And speaking of bears, you're like one with a sore head yourself this morning.'

'You talk too much,' Fergus replied, wishing he'd taken to the bottle last night since he had such a head today he might as well have drunk himself into a stupor anyway. Of course, enduring a sleepless night tossing and turning and feeling guilty about Miss Court as frustration racked him was guaranteed to make him short-tempered, but that was understandable.

'Quite an achievement given I currently share a house with you, Brother dear,' Brendan told him with enough edge on his insult to make Fergus wonder if he'd been unusually terse with his little brother and he'd missed the boy like the devil all the years he was far away.

'Don't call me that here,' he said gruffly, 'servants have ears as well.'

'As well as what? A fine feminine figure and large brown eyes a man could drown in if he let himself?' Brendan said with a knowing look that made Fergus want to punch him for noticing Miss Court's more obvious assets when why wouldn't he?

'Attempt to explore that particular servant's worst-kept secrets and I'll make sure you can't walk upright for a week,' he warned his brother so softly Brendan nearly choked on his vast breakfast and looked truly horrified for a moment.

'Ah, so that's how it is, is it?' he finally recovered enough to reply sagely and Fergus could almost see the cogs turning in his brother's busy head.

'Of course it isn't. You know I wouldn't foul my own nest.'

'How would I? You were never in it before and even now you're pretending to be your own steward.'

'Well, I won't,' Fergus said shortly. Of course the very idea was repulsive, but an image of Miss Court breathless, warm and heavy eyed in his arms last night still tore holes in his certainty he'd be a villain to teach her more about lovemaking than a virtuous governess could afford to find out.

'The truth is you can't see straight about this place or the Selford half of your family. Those old men made you so furious about their precious succession and the way they hated Ma for being a fine and lovely creature your father insisted on marrying that you can't see past what they did.'

'What can't I see, then?' Fergus asked disagreeably, wishing he didn't fear Brendan was right.

'What a mess they left behind them?' Brendan said frankly, looking about the ramshackle room with a frown.

Eyeing the ancient roof and chimneys of Berry Brampton House from the morning-room windows, Fergus couldn't help but agree there was a great deal wrong here and he'd done nothing much to put it right yet. 'What would you do in my shoes, then?' he asked gruffly.

'Send those girls to school, give your precious governess a good reference and go back to Ireland, but that's what I'd do, Fergus, not what you want to do.'

'How do you know?'

'You don't love the land there like I do, so why would you turn your back on all this and go back to being the nobody in particular you've pretended to be these last ten years? You didn't find peace thousands of miles away, so how do you expect to feel it wandering about your own country? You belong here, Fergus, whether you want to or not. Fight the idea until the truth seeps through your thick skull if you like, but you feel something for this place I couldn't if I lived here the rest of my life.'

'I was never wanted here,' Fergus said gruffly.

'Not by a pack of dead men, but they're all gone now, aren't they? You're alive and the Earl in possession, despite all they did to stop you inheriting. Time you learnt to live with who you are and where you come from, my lord.'

Fergus grimaced. 'No, thank you,' he said abruptly, threw down his napkin and stamped out of the room in an even worse mood than the one he came in with.

Riding off to view the next old-fashioned and under-capitalised farm on his list, he thought about the effort it would cost him to live here and make the changes needed to drag this ancient estate into the nineteenth century. He could find a substitute Mr Moss to do it for him, he supposed, but the original one proved to be a broken reed. Since everything his forefathers had left him so reluctantly was entailed he couldn't sell any of it, but he could rent the whole place to a nabob with more ruthless ideas about progress than he had. Or he could stay here and try to be a good master of this grand old house and all the estates he'd never wanted to inherit. He could build the schools and encourage the trades and businesses that might make this place more secure and prosperous for those who lived here than it was as a simple agricultural system unchanged for a hundred years or more. He saw the benefits of shared labour and common land, but growing up in Ireland had taught him a few lessons about holdings that were too small to weather a series of bad harvests or a glut on the market. Yes, Berry Brampton would be challenge enough even without his four wards and the hard task of finding a replacement governess they wouldn't loathe on sight—so could he truly be Lord Barberry for the first time in his life and make suitable arrangements for them as Brendan suggested?

With his true family living in Ireland and no wife at his side it would be lonely sort of enterprise without the girls and their governess here to make it an adventure though, wouldn't it? No, Brendan was right; they would be far better at a good school. Here the fact they were born female and unable to inherit was flung at them at every turn, even more so when he took up residence as his true self. They were as much victims of the Selfords' single-minded determination to keep the son of an actress out of the succession as he was. He was protected from their obsession by a loving mother and stepfather. Not just protected, doted on, he recalled with a guilty glance at those venerable chimneys under which four orphaned girls had lived virtually alone for so long. Gifted with a brother he liked better than any Selford ever did one of theirs, and two half-sisters a man could be proud of, he knew now that he had so much and they had very little. How could he ever have resented them for being living proof of how little his father's family wanted him?

His deception sat heavy on his shoulders this morning and he was tempted to turn about, ride up to the main house and openly declare himself the Earl of Barberry. His mouth lifted in a wry grin for the first time this morning at the thought of the response he would get. Even Brendan's word wouldn't be enough to convince Miss Court in her role as temporary guardian and protector of the Selford girls that he was exactly who he said he was. She would probably refuse to believe him and who could blame her? No, if he was going to do this, he must plan better and wait until he had this mysterious stranger after Miss Court's private papers in his sights. The Earl's arrival might cause a sensation and scare the woman off, so he could forget unmasking Moss for another day and concentrate on the next farm on his list, and the puzzle of reasoning out why anyone wanted to know even more about Miss Court than he did.

'What are you reading, Miss Court?'

'A private letter, Lavinia,' Nell said repressively. Trust her eldest pupil to see the dark shadows under her governess's eyes and try to take advantage.

'It hasn't arrived recently from the look of it. Either you take no care of your mail, or it's quite old and worn out with reading already.'

'I do expect a properly argued, fair copy of that essay by the end of the day and what I choose to read and the state of my letters is none of your business,

Lavinia,' she managed to say sternly before she point-
edly went back to her reading.

'I hate history,' her eldest pupil mumbled rebel-
liously.

'We know. Most eligible gentlemen have expectations of a house of some sort though, and not all
of them are newly built, so won't you look a fool if
a young man you admire has an ancient house and
you are ignorant about every age it had to survive to
be the place it is today?'

'I suppose so, but it's so very stuffy,' Lavinia said
with a mighty sigh.

'Everything a young lady needs to learn is stuffy,
useless or boring as far as you're concerned, but the
sooner you learn, the sooner you will be a young lady
and escape it all at last. Now, kindly get on with your
work and leave me to study some slightly less ancient
history in peace.'

Lavinia grimaced, tried to distract her cousins
from their own work for a moment or two, then went
back to the Tudor monarchs with an even louder sigh.
Nell fought a strong urge to close her eyes and nod off
in the now-peaceful room and forced herself to carry
on reading the letters she had set aside last night to
read more carefully when she could find time. The
ones her brother Colm wrote when they were children, then on his very active service in Spain and
France had been read and re-read so many times she
was certain there was nothing hidden in them, apart
from as lively an account of how it felt to be a schoolboy and then a soldier in extraordinary times as she
had ever come across. Maybe one day they could
be edited and published to give a colourful picture

of how it felt to be a young officer in the Duke of Wellington's army. Then schoolgirls far in the future could sigh to their teachers and moan about how stuffy it all was, until they read what Colm had to say about Portugal and Spain and the makeshift Allied Army who faced the great Napoleon across a muddy field last summer and changed the fate of Europe. Except Colm had been too ill from his wounds to write anything after Waterloo and Nell saw far too much on that battlefield herself the next day to want any reminders of such terrible slaughter.

She shuddered and made herself focus on the letters in front of her to divert herself from memories that would probably haunt her to her grave. Most of her school friends were faithful and often funny correspondents, but their letters were no different from those of any other group of like-minded people who once lived under the same roof. It was good to go over them again and value them as true friends, but otherwise their letters had nothing secret or startling in them.

She kept aside some letters between her mother and father that had found their way into her trunk when she left Linaire House for school. Maybe someone put them in with her things to stop her wicked uncle destroying them. Disappointed in what they had to say to each other and not really wanting another reminder they were both dead, she must have put them back in the box and forgotten all about them. With the eyes of an adult she could see her parents wrote of mundane matters when they were apart, but the easy and affectionate tone of their letters spoke of a far closer marriage than the one she had expected, given what her father did after her mother died. She was three years old when she lost her mother and all she recalled of the years before was a feeling of being warm and loved. So, her parents had been a lot happier than her uncle wanted anyone to think when his brother took up with a notorious woman to try to keep the loneliness away after his wife died. Papa was desperate to satisfy Pamela Verdoyne-Winterley's every whim so Nell had written her parents' marriage off and didn't bother to do more than glance at these letters until today.

What a mistake, she realised now. Her father had learned to love his rich and supposedly plain wife and Nell thought her mother the stronger character of the two, which might explain why Pamela could lead her father by the nose later. Anyway, never mind the old feeling she and Colm had been deserted for a ruthless siren, mutual affection came off the page in every letter and she wished she'd read them properly years ago. She had taken the late Duke of Linaire's word that her parents had a miserable arranged marriage. Instead it must have seemed to him that Lord Chris and his upstart wife had everything he deserved and they didn't. Her nabob Grandfather Lambury's fabled riches, Papa's famous good looks and charm, and, worst of all for a childless duke, children. Her eldest uncle was jealous of handsome, heedless Lord Chris Hancourt who had love dropped into his lap and a son he didn't even need, as fourth son of their noble father.

All this might be a revelation, but there was nothing here anyone would pay handsomely for. Her father might have been all but broken by the loss of his wife and perhaps he'd chased some sort of solace with a noble doxy, but it was an old scandal. Her possession of the letters gave away her true birth and her brother's latest ones spoke of restored fortunes, but how could that benefit anyone else but her? The bare thought of kidnap and forced marriage shook her badly. She managed to turn her gasp of shock into a sneeze and shook her head and apologised before waving her pupils back to their work with a severe look to tell Lavinia not to make it an excuse to disrupt her cousins.

No, she would have known if hard, speculative eyes dwelt on her when she ventured out. Shivering in the stuffy room, she tried to feel safe at Berry Brampton and as anonymous as ever. At least here in this high old schoolroom nobody could see in, unless they could learn how to sit on a cloud and not fall through. Maybe she ought to arm herself whenever she was out and about with the girls? She considered purloining one of the deadly looking duelling pistols locked up in the gun room and shook her head at the very idea. It almost made her smile to imagine herself armed to the teeth like a bandit whenever she took a step outside this room, then she looked at the row of dutifully bent heads in front of her and decided the Selford girls would seem a much finer catch for a kidnapper. It would be an absurd scheme, considering the wrath of the Earl of Barberry if he was forced to come here and meet his obligations for once. The Selford girls had a reluctant but powerful guardian to protect them. And why would a kidnapper want to look at Nell's letters anyway? Even with Mr Moss's fearsome frown and gruff impatience with her to contend with, she couldn't take that threat seriously.

Her letters were important to her alone, but for the small secret of her identity, so she laid them down and stared out of the window. Lavinia shifted in her seat and threatened to do the same if Nell didn't at least pretend to be occupied, so she turned to the only paper left in the pile she had brought into the schoolroom to puzzle over. This odd piece of doggerel seemed senseless, but nothing else would cause a stranger to spend a vast sum of money to get hold of it, so it must be looked at. She hadn't even found it until Colm was away at school and it never seemed important enough to tell him their father had left a message behind for her and none for him. It wasn't as if it made sense and he would have been hurt to be forgotten by the father he once adored.

For years the paper must have been at the bottom of her writing box, forgotten as her parents' letters had been. She had to rack her brains to remember where it came from until it came to her—she found it a few weeks after she and Colm were parted. The paper was a little tattered even when it fell from the roof of her doll's house after her nursery governess kicked it in a fit of pique. Apparently Nell had been paying more attention to her doll family than her lessons and she almost wished the Selford girls had to spend a week with the old dragon to realise they had quite an amiable sort of governess most of the time.

The few servants kept at Linaire House in the Duke's absence came running when Nell screamed, then burst into loud sobs at the sight of her imaginary home broken open and everything inside it flung far and wide. Miss Pitch was obviously in the wrong and not Nell, so her little house was picked up and reassembled as well as it could be. The delicate little figures inside were taken off to be mended by the night watchman and Nell comforted by a scullery maid not much older than she was. And this sheet of paper was left on the floor when everything else had been gathered up. It must have been hidden under the roof or between floors. Nell had never seen it before and felt sad now because she hadn't even recognised her father's writing at the time.

Thanks to his obsession with Pamela, Papa was a stranger to his children even before he died. It never occurred to Nell that it might be painful for Lord Chris to live in the home he'd shared with his wife until today. When it was closed and his children went to Linaire House and Uncle Augustus's less-than-tender care, Nell couldn't recall receiving a single letter from her father. Perhaps their uncle kept them back, of maybe Lord Chris really forgot his family and that other life in his lover's arms. Reading those letters between her parents made Nell doubt if her father would turn his back on their children so completely.

She frowned down at the rather dog-eared parchment in front of her. Whether he loved her or not, Lord Chris's scribbles made no sense. Perhaps she ought to show Colm this paper and see if he understood it better, but trusting it to the post made her feel uneasy for the first time in her life. If someone valued her letters so highly she was willing to pay poor Faith to steal them, what else would she do to get hold of one that contained the only mystery Nell had, besides her true identity?

She could show it to Mr Moss, she argued with herself, as she sat here feeling muzzy headed and weary after a sleepless night caused by the confounded man in the first place. Very likely it would make even less sense to him than it did to her, so she re-read the greeting at the beginning instead. No, it was too precious to share with a man so austere and aloof from her, despite the earth-shaking kiss they exchanged last night. He wasn't ready to trust her with *his* innermost thoughts and dreams, so why should she strip her thoughts and memories bare to appease him? Feeling vaguely guilty at wasting good teaching time on this nonsense, she began to doodle notes and questions about her father's odd little drawings and the series of numbers she'd never really tried to work out before.

'Finished, Miss Court,' Penny said cheerfully before she could get very far with that project and Nell looked up to find all four girls watching her expectantly.

'Excellent. Hand in your books and I will mark them tonight. Now it's nearly time for your luncheon, so please go and scrub the ink off your fingers, Georgiana. Lavinia, I hope you will oblige me by helping your Cousin Penelope tidy herself up before we eat.'

'I can do it myself, Miss Court,' her littlest pupil protested.

'You always skip the hairbrush and the washing bit of the list whenever you think you might be able to get away with it, Penelope.'

'Horrid brat,' Lavinia said mildly and Nell thought

her eldest pupil seemed ready to be fond of her cousins at last, although she was still a challenge to teach and be responsible for on a day to day basis.

After they had eaten the rather plain luncheon Cook thought fit for growing girls, the cousins were free to play for an hour or so and Nell drifted down to the library with her father's latest mystery because it seemed the most peaceful place to think. The numbers didn't have a logical sequence, but maybe it was some sort of code—if so, she didn't know how her father expected a three-year-old child to work it out and it occurred to her he meant it as some sort of insurance against the chance he would not come home when he hid it. He took a chance then, didn't he? Betting on the possibility she would even find that piece of paper he'd slipped between the cleverly made attic rooms of her beloved dolls' house was almost as huge a chance as him being able to survive a wild drive in an Alpine blizzard. If Miss Pitch hadn't lashed out at Nell's favourite toy his message might still be there now, or destroyed when the battered and much-mended toy was finally thrown on the bonfire. Still, he had gambled with his life; why shouldn't he take a chance his daughter would find his last message against the odds?

Nell shuddered at the memory of how terribly he'd lost the bet on his own life and his lover's. What a legacy for his children, she thought bitterly; an appalling image of her father lying broken and dying by his lover's side so many hundreds of miles away and beyond help as darkness fell and nobody came.

No, she refused to revisit the nightmares of her

childhood. Lord Christopher Hancourt chose to take that risk; he was an adult who ran away to live only in the moment of his own free will. Nell blinked away the memories of how it felt to be less important than the woman her father adored and frowned at the paper in her hand. The numbers made little sense, so what about the odd shapes her father drew around the sequence he set her? Surely he didn't expect a three-year-old child to unravel the numbers, but drawings would be a better bet. She tried to think of it as she might have done back then, if she had paid it this much attention. Perhaps it was something to do with their home at the time? No good, she couldn't even remember what the houses they once had in London and Brighton looked like. She had a sense of warmth and colour and an image of a wide sparkling sea on a lovely day, but that was all. Eyeing his squiggles from every angle, Nell decided whatever talents her father might have had, drawing wasn't one of them.

'Ah, so there you are,' a very different man from the late Lord Christopher Hancourt growled impatiently from the doorway.

'As if I would bother to hide,' she replied coldly.

'You might have; I came to apologise for all my sins last night,' Mr Moss said, sounding so like a schoolboy caught doing something he didn't regret at all that her heart almost softened towards him, despite every resolution she'd made last night to resist his unique sort of charm next time they met.

She nodded coolly to discourage any more folly and raised her eyebrows in what she hoped was a haughty invitation to expand on that gruff statement.

'I also wondered if you found a solution to the puzzle Faith set us yesterday. From the look of that paper you might have done,' he said stiffly, as if only the direst necessity had dragged him in here to confront her once again and he didn't really think he had anything to apologise for because it was as much her fault as his he'd kissed her last night and they both knew it.

Chapter Thirteen

❦

Tempted to hide the battered old document behind her back, since it was some sort of contact with her long-dead father, Nell wondered if it was safe to let Moss see it. It didn't make sense and there was no salutation other than the brief direction *To Nell* on the other side. He couldn't find anything much out about her from a few bad drawings and a senseless series of numbers, not when she had puzzled over them all morning and still felt none the wiser.

'I doubt it,' she replied flatly and held out the dog-eared sheet of hot pressed paper to invite him to see for himself how little sense it made.

'Hmm…' was all he said in reply as he did just that.

He walked over to the window with it to take advantage of what little light there was from the leaden sky on yet another day without sun. Feeling bereft and a little bit piqued at his inattention to her, Nell was free to study him instead of her father's nonsense, since he seemed to be totally absorbed and wouldn't even notice her eyes were on him.

He still wasn't classically handsome, was he? With the clear eyes of a critic she assessed his long-limbed frame with an almost-smile that worried her every bit as much as it would have him if he looked up and saw her grinning at nothing. Resetting her expression to governess-like blankness, she looked away and thought despairingly that she would never need a fine miniature or book full of sketches to recall how Moss looked in his prime.

Staring at the exquisitely carved mantel some long-dead Selford had commissioned for his splendid new library instead of his descendant's land steward this time, she went over her private images of the man still frowning at Lord Chris Hancourt's hieroglyphs because she couldn't seem to help herself. He had those acute and improbably clear blue eyes, of course, they were the first thing you noticed about him, after the general impression of a tall man with power and fitness in every line and sinew of his body. It wasn't just the surprisingly pure colour of his irises that held her attention whenever he was in a room, it was the glimpse into his acute and restless mind they gave her whenever he wasn't wary enough to shield his every thought. Once she had wrenched her gaze away from his azure gaze, she told herself the rest of his face was just a mix of arrogant cheek bones and mismatched features. His nose was craggy, even his own mother would have to admit that. Having been broken once upon a time did little for its patrician haughtiness. His mouth was… well, it was simply his. Nell couldn't even think about it without wanting to feel it burn and need on hers again, so she moved on as rapidly as she could. His chin—now that was firm to the point of stubbornness.

So how did such a man fare as third son of a country squire? Take those features and quirks one by one and Moss was a mixture of iron determination and secrets, put it together the whole added up to more. Nell doubted he took to being the second spare to his eldest brother very well as a boy. His boyhood must have been challenging for all concerned, she decided as she imagined him a clever and argumentative boy with a stubborn streak a mile wide and had to aim another of those almost tender smiles into mid-air. Never mind how he fitted into his allotted place in his father's family then, he was an adult now and somehow she doubted he'd wanted to be a nobleman's land steward since he was in his cradle. As a man he was compelling and unique and she defied a sentient female to forget he was in a room full of his supposed lords and masters and pay them proper attention when he was by, so perhaps he ought to consider a different future before those lords and masters learnt to envy him that quality?

'Where did you get this?' he barked as if he had every right to demand the information, but at least he'd interrupted her wayward thoughts.

'I have always had it,' she exaggerated slightly, to prove to herself he didn't have that right at all.

'Then you must know who it's from.'

'True, but that's my business.'

'Not when someone is trying to get hold of your papers it isn't.'

'I can't see how an old piece of paper that makes

no sense can have any bearing on the matter,' she said defensively.

He sighed and looked as if he wished she was Penny's age so she could be dealt with accordingly. 'I know you are angry with me, but could we at least try to be cool and rational about this problem? What I did last night must have made you hate me, I do understand,' he said with the sort of weary patience she used when Lavinia was at her most rebellious.

'No, you don't, you don't understand at all,' she said bitterly, feeling as if she might break if he didn't stop looking at her as if she was a promise he didn't dare make himself. Anyway, he didn't understand, not when he had no idea who she really was. Lord Chris Hancourt's daughter was the least suitable wife a hard-working man could find himself saddled with if they weren't very careful, heiress or not. They could afford one another in the strictest definition of the word, but would he be able to live off his wife's fortune and not learn to despise himself and her while he did so?

'Mr Moss and Miss Court can't afford to marry so burning for each other is wrong. It was cruel of me to kiss a woman I cannot wed,' he said rather starkly.

Nell supposed she couldn't have put it better herself, in reverse. Except of course they *could* afford a house and estate twice the size of his father's, with her dowry.

And what of his pride, Eleanor Hancourt? she asked herself and stamped on the tiny spark of hope the look in *his* tired eyes lit as they met hers.

He looked as if he was saying goodbye to a dream he couldn't afford to have. The daughter of one of the most scandalous men of his generation wasn't a fit wife for Mr Moss. There, if she told herself that often enough it might even sound impossible. Her fortune would be a bitter pill for such a proud, contrary man to swallow; the scandal of her father's wild life and death with his infamous mistress hanging over their heads all the time would suffocate him. She ought to tell him, perhaps make them both feel better about the heartache that would dog her footsteps, whether she stayed here or went to London to admit she was Miss Hancourt.

'I am…' she began. Too late when he turned away from her impatiently and began to pace the room. How could she shout something so crucial after his retreating back across half the width of the room?

'I am a clumsy idiot,' he told her from the furthest corner of the room. Any further away and they would have to yell and she wasn't prepared to proclaim her identity to anyone within earshot just yet.

He was, of course, but what if he was her idiot? Her heart lurched at the notion she might let the only man she could dream of marrying go because of a silly fancy about money and her father's black reputation. They were rational adults, weren't they? No problem could be insurmountable if there was a chance they might manage to love each other for life.

'True,' she mouthed, smiled sweetly and waited for him to come close enough for them to speak softly and not be overheard.

Too late, with the warning of another set of hasty male footsteps sounding overloud in the tacked-on enfilade that Mr Rivers was here and why the devil must the handsome great fool interrupt them right now? Nell glared at the man and wondered if she dared tell him to go away. He was the brother of Moss's employer and even a rich woman's husband might want to work to feel better about her fortune, so she stayed silent with an effort it was as well he didn't know about.

'What's this Mrs Winch tells me about one of the maids being paid to steal your papers, Miss Court?' the Earl's brother demanded before he noticed Moss standing stiffly in the opposite corner with a start, as if he sensed something more between them being on opposite sides of the room suggested.

'The work of a madwoman,' Nell said dismissively. Even if it wasn't it didn't seem important next to what might have been said, if not for Mr Rivers's arrival.

'Not necessarily,' Moss argued with a frown in her direction.

'What else can she be but mad to offer so much for so little?'

'In search of something you don't know you have?' Moss replied impatiently and whatever possessed her to think he was struggling to hide deep and tender feelings for her under a gruff manner? He obviously didn't care about her at all, he was just interested in the problem she'd presented him with.

'And what do I have that could be of any interest to anyone but me?' she sparked back at him.

'This,' he said baldly and held up the worn and battered paper she didn't understand when she found it all those years ago and still didn't understand now.

'It's nothing,' she said, shaking her head at the very idea it was worth five pounds to anyone.

'We won't know that until we've at least tried to work out what it means.'

'It's a meaningless series of numbers and doodles done to amuse a child.'

'And someone seems to think it worth a maidservant's wage for an entire year, so we would be foolish to disregard it so lightly, don't you think?'

'Well, *I* have no idea what it means and if I can't understand it, why would anyone else?'

Moss turned the paper over and read the shortened form of her name on the back. 'You are Nell then, Miss Court?' he asked with raised eyebrows.

They had kissed passionately and risked far too much in the candlelit intimacy of Mrs Winch's room last night and still they were Mr and Miss to one another. Nell was used as a short form of Helen and she didn't want to confess who she was with her employer's brother listening, so she waited warily for the next question.

'Who sent it?' he persisted, of course, and that was the next question she didn't want to answer. A plain Mr Court couldn't have secrets because he didn't exist. The idea of untangling lies and half-truths when she had never bothered to create a Mr Court to lie about kept her silent for a long moment as she tried to decide if she had the ingenuity left to invent one right now.

'A friend of my mother,' she prevaricated instead.

'One who knew you very well,' he said, as if he suspected her mama of conduct unbecoming a lady.

'Or perhaps he only thought he did,' she lied, crossing her fingers behind her back because it felt wrong to deny her parents when she'd only just re-discovered them through their letters to each other.

'I suspect this is meant to mean something to you, however well or poorly this man knew you as a child. You need to think harder about who he was and why he left you a coded message you won't take seriously.'

'He must have had more faith in me than he should have done,' she said crossly, because this really was none of his business. Disappointment was gnawing away at her good manners with every moment Mr Rivers stood listening to their argument with that knowing look on his face.

'Perhaps there's a reason you refuse to look more deeply into this puzzle?' Moss said as if he could read her mind. 'And why don't you write and ask him what it means?'

'He's dead,' she said flatly.

'Then you have even more reason to solve the problem he left you, in the mistaken belief you would bother to decipher it.'

'You are very rude, sir. Both the problem and solution are my business and not yours.'

'When it intrudes on Berry Brampton House and the safety of Lord Barberry's wards it is mine and his lordship's,' he said with an impatient glare at Mr Rivers, who was listening attentively but leaving him to ask all the awkward questions. 'The welfare of four vulnerable young girls trumps your privacy, Miss Court.'

'As if I haven't been putting them first for the last two years when you didn't even know they existed,' she snapped back sharply, near the end of her tether now he was intent on solving this puzzle rather than the bigger one of how a steward and a governess could find a way to love each other after all.

'I do now and it's my duty to safeguard them if some fool is trying to prise this away from you and they might get in the way.'

He was right, she decided reluctantly. It seemed insane anyone would want that hasty note from her father, but there was nothing else in her papers to explain why someone had such a burning desire to read them.

'I don't understand it at all,' she admitted with a shrug because she still couldn't see any sense in random numbers and squiggles.

'Then try harder. How old were you when this was written?'

'Three or four years old, I suppose.'

'Why don't you know precisely?'

'Why do I have to, Mr Moss?'

'You think I'm being rude again?' he said impatiently.

'I know you are.'

'Then I need not worry about losing your good opinion, need I?'

Nell wanted to slap his arrogant face, but somehow controlled herself and shot a glare at Mr Rivers, standing with his hands in his pockets as if he hadn't been this well entertained for months. 'No, but the girls are likely to realise I've been gone too long at any moment and come to find out what's going on,' she warned with a frown for both of them this time.

'Then we'd best hurry up and find out what this is about before they get here. Where did you find it?'

'Hidden in the roof of my dolls' house. I only

found that slipped under the roof when it was damaged and I have no idea when it was put there,' Nell lied again, because she could probably find out if she wanted to.

'When did this eccentric gentleman of yours die, then?' Mr Rivers chimed in as if feeling it was time he took a part in this odd comedy.

Ah, that was the question she'd been dreading, but why should they connect her with Lord Christopher Hancourt's and the first Viscountess Farenze's scandalous and tragic death in the same year?

'1799?' she said, as if she didn't know all too well.

'Why would anyone wait so long to chase this down?' Mr Rivers asked them as if they ought to know.

Nell shrugged and Moss began to pace the room again with that odd missive in his hand, staring at it as if he might wrench Papa's secrets off the page by willpower alone. 'These drawings are trying to tell a story. If the man had any skill with a pencil it would be a damn sight easier to work out what they're meant to be.'

'Don't swear and give it back to me,' Nell demanded, suddenly desperate for another look. 'Come, Mr Moss, you said yourself I alone can solve this problem—you must return it if I'm to stand any chance of doing so.'

'Yes, give it back to her, Moss,' Mr Rivers prompted with a laugh in his grey eyes Nell didn't even begin to understand and he seemed to be taunting Moss with some secret of his own.

'Very well, but don't forget someone else wants this puzzle solved more than you seem to, Miss Court.'

'Yes, you do,' she snapped and saw the sudden revulsion in his blue gaze that she could even think he was behind this. 'I didn't mean I think you so devious you might pay an intermediary to find this,' she said hastily. 'Not that your insistence I look hard for its meaning when I might not want to isn't both intrusive and annoying of you.'

'We'll take that as a given then, shall we? I seem to have been annoying you since the very first moment I set foot on Selford land.'

'Perhaps you're a very annoying man,' she said softly, looking up at him almost fondly as she forgot Mr Rivers's presence for a moment.

'Or maybe you are a pernickety female, over-protective of her charges and suspicious of anyone who comes within their orbit?'

'Arguing about which of you is most unsociable is going to help us solve this then, is it?' Mr Rivers asked with the wave of an elegant hand at the parchment in Moss's more work-worn one.

'No, but it might stop worse things if we work hard enough,' Moss muttered as he passed her in one of those restless lopes up and down the room.

'Don't,' she whispered so softly she hoped Mr Rivers couldn't hear and how badly she wanted him to go away. 'We can't,' she murmured when he turned not far away and began his pass back to that remote corner.

'Then think, woman, before frustration gets the better of one of us,' he muttered as if he was only managing to keep his hands off her because he had something else to do, even with the Earl's half-brother watching them as if fascinated by the spectacle they made as they almost quarrelled in his presence.

Comforted by the passion almost under control in Moss's intent gaze, the quirk of his firm mouth and the stern control he was trying to keep it under, Nell tried to think about quirks on paper instead and failed. He wanted her; the heat and promise of being feminine and desirable to him, despite her repressive gown and spinster's cap, burnt deep inside and made her breath come short. For a long moment he paused instead of passing her by and they both seemed spellbound by the chances of it, the possibility land steward and governess could make a life together if they tried hard enough. Then he handed the paper back to her and the crackle of expensive paper even after all the mistreatment it had been subjected to over the years reminded her how many lies and barriers still stood between them.

Stepping back, she stared unseeingly at her father's message for a moment. It was looking at them with only half her attention that must have let her eyes see the funny little stick figures Papa used to draw come to life again. Of course, he used to laugh and tell her their drawing talent was about equal back then, didn't he? She must have blocked the memory out, along with so much else about a man who left his children alone for the sake of a woman like Pamela Verdoyne-Winterley. Feeling the stirrings of what could be wild passion for a man for the first time, maybe she could understand what drove Lord Chris a little better, or perhaps those letters between her parents unlocked something too painful to remember until now. Whatever the reason, her favourite tale from *Aesop's Fables* was suddenly there—rendered in Papa's uniquely awful stick figures of two very familiar animals he'd danced around the edge of his message as if she was sure to understand him. Stuck in an echoing nursery with her elderly and embittered nursery governess, she must have made herself forget the life that went before. She spared a thought for that bereft little girl, but felt she had the father she'd once adored back at long last. He drew this direly executed message still loving her; this message said his every thought had not been of Pamela after all.

'It's meant to be the Tale of the Stork and the Fox, it was my favourite,' she said, delight softening her voice as she remembered him reading it to her night after night when he must have been bored by it even the first time.

'What tale; where is it from?' Moss demanded.

'I can't imagine how I missed seeing it all these years now. *Aesop's Fables,* of course,' she said and made for the stacks to find a copy. '*Mr Dodsley's Select Fables,* to be exact, as I suppose we must be if those numbers relate to the pages of a book.'

'Which they must do, or why leave a clue only you could understand?' Mr Rivers said as he got caught up in the mystery after all and followed them both to find a copy as fast as possible between the three of them.

'But what is it a clue to?' Nell mused.

She felt almost guilty for not telling either man she came from a far wealthier home than her current occupation argued. Even so, what could Papa have left her but some little present she was supposed to find while he was away? He had probably planned it as a diversion to keep her from pining, then forgot to tell her when he came back and she hadn't discovered it. Yes, that made sense. He must have done this when she was quite a small girl, before he dreamt of running away to France with his scandalous mistress and died there with her when Nell was not quite six years old.

'We won't know until we find it,' Moss said impatiently. He didn't deserve her guilt about deceiving him when he adopted his lord-of-all-I-survey manner, as if he'd taken on Lord Barberry's role as well as his own when he came here.

'He probably only hid a box of sweets or a toy at the end of a treasure hunt that doesn't exist any more,' she warned him anyway.

'Since you didn't find anything else to explain why this stranger wants your papers, this is the only clue we have.'

'Very well, but you'd best prepare to be disappointed,' she said to Mr Rivers and moved away from Moss to find the small children's section of Lord Barberry's neglected library. 'The girls have a newer copy than any in here, but I don't want them drawn into this,' she said in her best governess manner.

Unimpressed, Moss raised his eyebrows as if to remind her how un-governess-like she could be. 'Here it is, although I can't see how a series of page numbers will help us.'

'Neither can I,' she said, but her heartbeat speeded up anyway.

Tense now as he picked out the volume and turned to her favourite tale, she read it again over his shoulder and had to fight memories of being held safe in her father's arms as he read it to her with a catch in his voice she must have been too young to take in at the time. For a while he had tried hard to be father and mother to her when Mama and the baby died. Instead of feeling too little for his children, did Lord Chris feel too much? She cursed Pamela anew for taking him away and blinked back a tear for what might have been. Wrong to blame only her when Lord Chris fell under the woman's witchy spell and blithely walked away from any reminders of his late wife of his own free will.

'What else can these numbers mean?' she mused out loud, sure now that this was a wild goose chase.

'You might as well look at the pages and see if they mean anything to you,' Mr Rivers suggested helpfully.

'Very well, but I don't see how,' she agreed with a sigh, wondering what the girls were up to and if that hour she gave them to read or, more likely, gossip was up.

'Nothing ventured, nothing gained.'

Nell didn't even grace that cliché with a reply and signalled impatiently at the book so both men could see what a waste of time this was. Reading each page carefully, she got to the end of the list and tried hard not to say *I told you so.*

'Are you sure there's nothing in any of your other papers this mystery woman might pay for?' Moss said after a few moments of frustrated silence.

'Very sure.'

'You could always let me see your letters and papers and judge for myself?'

'They are private,' she said primly.

'Then we'd best hope this means something after all. Have you got your own copy of *The Fables*?'

'Yes, but it's very battered and there are quite a few pages missing. I used to get upset about some of the tales when animals ate each other so my mother decided to cut out all the pages that made me cry.'

'Then your numbers are different from this one,' Mr Rivers said triumphantly and, of course, he was right. 'You must send for it immediately,' he added, now so caught up in the thrill of the chase he had forgotten to be amused by the foibles of his fellow men.

'No need, I always have it with me. It may seem foolish of me, but my brother coloured in many of Mr Bewick's illustrations as carefully as he could for me before our guardian sent him to school, so I treasure it even now.'

'That doesn't seem foolish at all,' Moss said gently and here was the man she had been so terribly tempted by last night again and she had to remind herself Mr Rivers was still here to make herself turn away.

'I will try to steal upstairs without the girls knowing,' she said to get out of my lord's library before she disgraced herself.

Upstairs she glanced at the small square of mirror provided for a governess. The flush on her cheeks and the slight breathlessness she seemed to be suffering from lately could be explained by a rushed search for her book. She tucked a stray curl back into her cap and nodded sternly at herself before going back to the library.

How tempting to stand and stare at Moss's straight back, broad shoulders and narrow hips without him knowing, but Mr Rivers's grey eyes saw more than she would like them to if he turned and caught her at it, so she nobly resisted. 'Here it is,' she said brightly to interrupt their murmured conversation in the far corner of the room where she couldn't hear a word of it.

'Good, maybe we can get to the bottom of this strange business at last,' Moss said as if he had a hundred better things to do this morning.

'I'm sure I can work it out for myself now, gentlemen,' Nell said with an inviting glance at the grey sky outside they wilfully ignored.

'You won't get rid of us that easily,' Mr Rivers said with a mocking grin.

'Like a couple of burrs,' she mumbled disagreeably, but handed over her precious book all the same, before she could give herself time to think about not being rid of Mr Moss ever again and liking it all too well.

'Very like,' he agreed and seemed almost as jarred as she was by the flare of something bright and hot flashing between them when their fingers touched on the worn leather binding. He cleared his throat as if that might help. 'Read out that list of numbers, if you please, and we'll soon see if this makes more sense,' he ordered as if he had every right.

'How will we know?' she asked lamely.

'I suppose we must have faith in this friend of your mother's, since there's no other explanation for Faith's rich stranger taking such an interest in you,' he said.

'I suppose you're right.'

'Even if you don't want me to be?'

There was compassion as well as curiosity in his

acute blue eyes this time. Eleanor Hancourt, who braved the world alone, felt something aloof and a little bit frozen inside her threaten to melt. 'Even then,' she replied softly and never mind their un-wanted listener.

'Why not tell me about him?' he invited, laying the book he had been in such haste to see on the window seat behind them. 'You can trust me, I promise you.'

'I know I can,' she said.

'And Mr Rivers will give you his word as a gen-tleman not to tattle if you don't want him to, won't you, sir?'

Rivers nodded obediently, 'Word of honour, Miss Court.'

'I have managed for myself for almost as long as I can remember,' she said as if that explained every-thing, and perhaps it did.

'Poor little girl,' Moss said softly.

'I was well enough and never hungry or in need,' she argued half-heartedly.

'You sound lonely as the man in the moon,' he replied.

'My brother loved me and I was very happy at school,' she said, unable to look away from his blue, blue gaze this time and never mind if Mr Rivers was watching them with a worried frown.

Here was the magic and promise of last night almost within reach again. Her breath caught in a strange sigh that stuttered out between her parted lips as if they wanted to invite him to breathe with her, kiss her, be part of her and whatever else it meant for two people drawn to be more than the world saw when it looked at them.

'Miss Court, there you are at last. Georgie stole my book and now she won't give it back. I was almost at the end of it as well, so she only had to wait an hour or so and I would have given it to her,' Lavinia informed her from the doorway.

Nell jumped as soon as she heard her voice and stepped away from Moss and Mr Rivers as if she'd been scalded. She had nearly been caught kissing Lord Barberry's steward, in front of his lordship's uneasy and embarrassed brother, by one of her pupils. That would have almost rivalled her late father's sins if the story of what Miss Hancourt got up to before she met the critical gaze of the *ton* ever got around.

Ordering her inner demons back into their box, she raised a hand and found her cap disappointingly straight and proper. Wrong to be frustrated and cross because she was missing a chance to repeat her bad behaviour of last night, so she did her best to pretend he wasn't here and talked to Lavinia instead, because she usually understood her and Moss was a brooding mystery right now.

'It's high time we got back to our lessons, but I wish you two wouldn't quarrel like fishwives whenever my back is turned.'

'It wasn't my fault.'

'I didn't say it was. I will get your book back for you and make Georgiana apologise, but you two are setting the younger girls a bad example.'

'They don't need any help,' Lavinia muttered as if there were things she could say about Penny and Caro, but didn't want to be accused of tattle-mongering.

'Excuse me, Mr Rivers, Mr Moss. I must get back to my duties,' Nell said and swept her eldest pupil out of the room before they could argue.

Chapter Fourteen

Fergus stood looking at the worn and obviously much-loved book in his hand and wondered why he thought the key to Miss Court herself might lie inside it, as well as a solution to her latest mystery. He heard her and Lavinia's voices fading as they went up the intricately carved oak staircase and wondered why he'd spent so long listening to a woman walk away from him of late. He tried to shrug off an uneasy feeling it would be impossible not to listen for her step long after he escaped from this ridiculous position and made sure she was employed a long way away.

'We had best do this without her, Fergus,' his brother said uneasily.

Because Brendan had said nothing about what had almost happened just now Fergus knew how bad it was as his heart sank into his work-worn boots. The Earl of Barberry had been about to misbehave so spectacularly even his little brother couldn't find the words to say what a selfish fool he was. Unable to find the words to explain what was in his heart, because he didn't understand it himself, he opened the book in his hands and froze stiff as a statue as he took in the name so proudly written on the first page he could almost imagine a tiny version of the woman claiming her book with the deep concentration of a girl who had only just learned how. Damnation take the woman; she was in danger of charming him even as his inner man was screaming at her for what she'd done—how could she have lied to him so heinously it felt like the worst betrayal he'd ever suffered to stare down at the words as if they'd been written by the devil himself?

'This Book Belongs to Miss Eleanor Hancourt of Lambury House, Hanover Square, London, England, Great Britain', it stated in childishly self-important capital letters.

My God, Fergus, she's not only your equal, she could easily be your superior in both birth and *fortune,* his inner Earl whispered with a snarl of noble temper.

Fergus felt the pain of her deception sear through him and down to his very toes—how could she have deceived him so brazenly? She'd kissed him as if she meant it last night; left him racked with guilt and sleepless as he fantasied about promises he couldn't make to a governess and hated himself for breaking her heart. Clearly she didn't have one to break or she wouldn't have let a mere Mr Moss hope for a future he could never have with her. A marriage between the impoverished younger son of a country squire and Miss Eleanor Hancourt, granddaughter of a duke on one side and the richest nabob of his generation on the other? The very idea was laughable, but oddly enough he didn't feel like laughing. Crying and beating his breast was out for a hardened nobleman of one and thirty, so that only left him with fury, didn't it? Good, he felt the vigour of it sweeping past the desolation of knowing he'd been taken for a fool by a woman he'd come perilously close to loving.

Even in Ireland he'd heard the fuss this last winter when her brother inherited the huge fortune everyone thought lost by his notorious father on his twenty-fifth birthday. Hancourt's sister must have been an heiress in her own right when she wrote this inscription as a child and to think he'd been feeling sorry for her until he read that childish assertion and realised she meant something in the world.

Tempted to throw the book into the darkest and most dusty corner of the room and march away from this place without a word of explanation, he let his imagination get to work on what might happen if he did and frowned fiercely at the battered old tome instead. If Moss vanished like a thief in the night, Fergus's young cousins would be caught up in any misadventure the lying jade stumbled into because of her determination to stay here and brazen things out. If he had to stay as he was until he got rid of the confounded woman, he didn't dare risk seeing her right now. He might let out something crucial as he raged at her for not being humble Miss Court at all. He might even be tempted to forgive her and that would never do, would it?

Fergus scooped up the now rather battered beaver hat from where he'd flung it when he entered the room, so eager to see Miss Court again he had almost forgotten the gulf between the lord of all this and a mere governess. Sneering at himself in the watery old mirror over the fireplace, he gave a wordless shrug of apology to Brendan, then waved the inscription under his brother's nose to explain his silent fury. With Miss Hancourt's book under his arm he marched out of the house without another word to anyone. Never mind if it was uncivil of Moss to ignore his fellow servants as he stormed through the kitchens and out of the back door, he felt uncivil.

More than that, he discovered as he strode back to the land steward's house as if his feet were on fire, he felt furious and hurt and outraged all at once. A terrible anger salted his regret for a life he could never have with a woman who didn't exist. It didn't make a grain of sense, but that didn't matter—she'd lied to him. The fact she'd deceived everyone else here for a lot longer didn't matter right now. Once he had unwrapped this last mystery and made sure his wards were safe he was going to make sure the whole neighbourhood knew who had really been living under his roof all these years, so they couldn't condemn him as an arrogant beast when he sent Miss Court to the right about the moment he was his true self again. The fine Irish temper he'd got from his mother, mixed dangerously with her first husband's English certainty he was always right, and now flared into full, fearsome life because Miss Court's betrayal felt so very personal it hurt. With all those fierce emotions rattling in his head Fergus managed to ignore the voice of reason that whispered, even if Eleanor Hancourt neatly deceived him and everyone else at Berry Brampton, he was just as guilty of double dealing as she was. When this didn't hurt any more he might listen. For now, being in a raging temper felt a lot better than the raw feeling underneath it that he'd been on the edge of something deep and dangerous with Miss Eleanor Hancourt, until he found out who she really was and jumped back from a precipice he hadn't even realised he was on the edge of until Miss Court vanished into it like the wraith she truly was.

'Mr Rivers wishes to see you, Miss Court,' Parkins the butler informed Nell disapprovingly later in the day. 'The gentleman is in the library.'

'Very well, I will come down as soon as I can be sure the Misses Selford are usefully occupied.'

'I will inform the gentleman,' Parkins said stiffly, distancing himself from the whole sorry business.

'What do you suppose he wants?' Caro asked, still a little bit infatuated with her guardian's brother, even though he treated her as the child she still was and that had taken the fervour out of her girlish crush.

'No doubt I shall find out shortly, Caroline,' Nell said repressively, wondering how she was to preach propriety at her charges when the Earl's brother ordered her to meet him alone in the middle of a working day. 'Now, Lavinia, you will read this passage out for me and the rest of you must do your best to understand it, girls. I want to hear your explanation of the ideas it contains when I return and you will do as your cousin tells you to, or I shall have to be very cross with you indeed when I get back and there will be no sweet course at dinner tonight if that happens.'

With many assurances they would be good as gold echoing in her ears, Nell went to see what Mr Rivers wanted with an odd feeling of dread deep in her belly.

'Ah, Miss *Court*,' the gentleman greeted with

undue emphasis, so she wasn't as surprised as she might have been when Mr Moss appeared out of the shadows to snap the door closed behind her and stand glaring at the floor, his face like thunder and her copy of *Aesop's Fables* held out accusingly in his hand.

How stupid of her to have forgotten her real name was written all over the frontispiece. She was so proud she could write her name and address back then that she'd scrawled it anywhere she could find space until even Colm protested. All sorts of contrary emotions threatened as she tried to take in the fact Mr Moss knew who she really was and Miss Hancourt couldn't wed a steward without making him a laughing stock. Since he was far too busy frowning into the middle distance now to even look at her, she had no intention of letting him know she cared how he felt about her true identity.

'This meeting is rather singular, gentlemen,' she said with a nod at the closed door to let them know it was improper as well.

'Do you want the entire household to know your secrets?' Moss asked as if he had every right to be furious with her.

He almost had, since she kissed him back last night as if they were equals. Six months ago they would have been on a par for poverty, if not rank, and it felt unfair that he should cast their differing fortunes at her as if it was her fault. Why should she be made to feel ashamed of being her true self again? She would have to disown her brother and the rest of her family to do that and not even the almost magic she had spun about in when locked in Moss's arms last night could make her do that. It had only been an air dream though; he couldn't feel anything enduring for her if he could stand there glowering at her like the sternest judge in the land and not a hint of softer emotions in his hard blue gaze.

'I suspect they soon will, whether I like it or not,' she replied as lightly as she could to his harsh query.

'I'm no rattle-pate,' he said shortly and why was the Earl's brother letting him take the lead in this embarrassing meeting?

'Neither am I, so your secret is as safe as you want it to be, Miss Hancourt,' Mr Rivers said quietly, with a hard look at Moss to say he might be wondering the same thing himself.

'Why? Why did you pretend to be Miss Court when you are a lady of high birth and fortune?' Moss burst out, as if not even his employer's brother had a right to silence him on the subject of her crimes.

'I'd rather not tell you, sir,' she said haughtily as if he had no right to question her and even good manners told her she was right as he backed away from her as if she'd turned into the Medusa. 'I had a living to earn and a strong dislike of those who are always so curious about my late father's exploits that I would have got very little peace here if I admitted being his daughter.'

'You certainly don't need to earn a living now,' Moss muttered darkly.

'Yet the Misses Selford still need a governess and I didn't want to desert them. I am sorry to be blunt, but your brother did that when he refused to come here and meet them, Mr Rivers, so how could I abandon them as well when my fortunes took a sudden turn for the better?'

'I still can't see why you didn't confide all this to me when I came here in his lordly lordship's stead,' Mr Rivers said quietly, exchanging a complicated look with Moss that Nell didn't even want to understand right now.

'If you or your brother only had a lady I could have told her and trusted her to find a suitable replacement,' she said stiffly instead. 'A single gentleman cannot ask the same questions as a lady can of a potential governess.'

'*You* certainly took a wily lawyer in without much trouble,' Moss interrupted as if he had the right to sneer at her in front of their employer's brother.

'If this was any of your business, Mr Moss, I could point out I never lied about my education, teaching experience or willingness to work as hard as I can to help the Misses Selford learn what they need to know to live a useful life as ladies of rank and fortune one day. Lord Barberry's lawyers seem to have a great deal of practice at hiring his upper servants, don't they? So I doubt they are easily deceived by those they must trust to run the household and keep his lordship's wards happy and usefully employed in his absence after all those years of putting his wishes into place by proxy, do you?' she countered. He must have fooled them he was a patient and calm land steward and he didn't look anything of the sort right now.

'I'm trying not to think them a pack of fools,' he said through gritted teeth.

'I don't believe you have the right when you must have fooled them you a quiet and biddable soul, sir. And it makes no difference who I am; I am here and I'm ready, willing and able to carry out my duties, just as I have been for the last two years. You are not in any position to object to my presence, Mr Moss, any more than I can have *you* hired or dismissed on a whim. I leave it to you, Mr Rivers, to decide what you will tell your brother about me. I doubt very much that he cares much who instructs his wards, since he's avoided being a stand-in father to them for a decade.'

For some reason that not very tactful reminder seemed to have more effect on Moss than it did on his lordship's half-brother. He grunted something furious under his breath and went back to pacing the book stacks again, as if he might find his lost serenity hidden down one if he looked hard enough.

'True, if not very diplomatic, Miss Hancourt,' Mr Rivers said mildly.

If he could seem almost amused by her forthright criticism of the absent Earl, why must Moss take it so badly when he'd never even met him? Because he felt betrayed by her lie in a way he couldn't express in front of his employer's brother, Nell supposed, with a sinking feeling he had some right to resent her position in society when she'd matched him kiss for kiss and never said a word about her recently returned wealth. If only Mr Rivers hadn't interrupted them before she could get that crucial explanation out, how very differently Moss might feel about her now.

'You're a coward, Miss Hancourt,' Moss accused as he paced back towards them again. 'Instead of playing out this pantomime of a dutiful governess at Berry Brampton House you should be in London with your brother and his new wife, making a much-delayed debut in the world where you truly belong. You have no right to risk bringing trouble down on your pupils by continuing to lie about who you are. By staying here in such a guise you made yourself a target for kidnappers and fortune hunters. Either breed will exploit your ridiculous charade if they can and you set yourself up for it by refusing to re-join your family.'

Nell gasped in shock at the notion of being abducted and forced into marriage. Somehow even the thought of such wickedness tarnished her life here as the very real possibility he was right sank in and made her shiver. 'You think that's why someone wanted my papers?' she asked him before she could stop herself.

'It seems an obvious answer to me.'

'Yet you doubt it?' she asked as he frowned at the very plainness of it.

'Yes, your father's conundrum can't be designed to make you tell the truth to your employer, since he didn't know what a clever little liar he'd sired when he wrote it,' Moss said, waving the old paper Nell wished he'd put away and forget, now there were more important matters to discuss.

'How do you know my father wrote it?'

'Who else could have done so? The current Duke of Linaire was in the Americas by the time you were born and the last one was well known to have no time for *his* wards. Rumour has it the late Duke actively hated you and your brother, so your father is the obvious man to be sending coded messages to his daughter.'

'My brother might have done so,' she said defensively. It seemed cruel of him to point out how bereft she and Colm were when Papa died in that stupid accident somehow, despite the hurt she had obviously dealt him with what he must see as her lack of trust and dishonesty in not telling him who she really was last night, when it might have been said and got around if only he loved her.

Which he obviously does not, Eleanor, her inner realist pointed out rather unhelpfully when she felt as if a chasm had opened up between them and she was swaying on the edge of it, not wanting to look down and see a bleak future as Aunt Eleanor, blue-stocking spinster of the Hancourt family, stretching ahead of her.

'This isn't the work of a child,' Moss pointed out implacably and why did she still long to be on his side of that divide when he was being such a steely judge of her sins?

'It might as well be for all the sense it makes,' she said sulkily, sounding very much like Lavinia did when she was confronted by something she didn't want to do.

'Then look it up yourself,' he ordered her impatiently. 'Find those references in your copy of *the Fables*, then tell me the riddle isn't serious.'

'Give my book back then,' she demanded and waited for him to hand it over with what she hoped was chilly dignity, because she felt as if a part of her had been ripped away and the hurt might not heal for a very long time.

'I wrote the solution down in my pocketbook, for all the help it is.'

'There you are then; it *is* only nonsense,' she said as he handed over her book and Papa's scrap of paper.

She drew back as if he'd burned her when he went to hand over his leather-bound notebook as well.

'Oh, do it yourself, then,' he said bitterly and went back to his pacing.

'Do you mind if *I* join you, Miss Hancourt?' Mr Rivers said with a polite gesture towards the map table by the window where they could see what they were reading a lot better.

'Certainly not, your help will be very welcome, Mr Rivers,' Nell said sweetly.

The tension in the room was almost thick enough to slice when Moss let out a curse he should keep to himself in feminine company and paced harder. Let him think she was doing her best to flirt with the handsome brother of an earl if he liked. Now her true rank and fortune were out in the open, why shouldn't she? She couldn't let the bad-tempered bear see he'd hurt her.

Mr Rivers calmly wrote down the series of words she read out as she found them underlined after counting her quota of pages instead of the numbers they began life with. It sounded as if the riddle made a sentence, but Moss was right, it still didn't make much sense. Nell took the paper Mr Rivers handed her at the end of it all and frowned.

'I don't know what he meant,' she told him.

'Your father had faith in your intelligence when you were too small to know half what you do today. Not that you seem inclined to make use of the brains I suppose you must have been born with,' Moss pointed out unhelpfully when he came to another halt beside them.

'Now that's going too far—in fact, it's downright uncivil of you, Moss,' Mr Rivers said sharply.

It sounded as if his gentlemanly soul could bear no more, even if there was a frustrated love affair to account for Moss's fury with the unmasked heiress in their midst and almost justify him being so rude. Nell flinched at the idea their feelings were on show for even one member of the aristocracy to see. She truly hoped the Earl's brother would keep the chance she might love his lordship's steward to himself.

'I apologise, Miss Hancourt,' Moss said with a cool bow, as if that might make his bitter hostility feel better as he shot her a dark look to say they were only words.

'Thank you, Mr Moss. Perhaps we can be a little less childish about this business from now on.'

'Maybe that's it,' Mr Rivers broke in as if her words had sparked off a solution to all this in his head.

'Maybe that's what?' Moss barked gruffly, obviously forgetting his faux humility the moment a chance to take over again hove into view.

'We are looking at this through adult eyes and he was showing a child,' Mr Rivers said, almost as if this man taking over was something he expected and Nell wondered about the younger man's spinelessness even as she let half her mind think about his theory and wonder if he might not be right.

'Hmm,' Moss said thoughtfully, as if it was his secret to uncover. 'Let's see what he said again,' he went on, leafing through his book to find the page she had rejected just now. 'Through the eyes of a grandfather clock everything that is hidden will be found again,' he read out and Nell gasped as an image of the slow-ticking clock in the smallest drawing room of Linaire House came into her mind for the first time in years. 'You know what he means, don't you?' Moss asked.

'I may have some idea, but the clock he means is in London.'

'Then you must go there and find what he hid for you to find, must you not?'

'I am still responsible for four girls. I cannot order a carriage, jump into it and blithely demand the horses gallop headlong for the capital on a whim, sir.'

'Maybe not, but I could,' Mr Rivers intervened before his brother's steward could argue as if he had some right to dictate all their actions.

'Even if you ordered it so, Mr Rivers, I can't leave the girls here unprotected with this strange woman probably still in the neighbourhood,' Nell protested. She didn't want to leave the Selford girls—for all the trouble they gave her she was fond of them. And she was a coward, of course, so she would far rather stay here as the governess than be Lord Christopher Hancourt's daughter again under the critical gaze of the *ton*.

'You could take them with you, if you feel you cannot go unless they do. From what I could see last time I was in London, your aunt and uncle are not the sort of people who would turn them away if that's the only way you can be convinced they are safe,' Mr Rivers said, as if he was trying to find logical solutions to problems she wasn't sure she wanted solved. Moss's brooding impatience for her to leave here was too heavy a presence in the room for her to want to oblige him as well. She shot him an impatient glance and got ready to argue with Lord Barberry's little brother as well.

'According to Winch, you went dashing off to Brussels with your uncle a few days before your brother was injured at Waterloo. You can hardly claim the current Duke doesn't look kindly on you both after that, Miss Hancourt,' Moss pointed out and chopped even more ground from under her feet.

'Do you think the Earl will want to be rid of me?' she asked Mr Rivers, since he was more likely to know than anyone else.

Mr Rivers shot Moss a sidelong glance, as if he might offer him inspiration, but the man was staring at the Selford coat of arms at the centre of the elaborate carved over-mantel and didn't even look their way.

'Now an outsider knows you're here I expect he would say you are safer in London with your family, Miss Hancourt,' Mr Rivers said at last.

'Aye, and you'll be confoundedly in the way if you stay,' Moss growled even as his employer's brother glared at him, as if he might just dismiss him for being so rude to a lady and risk his elder brother's displeasure at being robbed of such a perfect land agent when he needed him most.

'And how will I get there without being waylaid?' Nothing could make her want to stay more than being told to go by this rude barbarian.

'Easy enough,' Mr Rivers went on as if she and Moss weren't still frowning darkly at each other from opposite corners of the room. 'Winch can chaperon you and the girls, whilst Moss and I act as outriders. I'm sure we'll terrify law-abiding citizens going about their rightful business, let alone any villains you manage to attract, Miss Hancourt.'

'You're determined to unmask me?' she asked.

'What else can he do?' Moss barked impatiently. 'You can hardly pitch up in Grosvenor Square and announce your identity at the last possible moment. You're the one who claims to care so much about them, but I suppose you'd have an uncomfortable time if you were shut up in a carriage with the Selford girls once they know about your deception and you wish to avoid such a tense journey.'

The girls would indeed be shocked, but how dare he imply she had such a selfish reason for keeping them in the dark for a few more days? 'How long have I got?' she asked Mr Rivers, who seemed rather young and helpless in the face of Moss's unyielding fury at her for flying under false colours.

'You can pack tonight and be ready at dawn,' Moss said brusquely.

'Luckily I don't take my orders from you, Mr Moss. Mr Rivers?' she questioned with as much steely dignity as possible when she had to clasp her hands into fists at her sides to stop them visibly shaking.

'It would be the best way out of this muddle,' the Earl's younger brother said with an apologetic shrug and Nell turned on her heel to leave the room in disgust.

'Don't say anything about Faith or your father's puzzle,' Moss ordered before she could open the door.

'Good day, Mr Rivers,' she said coolly and left before she lowered herself to throw something at the infuriating man and rage at him for being such a mannerless and unforgiving great oaf.

Chapter Fifteen

❧❧❧❧

'What the devil did you rip up at her so stiffly for?' Brendan demanded before the echoes of a door being closed painfully softly could die.

'She's a liar, why shouldn't I?'

'Because you aren't Moss any more than she is Miss Court?'

'That's got nothing to do with it.'

'If you truly think that, I'd hate to be in your shoes when she finds out who *you* really are.'

'That's different.'

'Is it now?'

'Yes, I had to find out what was going on and it all turned out to be her fault.'

Brendan shook his head and looked as if he didn't know where to start arguing with that statement. He knew Fergus's hot temper of old, though, and seemed ready to let him stew, since he murmured something about warning the coachman and grooms of the hasty journey they must make to the capital tomorrow.

Fergus still paced the neglected old library. Why the devil *did* he feel as if this was the worst betrayal of his vulnerable inner self ever committed?

'Or maybe it's because I'm a damned fool and cool, vulnerable Miss Court was a fiction I almost fell for,' he added, paused in his hasty march and considered Miss Hancourt's life as a governess and the blight her father's sooty reputation would have cast over it. 'I ought to pity her for the scandal that wound itself into every strand of Lord Christopher Hancourt's life when he set up another man's wife as his mistress, I suppose,' he said as he set off again and his brother lounged back against the library table and listened with an infuriatingly knowing smile on his face.

'If she didn't inherit a fortune the day her brother turned five and twenty I might be able to forgive her, but she chose to stay here and draw poor Edward Moss into her web of deception.'

'Lucky you're not Moss, then,' his brother pointed out laconically.

Fergus snorted rudely and went back to his pacing. To think he had even considered the wild notion of wedding an upper servant for her sake and all the time she must have been laughing at him behind his back.

'You know how hard her so-called betters were to Ma when she wed above what they considered her place in life, Brendan. She's worth a hundred of the idlers who look down their long noses at her, but how could I subject a woman I almost let myself fall in love with to what she's had to endure since before I was born?'

'Hmm, see what you mean, but Miss Hancourt's not really a governess.'

'She's not the woman I thought her though either, is she? She played me for a fool, Brendan. How can I forgive her for that?'

'With difficulty, I should imagine, since you're a pretty big fool without her help.'

'Moss was her primer for finding a husband. She's had no chance to try out her wiles until I came along. A lady of her breeding, looks and fortune will have a whole troop of suitors falling over themselves to win her during the next London Season if she did but know it, but they're welcome to her.'

'Are they now?' Brendan asked with a sly grin Fergus might have been tempted to wipe off his handsome face if they were a decade younger.

'Yes,' he said between set teeth, 'they damned well are.'

Brendan held his right hand up as if conceding the argument, but Fergus knew him a little too well for that and glared at him for good measure.

'Perhaps I'll remind you of that when we see her engagement announced in the London papers,' Brendan said as he inspected his already immaculate fingernails for hidden damage.

'If you want your teeth rearranged, you do just that,' Fergus snapped and felt his much-tried temper tug a little harder at its tethers.

'Pistols or swords?' Brendan challenged with a dare to beat him at either in his laughing grey eyes he knew Fergus wouldn't be able to resist.

'Pistols,' he agreed with a glance out of the windows to see if the usual grey clouds were about to produce rain, but, no, it was fine enough for what they needed.

'Best of ten?'

'A hundred might make my head ache enough to distract me,' he said with the barest hint of rueful humour breaking through his own personal thunder clouds.

'Fifty and I hope your bad temper about Miss Hancourt will distract you, so I can get my revenge for you beating me hollow last time.'

'Best of fifty, then,' Fergus said and they went to fetch the best of his late lordship's guns and enough ball and powder to keep their contest going.

It had helped, he decided, when they declared it a draw and resorted to the gunroom again to clean and put the weapons away again, until tomorrow.

'Are you going to forgive her then, Fergus?' Brendan asked at last.

'No,' he said baldly and even now the white heat of his fury was dying down a little he couldn't see a day coming when he would. She had almost been a dream the Earl of Barberry was never going to let himself have before he met Miss Court in the gloom that first day. Miss Hancourt had turned that dream into a nightmare and why should he forgive her for it when she could only have been playing with Moss? He wasn't Moss, but he might have been. No, she had shown him the true meaning of betrayal so why would he ever forgive her for putting another layer of cynicism around Lord Barberry's already frosty heart?

'I still can't believe it's true,' Caroline said as their carriage finally rolled its weary way through the outskirts of London and even the novelty of it all couldn't distract her from her former governess's sins for very long.

'Nor can I, but Miss Court seems quite certain she

is really an heiress and a niece of the Duke of Lin-aire, so who are we to argue with her when we spent two years trying to believe every word she's told us?'

'Thank you, Lavinia,' Nell said as firmly as she could when her eldest pupil was subtly calling her a liar and she really couldn't argue, 'but you must get used to calling me Miss Hancourt if you truly want to stay at Linaire House and not with your own aunt and uncle in Cavendish Square.'

'Oh, no, they wouldn't want me even if I wanted to go there.'

'I'm sure that's not true,' Nell argued, although if Lavinia's maternal relatives had a scrap of love in their aristocratic hearts for their niece they would have taken an interest in her happiness before now.

'And I want to see how you behave when you're not pretending to be a governess, of course,' Lavinia said, as if she was looking forward to watching her former teacher feel uncomfortable in own her skin for once, instead of the other way about.

Nell wondered if she'd made a rod for her own back when she insisted the Selford girls come to London. Too late to regret it now, the mud-spattered carriage was turning into the broad streets of Mayfair and they were nearly at their destination. Far too late to argue again with the stiff, aloof man riding alongside the Earl's travelling coach as if he didn't trust her to go unmolested in the most exclusive area of the capital city.

'So do I,' Penelope said with a stern nod at her one-time teacher.

Georgiana said nothing; she had refused to speak to Nell since she'd confessed she wasn't Miss Court but a well-connected heiress. At least she hadn't stopped talking altogether, Nell reflected philosophically. It would be awkward to introduce a girl who refused to speak at all into her uncle's home. The Selford cousin who had always seemed most damaged by her family's folly and neglect was Lavinia, but Nell was beginning to wonder if Georgiana hadn't been hiding her hurts under a quieter manner. It felt wrong not to find out why she was using silence like a weapon, but she wasn't the girls' governess any longer and had lost some of the natural authority a grown-up held over a girl by admitting she'd lied to them all. Perhaps Aunt Barbara or Eve could break through the silent defiance Georgiana had put up against her former governess.

'Now this house really is grand,' Penelope said when the horses turned into Grosvenor Square and the coachman halted at Linaire House.

'Yes,' Nell agreed hollowly, 'it really is.'

As a child she was convinced the mansion had a stiff and disapproving soul and saw her as an unwanted interloper. It was Uncle Augustus's house then—cold and austere and the perfect reflection of his dour personality. Nell shivered; even on the hottest days of summer coming back here had felt like stepping into an icehouse. It was a wonder she didn't freeze during the two years she'd spent alone here.

'Nell! Oh, you darling, stubborn girl. It's so lovely to see you again,' the Duchess of Linaire exclaimed as she bustled down the grand steps of her latest home as if she wasn't a duchess at all and took Nell's dread of coming here clean away.

By the time she had been hugged and scolded and

exclaimed over and her four companions made welcome, Nell felt this grand classical mansion could be home after all. It was a lesson in not blaming a place for the temper of its owner and even Georgiana's stony silence hadn't survived long in the face of Aunt Barbara's warm interest in her guests.

'Now I must thank you two gentlemen for escorting my niece and her charges here safely,' the Duchess of Linaire said when she could spare the two men the time of day. Nell felt unworthily smug about her aunt's priorities and hoped it would put surly Mr Moss, her judge and jury, firmly in his place.

'My name is Rivers, Your Grace, and this is...'

'He is Mr Moss, Lord Barberry's land steward...' Nell heard herself introduce the wretch at the same time as Mr Rivers and stopped. She flushed and waved a hand at that gentleman to continue, but this time her aunt beat them both to it.

'Nonsense, Eleanor, this young man is quite obviously Mr Rivers's brother,' Aunt Barbara said, seeing the fugitive likenesses between the two men Nell ought to have spotted the first time she'd laid eyes on Mr Rivers.

With her piercing artist's eye Aunt Barbara saw more than any person Nell knew—when she chose to truly look at a person with it, instead of letting her gaze drift over their head to something more interesting. Was Nell glad or sorry the Duchess had come out of her artist's studio long enough to welcome her here and subject the Earl of Barberry to an eagle-eyed scrutiny? Hard to tell with the truth still ringing in her ears as if they'd been boxed by an angry hand.

'Of course he is,' Nell heard herself say numbly.

'Don't you *dare* faint,' she heard her aunt whisper as the possibility occurred to Nell as well and pride ordered her not to give him the satisfaction.

The Selford girls had gasped, then clung together on hearing this latest betrayal of their trust. Who could blame them for only relying on each other after the two huge lies Nell and Lord Barberry had told them? And she'd been doing penance for much lesser sins for the last two days. Nell glared icily into the middle distance instead of lowering herself to look at the lying toad.

'I won't,' she whispered fiercely.

The similarities between the brothers outranked the differences when she finally managed to glance disdainfully at his lordship instead of ranting at him for what he'd done. Mr Rivers was fair and his eyes were grey rather than blue; his handsome features had some of the softness of youth that his brother's emphatically lacked, but standing side by side on the carriage sweep in front of Linaire House with the reins of their weary horses in their gloved hands, it was so obvious they were brothers she had no idea how she'd managed to miss seeing it for so long.

'You had best come inside and talk about it without any onlookers,' the Duchess said with a glance at the grooms and coachmen as well as the bland, blank windows of the other grand houses in the square.

'But we're still in our dirt, Your Grace,' Mr Rivers protested half-heartedly.

'We have more important things to worry about than a little mud and the odour of horse, young man,' Aunt Barbara said magnificently and ordered their

mounts to the mews to be pampered until their own-
ers were ready to take them away.

Nell saw the brothers exchange glances as if assessing their chances of escape, then shrug, as if resigned to a scene and resolved to get it over with. How
had she missed the cool devilment in the so-called
steward's blue eyes, the imperious nature betrayed
by his haughty Roman nose, not to mention his arrogant stance that said no man was his master? Fool,
she chided herself as she followed her aunt inside the
grand Palladian mansion and reminded herself it was
still her duty to put the Selford girls' feelings first,
but how she wanted to rage at the man for kissing her
so passionately he woke up a Nell Hancourt even she
hadn't recognised and how he'd condemned her for
it when he found out she wasn't a poor little dependent governess after all. He was the Earl of Barberry
and a far bigger liar than she was, but perhaps he'd
hoped to set her up as his mistress? What a lucky escape they'd both had, then. But if she felt betrayed
by the false rogue, how must his wards be feeling?
First their governess hid her true self for two years.
Now the Earl of Barberry was unmasked as a man
who had skulked about Berry Brampton acting as his
own land steward, instead of finally shouldering the
responsibility he'd dodged for so long.

'What a shame my nephew and his wife are spending a few days at Darkmere to celebrate the arrival of
Eve's new half-sister. Colm will be so annoyed that
he's missed you, my lord,' Aunt Barbara informed the
Earl with a regal irony that made Nell want to hug
her, even as she shuddered at the idea of her brother
meeting this brute at dawn to shoot him for her sake.

She had no doubt Colm could put a bullet in the Earl's sorry hide wherever he chose, for he was a famous marksman under his other name. Her shiver was for her brother's horror if he had to fire in anger once again. Colm would suffer if he hurt another human being after the endless carnage of Waterloo and all the battles he'd somehow survived before it.

'Mr Hancourt will find me at Barberry House in a week or two if he still wishes to make my acquaintance,' Lord Barberry said, as if quite ready to be challenged when he had the leisure to spare for such a minor matter as his improper intentions towards Colm's little sister when he'd thought of her as a mere governess.

As if she would tell Colm exactly what they had got up to at Berry Brampton when his lordship thought her fair game. Nell felt so furious on Miss Court's behalf she wanted to slap the wretch, then rage at him for his sins, but it would take too long to list them and lower her to his level, so she decided a sniff of chilly disdain would have to do instead.

'You intend to stay at Barberry House and grace polite society with your presence at last then, my lord? The *beau monde* will be so delighted I dare say you'll be nigh crushed in the stampede,' Aunt Barbara said, as if she routed pretenders like him every day before breakfast. 'Meanwhile, here is my husband; he might be eager to bid you welcome as well, my lord.' The words *if you're very good* sat unspoken in the air as if he was a small boy who hadn't washed his neck.

'Were we expecting visitors, my love?' the Duke of Linaire asked amiably.

Nell smiled warmly at her eccentric scholar uncle,

even with the Earl of Barberry looking on as if at a play. She was too fond of her Uncle Horace to pretend not to be in front of strangers and Lord Barberry was one of those, wasn't he?

'I'm sure you're as delighted as I am to welcome our dearest Nell home, Horry,' the Duchess said with a fond smile at her husband.

'What, you're actually going to grant us your company despite all the past rebuffs, are you, miss?' the Duke asked and hugged her.

'I am, and these are my former charges, Uncle Horace,' Nell explained. She managed a smile, despite the Earl's stormy glower. The girls were his wards, but Nell beckoned them forward to be introduced, despite his lordship's silent disapproval. 'This is Miss Lavinia Selford, Uncle Horace. Miss Georgiana, Miss Caroline and Miss Penelope Selford are doing their best to hide behind her for some reason best known to themselves.'

'No need, my dears, you're very welcome here *and* you managed to bring my stubborn niece with you. That's something the Duchess and I haven't managed this last year and more, so we're very grateful,' the Duke said and made Penny laugh at the idea they had brought Nell here rather than the other way about.

'We must contain our joy for now, my dear,' the Duchess intervened, 'the Earl of Barberry and Mr Rivers are waiting to be noticed.'

'Pleased to meet you, Rivers, I knew your father at Eton.'

'I doubt he learned very much there, Your Grace. I hear he was as wild as a mountain pony until my mother tamed him as best she could.'

'True, but he lacked patience rather than kindness or good humour. I dare say time has taught him that.'

Mr Rivers chuckled. 'He hasn't changed very much from the sound of it.'

'Then be sure to tell him I'll be delighted to see him if he ever feels like crossing his beloved Irish Sea for a week or two.'

'I'll be sure to do that, Your Grace,' Mr Rivers said, a coolness coming into his eyes as they rested on his half-brother, perhaps recalling why Sir Graham Rivers stayed away from London after he wed the widow of the last Lord Barberry's youngest son.

'So you're the elusive Earl of Barberry, are you, young man?' the Duke said as if Moss's worn riding coat and breeches were in no way remarkable on an earl.

Seeing the fine cut and expensive fabric of the old and slightly outdated clothes he must have sent for after she christened him Mr Moss, Nell wondered how she could have deceived herself he was the man and not the master. She recalled the way she'd behaved in his arms only a few nights ago and shuddered at the idea of him smirking at her as he walked away to share her silly, willing vulnerability with his younger brother and perhaps laugh at her in his cups.

'I am indeed,' the wretch admitted coolly.

'Then whilst you may have had a hard journey escorting my niece and these delightful young ladies here and are currently a guest under my roof, I have a good many quarrels to pick with you, sir. The first is why you have let our Nell take your responsibilities on her shoulders for so long? My wife and I have been pleading with her to live with us ever since we got back to England, but, no, she must stay with your wards because nobody else cared tuppence about their happiness and well-being. Now I've met you all I can see why our girl here refused to abandon you, but it defeats me why she didn't bring you here a year ago. There's room enough for twice as many girls to stay and still leave room to billet an army.'

'I would not have permitted such an arrangement,' Lord Barberry argued.

'Everyone knows you ignored your cousins from the day you inherited Berry Brampton House,' Nell said hotly. 'If you have a scrap of feeling in you, then you'll stay out of their lives now and send them to a good school so they can make friends their own age and learn to enjoy life, instead of always being conscious they were born female so you are the Earl of Barberry and not one of them. It's far too late to pretend you care about anyone but yourself, *my lord*,' she finished with a regal glare she hoped would cinder any memory he might have of her eagerly returning his kisses as if he was a good and decent man.

'It's never too late to put things right,' he snapped.

'That's up to your wards. Affection and respect cannot be demanded like a ton of coal or a baron of beef from a tradesman,' she said so coldly even she shivered.

'If the Duke and Duchess will have us, I would like to stay here with Miss Hancourt,' Lavinia surprised Nell by saying, then moving to stand at her side. The other three girls looked at each other and Penny went to her eldest cousin's other side while Caroline and Georgiana took Nell's and their loyalty brought tears to her eyes.

'I should be delighted to welcome your wards to Linaire House until an acceptable compromise can be reached about their future, Lord Barberry,' Aunt Barbara said blandly, prepared to be diplomatic now she'd got what she wanted. 'Barberry House has been rented out for a decade, I believe, and must need a great deal of work before it's ready to house four young ladies and their maids, plus a governess to continue their education *and* a suitable chaperon for you all.'

The stubborn line of the Earl's mouth looked set as worked stone now. Nell was sure he would refuse, however sweetly the Duchess of Linaire pointed out he was ill prepared to house four growing girls. They'd resented Nell's authority when she arrived at Berry Brampton House—how much worse would they be with the guardian who had wanted nothing to do with them for a decade? She was tempted to stand back and let him try, but she loved the girls too much to inflict it on them if there was any chance they could stay here instead.

'The Duchess is right, Fergus,' Mr Rivers said rather apologetically.

Nell wanted to shout at him for pacifying the stubborn liar instead of telling him not to be an arrogant fool. Yet her inner idiot treasured the gift of his true name and silently tried it out on her tongue. *Fergus.* Foolish Nell felt every syllable on her tongue as if it was unique.

'Barberry House must be threadbare and out of fashion by now,' Mr Rivers went on. Maybe he was used to finding ways around impasses for his arrogant brother and no longer even realised he was doing it. 'We have no lady with us to make all right either.'

'We're not related to the Hancourts—what reason can there be for them to take the Selford girls into their home, even if I were to allow it?'

'The world knows my niece had to earn her living before the blind trust her father set up matured on the day her brother was five and twenty. At the moment it's considered a fine and romantic tale: a poor orphaned girl forced out into the world penniless by her own wicked guardian, my late brother,' the Duke said in a shrewd summary of the whispers going about the *ton*. 'All *you* need do is go and live at Berry Brampton House for a few weeks, my lord. No more explanation of why your wards are living under my roof instead of your own will be needed. You will seem like a kind guardian and my niece a right-minded and careful lady to come here the moment you put in an appearance there at long last. You could thank her for her care of the girls she has grown so fond of by allowing them to take a holiday here while arrangements are made for their future. That would show how wrong everyone is to call you a care-for-nobody, wouldn't it?'

'I seem to have very little choice in the matter,' Lord Barberry said. 'As well I don't want to stay at Barberry House until the upholsterers have been in for a month or two. If we go now we'll be back at Berry Brampton House by tomorrow evening and you can spread this unlikely story while I catch up with my sins and omissions of the last ten years.'

'And what a thankless task that will be,' Mr Rivers said. 'I can hardly wait to be back in the saddle after our long and uneventful journey here,' he added ruefully and Nell silently blessed him for trying to lighten the mood.

'Needs must when Miss Hancourt drives,' the Earl said disagreeably.

If they hadn't managed to stop making love in his housekeeper's sitting room she might be planning their wedding right now. Feeling sick at the very thought of enduring such a hasty and hollow marriage, Nell got through the next few minutes by pretending this was all happening to someone else.

'And thank goodness *we* don't have to make that awful journey again today,' Caroline said as she watched from one of the drawing-room windows as the half-brothers waved goodbye to the Duke and rode out of sight on lively new mounts provided by the ducal stables.

'Would you rather have gone home with Lord Barberry?' Nell asked guiltily, wondering if she had robbed the girls of a chance to know their guardian.

'No, he doesn't want us and we'll have far more fun here,' Penny said happily.

When the Duke came back in with a procession of footmen bearing food, Penny sat down to toast a muffin by the fire and never mind if she hadn't had her hair brushed or her travelling dress changed yet. As the Duchess pointed out, they had come a long way and there hadn't been children at Linaire House for far too long.

'Plenty of time to sort things out when his lordship has his feet under the table at Berry Brampton and these young ladies aren't cold and hungry after a long journey, Nell. Sit for a while now and stop fussing, my dear,' the Duke said and took over toasting duties when Penny almost dropped a muffin in the fire. 'Ring the bell and tell Biggins we're not at home to visitors for the rest of the day would you, my love?' he asked his wife, 'We're far too busy to entertain this afternoon.'

Uncle Horace would have made a wonderful father, Nell decided, as she finally took off her bonnet with a sigh of relief. Between the fire and hot tea and muffins she should be warm, but part of her felt cut off from the lively scene around the ducal fireplace. Maybe that bit of her would always feel chilled now the rightful owner of Berry Brampton hated Miss Eleanor Hancourt with such stern passion.

Chapter Sixteen

'What, the chit is in London with her confounded family now and you're no nearer to finding out where those damned jewels are?' Lord Derneley whispered furiously and he could fit a lot of fury into a mere whisper.

'They suddenly packed, upped and left, Derneley. I could hardly stop them,' his lady said and looked as if she preferred his room to his company for the first time in their joint lives. 'It *was* quite pleasant to get out of this horrid house for a few days, though,' she added sulkily.

'You'll be stuck here for good if we don't get hold of those jewels. One day even those fools on my tail will get in and find me and I'll be hauled off to the Fleet.'

'Oh, no, Derneley, we can't stay here. It's not at all what we're used to.'

'And I can't rot in a debtors' prison, woman, so you'll have to do better next time, won't you? What did you do to find those papers I wanted?'

'I found a maid servant willing to search her room and bring them to me.'

Her lord's eyes narrowed against the dim light of a single tallow candle that was all the nip-farthing old lady allowed her niece when she thought the best use for darkness was to sleep. 'Why didn't she do so, then?'

'I don't know, Derneley. She didn't come to the place we were to meet and I waited for hours. Next thing I heard the Selford brats and that silly chit of Chris's were off to town and Barberry's brother and some manservant escorted them all the way here. Even if I could catch up, I could hardly pretend to be a highwayman and hold them up, could I?'

Derneley brooded on her tale for a few moments, then seemed to untangle the gist of it and arched over the weak candle light so he could look straight into her eyes. 'To guard them that closely, they must have been suspicious,' he told her harshly. 'You did something stupid, didn't you?'

'No, I was quite clever to find a girl whose family are even more miserable and in debt than we are.'

'Hmm, what did you offer her for the Hancourt girl's papers?'

'Oh, only five pounds,' Lady Derneley told him proudly. 'Just enough to tempt her and not enough to seem desperate.'

'Five pounds,' he echoed as if he could hardly believe his ears.

'Yes, she wouldn't do it for less.'

'You negotiated,' he said flatly, frowning so fiercely he looked as if he was only managing not to shout with a huge effort of will. 'You offered this cunning little doxy all she might earn in a year for one trivial task and expected her to keep quiet about it?'

'Yes,' Lady Derneley said, sounding a little uncertain now.

'You damned fool,' he said and she flinched away, looking terrified of the fury in his eyes as they glinted back at her in the semi-darkness. 'You brainless, feckless, stupid woman,' he managed with angry despair. 'What the devil are we going to do now?'

'Find that paper some other way?' she said with a desperate sort of helpfulness that somehow didn't look to be very helpful to her once-dashing lord.

'No, they know we're after it now,' he said and turned his back on her as if he could brood better on the misfortunes dogging him without the sight of her defensive, sulky face distracting him.

'Then we must stay here for ever?' she asked as his despondency made her realise they might be penniless for the rest of their lives. The sound of despair in her voice instead of her usual shallow optimism seemed to make even selfish and spoilt Lord Derneley consider someone else's miseries for once in his life.

'No, we'll find another way, Lexie, don't you worry your pretty head about it,' he said and she smiled brilliantly and he seemed to forget his ill temper. 'I'm not staying in the old cat's cellar for the rest of my life,' he went on. 'If they're on the hunt for the Lambury Jewels I could always let them find them, then snatch them out from under their noses at the last minute.'

'You're so clever, Derneley,' his lady said admiringly.

'Lucky one of us is, then,' he muttered under his breath.

* * *

'You're a success, Nell,' the Duchess of Linaire told her husband's niece as they travelled back to Linaire House one night with the dawn.

'My fortune has cast a wonderful gilt over me.'

'Nonsense, now you're dressed as befits Miss Hancourt everyone can see what a lovely, lively young lady you are at last. You are a refreshing change from the usual empty-headed young miss launched straight out of the schoolroom into the *ton*.'

'Fine feathers make fine birds,' Nell said, because somehow her success in the wider world meant far too little. She had been shut up in a large old house in the country with four girls for so long she should be eager for every new experience, but instead she felt as if she was acting in a play about someone who wasn't the real Nell Hancourt at all.

'That really is the most ridiculous saying. Not even a fine gown like that one would make you appear as you did tonight if you were not a very pretty young woman to start with. No, don't dismiss what I say as partial because you're Horace's beloved niece. Remember I aspire to be an artist and don't argue with me because I don't flatter, I simply report what I see.'

'Affection can distort even the clearest vision.'

'And false modesty can infuriate the most patient of souls. I am not one of those, Nell, so please don't try me any further tonight.'

'Very well, I shall accept all praise as my due from now on.'

'Hah! That's about as likely as Horace becoming prime minister.'

Nell chuckled at the idea of her uncle's face if such

an invitation came his way. 'He would drag you on to the next ship sailing to America and refuse to come back, however much we missed you, lest they ask him again,' she said.

'And now we've come all this way to be a duke and duchess it would be wrong of us to run away. These things have to be faced, as your Lord Barberry finally seems to have accepted, since he's firmly settled at Berry Brampton.'

'He does, doesn't he?' Nell said sweetly, refusing to rise to her aunt's bait and reveal her still-raw feelings for the stubborn great idiot.

'As well there are so many personable young men in town for you to choose from and you danced twice with Mr Rivers tonight, didn't you? Now he really is an Adonis and a knowing young rogue with it.'

'And very young and not in the least bit inclined to marry and settle down yet. I wonder Lord Barberry can spare him, though.'

'Perhaps he can't,' Aunt Barbara said and Nell could think of nothing to say in reply to such a cryptic comment.

For a while there was silence inside the luxurious coach and Nell wondered if her aunt had nodded off. Not so, she felt the Duchess's acute gaze on her face as they rattled over the cobblestones and surely they would be home soon, so she could go to bed and try not to dream of a man who certainly didn't want to marry her. Aunt Barbara smiled in the strengthening light with too much understanding in her eyes and Nell felt a wave of love for this strong, loving and clever woman who had taken her to her heart and given the Selford girls a temporary home as well.

'I have enjoyed the last few weeks, Nell dear, but I'll be glad if Eve or one of Lady Farenze's friends can chaperon you now you are properly launched and a success. I shall be far too tired to do aught but sleep in the morning, not that it isn't already morning and I'm far too old to be out half the night.'

'You know I'm always glad of your company, Aunt Barbara, but now Colm and Eve are back in town you can get some painting done at last.'

'Especially as they brought Eve's old governess with them. Now that scamp Verity is back at school while her father and stepmama sail the seven seas for a while, I'm glad Miss York has agreed to keep your girls occupied while Lord Barberry makes up his mind what to do with them, despite the fact she must be in need of a long holiday. The best thing Lord Barberry could do is consult you, of course, since nobody knows as much about his wards as you do.'

Nell was so tired after dancing all evening and trying hard to pretend she was happy she felt as if she'd smiled until her face ached. She had to blink her weary eyes several times to stop herself crying. It was ridiculous to let the wretched man affect her this way when he'd been back at Berry Brampton for a month and obviously didn't care about her. He'd certainly found it easier to forget her than she had him. Nothing seemed to erase the way he made her feel when they were close. 'I have no wish to speak with him ever again,' she said as soon as she could steady her voice.

'Do you not, my love? Well, hasn't the world changed since your uncle and I were courting? I longed for the next time we could speak and hated every event my mother dragged me along to if he wasn't there.'

'You and Uncle Horace were in love.'

'Yes, and it's wonderful to find the man you can be happy with for life, Nell. Are you sure you haven't met that man yet?'

'Very sure, I think I danced with half the young men in London tonight and my heart only beat faster because I needed to get my breath back,' Nell said lightly, telling herself it was stupid to feel so disappointed not one of her partners had outshone a man she hadn't danced with and now never would.

Fergus would have laughed, cynically and rather hollowly, if he'd been able to read Nell's thoughts. He'd spent three weeks camped out in his rather shabby London mansion with nothing much to do but think about Miss Eleanor Hancourt and how not to miss her as if half of him had been cut away. Of course, the contrary, stubborn, confoundedly popular female was never still long enough to pine for him. On the other hand, he had hours on end to watch her new home through the best spyglasses money could buy by day and lurk about the Square at night in the hope whoever was after her letters at Berry Brampton would try again. He was in the ideal position to know Miss Hancourt was so much in demand among the younger gentlemen of polite society that she was rarely at home for very long unless she was asleep. He caught glimpses of her dressed in the first stare of fashion and groomed to perfection as she stepped out of a fashionable town coach with some eligible man's sister or mother, or climbed the dizzy heights up to a dashing curricle. He frowned at the house across the Square and watched her being handed up into one so ridiculous the coachmaker ought to be shot for selling such a vehicle to a mere whipster. Tempted to run across and mill the flash young fool down, he hit the nearest wall to relieve his outraged feelings instead.

He was the best man to watch out for any mysterious strangers haunting Grosvenor Square because nobody here knew him, but he was slowly going insane while he pretended not to be here and Eleanor Hancourt ran about town pursued by eager suitors. And what would Miss Hancourt make of the fact her nearest and dearest were deceiving her for her own good as well this time? No doubt she would be furious and declare she could look after herself, thank you very much, and it was all his fault. Which was exactly why he was stuck here, trying to pretend he was nowhere near the capital, so she couldn't take a pet and ruin the whole enterprise, then insist on going about alone to frustrate him. Fear for Nell and his cousins' safety goaded him into coming back here to watch over them in case whoever was after her secrets got desperate enough to kidnap one of them. And life was devilish flat and empty at Berry Brampton House now anyway.

He'd been watching from the eyrie he'd made in one of the top-floor rooms overlooking Linaire House when Brendan arrived to escort Miss Hancourt and her aunt or sister-in-law to any events Hancourt or the Duke could not attend. At least his brother was welcome at Linaire House, but suspicion such dangerous proximity might make a marriage between his little brother and Miss Hancourt had got Fergus so desperately overwound with frustration and fury that he wanted to hit something very hard until his fists were as numb as the rest of him. He couldn't risk that because he might need them to protect her and the girls one day soon, but Nell wouldn't let him escort her if he begged on bended knee. If he came out into the open she would be more stubborn and uncooperative than ever just to prove she didn't need him, so he had to stay here and watch for her enemy to make a move and somehow he'd find a way to contain all this raw emotion and keep his temper before he punched his way out on to the roof and could watch her from out there as the rain dripped into his fine London house.

He glanced down at his latest less-than-aristocratic outfit. Whose idea had it been for him to pretend to be a down-at-heel footman? Surely he wasn't fool enough to want to spend his days in a shabby and mismatched set of livery in case he had to fool someone he was a willing conspirator in whatever mischief they had planned this time? So far he might as well have spent the time at his tailor's and strutted about the place in new clothes for all the good it had done him not to. He hadn't been entirely idle, though, and was beginning to get information from Poulson's sources now he'd put the right feelers out. As well to be certain before he moved against the man he suspected was behind this nonsense, so he waited and watched. At last his patience was rewarded when his most likely quarry left his lair in the depths of the darkest night Fergus had lurked in since he'd got home. Now it was time to bait his trap and wait for the desperate idiot to walk into it. He just hoped the man would leave his wife at home this time.

* * *

'Are you sure about this, my boy?' the Duke of Linaire asked his nephew a few nights later.

'No, but Barberry says Derneley is desperate for the Lambury Jewels and he might hurt Nell or Eve if they get in his way,' Colm Hancourt said grimly.

'Miss Hancourt won't be safe until we smoke the fool out,' Fergus confirmed.

'And he was behind that odd business at Berry Brampton?' the Duke asked.

'He seems to think that because his sister-in-law was given paste copies of the Lambury sapphires and emeralds he was defrauded of the fortune they should have been worth when she died and he found out they weren't real.'

'He's mad, then,' Colm said impatiently.

'No, he's selfish and vain and ridiculous, but he's not mad,' the Duke said before Fergus could argue it didn't matter.

'He's desperate enough to be dangerous and we need to contain him before he does any more damage.'

'Well then, we must do so, but he's no gentleman.'

'After what he tried to do to Eve last year we know he's nothing of the sort, Uncle Horace, and don't forget Lady Derneley fooled me into writing to Nell so they could find out her address,' Colm pointed out irritably.

'And she was the female who offered to pay my servant to steal your sister's papers,' Fergus pointed out.

'Is that why you're taking such an interest in my sister's affairs, Barberry?' Colm challenged.

'My wards seem to love her and this business did start under my roof,' Fergus said defensively, avoiding his gaze because somehow he didn't want to ask for Nell's hand with this farce hanging over them. He wanted her free and clear of danger and misunderstandings before he dared try to court her, because it would be hard enough to get her to believe a word he said without a shabby villain trying to steal the jewels she was so indifferent about and distracting him at every turn.

'No, it started here, more years ago than I care to recall,' the Duke said as if all this was his fault though he wasn't even in the country when Lord Chris set his little girl a funny little puzzle.

'Then why tonight?' Colm Hancourt asked as if he didn't care about the jewels either and they were a minor inconvenience he could have done without.

'Since I found him loitering outside your house one dark night it's taken me a while to wriggle into the man's confidence as your disgruntled former employee, Your Grace,' Fergus told the Duke. 'I told him I'd persuade my sweetheart to leave the garden door unlocked tonight, if he gave me the silver inkstand from your study as my share of his ill-gotten gains.'

'My grandmother gave me that,' the Duke said indignantly. 'It's the only thing I took to America and back again, apart from the Duchess, of course.'

'Just as well I don't really want it then,' Fergus said.

'Or my aunt, I hope?' Colm muttered.

Fergus had to muffle a surprised laugh at that wry comment and wondered if he and Hancourt had something in common after all, apart from Miss Eleanor Hancourt, of course.

'So he will get in once most of the servants are in bed and the light goes out in your study, Your Grace. Mr Hancourt is rumoured to be out tonight and the ladies are from home. I told him he would just have to risk the younger ladies all being asleep and I hope they don't hear anything from the schoolroom floor and come creeping downstairs to find out what's going on. That's why I needed you both on hand, in case we have to contend with more than Derneley tonight.'

'Hmm, that's wise, I suppose,' the Duke said. 'Just as well the ladies are out, though, or we would certainly have to contend with them.'

'True, now perhaps you could check the servants are all abed except the footman on duty downstairs, Hancourt? We need to get on lest the man gives up and goes home and it's all to do again.'

'Heaven forbid,' Colm Hancourt said, rolling his eyes at the elaborately plastered ceiling at the very thought of lying to his wife for much longer.

He'd told her he was meeting some old army comrades tonight and even Fergus could see how much it pained him to lie to her. How must it feel to love a woman that strongly? he wondered, then assured himself he wasn't the kind for such overwhelming emotions, even if a goodly part of him didn't believe it.

'And what happens once we blow the candles out in this room, my boy?' the Duke asked genially.

'We wait for Derneley, confront him with his sins and send him packing across the Channel where he can do less damage. Until he's in we only have Faith's

word that it was Lady Derneley who offered to pay
her for your sister's private papers and a lot of vague
suspicions he's after the Lambury Jewels.'

'Not much to prosecute him with, then, even if
we wanted to.'

'So long as he goes away for good that'll be enough
for me,' Fergus agreed.

'I'm not a vengeful man and they'll be miserable
enough with nothing in their pockets but what they
can earn for once in their lives.'

'Are you sure your niece hasn't already worked this
riddle out, Your Grace?' Fergus asked, wondering if
it might be cause to hope if she was too distracted to
search for the jewels because she ached for him as
much as he did for her.

'She would have told us if she had.'

'Yet her father's words seemed to mean something
to her at the time.'

'Will you show me?' the older man asked.

Fergus opened his pocket book to the page where
he'd scribbled the words so angrily when he'd discovered Nell Hancourt's secret, then lost his temper so
spectacularly he'd lost her as well before he'd finally
cooled down and realised what he'd done.

'Through the eyes of a grandfather clock everything that is hidden will be found again,' he read out.

'The clock in the red drawing room looks as if it
has eyes,' the Duke said with a visible shudder. 'Our
father used to make us explain our sins in there and
Chris always used to say the clock shared Papa's low
opinion of us both.'

'Is it still there?'

'Yes, although I've been meaning to have it taken

down and stored in a dark cellar ever since we got back to England, I haven't got around to doing it yet.'

'Perhaps we should see if we can make sense of it while we wait,' Fergus suggested.

'My brother did leave that clue for Nell,' the Duke argued uneasily.

'She hasn't pursued it though, has she? Hush, did you hear that? And we haven't even put out the light,' Fergus whispered, puzzled because the soft steps outside the Duke's study sounded too light for a man of Derneley's build and former habits. Surely the man hadn't sent his wife again?

'I knew you were all up to something,' an all-too-familiar feminine voice exclaimed and how the devil had she got wind of this?

'Nell, m'dear, whatever are you doing here? You're supposed to be dancing away at some ball with your aunt and sister-in-law until the sun comes up.'

'Colm is a terrible liar and we thought we ought to know what was going on here before one of you got hurt. If I don't send word within half an hour, Aunt Barbara and Eve will send Eve's Uncle James and half-a-dozen grandees to rescue us, so don't look at me as if I've run mad.'

'You'll drive me to Bedlam then, even if you don't end up there yourself,' Fergus told her in a furious undertone.

'And what are *you* doing here?' she said haughtily, the only female he knew who could manage it dressed in a governess's dull plumage and when had she found time and chance to put that absurd get up on again?

'Tracking down your family treasures, since you're obviously too busy to bother,' he told her and wasn't it satisfying to get under her skin again? 'You're a woman of so much substance you obviously can't spare the time to worry about it,' he told her with an ironic bow in the hope of doing it again. He hadn't wanted her to march into danger with her nose in the air, but his whole world felt wider and more vital with her nearby. God save them both, but he'd missed her.

'You look like a derelict,' she said with a disdainful look at his down-on-my-luck servant's garb.

'And you look like a governess,' he said with a humble bow, as if he really was the Duke's footman, before he did something disgraceful and was dismissed.

'Half an hour, you say, m'dear?' the Duke said with a glance at his watch to remind them time was a-wasting.

'You're not planning to go on with this now your niece is here, are you, sir?' Fergus only just managed not to yell as fear for her nearly felled him.

'If not tonight, Nell will get involved in some other way, when we're not by to stop her getting hurt. The Lambury Jewels were left to her as well as Colm.'

'But…' Fergus began to protest, but the Duke calmly went about snuffing candles before he could find words powerful enough to forbid it.

'My wife is a lady of iron resolution as well, so you might as well get used to it, Barberry,' the Duke told him kindly.

'I don't see why I should,' he managed to mutter grumpily before Miss Hancourt elbowed him in the ribs and he decided to save his breath, not sure if he wanted to kiss her senseless or leave her to find the Lambury Jewels without him, but very sure the idea of her being in danger made him afraid as he'd never been before.

'You're supposed to be at Berry Brampton,' she told him in an irritated whisper.

'And you're supposed to be at a ball,' he retaliated.

'Hah! A ruse to get us out of the way that a five-year-old child could see through,' she told him softly.

'Will you two be quiet?' Colm demanded irritably.

'I wasn't making a noise,' Nell muttered darkly and Fergus recovered his sense of humour and his delight at being close to her again at the same time as terror for her made his heartbeat gallop in his ears.

'And crows aren't black and fish don't swim in the sea,' he parried and this time it was his turn to nudge her in the ribs and surely it wasn't right to feel such joy at being shut up in a dark room with her and her closest male relatives? She *was* speaking to him again, even if it was in insults though, wasn't she? 'I missed you,' he informed her softly and somehow he knew she was smiling rather smugly about that, even in the stuffy darkness of this closed-up room.

'You two can croon at each other later, someone's coming,' Colm whispered sharply.

Fergus decided nothing about this evening was going to plan, but he might as well learn to reshape them, because Nell would never be a predictable female if they both lived to be ninety. He wouldn't want to spend all those years with her if she was, but he very much wanted all that time with her and they were in the middle of a dangerous muddle that could go horribly wrong. He listened for their quarry and wondered if it was too late to kick up enough row to make an intruder jump out of the window and dash back into the night. Anything rather than endanger Nell and her otherworldly uncle, although Colm Hancourt could obviously look after himself. The whole untidy business might still have gone smoothly enough if the Duke hadn't sneezed at exactly the wrong moment.

'There you are, Lexie, didn't I say it could be a trap?' Derneley observed as he uncovered the dark lantern he carried in his other hand and saw the Duke and two pretend servants plus the Duke's nephew not even trying to hide from the cocked pistols he had stolen from Lady Derneley's aunt. 'Keep Hancourt covered, my dear, but don't get close enough for him to get hold of your gun. He's tricky, that one,' he observed coolly, taking a closer look at the smaller servant as he put the lantern where it cast the best light to watch them all by, 'just like his sister.'

Somehow Colm managed to look amused by the fact he was being held at gunpoint by Lady Derneley. Fergus cursed himself for not taking this threat more seriously and getting the Bow Street Runners involved, whatever Hancourt and his uncle had to say about keeping it in the family. He wondered if it was worth trying to overpower the couple before they settled.

'I may not be clever or accomplished, but I am an excellent shot,' the lady boasted as if she could read his mind and he decided it wasn't worth the risk.

'It's true,' Derneley told them proudly. 'Once won me a pony by shooting the pip out of an ace at fifty paces. Wish I'd bet a monkey; I could do with it now.'

Fergus could imagine the wild and rather dashing couple they must have been thirty years ago, but look what all that fizz and sparkle dulled to after years of headlong pleasure seeking. 'Which brings us to business,' he said laconically.

'Who are you really, then?' Derneley asked, his long-barrelled and over-decorated old pistol aimed at him, and Fergus bit back a sigh of relief. If the fool shot Nell he'd rather die himself than endure seeing her hurt in any way.

'The Earl of Barberry's land steward,' Fergus lied. If he could keep the man talking long enough James Winterley and his cohorts would rescue them. On the other hand, the more people there were here, the more chance there was that someone might be hurt.

'What the devil are you doing here, interfering in my business, then?'

'My lord asked me to; his wards live here,' he said and watched the weight of the clumsy old pistols taking its toll. Another few minutes and Lady Derneley would need a flat surface and her other hand to keep her gun level. Derneley didn't look in very good shape after hiding from his creditors and a lifetime of dissolute living either.

'Tell me where the Lambury Diamonds are or I shoot the wench,' his lordship said as if he'd noticed that, too, drat him.

Lady Derneley narrowed her eyes at Colm as if she had a suspicion he was up to something she wouldn't like. 'And the rest of the jewels are here somewhere,' she reminded her husband.

'Nonsense, of course they're not. Do you really think a fortune in diamonds could be been hidden in a public room for so long without them being found long ago by the servants?' Nell asked scornfully.

'He must have hidden them very well,' Lady Derneley said with a shrug.

'So well that no maid, clock-winder or upholsterer has found them in all these years?'

'Even a fence couldn't hide having so many stones to cut up and as your father managed to fool Pamela with his tricks he'll have hidden them cunningly,' Lord Derneley told Nell, as if Lord Chris was the one at fault instead of him.

'My sister had the rubies inspected and cleaned. They were the real thing, so why would we have doubted them when he gave her the sapphires and emeralds as well?' Lady Derneley said indignantly.

'You stole them when she died, didn't you?' Nell accused with such bitter contempt Fergus was afraid Derneley might shoot her anyway and tensed to jump in front of her if the man's finger tightened even a shade on that heavy old trigger.

'I had to wait until that useless treaty in '02 and I searched for nearly three days up and down those mountains before I found them both lying at the bottom of a valley nobody thought they ought to be anywhere near. Finest stones I ever laid eyes on, netted us a fortune, didn't they, my lady?' Derneley boasted. 'How your sister would have cursed Chris for tricking us out of the rest if she'd known.'

'He was my father,' Nell said through clenched teeth.

'Left you behind for Augustus to neglect though, didn't he? Can't have loved you very much to do that,' Lord Derneley taunted and Fergus felt any mercy he'd been inclined to grant the worm seep away.

'This thing is heavy, Derneley, how much longer

must we stand here talking?' Lady Derneley asked querulously, bracing her gun hand on the back of a chair this time and looked ready to wilt into it if he didn't hurry up.

'Until we get what we came for,' he said impatiently. 'So where are they, wench?' he asked Nell. Fergus stiffened as the pistol in Derneley's hand swerved away from him to aim straight at her heart and fear froze every inch of his body for a long and terrible moment.

'I don't know. We only found his message when your wife came looking for it and I've been too busy to work it out,' Nell explained impatiently.

'Too busy for a fortune in jewels?' Lady Derneley sounded so incredulous her gun wavered from her own target until she caught Derneley's glare and steadied it on Colm Hancourt again.

'She don't need a fortune, she's got one, Lexie. You, steward—read me this riddle and if you've got a pistol I'd wonder if you can get it out and shoot me before I shoot her if I were you,' Derneley ordered.

'Which clock does he mean?' the man asked after Fergus did as he was bid.

'It's the biggest one in the small drawing room,' the Duke said mildly and Fergus hoped the man was a lot cannier than Derneley thought him.

'They're not in the clock,' Nell said wearily when they got to the old-fashioned room that looked as if it was rarely used even by family.

'Why does it say it is, then?'

'"Through the eyes of the clock…"' she quoted the puzzle Lord Chris left behind as if they were slow infants and she was an impatient governess again.

'Clocks don't have eyes,' Derneley argued and swung about to look hard at every dial he could see.

That was enough of a chance for Fergus. Every muscle and sinew must work to get him to that pistol in time, so he sprang and prayed at the same time. Almost, he thought in a daze, as the confounded thing fired anyway. He waited for the terrible reality of the bullet to strike him and hoped he'd expire in Nell's arms if that was all they were going to be allowed.

'Stupid great idiot,' his love all but shouted in his ears. He marvelled she'd got her breath back and could speak so abruptly to a dying man who had only just realised he loved her with everything he was when it was too late.

'Don't you love me, then?' he asked in a bewildered voice even he hardly recognised.

'Why the devil should I after you nearly got yourself shot like that?' she demanded furiously. 'And I don't know why the rest of you are standing there grinning,' she went on to accuse the Duke and her brother, who were now holding the Derneleys at bay with Lady Derneley's pistol.

'Would you rather we let them go then, Sis?' Colm Hancourt asked with a shrug that told Fergus he no longer figured in the man's list of enemies he must have banished to a dark corner of the earth.

'No, but I don't know how we're going to explain this to the rest of the world,' she said a little more reasonably.

'Explain, my dear? Why would we Hancourts lower ourselves to enlighten the curious?' her uncle asked haughtily.

'Ah, I see,' Fergus heard Nell say and groaned.

'You need to marry me,' he argued. 'Before I die.'

'We'll have time to sort you two out later,' the Duke said soothingly.

'You're not going to die, you idiot,' Nell said once she finished poking and prodding his helpless form as if he was related to the sofa he had refused to lie on. 'The bullet went through your coat sleeve,' she pointed out as she helpfully pushed her index finger through the hole it left behind it to demonstrate. 'You're not even grazed,' she added kindly, as if she was humouring a half-wit.

'You need to marry me anyway,' he said gruffly as he got to his feet feeling very sheepish, but determined not to let her off that easily again.

'No, she doesn't,' the Duke argued calmly. 'Unless you want to of course, my dear?'

'Not if he can't do better than that,' Nell said grumpily and Fergus wished everyone else would go away so he could kiss her breathless and persuade her he loved her with everything he was, Earl or not.

'Ah, well, that's sorted out then. We'd best get these two turned over to the Runners and go to bed, I suppose,' the Duke said as if nothing very much out of the way had happened tonight.

'On what charges?' Derneley managed to ask gloomily.

'Breaking and entering, being a greedy worm who never did a decent hour's work in his life let alone a day of it? Owing your creditors a fortune will do if nothing else sticks,' Colm Hancourt said briskly.

'And don't you ever even think about stealing the Lambury Jewels again,' Fergus said, feeling as if he ought to assert himself after making such a monumental fool of himself just now.

'We're still ruined, then?' Lady Derneley said wistfully.

'The diamonds aren't here anyway,' Nell said comfortingly.

'Why don't you give them a pat on the head and invite them to supper?' Fergus demanded caustically.

'Don't be rude,' she told him with a militant look in that made Fergus groan out loud as he sensed her spotting a cause in Lady Derneley that the foolish and heartless creature did not deserve to be.

From the sound of it Mr Winterley and his bevy of powerful friends had just arrived and Fergus wished he cared enough to find out what they were going to do with Derneley and his wife as the Duke and his nephew shepherded them out of the room and at least now they were out of Nell's orbit and they could concentrate on more important things.

Chapter Seventeen

Before anyone else could come in Nell stood in front of the clock and stooped far enough to make her eyes on the same level as the holes where the key went in. 'If Papa left something for me to find it must be in there,' she said as she eyed the case where an automata a past Hancourt must have brought back from his travels stood. It represented a czarina in full coronation regalia and she had never found time to study it closely before, but the incredible detail and opulence of it almost distracted her from the quieter beauty that finally gave her father's mystery away. 'There,' she said softly at last and felt her smile wobble and tears threaten at the thought of Lord Chris hiding it for her before some trip he was about to make, knowing how much she would miss him and hoping to distract her.

'The belt?' Lord Barberry asked.

'Yes, or at least what looks like a clasp on it—it's my mother's locket,' she said reverently. 'I thought I'd forgotten her, but now I see it I remember how she always wore it. Of course he couldn't take it with him on an adventure with Pamela, she would have thrown it in the nearest midden.'

'It's very fine piece of workmanship,' he said as he came up beside her to peer at it through the glass and Nell shivered at the image of them reflected in the polished glass. They looked right, she decided and never mind clothes, lies or rank.

'Can we take it out?' she whispered, feeling as if she hardly dared breathe on the case lest it shatter and take her newly discovered memories with it.

'Do you know where your uncle hides the key?' Fergus asked and how could she think of him as a stiff and stubborn earl when he was standing by her looking as if he wasn't fit to clean his own steps, and he'd just made such a fool of himself in front of Colm and Uncle Horace surely he felt something out of the ordinary for her? They had told each other so many lies she wasn't sure she trusted words any more, but this time maybe his actions spoke for him and they were saying something silly and un-Moss-like and quite wonderful. This lurch of heat, tenderness and awe she felt when she thought of a possible future for them must wait a few more minutes though, so they could finally admit it to each other without someone interrupting.

Uncle Horace eventually found the key to the czarina's cabinet in a puzzle box he and Chris used to play with as boys. 'Racked my brains to think where he might have hidden it as soon as I realised where that villainous old clock was pointing us,' he said as he watched Nell unlock the cabinet.

A small gilt pin held the belt in place at the back and it was the work of moments to tug it out and there, at last, it was in Nell's hand. 'He used to show me the trick of it until I could undo it,' she said softly and pressed the neat mechanism that held the clever thing together and there were her parents; young and happy and as full of life as if it had been painted yesterday.

No need for tears this time, not with Fergus at one side and Uncle Horace holding a candle aloft at the other so she could study the finely painted images more closely. Aunt Barbara was warming her toes on the hastily lit fire and Eve had gone to bed, since Colm was still busy arranging the Derneleys' future with the lords of creation who had marched them off to some anonymous place they kept for awkward problems before they were quietly exported some-where more convenient.

'You are very like them,' Fergus said.

'Hmm, my father was accounted very handsome and my mother quite plain.'

'Then account was wrong,' he argued, his gaze steady as he met hers to assure her that her mother certainly wasn't plain and nor was she. 'The very fine artist who painted this took the trouble to see her as she was, instead of listening to such jealous nonsense.'

'Yes, it's very like,' Uncle Horace said, 'Come and look, Barb.'

'It is,' her aunt said as she joined them, finally warm after an anxious wait to find out if all was well with her nearest and dearest. 'And Barberry is right, you do have a strong look of her.'

'I'm glad then; he loved her back, didn't he?' Nell said. 'And I suppose he was terribly lonely after he lost her,' she added with a shake of her head to say it seemed a very small excuse for his obsession with Pamela.

'I wouldn't do that,' Fergus protested as if she'd accused him of a betrayal beyond even his record of them so far.

'No, you're too strong to need anyone that much, Lord Barberry,' she told him sharply and why must she snap at him when most of her only wanted to coo words of love and melt in his arms?

'Not strong, just stubborn, and I need you endlessly, my torment,' he whispered in her ear and it took a cough from Aunt Barbara to remind them they still weren't alone.

'Aren't you going to take a closer look at what Chris left behind?' the Duke asked as if he knew she and Fergus were too busy with one another to worry about jewels right now.

'Do you think there could be more than this then, Uncle Horace?' she asked half-heartedly and followed her uncle's gaze over the magnificent-looking czarina. 'Oh, heavens above, you mean the jewels in her regalia are *real*?'

'Are they?' Fergus asked and wrenched his gaze from her face to see for himself. 'If those are your mother's diamonds, please promise never to wear them in public without a private army on hand to protect you,' he added as if such a vast fortune in jewels was a liability, which looked very close to the mark, she decided, as the cold glitter of them made her shudder with disquiet.

'I'd sooner have this locket than all the Lambury Jewels put together,' she said at last.

'Truly?' Fergus said, one eye on the large stones that could outfit several countesses.

'They seem gaudy and rather soulless to me,' she said truthfully.

'From the look of them in the family portraits I have had nothing else to do but get acquainted with these last few weeks, the Barberry jewels can't hold a candle to these,' he warned softly, 'but you might like them better.'

'Never mind what you're going to do with them right now, let's lock the cabinet up until we can get a jeweller in to remove them and put them in a bank vault while you and Colm decide their fate,' Uncle Horace said with an expectant look at his duchess to say it was time to be tactful. Nell silently agreed with him and waited impatiently for them both to leave the room.

'And you will make sure Colm doesn't come after us with a horsewhip, won't you, Auntie dear?' she murmured as the Duchess was on her way to the door.

'Of course, my love, a lady should always be left in peace to dictate terms to the love of her life,' Aunt Barbara whispered back and sailed off to bed as if there was no single Earl standing in the red drawing room and staring down at their niece as if he couldn't get enough of the sight of her.

'Do you expect me to thank you for interfering in my affairs and nearly getting yourself shot?' Nell asked when they were alone at last.

'Not unless you've changed out of all recognition since you took up your new life, Miss *Hancourt*,' he said with a frown at her workaday old gown.

'I could have managed very well without you,' she

said crossly and shot him one of Miss Court's best frowns because this wasn't the most romantic of interludes so far and even Miss Court had her dreams.

'Are you as rude as this to all your suitors?'

'No, only you,' she said grumpily.

'And I recall you being so to poor Moss on more than one occasion as well.'

'I would never have been so discourteous if you hadn't goaded me into it,' Nell defended herself.

'You saved that for your noble employers, then?'

She snorted inelegantly at the description of my Lord Barberry as a noble in anything other than fact. 'Noble indeed, and it's just as well I don't intend to have any more of them, since you put me off the whole breed.'

'And your days of acting the governess are well and truly over, madam.'

'Perhaps I shall take to the stage instead,' Nell managed to say airily. He was holding her at a distance again, as if they had only ever been impossible together, whatever rank they were pretending to have at the time, and she didn't like it one little bit.

'My mother became an actress to save her family from want and went back to it to keep me fed and healthy. She's worth a dozen of any duchess I ever met except your aunt and I refuse to be ashamed of her even for your sake.'

Nell's heart thumped a fluttering, hard beat. He had just said *even* for her sake, hadn't he? So maybe he did love her. She stared up at him as if she might read the truth in his eyes and gasped in a great breath because she might faint if she didn't and this wasn't the time for such missishness. 'I truly admire Lady

Rivers for doing as she did. She is obviously a lady of spirit and resource; why wouldn't you be proud of her?'

'You really mean that, don't you?'

'Of course I do; why would I say it if I didn't?'

'Forthright as ever, Miss Court?' he said with a rueful smile she almost took as a compliment. 'I'm not ashamed of my mother and never will be,' he added as if he intended setting out rules for the future when this was all about trust for her.

'Lord Chris's daughter wouldn't have a leg to stand on if she wanted to condemn Lady Rivers because she once had to work for a living,' she said steadily and met his eyes with a challenge to stop judging her by polite society's rules when it had done neither of them many favours in the past.

'It's not your fault your father loved unwisely, Nell,' he said earnestly.

There it was; that real, true love and trust in his eyes and voice that she wanted so badly this felt like the most crucial conversation of her entire life. Of course, his rock-like determination to keep her safe came from the true heart of him. She could excuse it because he'd watched his beloved mother be sneered at and looked down on because she didn't fit the exact mould of a nobleman's wife, but she didn't intend to let him protect her until she was stifled. She had been an independent woman too long to meekly submit to being cosseted for her own good and put in a glass cabinet like the imitation czarina.

'My father would have done far better to love a lady who deserved his devotion,' Nell said absently because Fergus Selford was far more interesting right now.

'He ruined your life.'

'No, he ruined his own life and Colm and I had to become stronger than he was as a consequence.'

'Too strong to think the world well lost for love like he did?' he asked huskily.

'Too strong not to love anyway. We know we can live outside the tight limits of polite society because we've done it most of our lives. How many of our kind could say that, Lord Barberry?'

'I can,' he said rather unsteadily, as if this was another caveat they had to get out of the way before they admitted their feelings to one another and he was getting as impatient with them as she was. 'I made it my mission to live without my title and the trappings of an English earl when I went to Canada and stayed there although my little cousins needed me. Beware of a man with a mission, Miss Hancourt; he tramples on innocents to get what he wants.'

'I don't think your cousins are that easily down-trodden, my lord.'

'What about you, Miss Court?'

'Didn't I just finish telling you how hard I am to cast out and bring low?'

'So you did, then please will you finally agree to marry me?' he said. He looked caught between horror she might say no and hope she would agree as he stared down at her with so many complex emotions in his fascinating blue eyes she felt as if she could stare into them like a bewitched idiot for hours on end.

'Why?' she asked at last.

'I love you.'

'Hmmm, I wonder,' she said, forcing the words past her galloping heartbeat and a vast, dangerous hope that was making her clench her hands into fists at her sides so she wouldn't throw herself into his arms and agree to anything if he'd only keep saying it.

'How can you doubt it? I have just made such a fool of myself when I thought he was going to shoot you that I suspect even your brother has to know I love you more than life itself by now.'

'You were either furious or mocking most of the time I was Miss Court and not much different since I owned up to being my true self,' she argued.

'You always were your true self, isn't that what you just told me?' he said impatiently. 'And you don't look that different to me, if you're dressed in Bond Street's finest or that gown you wore back at Berry Brampton.'

'I look completely different when I'm dressed up in all my finery,' she said defensively.

'Your hair is beautiful, but it always was,' he said coming to stand behind her and looking at the only traces of the new, fashionable Nell available tonight.

She felt the heat and proximity of him and forgot what they were talking about, until he cocked his head on one side as if eyeing up a masterpiece in need of some restoration. 'I would like it a lot better if it was down about your shoulders, of course. I've always wanted to run my hands through it and find out if it feels as soft and seductive as it looks.'

'I'm not beautiful, Fergus,' she said stiffly.

'You are to me; I can't look at any other woman and think her anything but pallid and uninteresting next to you and I want you endlessly, Nell. You're lucky my mother knows a bit too much about lusty young gentlemen and taught me to control my urges and burn in duchesses' drawing rooms. I want to throw you down on the *chaise* over there and teach you how bitterly a man can long for you and you alone right now, so be more careful what you say because I'm too close to proving how lovely you are to me by actions if you won't believe the words.'

'Oh, you idiot,' she said, with a soft sound between a laugh and a sob. 'I want you so much I feel as if every inch of me is screaming for your touch. I don't know how to say it more politely, but if you really mean to love me I wish you would just get on with it, Lord Barberry.'

'What, here and now?' he said as if startled the notion could enter her head.

Nell turned away from the shadowy look of them in a nearby mirror the wrong way around and felt Miss Court was being left behind in that fine old Venetian glass, frowning with disapproval as Nell's inner demon boldly stared up at the Earl of Barberry and considered the idea very seriously indeed.

'Best not, perhaps, Colm might not take to you as I want him to if he catches us being very improper indeed on one of my uncle's fine couches.'

'Come and be improper on one of mine then, Nell?' he breathed as if one of them might shatter soon if she didn't.

'Haven't you got the upholsterers in? That's what you told my aunt and uncle just now.'

'One or two of them are still serviceable and I seem to have slept on most of the ones that are this last fortnight, so at least I know which will not shoot a spring out of place at the worst possible moment.'

'Arrange it then, my lord,' she demanded boldly,

still not quite sure why she still hadn't admitted she loved him and felt truly desperate to marry him now she knew he loved her back.

'I ought to demand you wed me first.'

'I dare say you ought,' she said, examining her highly polished fingernails as if it didn't matter very much if he refused to be scandalous with her tonight or not.

'Meet me at the side gate in half an hour and don't forget to bring keys, because you'll have to creep in and get yourself into the right bed on your own tonight. I'm not inclined to let your brother shoot me if I have to break into your uncle's house to let you back in with the dawn.'

'An hour,' she challenged, because it would take her that long to wash, pretend to take to her bed then redress as soon as her maid had gone to bed herself.

'Three-quarters,' he argued as if that was the outside limit of his patience.

Nell wanted him so urgently and was beginning to read his darkest frowns and grimmest glowers as the sign of the controlled emotion they truly were. She nodded and agreed to their first compromise as lovers, then went off to get ready to seduce and be seduced by the first and last one of those she ever intended to have.

Chapter Eighteen

'At last,' Fergus murmured in Nell's ear and drew her close for the brief tiptoe across the square and up the steps to his own nearly splendid again mansion.

Nell caught her breath and wondered nobody could hear the thunder of her heartbeat as they crept through this merciful, cloudy darkness to the side door of Barberry House. She didn't dare speak, but felt him move next to her and her breath caught with the hugeness of what they were doing. If she lost her nerve he would let her turn tail and say *no* to such a final commitment between lovers, but she refused to damage this wondrous feeling at the outset. So there was no stumble of maidenly hesitation for her and Fergus had to stop her running up the side steps to get herself ruined all the faster and giving them away.

'Have all your servants gone to bed?' she managed to whisper softly when he had the door open, at last, then locked it hastily behind them.

'The few I have left here are enjoying a holiday at my expense,' he managed to murmur in a fairly normal voice, although it was rasped by powerful emotion as she snuggled against his side as if there was nowhere else she longed to be and wasn't that the truth?

'How convenient,' she said coolly as a woman could when she was plastered against her man's torso so tightly he might as well wear her as a shirt.

'It won't seem so when you have to live among the debris.'

'Why would I do that?'

'Because you're not going to get away with a splendid marriage in Hanover Square and a six-month viscount after tonight, my lady,' he said a little bit too seriously even as he lit a branch of candles waiting on a dusty side-table and turned to meet her hot eyes as if even now he'd say them nay, if she wouldn't agree to wed him as fast as they could obtain a special licence.

'I might like being the most notorious Hancourt since my father,' she objected half-seriously.

'You might, but I wouldn't and you haven't met my mother yet. I doubt she would speak to either of us until after the babe was born if we disgraced her like that,' he said with a warm chuckle that changed into a groan as even the thought of bearing his child made Nell forget they were standing in a chilly hallway in a dusty and deserted mansion and writhe her body against his in a silent demand they start the project right now.

'Are you certain it's me you really want as a wife, Fergus?' Nell made herself ask and even managed to set a few fractions of an inch of space between them against all her instincts never to let him go again.

'Certain of myself, Miss Eleanor Hancourt, not quite as sure of you,' he said unsteadily and led her into the little sitting room he must have been using as his base to watch over her these past weeks, when she'd thought he was long gone and forgetting her.

'Even when I'm behaving like a wanton *houri* in your arms, my lord?'

'Even then,' he said seriously.

'I'm sorry,' she said and felt him flinch, then cursed herself for making him even think it could be a refusal. 'No, sorry I find it so hard to admit I need anyone, not sorry about you and I'll just creep back to my lonely bed, thank you very much, my lord. I spent so long telling myself it was better not to rely on anyone it seems nigh impossible to admit I need you so desperately now. For most of my childhood and adult life I have had to walk my own path, you see?'

'So you need me, do you?' he said and his soft sigh at her intransigence spurred her into saying what she meant at last, because it sounded as if he was trying not to hurt and that was the last thing she wanted.

'Need wouldn't be enough. What I feel for you is fierce and hungry and far more powerful than anything I ever expected to feel. I always thought I was cold and immune to loving to the edge of reason, but I wouldn't be here now if I didn't love you to distraction, you great fool.'

'You would make me wait until after the wedding, then?'

'No, I wouldn't marry you at all.'

'Thank heaven you love me, then,' he said with another of those heartfelt sighs she felt guilty about wringing out of him. 'And why not you? You deserve to be happy,' he added as if the rest of her words had taken that long to get past his relief at her final, life-changing admission she loved him.

'But I'm Lord Christopher Hancourt's daughter.'

'An aristocrat who shouldn't love Kitty Graham's son?'

'No, she loves him beyond her wildest dreams, but my father really did disgrace the Hancourt strawberry leaves—trust my eldest uncle to make sure I knew that every day of my younger life.'

'Ah, but he's dead and done with and we're alive, with a lifetime of proving him wrong in front of us. Don't let him win, Nell.'

'Only if you promise to forget your grandfather and uncles' foolishness as well, my love,' Nell said and finally gave into the desperation she'd been fighting since she saw him again, frowning back at her as if he was daring her to hate him for being there.

She rose on her toes to meet his hungry mouth with hers and to the devil with propriety and maidenly modesty. Their kiss was even more hot and urgent than the ones they exchanged at Berry Brampton, but this time there was a confidence, a sweetness behind the passion that made Nell's toes curl into her kid slippers, then flex with sensual pleasure. She locked her arms about his powerful neck and pulled him closer.

'I can't stand up,' she whispered when he raised his head to breathe.

'Do you want to?' he demanded hoarsely and walked them to the nearest flat surface as if he couldn't wait to get there either.

'This *chaise is* up to our weight, isn't it?' Nell asked with a hint of a breathless giggle in her voice that sounded girlish and giddy and delight shot through her like champagne bubbles because this was real and he was here and how very much she loved this man.

Fergus took her attack of giddiness in his stride. There was a lightness, almost a boyishness in his deep chuckle that made her realise how much of himself he'd been holding back since they met as well.

'It's far too uncomfortable to get worn out,' he told her as he found time to reach blindly for a tumble of cushions and a softly expensive blanket to guard them against stiff old leather and horsehair stuffing.

'Let's try anyway,' she murmured and pulled his head back down so he could kiss her into forgetting their surroundings altogether. 'Oh, yes, I think we should start as we mean to go on,' she murmured into his ear, then explored it with her curious tongue while she was up there. She felt him twitch with a shock of manly desire, so of course she did it again.

'You'll unman me if you're not careful,' he warned unsteadily when he'd got enough breath back to speak.

'I'm tired of being careful,' Nell murmured. Fumbling the knot in his frayed neckcloth undone and throwing it into a corner, she was glad he wasn't in full gentlemanly fig. She knelt upright on the unyielding old couch to try out what kissing her way down the intriguing chord of tension in his neck and down to the hollows at the base of it might do. Luckily he remembered what his hands were for before she got there and he found the laces of her gown and undid her even more completely while she was so busy undoing him.

'Shift,' he demanded and she was delirious with

love and delight and anticipation and frowned in puzzlement that he was troubling to name her garments at a time like this.

'Yes, I know,' she said blankly, sparing her fingers long enough to smooth the fine silken stuff of her very expensive underwear with absentminded approval.

'No, shift your knees, unless you would like me to rip this very respectable gown off you right now and ruin it, Miss Hancourt. We need to get you home before the house is stirring, don't forget, and it'll be a lot easier to do that if you're not naked,' he said, laughing as she hastily did as he said and let him slide the mundane stuff gown out from under her then it was off and over her head in one smooth move.

'Are you sure you're not a rake?' she said, frowning at the very thought of him doing this with anyone else.

'If I ever was I would have met my match in you,' he said with only half his attention on what they were saying. His hot blue gaze was intent on the whisper of silk that made up her new shift and her rather exotic short corset, rich with satin and lace and shaped by a mistress of the art. Eve had insisted such a fast garment would make her feel as well as look a very different female from sternly practical Miss Court and she was so right. 'Whoever made that ought to be locked in a tower and ordered to make one in every colour under the sun only for you, since I doubt this one will survive the night,' he said hoarsely.

'I like it,' she protested and wriggled about to undo it before he could rip the delicate laces open.

'Did I say I didn't?'

'No, and why are we arguing about my corset?'

'Because that's what we do; I doubt we'll give it up simply because we love one another,' he replied and somehow made himself tug the bow undone and loosened the laces so she could wriggle out of it although his wonderful eyes were blazing with need and something close to desperation as he watched ever more of her emerge from its rather sensuous embrace.

'We might get bored with each other if we lived in sweet harmony,' she agreed absently, revelling in the feel of his work-hardened palms abrading her tightly needy breasts with only this whisper of silk left between them now. 'Oh, please, give me more, Fergus,' she managed to gasp as the absolute pleasure of his touch there shot flames of merciless need right through her. 'Please?' she asked as he lowered his dark head and suckled on her frantically needy nipples until she keened with desire. In the shadowy gloom of one branch of candles and the fire she watched his dear, dark head as he feasted on her blatantly aroused breasts as if he was desperate for the taste of her. Even as she felt the flick of his wicked tongue on her wet, silk-veiled nipple she gloried in the chance to know his powerful neck and the sensitive curves of his head and brow by touch. He felt as if he was hers every bit as surely as she was his. He felt hot and passionate and possessive as he gave her tightly demanding breasts one last, lingering caress and worked his way back up, meeting her gaze with a rather self-satisfied grin.

'Is that it?' she teased as if she didn't know there must still be a banquet of some sort waiting for them. She couldn't be this tense and hot and needy for something even more incredible if this was all men and women did together in a bed.

'It should be until we're wed,' he said with a frown and she cursed herself for finding words instead of kisses at such a time.

'Don't be silly, my lord,' she said brusquely and decided it was high time she satisfied her curiosity about the intriguing differences between him and her. 'I am three and twenty and know my own mind, and my mind wants you nigh as much as my body does right now,' she said, as if he didn't already know.

'Soon you will be my lady and you won't be able to throw my title in my face like an insult,' he said even as his mighty body quivered when she ran a curious, exploring finger over his tightly muscled torso and down over his own tiny nipples to linger briefly and see him tighten with desire as well. Too intrigued to linger for now, she moved on and felt his breath hitch. She felt satiny skin shift under her touch, as if the almost not there sensitivity of her touch made him more of everything. More aroused, more delighted they were here together like this, more Fergus Selford than ever before and he was *her* lover.

Even as she thought he couldn't be more than he already was, her wandering finger slid further down and the stark evidence she was wrong reared rigidly against his flat belly. He was mightily aroused and mighty indeed, it felt as if every muscle and sinew he possessed in this very impressive body of his was clenched with driven need for something very intimate indeed with her.

'Do you know how a man and woman mate, my love?' he whispered into her gasped open lips as he leaned his forehead against hers to look the question into her love-dazed eyes.

'Like the wild animals, I suppose,' she said, having long ago decided the more fanciful of her fellow pupils at Miss Thibett's School had to be wrong about husbands and wives for the human race to have lasted as long as it had.

'Not entirely,' he qualified with a tender, secretive smile that promised a great deal more than the simple urge to mate and a few harsh grunts.

'Like tame ones, then?' she whispered provocatively.

'Why not let me show you? Telling is much less fun,' he murmured against her mouth and kissed her so deeply and passionately she forgot what the question had been.

Heat was pulsing through her in ever stronger waves and she wondered if she might faint from the sheer, edgy pleasure of it as her body seemed to know what it wanted better than she did. It rose against her lover, back bowed so his rigid sex was emphatic against her roused core, the feel of him there sending shivers of hot anticipation through her until she felt as if she'd been half-tortured, half-pleasured as the knot at the heart of her got ever tighter and hungrier to be unknotted by him.

'Careful, my love,' he whispered and she was impressed he still could.

Lost for words herself, she gasped open her mouth to try and moan out some sort of question as he stroked his index finger over parts of her she never knew wanted his caress so badly until this very moment. Even as he brought her to the edge of wonder he seized her mouth with his and plunged his tongue inside it, setting up a beat as strong as life itself. She shifted, smoothed out her cramped legs to fall back against the silk and velvet cushions until she was open to whatever came next because she trusted him that much. Her breath coming in gasps now, she heard it hitch even more as he followed her down and his sex butted against hers. If not for the fact she could hear his lungs labouring to get breath into his body against the power of wanting her so much, she might have hesitated and learnt to fear, but his desperation rekindled her own after that moment of wondering how she could endure sharing any more of herself even with him. There, now, he was inside her. Gentling as best he could as he tried his hardest to let her grow accustomed to having a man inside her for the first time; her man inside her for the first time, she amended smugly somewhere in her head.

A flood of warmth, a softening she couldn't quite describe and he was even further in and she purred and raised her knees beside his paused flanks to demand yet more of him. Still for a long moment, taking his weight on his elbows and caressing her hungry mouth with his busy tongue and lips, he seemed almost reluctant to go on until she bit his upper lip gently and licked it better with a sensuous satisfaction that seemed to snap his last tether. Still bowing back his head in an effort for self-control, he broke through the fragile barrier of her maidenhead and she knew why he had hesitated, why he seemed almost on the edge of keeping her out of the land beyond it until their wedding night for a long, desperate moment. Glad he wasn't as gallant as he wanted to be, for both their sakes, she rode the wave of a brief pain that subsided to soreness as her inner and most sensitive Nell adjusted to not being alone any more. She felt him holding his breath, waiting for any sign she didn't want him to go on. He would stop even now, whatever it cost him; she knew that as surely as if he'd sworn it on paper and signed it in blood before they began.

'Idiot,' she muttered into his dark, sweat-dampened curls and made him lift his head to face her gaze by gently cupping his chin as if he was the one new to all this and not her. 'How could I not want you?' she asked huskily.

'I'm told it hurts.'

'Who by?' she asked, almost sharpened out of pleasure by the most acute jealousy she could ever imagine before he became her one and only lover.

'One of my sisters,' he said flatly, 'but don't you dare tell her I said so.'

'I won't,' she said and lay back on her seducer's shabby old couch again and gave him a heavy-eyed gaze of what she hoped was sensuous encouragement.

Seeing him frown as if he still wasn't sure if he ought to stop right now anyway, she managed an experimental wriggle and contracted her internal muscles about his rigid manhood. It jerked inside her as if it had a life of its own and she heard him groan with need with a very self-satisfied smile on her face.

'Show me everything,' she demanded.

'That will take years, love,' he protested with a chuckle that felt wonderful as his muscular torso shifted against her pertly demanding nipples and reawakened another wild need inside her.

'Then show me some more,' she whispered with the wild lure of all those years to come making her catch her breath and yearn even more.

He withdrew almost all the way out of her and flexed his tight buttocks to thrust all the way back in again and this time she knew there was nothing in the way of their driven exploration of each other. Feeling him fully engaged inside her for the first time as he rocked all the way into her, she let herself believe this was really happening with the love of her life and opened herself up to him completely. She felt her muscles contract and relax around him and she forgot questions and murmured words and let her body have its head. It knew how to rise and fall to the tune he set for them, it felt the pulse and glory of life itself draw her on and, most of all, it cherished and trusted this mighty man who took so much care for her pleasure he was using every muscle and breath he had to make this good for her. At last his mouth was set with effort, his breath rasping as he used every ounce of self-control he had left to hold himself back from some goal she could sense but not know. She reached an unsteady hand to smooth the frown from his fierce brow and it seemed to break his chains. On a gasp of manly protest, then he bucked and moaned even as she felt the first almost fearsome contractions of something strange and new threaten to drown her.

'Go with it, love, don't fight us,' he ground out between clenched teeth and how could she *not* trust him to know what was coming and cherish her through every beat of it?

'I will, I do,' she whispered on a gasp of wonder and trusted him and her body to know what to do, even if this felt too enormous to cope with on top of all the other novelties he'd shown her tonight for an awed moment. Such power, such light, such uncanny warmth and *oh, oh, ooh*, this was way beyond any words she could conjure up as she flew in his arms.

Nell reached for her lover and clasped his strong shoulders since she seemed about to drown in endless pleasure while her body bowed and jerked in time to his. Wave after wave of it swept through her like the force of life itself and with any man but him it would have been so lonely. Instead it was joy and love and their soft moans of exquisite pleasure sounded right in the intimate warmth of this half-dismantled room. Just when she thought she was drained of all wonder, his sex seemed to harden even more as he surged into her ever more powerfully, until she wrapped her slender legs about his hips and hung on to his shoulders as he thrust into her with a huge, driven groan and she felt the surge of his seed inside her for the first time while ecstasy finally wrapped them both in a long, hot glory that went on and on and was over all too quickly at the same time. Now their gasps were of sated wonder, hers almost a whimper of protest as she felt the last echo of absolute pleasure and unity fade. Still surprised by the occasional spasm of ecstasy, she sucked in air as if she had just run from here to Berry Brampton and yet suddenly she felt absurdly shy as she met his gaze in the fading firelight.

'I, well… I don't know what to say,' she managed to say at last.

'Miss Court silenced? Isn't that a marvel?' he whispered teasingly and she laughed even as she felt a little bit sorry for that poor, lonely governess.

'You'd best ask my pupils.'

'I'd best not, I hardly think it's a guardian's lot to tell his wards what a fraud their teacher has proved herself to be, in so many ways,' he said and raised a wicked eyebrow to encourage her to ask the question she was too wise to say out loud. 'You never were cold or restrained or wrapped up in icy propriety, were you, my love?'

'No, and I always wanted you,' she said with a contented sigh and tried not to regret it when he withdrew from her body and she was one and a little bit lonely again after that triumphant coupling with this man she never wanted to live without. 'Miss Court was horribly lonely at times, my lord,' she added with a frown, 'but she nearly drove herself mad with wanting you and knowing it would it would be seen as a sad misalliance and damage his pride if she stole into Mr Moss's rickety bed one night.'

'Would that you had then; my ancient bed was rendered hideous by the lack of you in it most of the time I stayed at the steward's house.'

'Would my lord have been able to take Miss Court's hungry heart and trample on it like that, though?' she asked, almost offended by the idea that the woman she was not might have been seduced by a man he wasn't either, if they hadn't been so wary of each other.

'No, and my lord wouldn't have been so bad tempered and gruff if he hadn't wondered if he could and come up with a firm *no* every time he wanted to.'

'Good, I don't want the man I love seducing any more virgins.'

'I'll never love any other virago but you, my darling,' he said and shifted her to lie across his torso where she could feel him breathe under her for a luxurious few minutes before she had to go home and pretend none of this had happened somehow or another.

'If anything ever happens to me, promise me you'll not love a heartless jade and put our children through the loneliness Colm and I endured, Fergus?'

'Hard to imagine anything worse than being caught in the toils of a Viscountess Pamela, but the best way to make sure our children live happy lives is for you to live them with us. Don't expect any such promises from me, Miss Hancourt. You're going to have to be here to look after them yourself because I'm not willing to do any of it without you and my wards can't spare you either.'

'Be serious, love.'

'I am,' he said implacably and Nell let herself know this wasn't going to be a conventional marriage and who would want one of those when she could have him as her husband instead?

'Very well then; I won't accept you leaving me alone and bereft and with a son to bring up alone as your father did your mother either.'

'If I decide to sail the Irish Sea in the teeth of a gale I promise to take you and our offspring with me,' he conceded and kissed her disordered curls, then sighed with such total contentment it brought hot tears to Nell's eyes.

'Better still, don't set out so recklessly in the first place,' she ordered him as sternly as she could when she was lying in his arms and appreciating every vibrant inch of him.

'And welcome back, Miss Court,' he said with a

mock sigh and shake of the head to argue he didn't enjoy the idea of having two strong-minded ladies in his bed when it was very obvious to her that he liked it very much.

'Hmm, shall we keep Mr Moss as well d'you think?' she asked with a delighted shiver at the idea of that short-tempered son of the soil making the odd guest appearance in her wildest fantasies once again.

'At your own risk,' he growled and ungallantly pushed her off his chest and on to the rather thread-bare hearth rug when she purred a long moan of antic-ipation at the very idea of risking it right now. 'Home with you, woman, there's too much to do for us to have the time to undo you all over again right now,' he said as if he wasn't on fire again as well and she knew perfectly well that he was.

'A man is at a distinct disadvantage with his lover, isn't he?' she said smugly at the sight now as well as the feel of all that masculine fire and need blatantly wanting her all over again against her bare body. He was being gallant, despite all that fire and need, and she was torn between feeling touched and frustrated.

'Yes, now stop talking and keep dressing, it's nearly morning.'

'Would you mind if I gave them away, Fergus?' she asked seriously this time as she reluctantly did as he asked.

'Gave what away?' he asked absently, his eyes hungry on her still near-naked body and she almost gave up and encouraged him to be even more absorbed in it and forget the daylight beginning to steal around the shutters and chase away the night.

'The diamonds,' she explained instead, since she

didn't want to be caught stealing home by the servants either, or for Colm to catch them and kick up some silly masculine fuss because his sister had chosen the man she wanted to spend a lifetime with and couldn't wait to begin it.

'They're worth a fortune,' he cautioned and why wouldn't she love him when he seemed more concerned she might not have grasped their worth than he was by the fact she wanted to give them away?

'I know; one day our children might curse me for doing it, but there are even harder times than usual coming for the poor, are there not?'

He nodded and frowned at the thought of the terrible prospects for the harvest after such a wet, cold and cheerless summer. 'Aye,' he said seriously, 'it's been bad enough for them since the French wars ended, but this winter will be terrible with so little grain to be gathered in and not a lot else to take its place. Even the Lambury Diamonds couldn't fill that mighty a gap though, love.'

'But they might help,' she argued and it felt right to put the chilly, dangerous things to good use at long last. 'I don't want them and I don't want our children to be burdened with them either. There's something wrong with them, they only ever cause bloodshed and tears to those who own them. It's time they did some good in the world. Maybe they can lie easy in some princess's crown because I really don't want them.'

'Your brother says they're yours to do with as you wish, love, and I won't argue with bidding goodbye to them if that's what you truly want.'

'I think I shall like you as a husband nearly as

much as I do as my lover, Lord Barberry,' she said with a come-hither smile.

'No, stop it, you witch; your brother might kill me if he catches you coming home after the dawn.'

'Or he might be asleep and you're worrying about nothing.'

'In three weeks we'll have every right to sleep in the same bed, but right now I'm not willing to be compromised by you or shot by your brother. No kindly get yourself dressed and back in your own bed before he finds out where you've been tonight.'

'Very well, my lord,' Nell said meekly and thought three weeks a devilishly long time for them to make love on the most uncomfortable couch in Britain. 'You won't ever get rid of this monstrosity, will you?' she asked with a sentimental sigh.

'Never,' he breathed, with a long look back at the nest they'd made to love each other on for the first night of a lifetime as lovers and a very fond smile.

* * * * *